HER
HOUSEKEEPER

BOOKS BY SAMANTHA HAYES

The Reunion

Tell Me A Secret

The Liar's Wife

Date Night

The Happy Couple

Single Mother

The Trapped Wife

The Ex-Husband

The Engagement

The Inheritance

Mother of the Bride

HER
HOUSEKEEPER

SAMANTHA HAYES

bookouture

Published by Bookouture in 2024

An imprint of Storyfire Ltd.
Carmelite House
50 Victoria Embankment
London EC4Y 0DZ

www.bookouture.com

Storyfire Ltd's authorised representative in the EEA is Hachette Ireland
8 Castlecourt Centre
Castleknock Road
Castleknock
Dublin 15 D15 YF6A
Ireland

ISBN: 978-1-83525-898-9
eBook ISBN: 978-1-83525-897-2

For Ben, Polly and Lucy,
with love always xxx

PROLOGUE
SARA

It's funny – I never thought I'd watch myself die. Especially not aged fifteen.

There comes a point when you know, without question, that it's going to happen, that there's no turning back, where the end, literally, is nigh. Witnessing yourself taking your last breaths is some kind of drug as you look down from above. Even in such a murderous situation, my senses were letting me go gently, like a fond caress goodbye. Numbing me to all the bad. And I found it quite liberating to relinquish, to end the pain, to free myself from fighting back. Not that I was able to fight much. He was way bigger than me.

It had begun with a hand around my upper arm. I'd sensed trouble simply from the way he'd gripped me. Rougher than usual.

'Oh no you don't,' the voice had growled in my ear, sending fear spiralling through me. He'd yanked me round.

Keep walking, keep walking, I'd told myself. It wasn't me he wanted, after all. I'd been out searching for her, wanting to bring her back to safety, though there was little chance of that because where we came from was not safe at all. It wasn't the first time she'd run away.

It was pure bad luck that I'd bumped into him while I was out looking.

'If I can't have *her*, you'll have to do,' he said as he forced me to stumble along beside him. 'Punishment.'

He wasn't walking fast – he wasn't capable of that – but he was strong. There was no way I could escape the hold he had on me. His hands were big and insistent, and I knew they'd soon be all over me. As we marched on, I was resigned. It wasn't the first time this had happened.

At first, I thought he was taking me to his house. I didn't like it there. It smelt musty and old, and it was too big and dark. But we ended up close by – at a spot that, sadly, I knew too well. As he unzipped himself, made me do things to him, I thought of my sister, I thought of my friends, I thought of my boyfriend. While my body had to do these things, my mind was elsewhere – living a life I didn't have. A life I was never *going* to have. I shivered from the cold.

When it was over, he grabbed me, dragging me through the undergrowth. I knew this wasn't good. Usually he just walked off and left me, or put me outside his front door, shoving me into the night like an alley cat.

Then came the punishment. I was screaming. Thrashing. Begging for my life. This time, as I looked down on myself from above, seeing myself helpless below, I knew the end was coming. It seemed to go on forever.

But then it stopped. I was back in my body.

Was someone else there?

Truth was, by then I didn't know if I was alive or dead.

ONE

GINA

I rush to the front door as the bell sounds for the third time – the old-fashioned chime resounding through the entire ground floor of the grand Georgian townhouse. The townhouse near the sea in Hastings that I still can't believe we're living in – albeit temporarily.

And if not for the reason behind us having to move here, then I'd say life feels pretty damn good right now. What's not to love about living in a house on the South Coast with my husband and two children, all for free?

When I pull open the door, there's a woman a few years younger than me – perhaps mid-thirties – standing on the step below, beaming a perfect white smile as she looks up at me.

'Hello... hell*ooo*...' she croons, her smile stretching even wider.

I stare at her for a moment, bemused and wondering what I've forgotten.

'Hi,' I say back, feeling somewhat less-than as my eyes scan her up and down. I catch sight of the baby sick on my T-shirt as I hitch Tommy, my three-year-old, higher on my hip. He yanks a handful of my unbrushed hair, making me wince and jerk my head sideways. 'Can I help you?'

'I'm Mary,' the woman says sweetly, looking up at me as if I should know exactly who she is. She's wearing an above-the-knee, pale blue fitted tunic dress with short sleeves and a starched white collar. She's slightly shorter than me, but she's standing a step down with flat black ballet pumps on her feet. Her blonde hair is neatly tied up in a tight bun on the top of her head, and her pale skin is flawless and make-up free. I can't help thinking that if *Kill Bill* and *Maid in Manhattan* had a film baby, she'd be playing the lead role.

But it's her eyes – wide-set and piercing, with something deep and unfathomable lurking behind the cobalt blue – that, even with my newborn baby's cry starting up again in the kitchen, draw me in. A shiver runs down my spine.

'How can I help you, Mary?' I ask, shifting from one foot to the other with the hems of my old navy sweatpants frayed around my bare toes.

'Did Annie not tell you?' she says, reaching out her slender fingers to Tommy, who instantly stops grizzling and begins to laugh when Mary tickles his palm. 'About me?'

I shake my head vaguely, my baby-fuzzed brain trying to find something in its murky depths that might explain why this woman is standing on the doorstep not twenty-four hours after we arrived at our new home. Well, not *our* new home, exactly, but it's ours for the next couple of months while Annie is away travelling – finding herself or 'resting', as she put it in her WhatsApp message – while our house is being renovated. Or rather, being rebuilt. The fire destroyed much of the structure as well as everything inside it.

'No, no, she didn't say anything about you.'

Which is the truth. In fact, Annie told me very little when she first texted with the idea of us moving in here. I even had to remind her to send me the lock box code for the front door keys.

Impulsive, reckless, forgetful and wild have always been Annie's middle names. At school, we all used to tease her that her last name, Stone, was the opposite of what she *actually* was – her mind always alight, her brain constantly creating, her body vibrating with energy. She told our friendship group it's why she chose the last name Wilde as her professional name – the nickname we'd given her back then. *You're a wild one, Annie.*

Mary laughs and tips back her head, exposing her sinewy neck. 'Typical Annie,' she says, taking a step up to my level. Our faces are close, and I feel the warmth of her breath on my cheek as she speaks. 'She'll forget to turn up for her own funeral, that one,' she adds with a laugh.

A strange choice of words, I can't help thinking, but I don't want to seem rude, so I give her a smile back.

'I have my own set of keys, but didn't want to startle you. Mind if I come in? It's kind of necessary if I'm to do my job.' Another perfect smile.

'Job?'

Somehow Mary slides past me and glides down the long, chequerboard-tiled hallway until she reaches the kitchen doorway. She turns, her slender frame silhouetted in the light pouring in through the expanse of glass in the huge kitchen-dining-lifestyle-don't-need-the-rest-of-the-house extension that Annie had built across the back of the house. It was only finished a few months ago in the spring and no expense was spared.

'Shall I just follow my usual routine?' Mary asks, the shroud of light around her making her appear angelic.

'Go on, get down then, Tommy,' I say with a sigh, lowering my squirming son to the floor. 'And be careful around Gracie!' I call after him as he zooms off into the kitchen making roaring noises and holding up his toy car.

Mary laughs. 'He seems like a live wire.'

'I tell you what, Annie is a brave woman letting us lot stay here.' I close the front door and match Mary's laugh, heading down the hallway to join her. 'And look, I'm sorry for sounding so vague. Annie might well have told me about you coming but, you know...' I tap the side of my head, 'I probably forgot.' Then I squeeze past and head over to the glass bifold doors leading to the garden, checking on Gracie, who's stirring in her baby carrier. 'Hello, sleepyhead,' I croon before turning around again. 'Oh...!'

Mary is directly behind me, peering down at my baby.

'What a darling,' she says, not taking her eyes off her. 'How old?'

'Seven weeks tomorrow,' I say, bending down and unbuckling her from the carrier. She was asleep when I came back from dropping Matt, my husband, at the station half an hour ago so I could keep the car for the day, and I'd kind of hoped she'd stay that way while I cleared up from breakfast and did a bit of unpacking. Everything was so fraught yesterday when we arrived, and I barely got a chance to do anything.

'Such a little poppet,' Mary says, holding out her arms before I've even taken my now whimpering baby from her carrier. 'May I?'

I look at her for a second. 'Oh, sure,' I say, handing her over. When Tommy was a baby, I'd have found any number of reasons not to allow a stranger to hold him – I was so protective, being a first-time mum. But I'm much more relaxed with Gracie, and, as a result, my baby seems much more laid-back too.

'Ooh, aren't you a gorgeous little girl?' Mary says, deftly taking her from me and supporting her head with a skill that tells me she's no stranger to infants. 'You're going to be a right heartbreaker when you're older, eh, Mummy?' She glances up at me, a sparkle in her eyes.

'Oh, definitely,' I say with a laugh, wincing as Tommy drags the wheels of his toy car along Annie's immaculate white walls. 'Tommy, no, stop that!' I call to him. 'Play on the rug, there's a good boy.'

My son scowls and hurls himself onto the thick cream rug beside the huge, modern fireplace.

'So, um, tell me, Mary... sorry. You mentioned your job?' I watch her rocking Gracie in her arms, her head nestled in the crook of her right elbow, her other hand gently supporting the length of her back. She bobs slowly up and down, swaying a little. Gracie makes contented gurgling noises, blowing bubbles through her rosebud lips as she gazes up at the unfamiliar female face.

'I've been working for Annie just over a year now,' she explains, adding in a cooing noise directed at Gracie. 'And now I'm at your service, too!'

'At my service?' Something inside me stiffens. I'm not used to having anyone around.

'I'm her housekeeper, of course,' Mary says, leaning forward to give my baby a kiss on her downy head, while keeping her eyes firmly fixed on me.

TWO

GINA

'A housekeeper?' Matt says later, shaking his head incredulously. 'You're joking, right?'

'Nope. Uniform. Feather duster. Gleaming smile. The works.'

He blows out a whistle through his front teeth before swigging from his bottle of Peroni. 'Didn't see that one coming.'

'Me neither,' I say, listening out for a moment. 'She was a bit... *intense*,' I say, trying to think of the best way to describe Mary without sounding mean.

I get up to fetch the baby monitor from the white marble kitchen island at the other end of the huge, glass-sided extension, bringing it back to where we're chilling on the L-shaped sofa by the fire – the *white* sofa that I'll have to cover with some throws before Tommy destroys it. And there's no humping logs in from the shed or sweeping out the ash pan here – oh, no. A single flick of a remote control brings an ultra-modern inset fire to life with flames licking at giant faux pebbles.

'Feels a bit weird, with Gracie and Tommy being so far away upstairs.' I put my ear to the monitor, listening. 'I hope it's working. The house is so huge, the walls are bound to be really thick.'

'Love, relax. We tested it last night, and it worked fine.' He passes me my chamomile tea. 'Here, I made you this. It's been a hectic few days.'

I snort. 'Hectic few *weeks*, more like.'

It's true. It's been horrific and, frankly, I don't know how we've made it through – especially with having a new baby to look after. A day hasn't passed that I haven't thanked my lucky stars that we weren't in our home the night it burnt down three weeks ago. For once, having a bit too much to drink at our good friends Laura and Patrick's place, resulting in us stopping the night at theirs – kids, travel cot, pumped breast milk and all – was *very* much worth the next-day hangovers. It saved our lives.

'Where are you going now?' Matt asks as I leap up again, unable to settle.

'To see if I can figure out how the window blinds close,' I reply. 'I feel exposed, sitting behind all this glass in full view of whatever is out there.' Or *who*ever, I can't help thinking as I glance out into the pitch-black night, a shudder winding down my spine. But all I see is myself and the room reflected right back at me with the night sky beyond.

'Who's going to be out there on a drizzly autumn night staring in at *us*? It's just that patch of derelict land behind the garden. No one can get in. We're hardly interesting, as couch potatoes go.' Matt pats the seat beside him.

I pause, remembering the senior investigating officer's words when he first mentioned the possibility of arson, the tactful way he'd asked if anyone might be holding a grudge against us, if we'd had any spats with the neighbours, or any disagreements at work – and if we'd noticed anyone lurking in the area, perhaps watching our movements. Until then, I'd never have thought anyone would want to spy on us either, let alone destroy our house. The thought seemed impossible.

'Alexa, close the window blinds!' I call out in desperation.

'*Sorry, I didn't find a device named window blinds...*' a saccharine voice replies.

My eyes scan the room as I search for another remote control, but I can't see anything that we haven't already discovered. And then, as happened this afternoon, the ceiling lights start to flicker. 'That's what I meant from earlier,' I tell Matt, freezing as I look up, waiting for it to happen again. 'There... like that,' I add after they flash on and off for another couple of seconds.

Matt stares at the inset spotlights and shrugs. 'I doubt it's anything to worry about. You're bound to feel twitchy, though. I understand that.'

I don't say anything for a while, waiting to see if it happens again, but it doesn't. I can't stand the thought of staying somewhere with dodgy electrics – not after what happened to our house.

'Look, love, these lights are virtually brand new. And fitted by an electrician,' Matt continues, seeing my concern. 'You could just text Annie and ask her about the blinds,' he suggests, patting the sofa beside him again. 'Then come and relax.'

'But Annie is busy *finding herself*. She's made it perfectly clear she doesn't want to be disturbed while she's on holiday,' I say in a silly voice, mimicking Annie's message when she told us about her Kenyan-Thai-Japanese adventure. 'Though knowing her, she'll probably be home next week desperate to get back to work.'

'If she can't find a moment to tell you how to close the blinds, then she's got eff-all chance of finding herself, hasn't she?'

'Fair point,' I say, reaching for my phone and tapping out a quick message.

A few moments later, as we're scrolling through Netflix trying to find something to watch, Annie replies.

Blind control switch on main light panel xxx

Then, a second later, a photo of some zebra in a scrubby landscape with a stunning sunset appears on my screen. 'Looks like she's been on a safari,' I say, flashing Matt a look before going over to find the switch. 'Magic!' I say as the blinds lower within the double-glazed glass units. 'Privacy at last.'

I drop back down beside Matt, sinking into the soft feather cushions as he loops an arm around me, but I still find it hard to settle and get comfortable.

'What's up?' he asks, pressing pause on the remote. 'You're not yourself.'

'Sorry,' I say through a sigh. 'I just feel a bit... *rattled*. You know, uneasy inside.'

Matt faces me, his eyes wrinkling softly at the corners as he gives me a look. 'Unsurprising,' he says, squeezing me and kissing me on the forehead. 'You had a baby seven weeks ago and our house burnt down when she was a month old. That'll do it.' *And being in this place,* I swear he mumbles.

'I know, you're right.' I rest my head on his shoulder, thinking of our two precious little mites asleep upstairs, thanking God for the millionth time that they're safe. 'But it's not that making me feel weird. It's that woman from earlier...'

'I'm Gina, by the way,' I said to Mary this morning as she held Gracie. I was itching for her to give her back. I'd basically allowed a stranger off the street into our home and, within a couple of minutes, I'd handed over my baby.

'Yes. Gina. I know,' Mary said with a smile, looking at me with those blue eyes as she swayed from side to side. Gracie seemed besotted, staring up at her and gurgling. 'Annie told me all about you. I'm so sorry for what you've been through. It sounds awful.'

'Thank you, it was,' I replied. 'I think we'd have gone crazy having to spend another night in that hotel room while we searched for a rental. Thank God for Annie's generosity.'

At first, we'd tried to look on the bright side – simply relieved that we were all safe and unharmed, and at least hadn't had the trauma of escaping a burning house in the middle of the night with two terrified children. I've woken to that very nightmare several times since the fire, my brain playing out the worst-case scenario as I've processed events.

Thankfully, the house insurance covered our hotel stay until a rental property could be secured, though finding anywhere was proving tricky. While our phones, laptops and other essentials were replaced quickly, the full assessment and pay-out were going to take a lot longer and, at the time, were largely dependent on the investigation's findings. Though no amount of money can replace the sentimental items we've lost.

The chief of the fire investigation team wouldn't let us go inside the shell of our house in the following days – an unremarkable 1950s three-bedroomed detached on the edge of Crawley – deeming it too unsafe. Once the investigators and police had done their work to establish the cause of the fire, they rescued as many of our belongings as they could – but most things were either destroyed by water, or, if the flames hadn't consumed them, they were completely ruined by smoke and covered in a tarry black film.

'It was perfect timing then, wasn't it?' Mary said, hush-hushing my baby as she held onto her, rocking and cooing down at her. 'What with Annie going away and offering you her place to stay.'

'It was,' I replied, remembering how, at that point, Mary's expression changed from sweet and kind to blank and staring. I held out my arms to take Gracie back. The rocking had stopped, and I wondered if she'd even forgotten she was still holding my baby, concerned Gracie might roll out of her arms and onto the floor. But Mary wouldn't let go of her.

'It was so weird,' I tell Matt now. 'When I went to take Gracie, I swear for a few moments, we were literally having a tug of war.'

'She was probably just being overly careful. I wouldn't worry, love. She's Annie's cleaner. She'll have been vetted to within an inch of her life.'

I muster a laugh. 'You're right. Though when you meet her, for God's sake don't call her a cleaner. She made it quite clear to me that she's her *housekeeper*.' I laugh, grabbing a couple of Maltesers from the bag that Matt has opened.

'Same difference,' he replies, jabbing the remote at the TV again. 'How often does she come?'

'That's the thing,' I say, biting my lip. 'Most days, by the sound of it. Though she said she has a few days off a month on a rotating basis.'

Matt swivels round to face me, frowning. 'I suppose Annie has to spend her vast riches on something.' There's a tinge of bitterness in his voice, and it's not the first time I've wondered if he's a little bit jealous of her.

'Oi, don't be mean,' I say, prodding him playfully. 'Annie might be well-off, but she supports loads of charities. *And* she's giving someone a job.' *Not to mention putting a roof over our heads*, I think, but decide to keep quiet, not wanting to imply that Matt isn't able to provide for us.

He's a proud man and at first wasn't keen on taking Annie up on her kind offer. He blames himself enough for the fire as it is. Since we had kids, money has been a bit tight, but we decided that I'd stop work until they're both at school – it just didn't make sense with childcare costs, given I wasn't earning a huge amount at the garden centre anyway. Matt has a good enough job as a building surveyor and we get by each month, *just*, but we don't have a lot left over.

'I was kidding, love. If a single woman who's hardly ever present at her vast seaside home feels the need to employ a full-time housekeeper to look after her, then who am I to argue? Especially if we get to reap the benefits.' He pauses, raising his eyebrows as if he doesn't believe a word he's saying. 'Anyway, what exactly did this Mary person clean today?' Matt glances around the beautifully furnished space.

'That's the thing,' I confess, 'I said she could have the day off and sent her home.'

Matt frowns. 'Surely she could have done *something*?'

'The whole house was pristine when we arrived, and we've only been here a day. Trust me, it won't be long before we've trashed it,' I say. 'I just needed some time to... settle in. Spend some time with Tommy. He might seem OK, but since the fire, his behaviour has been a bit... *off*. You know?'

'Understood,' Matt says, nodding. 'You did the right thing. So when is Mary Poppins coming back?'

'First thing in the morning,' I say, though I can't help wishing that she wasn't. Matt will be at work, so it won't affect him, but I'm not used to having people around when I'm taking care of my children. Especially people I don't know.

But what's been troubling me most is what happened after I explained to Mary that we needed time to settle in, and that she should take the day off.

She did not seem happy, giving me a terse nod before she left.

It was an hour after she'd gone when I happened to glance out of the front window as I checked on Gracie asleep in her pram. I swear I saw Mary standing across the road in the grassy square opposite. She was half hidden behind a tree, staring back over to the house. It was only when she saw my face in the window that she put her head down, turned and walked briskly off.

THREE
GINA

The next morning, I have my phone pinned to my ear and Gracie nestled in the crook of my arm as I busy about with our routine. Tommy is hanging onto my legs, grizzling as I attempt to walk across the kitchen to get to the coffee machine to make another espresso.

'*You are caller number twelve... please continue to hold...*' I roll my eyes at the automated voice. I was hoping to speed up the surgery registration process by asking the receptionist to email me the forms to fill out before we head down there, but I'm not sure Tommy will go the distance of holding for eleven more callers before a full-on meltdown has him kicking and screaming face down on the floor.

'Tommy, love, let Mummy walk, will you?' I sigh, dragging my leg with my son attached to it as I try to find the mugs. I still haven't got the measure of where everything is yet, having only visited Annie at this house once before.

Over the years, our friendship group has kept in touch, and, while all three of us don't always get to see each other as frequently as we'd like, Laura and I manage to meet up once a month given that we live closer to each other – Matt and I in

Crawley, while Laura and Patrick are based in Royal Tunbridge Wells. Since Annie's acting and music career took off in the last ten years, we've seen less of her as she's often busy filming or travelling, and especially so since she moved into this place and got stuck into organising renovations.

Though I can't help thinking that there's another reason we don't visit her as often these days – because she lives back *here* in Hastings... the town where we all grew up. The town where we were once a group of four. The town where everything went bad.

'No *way*!' I snap at my phone at exactly the moment a suspicious smell escapes Gracie's nappy. 'How can I be caller number *fourteen*? I'm going backwards! Sod this.'

I instantly regret swearing in front of Tommy, who, while still hanging onto my leg and wiping Marmite toast down my pyjama bottoms, is now singing '*sod this*' over and over and as loudly as he can.

'Good morning!' comes a chirpy voice from behind, making me whip round as best I can with two children attached to me.

Mary is standing beside the white marble kitchen island, dressed in her neat uniform with a pleasant smile on her face. Though I swear I see one side of her top lip twitch ever so slightly as she looks at us.

'Mary... hello,' I say, hanging up my call to the surgery as I try to shake Tommy off my leg. But he's having none of it. *Sodthissodthissodthis* turns into a meaningless chime spewing from my son's mouth in an endless grizzle. 'You're here,' I continue above the din, because I can't think of anything else to say that doesn't involve either excusing the scene of chaos that she's witnessing or letting her know that I'm annoyed because she let herself in.

'You don't mind that I used my keys, do you?' she chirps, giving me a sideways look. 'Lots to do today, so just pretend I'm not here. I'll try to keep out of your way.'

'Would you like a coffee first?' I ask, uncertain if I'm meant to give her specific jobs. I go to fill the machine with water, taking the canister over to the sink. 'God, not again...' I mutter when the water from the tap sputters and spits with low pressure. Then, suddenly, it comes back on full power and sprays all over me. I jump back. 'It keeps doing this,' I say. 'I think there's something wrong with it.'

Mary reaches for a towel, handing it to me. 'I don't usually stop for coffee,' she replies. 'But thank you. It'll give us a chance to get a little more acquainted.' She perches on a bar stool with Tommy peeking out from the side of the island unit, staring up at her.

I dry myself off and flick on the machine to heat up. 'Tommo, come here, let me wipe your mouth. It's covered in Marmite.' I wave a piece of kitchen paper at him, which he duly ignores, gurning up at Mary instead.

'Looks like you've got your hands full with these two,' she says. 'Would you like me to make the coffee while you try the doctor's surgery again?'

I stop, staring at her. How did she know who I was calling? I don't like the thought of her eavesdropping – I must have been talking to myself.

'Thanks, but don't worry,' I reply. 'I'll head down there shortly to register. Gracie needs her health visitor appointments booking in – provided the pair of them behave long enough for me to fill out the forms, that is.'

I decide not to mention that I have Type 1 diabetes and also need to set up my insulin pen prescriptions at the local pharmacy. I was diagnosed in my early teens and it's not something I even think about much these days – I'm so used to the routine of regular blood sugar checks and injections, it's second nature to keep it under control. I feel so blessed that both my pregnancies went without a hitch.

I press a couple of buttons on the space age-looking coffee

machine, suddenly realising I forgot to put a cup under the spout. 'Uh-oh...' I say, flinging open cupboard doors to find a mug.

As if by magic, Mary is suddenly beside the machine placing an espresso cup beneath the stream of coffee, wiping up the mess and, a few moments later, after she's finished making the drinks, we're sitting side by side at the island.

'You know, you could leave Tommy and Gracie here with me while you go out. The parking is terrible at the surgery, so I suggest you walk there. Much less fraught for you. You could even have a wander around the shops on the way back, too. There are some lovely clothes boutiques nearby.' She flashes a look up and down me.

It's the way she says my children's names that sets my nerves jangling – as if she's familiar with them already. That, and the way her nose twitches ever so slightly, just enough for me to cotton on to her hint.

But I don't get a chance to reply. 'Oh, Gracie, your nappy,' I say, leaning down and smelling her. 'Bad Mummy for not changing you yet.'

'Bad Mummy... badmummy...' Tommy chants, thwacking my legs with his toast and sending it spinning across the tiles.

'He suddenly hates Marmite,' I explain, getting up to find the nappy bag. 'And he's taken to throwing food, well, just because he can...'

'I think it would do you good,' I hear Mary say from where I'm kneeling on the rug beside the fire, spreading out the changing kit. 'It's a lovely day. When did you last have any alone time?'

I feel like laughing hysterically, unable to remember when I last had a moment to myself, but I can't get the image of her lurking opposite the house out of my mind. I peel back Gracie's nappy, sensing that Mary is standing directly above me now, peering down at my semi-naked baby lying in a dirty nappy on

Annie's expensive cream rug. Then I spot a Malteser from last night, crushed underfoot with the chocolate smeared into the deep pile. Just before Mary kneels down beside me, I flick it under the sofa, leaving a brown smear in its place.

'Ohh, look at you, you little cutie!' Mary sings, stroking Gracie's head. Instantly, my baby stops grizzling and flaps her arms and legs excitedly in a way I've not seen her do yet. 'I'll change her, if you like. You go and get ready to go out.'

I glance down at myself, feeling slightly ashamed that I'm still wearing what I slept in – tartan pyjama bottoms and a faded Green Day T-shirt that used to be Matt's. I admit, it's a tempting offer.

'I suppose I *could* use a shower,' I say, thinking it's a chance to wash my hair, too. 'Are you sure?' I only feel comfortable saying this because Mary is Annie's employee. She was probably just waiting for a lift or something when I saw her. Besides, she's already cleaning Gracie up with wet wipes, making it look so easy.

'A hundred per cent,' she says with a kind look in her eyes. 'And don't worry,' she adds, putting her hand on my arm, 'while you're out I'll sort the chocolate stain on the rug, too.'

FOUR

MARY

If Gina knew who I was, there's no way she'd have left her children in my care. No way she'd have happily skipped upstairs to the shower, enjoying the freedom of washing and drying her hair without interruption. And she certainly wouldn't have put on her coat, grabbed her bag and planted a kiss on each of her children's heads before leaving the house with a smile on her face and profuse thanks to me.

No. There's no way she'd have done any of that.

Soon enough, I imagine she'll have a moment of anxiety, perhaps messaging Annie to confirm that I am indeed a trustworthy employee, that my references are glowing, that I'm DBS-checked and as squeaky clean as the windows I'm currently polishing. And I'm certain Annie will confirm all of this to her in a glowing reply – because it's true. I'm as clean as they come. An exemplary housekeeper.

My domestic skills are not in question.

'Tommy, sit *down!*' I tell the annoying three-year-old yet again. I have no idea how to entertain a child of his age, but he seemed to like the cartoons I put on the television – for all of two minutes. Then he was up and roaring about and crashing into things, nearly knocking Annie's Murano glass vase off its plinth and onto the baby, who's in her bouncy chair nearby mindlessly staring up at some colourful plastic dangly things. I caught the heavy vase just in time.

I have absolutely no desire to have any children of my own, and I remind myself that this temporary period of babysitting is a necessity as I bide my time. Watching. Waiting. Ready to do what I must.

Thankfully, it's not long before Gracie has fallen asleep to the sound of the vacuum cleaner droning back and forth as I hastily shove it over the rug to make it look like I've been busy. Small mercies that the baby is placid. Gina informed me that there's a supply of breast milk in the freezer should I need it, though I stopped her when she started to explain how to prepare it.

'Done it all before,' I told her, putting her at ease, while feeling slightly nauseous. She didn't need to know that I have no intention of handling the stuff or feeding the baby. It won't kill it to go without for a couple of hours. 'I nannied for a few years before becoming a housekeeper,' I informed her untruthfully. It seemed to do the trick as her concerned frown relaxed.

'I'll get going then,' she said, though I could tell she was still a fraction nervous by the way she kept glancing at her children as she edged towards the door.

'You sit still and watch TV, OK?' I say to the boy now. 'Don't move.' He thrusts an action figure at me, letting out a demonic laugh.

'Datdan...' he says through a snotty grin.

'Yes, Batman,' I echo, and he seems delighted that I understand. I hand him a tissue, but he drops it to the floor, watching it flutter down. 'Just stay here.'

I hurry through the hallway and up the staircase, having already worked out that the thirteen-minute walk each way to the surgery, plus an estimated fifteen minutes inside for form-filling and queueing, gives me a worst-case scenario of forty-one minutes before Gina's return. In reality, it'll be more like an hour, and longer if she decides to browse the high-street shops as I suggested. I hinted at the idea of picking up some treats from the delicatessen, and maybe choosing something nice to wear from one of the boutiques, but I don't know her habits or tastes well enough yet to determine if she'll bite at the diversion.

Twenty-eight minutes left, given that I've already wasted thirteen of them cleaning downstairs.

I enter the bedroom that Gina and Matt are using – Annie's guest suite. They've only been here two days and it's already in a mess. How two people have created such carnage when most of their possessions have been destroyed in a fire is beyond me. But ultimately, I remind myself as I step between items of discarded clothing, I am *more* skilled at producing carnage. I'm also very good at cleaning up after myself.

As soon as I spot the laptop bag on a chair in the corner of the room, I make a beeline for it. It's no surprise when I'm denied access to the silver MacBook (Gina's, I assume because of the butterfly stickers on the lid), but it was worth a try. And of course, without her fingerprint, the touchpad is no use. It's no surprise, either, that her password isn't a combination of her children's or husband's names. She's way too smart for that. I know someone who could get into the laptop with ease, and I'll ask him if I have to. I haven't met Gina's husband, Matt, yet – not officially, anyway – but I will be making that happen before too long.

I shove the laptop back in its bag and slide my fingers into the side pockets, pulling out a few random receipts – petrol, a coffee shop, a hair salon, a pair of Nike trainers – snapping photos of them on my phone. They help build a picture, allow me to colour in some blank spaces, lay out the jigsaw of their lives. There's also a small spiral-bound notebook with some figures written on several of the pages – the workings of a budget by the looks of it. I photograph it all just in case it's useful.

I head over to the dressing table near the window over-looking the back garden. Beyond that, between here and the large houses on the next street, is an area of overgrown land that's choked up with trees, brambles, weeds and gnarled old shrubs. It's council-owned as far as I know, but since the modern flats on the western side were built a decade ago, there's been no direct access to it apart from through the gardens of the surrounding properties. And it can't be built on either, so it just sits there forgotten and overgrown. A relic of past times.

Of past horrors.

I stare out at it – imagining, picturing, working things out. Then I swear I see a little girl in the undergrowth, running free with a grin on her face, her head tipped back, her blonde hair flying in the wind. But I gasp when I see the blood on her face, that her smile is really a grimace, and her eyes are filled with terror, her hair matted and muddy. I grip the dressing table to steady myself, looking away and screwing up my eyes.

With only nineteen minutes left, I need to keep moving.

A quick listen out from the top of the stairs and all I hear is the sound of the cartoons keeping Tommy occupied while I do what I must.

I exhale slowly, balling up my hands at my sides, closing my eyes again until the anger passes. Then I rummage through the two toiletries bags on the dressing table – one containing a few items of cheap make-up, and the other stuffed with items such as hairspray, body lotion, cleanser and deodorant. Quite the opposite of the high-end products in Annie's bathroom.

A quick glance at my watch tells me I need to get a move on – and another quick glance in the bathroom tells me that apart from two toothbrushes, toothpaste, soap and some wet towels, there's not much to see in there either. But it's as I'm heading back across the bedroom that the glint catches my eye.

Something on the bedside table that I missed before – gleaming in a ray of sunlight now streaming in through the window. As I take a few steps closer, I see a brassy-coloured chain with a tacky, tarnished pendant attached – half of a heart shape with a jagged edge and the word *Best* engraved across the front. Like something you might buy for a teenage girl.

I stare at it for a moment, my mouth curling into a small smile, while my own heart clenches into a tight knot. *She's still got it*. I fight back the tears before swiping it onto the floor and heading back downstairs to deal with the children. It's not time to take it yet.

FIVE

GINA

I'm halfway to the surgery when I begin to wonder what the hell I've done. Leaving my baby and three-year-old in the care of a stranger suddenly doesn't seem like a great idea. The overwrought and anxious part of me plays out a scenario in my mind where I run back to rescue my children from Mary's evil clutches. But the sensible part tells me to get a grip, that they'll be fine, that Mary is reliable and kind, and I should use the free time wisely as it's such a rarity. That I should be grateful to Annie's housekeeper for helping me out when it's not even her job to do so.

But still, I swipe my phone from my bag and fire off a text.

Hi Annie! Just wanted to check that Mary's OK dealing with kids, yeah? She's got Tommy and Gracie for an hour or so. Big love etc xx

It's the longest five minutes of my life and my legs feel about twice their normal weight as I continue my walk to the surgery, my eyes glued to my phone – checking the route and waiting for Annie's reply. As soon as the notification comes in, I open it.

*Relax! Mary's a gem. Totally trustworthy with the kids and the
house xoxo*

I instantly feel my insides unknot as I approach the surgery.
I put my phone away and join the queue at the reception desk,
groaning when I see there are at least seven people ahead of me.

'Hey, it's me,' I say to Matt's voicemail half an hour later. We
usually check in with each other a couple of times a day. 'I'm
just heading back from the doctor's now. Hope you're having a
more exciting day than me. Maybe we can take the kids down to
the seafront later when you're back from work. Love you.'

I hang up, smiling, knowing it's the little things that have
kept me and my husband going the last few weeks. Gracie's not
seen the sea yet, and we both want to be present when we show
it to her – even though, at seven weeks old, she's not going to
remember a single thing about it. But it'll be a special moment
for us. And Tommy won't remember the last time he was at the
coast a couple of years ago, so his excitement at licking an ice
cream while watching the waves crash onto the beach will be off
the scale.

I tuck my phone away, deciding to take a quick detour via
the local shops that Mary mentioned, heading into the deli
where I pick up some ham for lunch and, on a whim, a couple of
steaks for me and Matt tonight as a treat. Then I pop next door
to the grocery shop.

On the walk back, it's clear the neighbourhood has tempted
Londoners south, giving pockets of the town an arty vibe. As
teenagers, the four of us in our friendship group never appreciated the area we'd grown up in or the joy of living on the coast.
We couldn't wait to get away, plotting how we'd spread our
adolescent wings in the wider world.

Except one of us never got the chance.

We weren't emotionally equipped to process the shock of losing our friend under such terrible circumstances. Between us, we dragged around the blame, the guilt, the biting pain that gnawed away at our young minds until we couldn't stand it any more. Getting away from where we'd grown up became less about adventure and more about escape.

But now Annie has returned to live here, and as much as I want to love the town again, however hard I try to forget what happened or work out who was to blame, there'll always be a dark shadow looming overhead whenever I visit. And as hard as I try to block everything out, nothing will bring Sara back.

As I go up the front steps of Annie's house, I realise my ability to blank things out has helped me deal with the aftermath of the house fire, too. I just wish Matt could stop blaming himself with all the *what if*s and the *should have*s... Neither of us could have predicted the fire, but once arson had been ruled out, Matt still needed someone to blame.

And that someone always ends up being himself.

When the cause of the fire was found to be faulty wiring in the hall ceiling light – the light that Matt had fitted only a week before – my husband sank into a pit of self-loathing, virtually silent and refusing to get out of bed for three days when we were holed up in our cramped hotel room. I spent my time bringing him sandwiches from the little Tesco around the corner, and entertaining Tommy at the local park while rocking Gracie in her pram, leaving Matt to wallow in remorse.

I couldn't let our son witness his dad like that, and while Matt's low mood has improved since he saw his GP and got medication, I know he still blames himself for what happened. For destroying the home we'd scrimped and saved to buy – all of it wiped out within a few hours.

'If only I'd waited for the electrician to come,' Matt has said a thousand times in various permutations. 'What if we'd not stayed over at Laura and Patrick's that night?' is another favourite self-blame mantra that he's chanted a thousand times more.

What if... what if... what if... I think now, unlocking the front door and heading inside.

'Hi, I'm back!' I call out, putting the keys on the hallway console. I can't quite bring myself to say *home.*

I listen out for a moment, but the house is silent.

SIX

GINA

'Mary... *hello*, I'm back!' I call out a third time, going through to the kitchen again, casting my eyes around in case I missed them the first time. The rug by the fireplace looks freshly vacuumed, and Gracie's bouncy chair sits empty beside the glass sliding doors. Then I spot Tommy's beloved Batman figure balanced on the arm of the sofa – odd, given it's his 'toy of the moment' and he carries it around with him everywhere.

Back in the hallway, I shout up the stairs. 'Tommy! Gracie! Where are you?' I feel stupid saying my baby's name – as if I'm somehow expecting a reply from her – but that same feeling soon turns into the first whispers of anxiety as, for the second time, I rush into the drawing room... the formal dining room... the study with its dark grey walls and bookshelves... flinging open all the doors, my eyes whipping round. I even check the downstairs cloakroom in case Tommy needed to go, but that's empty, too.

My children are not here. And neither is Mary.

I run up the stairs again, trying to hide my concern in case Mary appears with Gracie in her arms and Tommy at her side.

Maybe she's looking for toys to amuse Tommy, or hunting for a book, or getting her phone charger or... or...

'Mary, I'm back!' I fling open a couple of doors off the first-floor landing, then I check the bedroom where Tommy has his little racing car bed that we recently bought, as well as the few toys that we've managed to replace for him.

Empty.

Then I go into the bathroom, my eyes quickly scanning around, and I freeze when I see the red spots on the white floor tiles. I drop to my knees to get a closer look, wiping my finger across the dark red blotches, inspecting what comes away. There's no doubt in my mind that it's blood.

'Tommy!' I yell, my heart thundering in my chest as a burst of adrenaline spurs me on up to the top floor – the attic rooms that Annie said she hadn't got round to decorating yet.

'Anyone up here?' I call out, panting. 'Tommy, Mummy's back. Where are you?'

There are three doors leading off the small landing with its sloping ceiling – one a shower room, and the other two are bedrooms filled with boxes and furniture draped in white sheets, the half-light from the closed curtains giving it a ghostly feel. My eyes scan around, but it quickly becomes clear there's no one up here either.

Desperately concerned that one of my children is injured, I hurry back down to the ground floor. On the edge of panic, I fumble with the lock on the heavy glass doors leading to the back garden, sliding them open. But even before I step outside, it's obvious the garden is empty. Despite their Georgian grandeur and size, none of the houses on this street have huge outdoor spaces – but even so, I head down the stone path leading from the marble-tiled terrace in case Mary has taken my children behind the summerhouse for some reason – maybe going on a nature hunt or to find a lost ball. I don't know... my thoughts aren't making any sense as my anxiety peaks.

'Mary! Tommy!' I yell again, scanning around, my voice verging on a scream. The only sound I hear in reply is a few lazy yaps from a dog a several houses away – followed by my own whimper when I realise my children, and Mary, are nowhere to be found.

Then I spot it. The wooden gate in the six-foot-high fence at the end of the garden, barely visible behind a laurel bush and set off to one side.

And the gate is ajar.

My hand comes up over my mouth when I see the gap leading to the patch of wasteland behind the house. A gap about the size a child could squeeze through.

I run over to it, yanking it fully open – though it's hard because of the weeds. My mind races through all the terrible things that might have happened... Tommy playing out here alone, finding the gate left open and wandering through it... An intruder breaking in and kidnapping my son and baby... Or maybe Mary herself has stolen my children, making off with them through the barren land at the back of the house, perhaps knowing a secret way out to make her getaway.

'Shit, shit, *shit*,' I mutter, standing on tiptoe to survey the virtually impassable area. It soon becomes clear that no one with two small children in tow would make it very far through the thick brambles and undergrowth, so I pinball my way back up the path and into the house, praying that my children will have magically appeared in the kitchen. But no – it's still empty.

I career into the hallway to grab my phone from my coat pocket. I'll call Annie first to get Mary's number, then if that's fruitless, I'm calling the police. This is beyond a joke now. There might have been an accident... anything could have happened.

'I *knew* I should never have left them,' I wail, skidding to a stop beside the coat stand. 'Oh!' I exclaim, a waft of cool air from outside suddenly hitting me as the front door opens. It's accompanied by the sound of squealing and giggling.

'Ahh, look, Mummy's beaten us back!' Mary says as she leads Tommy inside by his hand. He jumps over the threshold, a grin on his face. Gracie is wrapped up in her padded onesie and nestled in the crook of Mary's arm, her eyes drooping closed on the cusp of sleep.

'Oh my God, *Tommy*!' I cry out, crouching down and giving my son a tight hug. Then I'm up on my feet again, reaching out for my baby. 'You... you really didn't need to take them out...' I say to Mary, unable to hide the quiver in my voice or the tremble in my arms as I take Gracie back, pressing her soft head against my lips and drinking in her sweet smell. I'm shaking and flooded with relief. But also angry as hell.

'Oh, it was no bother,' Mary trills breezily, placing her hand on my shoulder. 'Tommy fell over in the garden and cut his knee, so I cleaned him up and took them down to the promenade to see the sea as a treat,' she says in a soft yet clipped voice. 'They loved it, and Tommy even had an ice cream, didn't you, sweetie?'

She ruffles my son's hair just as I spot the plaster on his knee.

'I hope that's OK with you, Gina?' she adds, tipping her head sideways, giving me one of her small smiles.

SEVEN

GINA

It's Saturday, almost the end of our first week staying at Annie's house, and Matt and I have fallen into a familiar rhythm: Matt leaving for work early – thankfully his latest project is under an hour's drive away – with me getting the kids up, dressed and fed before Mary's clockwork-like intrusion at 9 a.m. If nothing else, my steps have increased these last few days as we've been going out on long walks – thank God for double buggies – ambling over to Alexandra Park, sometimes strolling along the promenade or up to the headland, and we even hopped on a bus to Bexhill-on-Sea for a change yesterday. It burns off the entire morning so that when we return, Mary is almost done with her cleaning.

I think she prefers to work without the bother of us being in her way, though I don't know what she finds to clean for four hours each day. If it were up to me, I'd ask her to come once a week, but seeing as Annie is letting us live here for free, I don't feel it's my place to interfere with her routine.

'Your mum looked a bit harassed,' Matt says now, reversing the Toyota off the drive. I peer through the windscreen as we leave, seeing Tommy's face at Annie's living room window as Mum holds him up to wave goodbye. Behind her, I see Dad's outline as he rocks Gracie in his arms, cooing over her like the doting grandad he is.

'They'll be fine,' I say, more to convince myself than Matt. 'Mum will cope.' I give a final wave to my son, blowing him a kiss. 'It's only for a few hours, and there's no way I want Tommy seeing the house in the state it's in.'

If I'm honest, I don't want to have to see it again myself, preferring to remember it how we left it as we shut the front door for the last time and headed out to Laura and Patrick's for the evening. Having recently had Gracie, we'd not been out socially for weeks, and I'd been so looking forward to a night with friends. Never had I imagined that our lives would be turned upside down all because of a do-it-yourself light fitting job gone wrong.

I glance at the time. 'I reckon we'll be back by seven. Let's take Mum and Dad to that Italian place round the corner this evening. Treat them to a nice meal.'

I want to show them how grateful I am for looking after Tommy and Gracie. Matt's parents died within several months of each other two years ago, having moved to Scotland to retire a few years before that. Matt swears his mum died of a broken heart after his dad lost his battle with cancer. With Matt and I both being only children, childcare duties have fallen heavily on my mum and dad when they're able – though I know they enjoy the time with their grandchildren. And we can't bury our heads in the sand any longer about dealing with the house repairs.

Matt gives me a sideways look. 'Better check they have gravy on the menu for your dad,' he jokes. 'Maybe a takeaway is best. Then we don't have to worry about the kids kicking off either.'

I try to hide my disappointment. For me, getting out of the

house and wearing something other than joggers and a sweat-shirt will feel like a night out at the Ritz. 'Mum will help with any Tommy tantrums,' I say. 'And I know Dad's a bit meat and two veg, but I'm sure he'll find something to eat.'

Matt laughs, leaving me thinking that even if we're back drinking tea in our pyjamas by nine o'clock, after everything, I just want to feel normal again. I don't think he quite under-stands the claustrophobia of being cooped up with the kids in a house that isn't ours, given that he goes to work every day and mixes with other adults – but then I feel bad for even thinking that, as he suffers from *actual* claustrophobia and is working hard to support us.

To pass the time, I switch on the car sound system for some music, but it's already linked up to a playlist on Matt's phone.

'No way!' I say, giving him a look when I hear one of Annie's latest songs blaring out of the speakers – an upbeat poppy track that I'd never have had Matt down to listen to in a million years. 'You're a dark horse, Matt Dalton.' I give him a nudge. 'Liking her stuff.'

'I *don't* like it,' he's quick to say. 'I've no idea how this got on my playlist. You must have added it,' he says sourly, flicking off the stereo. 'I'm not in the mood,' he adds, focusing on the road ahead.

The rest of the drive to Crawley is uneventful, mainly filled with us discussing plans for the house renovations, plus we're toying with adding some of our savings to the insurance money to build the extension we've always dreamt of.

'It's going to be increased mortgage territory to get anything like what we want,' Matt says, breaking into a lengthy explana-tion about loan-to-value ratios, as well as how much garden we'd be left with.

Being a surveyor, he knows about this stuff. After he left school, Matt began an apprenticeship with a builder, learning all aspects of the trade including plumbing and electrics. But then in his mid-twenties, he retrained and, while he won't admit it, I know it was partly because he hated having to crawl into small or dark spaces that made him change career. He couldn't deal with the panic attacks and nightmares.

'I'm not sure getting into more debt is a good idea,' I reply vaguely, peering out of the side window as we head into our area on the outskirts of town. It seemed like the perfect place to raise our family when we viewed the property not long after we were married eight years ago, and close to Matt's head office, too. A few months after we moved in, Tommy was born, and then with my fortieth birthday looming, I fell pregnant with Gracie. We felt blessed to have completed our family.

Matt turns down our street – a pleasant road of unremarkable 1950s stuccoed houses, mainly semi-detached in matching pairs with neat front gardens. Some of the houses further along the road are, like ours, small but detached. We bought the worst house on a good street, and when we viewed number seventy-three Brockton Lane, we fell in love with its potential. It wasn't flash or grand, but from the moment we stepped inside, it felt like home.

After we'd moved in, we worked late into the evenings stripping peeling wallpaper, to save money by doing much of the work ourselves. When I was nine months pregnant with Tommy, I was glossing skirting boards, ending up in the labour ward with paint under my fingernails.

'Oh *no...*' I whisper now, covering my eyes as Matt pulls onto our small parking area.

It's only the second time I've seen it since the fire. Above each window, the brickwork is stained a sickening black, and I know that behind the metal hoardings covering the windows, many of the glass panes are broken from the heat. The yellow warning tape strung around the boarded-up front door flutters in the wind, and a 'Danger – Keep Out' sign has been nailed up on the front wall of the house. The charred roof timbers where the rafters collapsed hang precariously like burnt-out matchsticks.

'Come on, love,' Matt says, putting his arm round me as we get out of the car, tears filling my eyes. 'Let's get stuck in and have a productive day.'

I follow him up to the side gate, which he unlocks, and we head into the back garden where we've been told some of our salvaged items have been left, probably ruined by the weather now, too. The fire officer told us that some of our smaller items were left in the garage.

'Oh no, look...' I point across the lawn at Gracie's cot – once pristine white but now with black soot streaks up the side. The mattress has been chucked on the grass beside it and when I lift it up, it's sodden and muddy underneath.

'Oh, *love*,' Matt says, coming over and taking it from me, dropping it down again. We scour through the remains of our lives, picking over our possessions – everything from kids' toys to bedding to rugs to books, the microwave oven and even our melted plastic kettle. Not to mention the heaps of clothes and drawers that have been emptied out, with most things covered in a black, tarry substance.

I press myself against his side. 'I'm not sure I want to take anything back with us at all.' Sifting through our stuff was partly the reason for our visit, as well as meeting with a builder and architect about initial plans for putting our house back together. 'It'll just be a constant reminder.'

We're suddenly interrupted by a voice calling out from the front of the house – presumably the builder – as well as my phone trilling in my back pocket. When I look at the screen and see that it's my mother calling, my heart kicks up a gear.

'Hi Mum, all OK there? Are the kids all right?' I watch as Matt heads back through the gate to deal with the builder.

'Yes, yes, darling, the children are fine,' I hear down the line, instantly making me relax. 'But there's... well, there's a woman here.' Mum sighs heavily, and then I hear footsteps and a door banging as though she's gone into a different room. 'She scared the life out of us, to be honest, letting herself into the house like that. She says she's got nowhere else to go.'

EIGHT
THE PAST

The four of them were inseparable. Their teachers joked they should have been born sisters, and even though they all looked quite different, there was a telepathic quality to their friendship, as if their teenage minds had synced. If one was in trouble, the others seemed to sense it, rallying to their aid and doing what needed to be done to protect their group.

Of course, aged fourteen, this 'trouble' was usually something like missed homework, a lost pencil case, a clash with that mean girl from the year above, or not having enough pocket money to buy the current fad make-up item. Catastrophic things like that.

Mainly, they were just normal girls doing normal things in a normal town by the sea: Gina, Annie, Laura and Sara. Or GALS as they called themselves.

None of them knew it at the time, but soon one of them was going to die.

'Oh em gee, I nearly *died*, guys...' Annie spluttered into her can of Coke, her eyes wide and glittering as green as the sea that was just a few metres across the road from their table in the café window. 'I told Mr Bell there's no *way* I'm kissing him. Not on the lips, anyway.' She swept back her red-gold hair with her fingers, tipping back her head and shaking out her thick curls. Loving the cringe of what she'd just revealed to the others.

Sara watched on, jiggling the teabag in her mug as they sat in Davy's, the local café-cum-chip shop where they usually met up on a Saturday morning, wishing she was as striking and confident as Annie. There's no way she'd ever have the guts to audition for the school play, let alone be able to pull off the lead female part that involved a kissing scene. She literally *would* die.

She reached over to Annie with a paper napkin, dabbing the condensation dribbles from the bottom of her friend's Coke can.

'You'll be amazing,' she said in a soft voice that she wished more than anything was louder, more commanding, more powerful – anything to get her noticed. She was sick of blending in, of feeling not like the wallflower but the wall*paper*. Peeling wallpaper, at that. In the past, they'd all taken bets on which one of them would be first to get a boyfriend, and while Sara couldn't be sure who'd strike it lucky first – she figured Annie, but possibly Gina – she knew for certain that it wouldn't be her.

'You've *got* to do it,' Gina squeaked, clapping her hands together while trying to ignore the pang of jealousy inside. She'd got a berry slushie and her tongue was a diseased shade of blue, which she stuck out at three lads from their year as they sauntered past the café window, with the tallest of them, Matt Dalton, grinning and banging his fist on the glass, making it rattle in its frame.

'Oh my *God*, talk of the devil,' Gina continued, giving the others a wry smile. Gina tracked Matt as he passed, knowing she was only voicing to Annie what they were all thinking about the play. 'You have to take one for the team and tell us what it's like to snog him, yeah?'

Annie laughed, making a silly face and flipping her middle finger at Matt as he passed, but, strangely, his eyes were on Sara, where they remained for a few moments, his gaze lingering, his head turning back as the boys walked by.

'You do realise that you don't properly snog for a stage kiss,' Annie said, rolling her eyes as if they were all stupid.

'If only he knew we were all talking about him,' Gina said with a sigh as Matt disappeared down the road. 'Anyway, once word gets around that the hottest boy in Year Eleven has got a lead part in the school play, and the legendary Annie Stone is his leading lady, those tickets will sell out in minutes.'

'Oh, trust me – he knows,' Laura said confidently.

Outwardly, Gina laughed again, but there was a sting deep inside her as she slurped the remains of her slushie. Matt had barely glanced at her just now. She leant closer to the window to see if she could still see the boys as they headed further along the seafront. Or rather, to see if she could still see *him*. She wondered why he'd stared at Sara for so long as they'd passed, but then maybe she'd been mistaken. It felt mean to think it, but she doubted he was interested in her. The problem was, Matt didn't seem interested in *any* of them. They were beginning to think he didn't like girls.

Annie continued to protest and fluster about the on-stage kiss with Matt, making certain everyone else in the café knew that she was going to be snogging him in front of four hundred people in the end-of-term play, her arms gesticulating wildly, her mascara-laden lashes beating like insect wings. The other three knew she was lapping up the attention.

Classic Annie.

'Hold still, you've got a hair,' Sara said, barely audible beneath the cacophony of chatter that bounced between the other three. She reached over to Annie and gently lifted the errant eyelash from her cheek, blowing it from her finger. 'Make a wish,' she said, but Annie didn't hear.

'Just to be clear, it doesn't mean I'm *into* him,' Annie continued in a loud voice, leaning forward and ushering everyone close – which they all knew meant that she was into him. She was giving side-eyes to another group of girls at the next table, which only served to pique their interest in whatever the GALS were discussing.

'Well, *I'm* into him and totally would snog him,' Gina said, deadpan. 'Feel free to put in a good word for me when you have your tongue down his throat in rehearsals, Annie. I'm not too proud to admit it.' She flicked a glance out of the window again, but Matt was long gone. She just liked looking at the space where he'd recently been.

'Clearly,' Sara said, but it came out as a whisper, and no one paid any attention. She hadn't dared mention it to the others, but she'd felt Matt's stares over the last few weeks, had sometimes caught him looking at her. She thought he'd smiled at her once in the canteen, so she'd flickered a nervous grimace back at him, her heart pounding, not knowing how to act. And she hadn't failed to notice him staring at her just now when he'd walked past the window with his friends. After everything, it was weird.

Half an hour later, they left the chippy. Before they went their separate ways, the four shared a group hug, doing their GALS fist bump routine before Laura and Annie went off home. Sara and Gina, who lived in a similar direction, ambled the first part of the walk together.

'What do you know about Matt Dalton, then?' Sara asked Gina, instantly wishing she hadn't. For once, she was grateful that her words seemed to be swept away on the stiff sea breeze as they walked up the hill away from the coast, their legs quite used to the steep climbs in the town. She was forced to repeat herself when Gina didn't hear.

'Matt? He's cute,' Gina said with an upward inflection.

'But what's he *like*?' Sara said, surprised that she didn't have to repeat herself this time. Her words came out with purpose and precision.

'Yeah, he's nice,' Gina replied. 'He helped me pick up all my books when I dropped them. *Accidentally*, of course,' she said, giving Sara a nudge. 'He smells good, too.'

Sara didn't think that was the answer she was looking for, either. No, she wanted to know what made him tick, things that would help her understand him.

'*Ohh emmm geee*, Saz, you've got a massive blush on.'

Sara jumped as she felt something poke her in the ribs.

'No, scratch the blush. You're on *fire*.' Gina laughed, linking arms with her and pulling her close. 'You fancy Matt Dalton, don't you?'

'No, I do not,' Sara said as loudly as she was able. She didn't sound convincing. And she didn't *fancy* him as such, not like the others did. It was more that she wanted something to confirm that he was a good person, something to add a happy ever after to the thoughts swirling about in her head.

Silence for a moment as they continued walking, the energy between them suddenly feeling like similar poles of a magnet. Each of them sizing up what this non-confession meant.

'Just so you know,' Gina eventually said, 'his breath smells a bit.' She looked sideways at Sara, pinching her nose.

'Yuk,' Sara replied, and the girls walked on, each of them quiet, until they veered off towards their own streets – with Sara wondering if she dared smile back next time Matt looked at her, and Gina wondering if she should hurry up and ask Matt out herself.

NINE
GINA

'What woman?' Matt says, sounding annoyed and giving me an impatient glance as I interrupt his conversation with Steve, our builder. The pair are peering up at the burnt roof – Steve making suggestions about the extension, while Matt jots things down on his clipboard. 'Can't it wait?' Another scowl.

'I'm not sure. Mum said a woman has let herself into the house saying she has nowhere to go. Before I could ask who, she said she had to go and hung up. I heard Dad in the background, so hopefully he's helping deal with it.'

'Can't you call her back?' Matt turns back to Steve, who's now on about Crittall doors and various colour options, so my frustrated *of course I bloody well called her back* goes unheard.

I leave yet another voicemail message for Mum, repeating the same on Dad's number: 'Call me asap! Worried – what's going on? What woman?'

While Matt talks through plans, I pick through the soggy remains of our lives on the lawn, bagging up anything I consider salvageable. But I just want to get back to Hastings to find out what's going on.

'Oh, *Bunny...*' I say, spotting Tommy's favourite soft toy

lying in a heap of smoke-damaged bedding. The soft beige rabbit was grubby before, but now he's a barely recognisable sooty mess. Into the rubbish bag Bunny goes.

There are a few items I might be able to wash and clean, but not many. It's the smell that's the worst – an acrid, bitter stink that's as haunting as the panicked call we got from our neighbour late that night, informing us our house was burning down while we were on our third bottle of wine and eating a Thai takeout at Laura and Patrick's place.

'I'm nearly done here,' I tell Matt as I dump some rubbish sacks in the skip we hired. Mum's call has rattled me, and while I trust her and Dad to look after the kids – calling the police if needed – I just want to get back. A nagging feeling inside tells me I know *exactly* who the woman is.

We stop for petrol on the way back to Annie's later in the afternoon, adding another ten minutes to our journey, seeming to get stuck behind every slow-moving vehicle in the county.

'Still no reply,' I say to Matt as I try Mum's phone yet again. 'She usually answers straight away.'

'They'll be dealing with the kids, not glued to their phones, love. Try not to worry. We'll be back in under an hour. And at least we took care of a few jobs at the house. Steve's going to get his team started a week on Monday. He's liaising with the insurance company, too.'

'That's something,' I say, staring out of the window as, finally, we hit a stretch of clear road.

I try calling Mum and Dad several more times but give up once we're close to Hastings. As soon as Matt pulls up in front of the semi-underground garage at the side of Annie's house, I leap out of the car and rush up the stone steps, fumbling my keys into the lock. 'Hello! We're back!' I stride down the hallway and into the kitchen. But it's empty.

'In here, darling!' Mum calls out – her voice sounding cheery, which makes me relax. In the drawing room, I find my parents sitting on the sofa, Gracie asleep in her bouncy chair and Tommy on the floor playing contentedly with Duplo. There's a tray with a pot of tea and a plate of cakes, and on the sofa opposite Mum and Dad sits a woman.

Mary.

'Hi...' I say, lurching to a stop in the doorway, my eyes flashing around the room. 'Everything OK, Mum?' I give her a look that hopefully she'll pick up on.

'Everything's fine, darling,' she replies – a complete contrast to how she sounded on the phone. 'Mary here is just telling us about the history of this house. Fascinating.'

'Built in 1820, apparently. Once owned by a retired naval officer from Portsmouth,' Dad says, nodding at Mary.

'Right,' I say, totally confused. 'And all this has to do with...?' I go over to Gracie's chair, kneeling beside her as she sleeps.

'Absolutely nothing at all,' Dad says with his trademark guffaw. 'But interesting for an old history buff like me. Mary gave us the grand tour of the house when she arrived. Fabulous place. Our little Annie did all right for herself, eh? I always watch her in that cop drama... oh, what's it called now...?' Dad pulls a face.

'*No Limits,*' I tell him, not having the heart to say that it was one of Annie's earlier shows, that she's been in a load more stuff since then, including many award-winning movies. 'It's not your day to work today, is it?' I ask Mary, turning to her.

An awkward look flashes over her face as she studies the teacup balanced in her lap. Then she places it on the tray and stands up, zipping up her black hoodie. For some reason, it seems strange to see her in clothes other than her uniform – as if I'd never considered that she had a life outside of working here.

'You're right. I'm so sorry, I shouldn't have come,' Mary says in a sad voice. She shoves her hands deep inside her hoodie pockets. 'You've got family here. I'm intruding. It's just that...'

'Nonsense, dear,' Mum pipes up. 'You've done exactly the right thing, hasn't she, Ron?' Mum nudges Dad.

'The right thing, Joyce, the right thing.'

When I see the pitiful expression sweep over her face and tears collecting in her eyes, I let out a small sigh. 'Mum mentioned that you have nowhere to go, Mary?'

She nods.

Another sigh from me, inaudible this time. 'Well... I'm sure Annie wouldn't mind if you stopped here for a night or two. We can't have you homeless.' I'm already inwardly cursing myself for offering as there's something about her I don't fully trust, even though I can't fault her work here at the house. But given Annie's generosity, I don't feel I can chuck her out either.

Mary picks up her canvas bag and slips it over her shoulder, heading for the door.

'Thank you, that's kind,' she says, lowering her gaze. Tommy runs over to her, throwing his arms around her legs before holding up his Duplo model. 'But my problems run a little deeper than just a night or two.'

'May-*wwy*, look!' my son shrieks, pulling at her trousers.

Mary smiles down at him, ruffling his hair. 'Wow, you're so clever, Tom-Tom!' she croons. 'That's an amazing spaceship you've built.'

I don't fail to hear Mary's sniff, followed by her taking a tissue from her bag and blowing her nose. 'Anyway, look, I'm so sorry I interrupted your day,' she says. 'I didn't mean to foist my problems on you. I just thought that with me working here every day, that it would make sense if I...'

'If you moved in,' Mum finishes for her as she trails off. 'It makes perfect sense to me, dear,' she adds. 'And Gina would love the company, plus the extra help with the little ones. She's been struggling a bit since Gracie was born, what with the fire and all.'

'I am here, you know, Mum,' I say, getting up off the floor. 'What sort of problems, Mary?' I ask just as Matt joins us.

'It's OK, really,' she says, her cheek catching in a shaft of early evening sun as she angles her face slightly. 'I'm just stuck for somewhere to live right now.' She forces a laugh and it's only then that I notice the bruise under her eye. 'But I'll find somewhere to crash, so don't worry at all. And I'll be here as usual at nine o'clock on Monday morning. Can we just forget today happened?' She turns to me, clasping her hands under her chin, making her appear almost childlike.

'Hi Joyce, hi Ron,' Matt interjects quickly, giving my parents a nod and a smile. 'What have I missed?' He grabs Tommy under the armpits as he comes over to me, hoisting our son onto his hip. 'Hey, Tiger!'

'Matt, this is Mary, Annie's housekeeper. I told you about her, remember? And Mary, this is my husband, Matt. I'm sure I've probably told you all about him too!'

I'm trying to keep things light and breezy while thinking up a reason not to offer Mary more than just a night or two. I'm drained after today and just want to treat Mum and Dad to dinner out then get the kids settled and chill with Matt, not sort out Mary's housing problems. Though it's not as if there isn't any space for her here, I think, arguing with myself. There are two bedrooms doing nothing on the top floor – and Mary knows this. Besides, I won't be able to sleep tonight knowing the poor woman has nowhere to go. The thought of her sleeping in a bus stop or shop doorway seals it.

Then I'm aware that Mary is still staring at Matt – almost unpicking him with her eyes. Her hand comes up to shake his, but Matt is slow to respond, seeming distracted as he returns her stare, his head tipped to one side as she holds his gaze.

'Nice to meet you, Mary,' he says finally, sticking out his

hand. 'And thanks for everything you've done this week. House is looking tip-top.'

'You're welcome,' Mary replies, turning her head away as she smiles – showing her bruise again. But it's also a smile that tells me she's quite used to men acting slightly weird in her company.

In her uniform, Mary has a precise, symmetrical and flawless beauty. Now, in casual clothes, there's something even more appealing about her – seeming small and vulnerable inside her baggy hoodie, her shy mannerisms and the slight bow of her head with her long, ash-blonde hair hanging loose. She's one of those types of people who give off a magnetic aura without trying. A rare charm.

'Mary was just telling us that she's homeless,' I whisper to Matt, hearing Dad's grunts as he hoists himself off the sofa.

'And Gina was about to offer her a room, weren't you?' Mum explains further, giving Dad a hand up.

'Only if you're totally sure,' Mary says with an expectant look on her face.

I'm suddenly encircled by my parents, by Matt and Tommy, and by Mary – all eyes on me as they wait for my reply. I desperately want to say that Matt and I will need time to discuss it, that I should ask Annie's permission first, searching for the words to put her off any way I can.

But instead of any of that, I find myself reaching out and taking Mary's hands in mine, smiling and saying, 'Yes, yes, of *course* you can stay. For as long as you need.'

TEN

GINA

'I found this on the floor almost under the bed,' Matt says, holding something out. We're upstairs getting ready to go out for a meal, and also waiting for Mary to return with her belongings. She said she didn't have much to fetch.

Matt presses something into my palm – the little chain and pendant that I've had since forever. I smile, grateful that the superstitious side of me prevented it from being lost in the fire. I usually have it on me – either tucked inside my purse or double-looped around my wrist as a bracelet. I always keep it safe.

It's not much to look at with its faded brassy colouring – I'd never wear it around my neck any more – and the friendship pendant isn't exactly unique, but it's the little things like this that mean the most now. Familiar items with memories attached. It must have somehow got knocked onto the floor.

'It was good of you to invite Mary to come with us tonight,' Matt says, taking off the grubby sweatshirt he wore today. He presses it to his nose, smelling it and pulling a repulsed face. 'That stink of smoke. It'll be in my nose for days.'

'We could hardly leave her here while we all go out, could

we? Especially not after she explained about her abusive ex. He sounds evil.'

'Even so, do you think it's worth checking with Annie?' Matt says, ducking into the bathroom to turn on the shower. 'We don't want to piss off our landlord.' He peers out of the en suite, giving me a nervous look. I know he doesn't like the feeling of being beholden to anyone, least of all Annie. 'Water pressure seems to be OK up here, by the way,' he adds. I asked him to take a look at the kitchen tap earlier, explaining how it had been playing up.

'You're right, I should let her know,' I say, grabbing my phone and sitting on the end of the bed as I type out a quick message to Annie while Matt has a shower. 'Maybe we should call a plumber anyway,' I say back, though I don't think he hears.

Hey Annie... hope all good. OK with you if Mary stays here a night or two? She's had a bad break-up and we felt sorry for her. Big love TFNS xx

I swing my feet up on the bed and lie back, waiting for Matt to finish his shower, but quickly leap up when I feel something lumpy beneath the duvet. When I whip back the bedding, I gasp, not quite able to take in what I'm seeing at first.

'What the *hell*...?' I reach out to touch what looks like a pile of dirt on my side of the bed. Matted hairs, dust, crumbs and all kinds of filth is spread on the crisp white sheet, the dust wafting into the air when I disturb it. '*Matt*...' I hiss towards the bathroom. 'Something weird has happened...' But he doesn't hear me in the shower, and I don't want to shout.

I pinch a bit of the muck between my fingers, confirming what I think it is – the contents of the vacuum cleaner canister emptied into my bed. I feel sick inside, knowing there's only one person who could have done this. And she's in the process of moving in.

By the time Matt is towelling himself off in the bedroom, he's as puzzled as I am. 'I wouldn't leap to conclusions,' he says, staring at the pile of dirt. 'There could be other explanations.'

'Such *as*?' I snap, hands on hips as I work out whether to confront Mary about it. If it wasn't her, then it will only make things awkward between us. But apart from my parents, there's no one else it could be.

'Maybe she emptied the vacuum with the intention of changing the sheets but then got distracted. Perhaps she was going to shake the dirt into the dustbin.'

'That's a wild stretch and you know it,' I say just as my phone pings with a reply from Annie.

Poor Mary. Tell her she can stay as long as she wants. Mi casa etc. All good here xx

I'm about to send a message back, telling her exactly what I think of her housekeeper, when a piercing shriek comes from downstairs, sending me rushing to the top of the stairs. But then I hear Mum's cajoling voice as she deals with my son, followed by the slightly deeper, sterner undertones of Dad as he chimes in to put a halt to Tommy's growing tantrum. I'm half poised to go and rescue my parents, but I now have to change the bedding. And I still need to give Gracie a quick feed before we go out.

Back in the bedroom, I reread Annie's text... As I expected, she's generous to the core, and I knew she wouldn't have any objections to Mary staying, though I'm hoping it really will only be for a night or so, given what she's done – and so brazenly. I have no idea why she'd have a grudge against me, but at least she mentioned the possibility of moving in with her mother soon, though it was said in haste as she was rushing off to get her stuff. All things considered, I decide not to fan the flames by confronting her yet, preferring to wait for her to leave instead.

As I change the bedding, Matt chats about plans for the house, rubbing his hair vigorously with a towel and not seeming particularly disturbed by what's happened. On top of everything, I'm sad that Annie keeps forgetting to respond to my messages in the way us GALS always used to – the four of us chanting our little motto in the school playground, at the games arcade, sitting in Davy's Chippy or at each other's houses. Thick as thieves we were back then.

Until we became a group of three.

'Cheer up,' Matt says, chucking his wet towel at me.

'I'm still rattled,' I say, grabbing it and shoving it at him as I walk past. 'Guess I'd better get changed,' I add, catching sight of myself in the mirror.

'Oh, I dunno. I've heard that ripped tracksuit bottoms are all the rage right now.' Matt grabs me by the waist and pulls me close to his naked body, lifting up my chin and kissing me. 'I actually find them quite sexy,' he says, pressing a kiss on my lips. 'And try not to be upset by the bed. I'm sure it wasn't intentional.'

I hate that I hold back from responding, not feeling in the mood for intimacy – as well as feeling bulky and unattractive against his lean body. But then I remember my body has grown a whole new human life in the time it's taken him to perfect his biceps, so it's hardly a surprise I'm feeling a bit battle-weary.

'Not now, love,' I say. 'I've got Gracie to feed before we go out.' I prise myself away from him and pull off my tracksuit bottoms, finding something smarter to wear – black cargo pants with a loose, dark grey top that's breastfeeding-friendly. It takes me a few moments to check my blood sugar and inject a dose of short-acting insulin before I eat, then I loop the friendship heart chain around my wrist before heading downstairs.

'She's such a good baby,' Mum says in the kitchen, handing

Gracie over to me. She brushes a kiss on my little girl's head of soft brown curls.

'She's not had much choice but to be good, what with everything going on since she was born. I feel like I haven't given her as much attention as I should.' For a moment, I consider telling Mum about what I found in my bed, but I don't want to worry her unnecessarily.

'Nonsense, darling,' she says, arranging some cushions on the sofa for me as I settle down to give Gracie a feed. 'You're a brilliant mum. I'll fetch you some water.'

'Thanks, Mum,' I say, tipping back my head as I call behind me. 'And so are you...' But I trail off, sitting bolt upright again and swinging round, causing Gracie to lose her latch on me. 'Who are *you*?' I say, holding my baby's head steady. I suddenly feel very vulnerable with a stranger standing right behind me.

The boy, perhaps in his late teens, stares down at us. He says nothing.

'Here you go, darling,' Mum says, handing me the water. 'Do you want a drink, Tyler?'

'Tyler?' I say, fumbling to cover myself up. I hold Gracie over my shoulder and stand up. 'Sorry, and you are?'

The boy, who could be anywhere between fifteen and twenty years old, just stands there, his skinny arms dangling down by his sides with the buttons of his pale blue check shirt done all the way up to the top. He's wearing brown trousers and black trainers, and I catch sight of a phone in his right hand. But it's the stare emanating from piercing blue eyes set in his ghostly white face that makes me take a few paces away from him, especially while I'm holding Gracie. He seems fixated on her.

'Oh, there you are, Ty,' a voice says from the kitchen doorway.

When I look over, Mary is standing there holding a cardboard box in her arms.

'God, I need to put this down.' She glances around before

dumping the box on the marble island, brushing her hands down her front. Then she comes over to the boy and slings an arm around his shoulder. He's about a foot taller than Mary and flinches ever so slightly when she touches him.

'Gina, this is Tyler, my... He's my son.' Mary beams up at the boy. 'You don't mind if he stays too, do you?'

ELEVEN

MARY

I see she's wearing the heart chain wrapped around her wrist. And she's staring at me, her mouth hanging open, not knowing what to say as I introduce her to Tyler – the last thing she expected me to turn up with when I said I was going to get my belongings. I stifle the smirk. If only she knew the truth.

'Honestly, Tyler's no trouble,' I tell her. 'You'll hardly know we're here. I can't thank you enough.' I give her a grateful expression, my arm slung around Tyler's shoulder as he stands beside me, tall as a grown man. And he eats me out of house and home – if we had a house or a home, that is. I'm praying he doesn't say anything that will turn Gina off the idea of us both staying, because we come as a package. Tyler is one of the reasons I'm doing this, after all.

'No, no, that's fine,' Gina replies cautiously, fussing about with her baby as it begins to squawk. A strange look washes over her face as, no doubt, her brain is busy doing the maths, her eyes flicking between me and Tyler, trying to work out how old – or *young* – I was when he was born. And she'd be wrong, of course. She's probably wondering why I didn't mention him earlier, realising that I'd purposefully kept quiet about him until she'd already agreed to let me stay.

'I'm sorry... I figured that Annie would have mentioned I have a son. We can find somewhere else if you prefer. There's a homeless shelter not far away.'

'She didn't mention your son, no,' Gina says, softening slightly at the mention of Annie. 'I won't hear of you going to a shelter, for goodness' sake. And hello, Tyler,' she says, finally holding out her hand to him. 'It's good to meet you. I hope you like boisterous three-year-olds.'

Tyler doesn't reply. He just stares at the baby, not taking his eyes off her.

'He loves children,' I say on Tyler's behalf. 'He really does.' I decide to leave it at that before I say something I'll regret. 'Ty, your computer is in the box over there. Why don't you take it up to the top floor?'

It takes him a moment to react, but at the mention of his computer, he turns to fetch the box, easily swiping it up in his arms and heading upstairs. Once he's out of earshot, I say, 'Look, I totally understand if you want to check in with Annie first about this arrangement. It's a lot, I know.'

'I suppose I should let her know that you're *both* here.' A pause as Gina thinks. 'Though I don't want to keep disturbing her on holiday. I'm surprised she's managing to switch off from work for so long. It's most un-Annie-like.'

'I've been trying to get her to take a proper break for ages. I'm glad she's getting a good rest.' I hesitate, not wanting to overstep the mark and cross the line from housekeeper to friend. God no, that wouldn't do. 'While we're staying, I'll have a chance to give the entire place a really good sort out and deep clean for her return.'

Gina's expression switches back to concerned again as she bites her bottom lip, wondering just how long we're going to be staying. At the mention of a deep clean, the one or two nights she offered is turning into a couple of weeks in her mind.

She'd be wrong. It's going to be way longer than that.

I take a step closer, putting a hand on her arm before glancing at the door again to make sure we're alone. 'It's... it's not the first time Tyler and I have needed a place to stay,' I explain. 'Ty's dad... he gets in these bad moods sometimes,' I confide, which is enough for her to cotton on to my meaning.

'Oh God, I'm so sorry,' Gina replies. 'That sounds awful. Don't worry, there's plenty of space here for you both. We'll make up the beds on the top floor.' She rocks her grizzling baby, eyeing me. 'We'll spend a couple of hours tomorrow straightening the rooms out.'

'You're a lifesaver,' I say, taking a deep breath before I engulf her in a hug, staring blankly over her shoulder.

Half an hour later and our group is seated at a round table in an Italian restaurant a short walk away. It sounds funny saying that... *our group*, as though Tyler and I are now part of the family – Gina, Matt and their two children, plus Gina's parents, Ron and Joyce. I watch Matt struggling with his baby since Gina, exasperated, plonked her in his arms. There's a full-blown crying session brewing, judging by the agitated noises Gracie is making as Matt rocks her in vain, trying different positions.

'Put her on your shoulder,' Gina suggests. 'Might be wind.' They're sitting opposite me, and I notice that Matt snaps a curt reply back. I have Tommy to my left and Tyler to my right, and I take the menu as the waitress hands them out, my eyes scanning the huge selection of dishes for something that Ty might eat as everyone else makes their orders.

'He'll have a bowl of plain pasta, please.' I smile up at the waitress.

'What sauce does he want?' the young girls asks, flashing a glance at Tyler.

'No sauce. Nothing on it. No oil, no herbs, no garlic or anything. Just a bowl of plain pasta. Fusilli if you have it, but anything will do. Just not spaghetti or anything... long.'

'Not a fan of Italian food?' Gina says across the table to Tyler, who is carefully unfolding his napkin. He picks up his spoon with his right hand and inspects it before placing it down again.

He shakes his head. 'Not really,' he says, staring at the water jug. 'But pasta is OK.'

'What's your favourite food?' Gina presses on. 'I'll make sure to stock the fridge with things you like.'

She's taking pity on us, thinking that it can't be easy for a lad to be uprooted because of a volatile father, perhaps having witnessed his mother beaten black and blue many times during an unstable childhood.

'Pasta,' Ty replies politely like I've taught him. 'And I like cheese. But not together. And crisps, plain ones. And chicken burgers, no sauce.'

'Can't beat a good chicken burger and chips,' Matt says from across the table. 'My kind of man.' He grins, taking a long swig from his bottle of beer, presumably to numb the increasing cries of his baby.

'Kids these days are too soft, if you ask me,' Ron pipes up loudly to no one in particular. 'Back in my day, we ate what was put in front of us or we'd get a clout round the ear and sent to bed early.'

'Well, we're not *in* your day, Dad,' Gina replies, rolling her eyes at her father. 'And you're not exactly adventurous with food yourself. Anyway, people have allergies and all kinds of different dietary needs, and you are simply allowed not to like something, you know.'

'Pandering, that's what it is,' Ron continues, shaking his head. His cheeks are red and veiny and his nose bulbous. 'They'd soon eat up if there were nothing else.'

'Ron,' Joyce warns as she gives his arm a squeeze. 'Enough, now.'

'Are you at school or college, Tyler?' Matt asks, attempting to change the subject.

I wait a few seconds just in case Ty manages a reply, before answering on his behalf. 'He's been home-schooled,' I explain. 'Or rather, he kind of home-schools himself now.'

'Needs a stint in the army,' Ron mutters, and Joyce silences him again, more sternly this time.

'That's so interesting,' Gina says, sounding genuine. 'How do you fit in teaching around working? You must be exhausted.'

I smile, making out that I'm happy to explain while avoiding answering. 'Ty's always been ahead of his years, so it made sense to let him learn at his pace. School was holding him back.'

What I don't bother explaining is that I have no idea about the first part of Tyler's life – where he was, who he was with, which school he went to. He rarely wants to talk about it.

'It's only in more recent years that I've been able to work longer hours,' I continue. 'Before that, I had to rely on benefits as childcare wasn't always available.' The benefits part is true, at least, but I pray they don't ask about Tyler's father.

'What's your favourite subject?' Gina asks Tyler.

'Maths and physics,' he answers, which I knew he would.

'He's crazy about particle physics and quantum mechanics,' I add as the perfect distraction. 'And computers, of course. He wants to go to university.'

'Wow,' comes Matt's predictable reaction, followed by a moment's silence around the table. It's certainly silenced the old boy with his sanctimonious opinions, and Gina looks genuinely impressed. There might even be tears in her eyes. *This poor woman and her son...* she's thinking. *She's cleaning other people's toilets, raising a genius in the face of adversity...*

I keep my laugh to myself, thankfully distracted by my seafood linguine when it arrives. Because silly, *silly* Gina... she couldn't be more wrong.

TWELVE

GINA

Before we had kids, the thought of Matt going away for work never bothered me much. In fact, I enjoyed a couple of evenings alone trawling Netflix, maybe having friends round for wine, and once or twice, Laura and Annie came to stay – a rarity given everyone is so busy these days.

But since we've had kids, all his work trips mean now is extra effort in the evenings, me scoffing Tommy's leftovers for dinner and no one to whinge at face to face about how exhausted I am.

'Have you got everything?' I ask Matt, coming up to him in the hallway. He's got his back to me, though it looks as though he's pressing his face into something.

He whips round, shoving whatever it is behind his back. 'Yeah, I think so.' His eyes are staring and wide.

'What's that?' I ask, looking down. 'In your hands.'

'Nothing,' Matt replies, sounding guilty as hell.

I go up to him, circling round behind. 'A scarf?' I say, taking it from him and looking at it. 'What are you doing with a *woman's* scarf, Matt?'

'I... I was just smelling it. Breathing you in before I go.' He gives me a sheepish smile.

'But it's not even my scarf,' I say, hanging it up on the coat hooks. 'I wish, though,' I add, noticing the 'pure cashmere' label. 'It belongs to Annie, love,' I add, rolling my eyes.

'Oh... right,' he says, clearing his throat and looking embarrassed. 'I shouldn't be back too late on Wednesday,' he adds with Tommy hanging off his leg. 'I'll try to get away from the site at lunchtime.'

I nod, doing my best not to reveal the heaviness in my heart that this trip has come at a really rotten time – the first time we've been apart since Gracie was born and the house went up in smoke. And not only are we still adjusting to life in Hastings – a place I really didn't think I'd be living in again – but now I have Mary and her son here in the house.

In theory, I know I should relish the company and extra help, and Mary has promised that I'll barely see Tyler because he'll be holed up in his room studying or gaming, but after what I found in my bed, I can't help feeling unsettled.

I follow Matt into the kitchen as he goes to grab his laptop. I have a sick feeling in the pit of my stomach.

'You sure you'll be OK?' he asks, hoisting Tommy up onto his hip. 'Hey, big guy, you look after Mummy, yeah? You're the man of the house now.'

Tommy grabs onto his hair, letting out a laugh.

'Ouch!' Matt yelps, giving our son a tickle. 'No throwing things or screaming or shouting, OK? Daddy needs you to be a good boy for Mummy while he's away.'

'That's difficult for the majority of three-year-olds,' a voice says.

Matt and I whip our heads round at the same time to see Tyler standing at the fridge, peering inside. Neither of us heard him come in.

'They lack impulse control and their behaviours are

governed by what feels good to them at the time rather than rational, considered reactions or the needs of others. The peak synaptic density of his prefrontal cortex is not yet fully developed. Of course, many of his behaviours are also learned responses. Should there be an overreaction by their main caregivers to an event, be it positive or negative, it simply reinforces his behaviour in order to gain a response. And in your child's case, this behaviour would seem to be regularly poor.'

Tyler closes the refrigerator and pops the top on a can of Coke Zero, facing us but not looking at us. When we don't respond – we just stand there with our mouths hanging open – it's Tommy who breaks the awkward silence by yelling, 'Dutt-up!' which Matt and I both know means *shut up* but, thankfully, doesn't much sound like it.

'Frustration also plays a large part in compromised social skills,' Tyler continues. 'Not being understood gives way to behavioural meltdowns.'

'Er... thanks for the heads-up, Tyler,' Matt says, releasing Tommy down to the floor as he wriggles. He runs over to the older boy, begging for a Coke, tugging hard at Tyler's trousers. His pesters soon turn into a grizzle and, when Tommy kicks the refrigerator, Tyler takes hold of my son's wrist and I swear he gives him a pinch before turning and leaving the room.

'Quod erat demonstrandum,' he calls back over his shoulder.

'Oh my *God*,' I say when he's gone, scooping up my son and checking he's OK. 'Remind me not to ask him to explain the remote control anytime soon,' I add, making a show of kissing my son's arm better until he's giggling again.

'Try not to worry about him,' Matt says. 'Swotty teenage boys can be utterly obnoxious. I was one once, don't forget.' He hesitates before saying, 'But... but to be on the safe side, I wouldn't leave him alone with the kids.'

. . .

After we've waved Matt off in a taxi to the station, Mary comes down the stairs.

'Morning,' she trills behind me, heading into the kitchen.

Tommy jumps up and down, still calling out, 'Bye-bye, Daddy,' over and over, while Gracie sucks on her fist, hungry in my arms.

'How are you today?' I ask, trying to sound normal while following her into the kitchen. I don't want there to be an atmosphere while Matt is away. Mary heads straight to the utility room and drags out a vacuum cleaner.

'OK, thanks,' she replies, though I sense there's a *but*. 'I've been concerned about Tyler sleeping in a new place. He doesn't cope well with change,' she explains. 'He sometimes roams about at night, and I didn't want him to disturb you. I've had one ear open the last two nights.'

'Oh... I see,' I say, not liking the thought of that, especially now that Tommy is sleeping in his own room. He'd be scared stiff if someone came into his room at night – not to mention how I'd feel if I woke to find Tyler looming over me.

'He'll adjust after a while, but it takes him a couple of months to settle into a new place.'

'A couple of *months*?' I say rather too abruptly.

'That's worst-case scenario,' Mary tells me, reading my thoughts. 'I'm sure I'll sort somewhere for us before then.'

While I'm left reeling at the prospect of them being here for that long, Mary heads to a cupboard in the hallway, next to the locked basement door. One of the first things Annie did when she moved in here was convert the large cellars below the house into a state-of-the-art recording studio. And the renovations didn't come cheap. Excavating to increase ceiling height, underpinning and tanking, let alone thoroughly soundproofing the entire space and kitting it out with professional equipment cost as much as my entire house. I regularly remind myself that Annie lives in a different world to Matt and me – and, indeed, to most people – and that dropping a few hundred thousand on renovations is perfectly normal in her circles. But what I love about Annie is that she's still... well, *Annie*. Still that same gawky, loud, loving, opinionated and irritating, creative and beautiful soul that she was at school.

Which reminds me... while Mary sets to work cleaning, I settle down to feed Gracie and fire off a message.

Just to let you know Mary's son Tyler is staying here too. Bit of a surprise! He's 17 going on 50 with a brain the size of a planet. That OK with you? Everything fine with house. Taking kids to park this morning. Send more safari pics. BLTFNS xxx

I feel bad bothering her but would feel worse if she had objections. It's not until I'm wriggling Gracie into clean clothes an hour later as we prepare to leave for the park that I get a reply. Mary comes into the kitchen and sets to scrubbing the kitchen sink as I'm reading it.

Tyler's a good lad, no problem at all! All fine here. Lunch on the plains. Love Annie xx

There's a photo of a picnic table spread with delicious-looking food, and the safari Jeep is parked nearby. In the background are the wide plains of Kenya, an azure sky and a herd of elephants beside some stumpy trees. There are a couple of other people milling around the vehicle, presumably also on Annie's safari tour. I have a suspicion it could be a singles-type holiday but haven't probed. Despite her fame and busy work life, I sense Annie's lonely. While she's never been short of male admirers and plenty of available company for a night here, a night there, she's not had a special relationship for a long while. I know it makes her sad.

'Look at this photo from Aunty Annie,' I say to Tommy.

'Elephants!' My son immediately makes a trumpeting sound. Then, with Gracie tucked in the crook of my left arm, I go over and show Mary the picture. 'Thought you might like to see where your boss currently is.'

'All right for some, eh?' she says, scrubbing the sink while glancing at it. 'And here I am in my rubber gloves.' She laughs, looking down at her hands.

'I hear you,' I joke back, thinking that Mary doesn't *sound* as if she hates me, or is capable of putting dirt in my bed. 'We're just going out for a bit,' I tell her once I've got the kids ready. 'See you later.'

Mary gives me a smile and a little wave, her eyes tracking me as I head into the hallway with my children. But it's not *her* eyes that raise the hackles on my neck. No, it's Tyler who makes me jump, his stare boring into me from where he's sitting at the top of the stairs, watching me as I put Gracie into the pram side of the double buggy and strap Tommy into his seat. But it's his silence that unsettles me the most as I shut the front door behind us, causing me to look back over my shoulder every few minutes all the way to the park.

THIRTEEN

GINA

'It was so weird, he just sat there staring at us.'

I'm sitting on a park bench beside the kids' play area, chatting on the phone to Laura, who's barely out of breath as she pedals her way through one of her exercise breaks on the Peloton bike in her office.

'Sounds creepy,' she replies. 'And you had no idea he existed until he turned up?'

'Nope. Mary never mentioned she had a son.'

'So weird,' Laura says, panting slightly as she echoes my thoughts.

'I'm just praying they won't stay long,' I say, keeping my eyes fixed on Tommy as he plays in the sandpit with a couple of other kids about his age – a boy and a girl. Gracie is sleeping peacefully beside me in the pram. 'He's insanely clever, and I do feel sorry for the poor lad if his father is abusive. It's just...' I shake my head, staring up at the sky for a few seconds to try to put into words exactly what it is that I mean. 'He seems far too interested in my children, if I'm honest. He's always staring at Gracie with a weird sort of intense look in his eyes, and I swear he tried to pinch Tommy earlier.'

I keep staring up at the sky, watching the gathering clouds, wondering if I should say anything to Mary. My plan is to stay out of the house until she's finished her shift, then at least there's more chance of her and Tyler being up in the attic rooms by then, or perhaps they might even go out.

I take a few deep breaths and close my eyes, trying to release some tension. The autumn air feels oxygen-rich and fresh with all the trees surrounding us. Gracie snuffles beside me, making me open my eyes again. I adjust her blanket so she's warm enough then glance over to the play area to check Tommy isn't burying one of the other kids in the sand.

He's not there.

'Shit,' I say, standing up. I scan around, trying to locate him, but in my growing state of panic, it's as if all the other kids morph into him and he's everywhere at once – while also being nowhere at all.

'Gina, you OK?' comes Laura's voice down the line.

'Tommy!' I call out. 'Tommy, where are you?' I flick the brake off the buggy and grab my backpack from the bench, chucking it in Tommy's empty seat. Then I hastily wheel around the perimeter of the sandpit. There are four kids playing in it now and none of them is my son.

'Gina, what's going on? You're scaring me,' I hear Laura say.

'It's Tommy,' I reply. 'I... I literally just looked away for a moment and now he's gone.'

I pin the phone to my ear with my shoulder and put both hands on the buggy as I manoeuvre it further around the play area, scanning around the whole time. But there's simply no sign of him. I've told him not to go on the big slide without me and, indeed, he's nowhere near it. Nor is he on the climbing frame, the swings or the monkey bars.

'Shit, Laura, he's gone. Tommy's *gone*! I've got to go...' and I end the call without waiting for her reply. I have a sinking feeling that I'm going to need my phone to call the police.

'Excuse me, have you seen my little boy? Green coat, blue jeans, light brown hair. He's three.'

I must look like a madwoman to the two women sitting on one of the other benches by the play area. They look at me suspiciously, slowly shaking their heads. 'No, sorry,' they chime in unison, giving a cursory glance around. Then they shoot each other a look that says, *You terrible mother*...

I approach several other people, but it's the same. No one's seen Tommy.

'Shit, shit, *shit*,' I cry, feeling as though I'm about to have a heart attack – my chest is tight and my pulse whooshes through my ears. Slowly and carefully, making sure I'm not missing him in my panic, I scan around the area again. There are about fifteen children here in total, all pre-schoolers given it's term time, and Tommy is most certainly not one of them.

Then I see the path leading away from the playground down towards a dark, shaded, wooded area, and I *know* that it would look like the most inviting place ever to my son. I'm certain he can't have got very far in the few seconds I took my eyes off him, so I set off at a brisk pace to look in the trees. If there's no sign of him in the woods, I'm calling the police. And then Matt.

'Tommy!' I yell as I bump the pram down the path at top speed. Gracie stirs and whimpers, her head lolling, but I can't stop now. 'Tommy, where are you?'

My voice seems suddenly lost, swallowed up by darkness as I approach the edge of the woods, the tree canopy blocking out most of the light. The air feels damp and cool on my skin.

And then I see something. A flash of bright green. I swear it was the same colour as my son's coat, disappearing deeper into the trees.

'Tommy, stop, *wait!*' I bump the pram over the uneven track. 'Come back!'

I press on, praying I'll catch sight of him again, but it's hopeless. I stop running and, with fumbling hands, pull my phone from my pocket, hardly believing that my pleasant morning out with the kids has ended with me calling the police.

It's just as the operator answers and says, 'Emergency, which service do you require?' that I see Tommy appear from behind a tree trunk. My heart floods with relief.

But then I'm quickly consumed by fear again when I see the male figure tightly gripping his wrist.

FOURTEEN
GINA

'Tommy!' I call out, charging up to him. 'Oh my God, *Tommy*, you scared me half to death.' I bend down and scoop him up in my arms, clutching him tightly. 'Are you OK, sweetie?' He makes a whimpering sound when I squeeze him. Then I glare at the person behind him.

Tyler.

'What are *you* doing here?' There's no holding back the anger in my voice.

'Nothing,' he says, staring into the pram with a blank expression.

'What do you mean, *nothing*?' I squeak, incredulous at how unconcerned he seems. 'Surely you know that taking a three-year-old away from his mother without permission is *not* OK? What the hell were you thinking?' I can't get my questions out fast enough.

'He followed me,' Tyler says, unfazed. A small smile creeps over his mouth as Gracie stirs. 'It's my special place. I do... I do special things here.'

'And you didn't think to bring him back to me?' I'm trying to stop myself yelling at him, but it's hard. I can't stop shaking.

'No. I wanted to do things with him.' Tyler does not look at me.

His words and what they imply make me feel sick. 'What... what *things*?'

Tyler shrugs.

'What the hell are you doing here, anyway? When I left the house, you were sitting on the stairs.'

'I am going for a walk.'

I can't help the snort. 'A walk in the woods by the kids' playground where *we* just happen to be?' I don't care if he thinks I'm rude or overreacting. I'm running on adrenaline. 'A bit of a coincidence, don't you think?'

'Coincidences aren't as rare as people make out,' Tyler begins. 'Statistics show that it's human nature to perceive—'

'Stop...! Just stop, Tyler. I thought I'd lost my son because of you, not to mention nearly having a bloody heart attack. I don't know *what* you were thinking.' I can't stand to say what's racing through my mind, that his intentions weren't as innocent as he's trying to make out. 'Don't ever do anything like that again, do you hear me?'

Tyler stares at me, a crestfallen look washing over his face. But he also looks perplexed at the same time. 'I'm sorry that you allowed your vigilance over your son to slip. And I'm sorry that he followed me while I was out on my walk. No harm done.' Tyler turns to leave.

'Go wiv, *go wiv* him!' Tommy suddenly squeals, wriggling frantically in my arms. When I don't let him down, he starts to grizzle. 'Want da sweeties wiv Tyler, Mummy! He said I can have *sweeties*!'

Two hours later and my anger and fear have turned into guilt at what I'm beginning to think was an overreaction on my part. After Tyler disappeared off into the woods, I strapped Tommy back into his pushchair and we went in the opposite direction, heading down to the seafront for an ice cream. We sat on a bench, watching the foamy waves wash up the pebbles then sink back again with a hypnotic *shoosh* as the tide gradually went out.

Of course, I asked Tommy if Tyler had promised him sweets as a bribe to go with him into the woods, and gently probed if Tyler had done anything to hurt him, but my son had long since lost interest in the topic and, instead of answering, he pointed excitedly at the seagulls as he licked his ice cream. He was completely oblivious to my panic.

I try to convince myself that Tyler being at the park was, as he was trying to tell me, nothing more than a coincidence – especially as I never mentioned to him or Mary where we were going. So he couldn't have known where we'd be.

Unless he followed me.

Out of the four of us, it was Laura who I'd have bet my term's lunch money on ending up making a shedload of money, rather than Annie. But Laura – who'd started her own T-shirt printing business aged fifteen and had won national debating competitions at school, later going on to study law – ended up in a slightly mundane but respectable job as a corporate solicitor in a large firm.

After leaving college without any qualifications, I bounced from one minimum-wage job to another – bar work, waitressing, retail, office admin – until I eventually slotted into my garden centre role for a few years. Before I had Tommy and Gracie, I was virtually running the place. And it was where I was working when, completely by chance, I reconnected with Matt. He happened to be passing through the area and had stopped off for a pot plant for his mum. We'd not seen each other in years.

Out of our school friendship group, Annie was the only one who'd seemed to dodge falling apart after Sara died. Good fortune had taken her by the hand and led her through the devastation, guilt and regrets that haunted me and Laura. So it was no surprise that Laura and I ended up as lesser versions of the ambitious teenage dreams we'd once had for ourselves. The edges knocked off our lives.

Sometimes it felt as though we were still stumbling about in the wreckage while Annie was off living the high life. As for Matt and his group of friends, we didn't have much to do with any of them after the night of the party. Eventually, we'd all gone our separate ways.

'Thank *God* you found him,' Laura says on the phone when I call her back later that afternoon to update her. 'You must have been out of your mind with worry.'

'Those few minutes felt like my entire life,' I tell her. 'Reason six hundred and forty-seven why you're very wise not to have kids,' I say, not meaning it of course. 'Premature grey hairs guaranteed.'

'As much as I love your two little darlings, I'm hanging onto my blonde highlights, thanks very much. Patrick's already got his sexy salt-and-pepper look and doesn't care for kids anyway. Thank God.'

I laugh. 'How is the old codger, anyway? Still cycling?'

'You ask as though it's something he'll one day consider giving up. He does two hundred miles a week.'

For a few moments, we chat about Patrick, also a lawyer and ten years older than Laura, and his upcoming cycling trip to Lanzarote. But predictably, our conversation drifts back to Annie.

'Did she send you that safari picture with the elephants?' I ask.

Laura is quiet for a moment, and I can't tell if it's because she's miffed that she didn't get the picture, or because someone has come into her office.

'No, no, she didn't,' she admits. 'Go on, forward it on. I want to see.'

'Just a sec.' I tap on my screen and the two blue ticks appear straight away as she opens it.

'Looks amazing,' Laura says, sounding slightly flat. 'I'd love to go on a safari in South Africa.'

'Then you should,' I say, knowing she won't. Laura and I have had this conversation many times over the years – that she works too hard, that she rarely takes a holiday, that she could go with Patrick on his many overseas cycling trips. 'But Annie is in Kenya, not South Africa,' I correct her.

Another pause. 'Are you sure?' is Laura's reply. 'The Jeep has a South African flag sticker on the bumper, and if you zoom in, the number plate has the same flag on it, too. You can clearly see the colours.'

I laugh. 'You're suddenly a flag expert?'

'Did you not notice the front of my fridge when you last came to mine? It's covered in flag magnets that Patrick collects on his trips.'

'Yeah, but I didn't realise you'd learnt them all by heart.'

'Trust me, when you open the fridge ten times a day, these things stick in your brain.'

'Well, Annie is definitely in Kenya right now,' I say, confused. 'She told me. Next stop Thailand.' I scan back over her messages to make sure. 'Yeah, definitely Kenya.'

'Knowing Annie, she probably chartered a private jet because she heard the animals were better down in the south.'

We laugh in unison.

'I still can't get over seeing her face pop up on Netflix,' Laura continues. 'And just the other day, Spotify recommended her latest album.'

'Who'd have thought, eh? Our Annie. One of the GALS.' I smile fondly, listening out as I hear a noise. 'I'd better go. I think Gracie's waking up,' I say, just as an idea comes into my head. 'Look, why don't you come down to the coast and stay for a few days? Annie won't mind, and it'll be just like old times and...'

I trail off. Neither of us wants it to be anything *like* old times, and I know Laura is thinking the same because of the momentary silence.

'Sure, I'd love that,' she says vaguely, her tone telling me that it's unlikely.

After I've hung up, I get up to go and check on Gracie, but I suddenly stop when I see Mary standing a few feet behind me. I have no idea how long she's been listening.

FIFTEEN

MARY

'I'm *really* sorry to have to ask,' I say, trying to sound genuine.

Gina's head tilts sympathetically, her frown growing when I explain about the threatening messages I've been getting from Tyler's father, how he's furious that I've left him and is demanding to know where I am. When I show her my bruised ribs, telling her he flung me against the wall – a shocking display of green, yellow and black – her mouth falls open at the sight of my injuries.

'I really don't know what else to do,' I add for good measure.

'God, no, it's fine, it's *fine*,' she says, finally taking her eyes off my battered body as she slowly pulls at a dust sheet, revealing the dressing table beneath. 'Of *course* you can stay longer.' She gathers the sheet up in her arms. 'Is moving in with your mum not an option any more?'

And there it is. A telling little probe as she tries to find out if I've really, truly tried my hardest to find somewhere else to stay because, when it comes down to it, she's not actually that fucking compassionate at all.

Gina looks expectantly at me, clutching the knot of fabric at her chest, wringing it out between fingers that almost look as though they're tightly crossed. She doesn't want me imposing longer than necessary, that much is clear. But also, she won't hear of me and my son being turfed out onto the street while a violent ex is hunting me down. The guilt would be too much.

I shake my head. 'Mum's not been at all well the last few months. The doctors are doing what they can, but the chemo is taking its toll. I really don't want to bring all my troubles to her door.' I pause for effect and wipe a finger under one eye, adding a sniff at just the right moment. Then I take in a deep breath and sigh it out in a way that makes me sound like I'm at the end of my tether but trying my best to hide it. 'And I just... I just thought that me living in longer term makes sense, given that the amount of cleaning has increased since you and your family moved in.'

'Mmm, yes, yes, of course... And I'm so sorry to hear about your mum...' Gina says, trailing off with another frown. I almost hear her mind whirring as it searches for reasons that don't make her sound like an utter bitch.

I tug on the sheet Gina is holding, sliding it from her hands. 'If Tyler is going to make it to university next year, he really needs a stable place to study. These attic bedrooms weren't being used, so I just thought...' I start to fold up the sheet, shaking my head and making sure I don't look Gina in the eye. Then I stop folding and face her full on. 'Look, forget I even asked. You've got enough on your plate, what with a new baby and the fire. The last thing you need to be worrying about is a homeless domestic violence survivor and her son.' I reach out and touch her arm.

I'm not sure if it's the word homeless or the mention of abuse that seals the deal, or perhaps it's my sick mother, but suddenly Gina's whole demeanour changes and, to my horror – and delight – she gives me a hug.

'Of *course*, Mary. You and Tyler absolutely must stay as long as you need, no question. I won't hear another word about it. There's so much space up here, it seems silly not to make use of it.'

I pull back without making it obvious that I'm pushing her away. 'Thank you, Gina,' I reply. 'It's such a relief to know we won't be on the street. As soon as I've saved up a bit, we'll get our own place and be out of your hair. Meantime, you really won't know we're here.'

Behind those dark eyes, I imagine her thinking back to earlier when she found Tommy in the woods with Tyler. I can't believe he was so stupid, taking the boy like that, and I'll be having words with him later, reminding him that he's not to do anything until I tell him. I won't have him ruining everything. Not when I've come so far.

'I'll make sure the spare room is fresh and welcoming for when your friend comes to stay at the weekend,' I tell Gina. 'I've put the sheets from when your mum and dad were here in the wash.' I give her a sweet smile.

'Friend?' she says, looking confused. Then the penny drops when she realises that I was eavesdropping on her phone call to Laura earlier. 'Oh... yes. I doubt she'll take me up on the offer, but I thought a few days at the coast might do her good.' Gina rolls her eyes and laughs. 'Laura is another workaholic, like Annie.'

Oh, Gina, always the do-gooder, the people-pleaser, smoothing over and calming. It's almost as if you're trying to atone for something...

'Well, let's hope she does,' I say. What Gina doesn't know yet is that Laura *will* be coming to stay this weekend. 'Annie loves it when the house is filled with people – family, friends and all their children. She hosts the most amazing house parties with her musician friends – some of them are quite famous. All-night drunken recording sessions in the basement aren't uncommon. It's been quiet since she went away, so I'm glad you and your family are here. The place has come to life again.'

Gina nods, smiling tentatively. 'Talking of Annie, do you have an itinerary for her? She's in Kenya right now, isn't she?'

'Yes, she is *now*,' I tell her. 'She flew to Cape Town and spent a few days in South Africa first.'

'Ah, that explains it,' Gina says, gathering up another sheet as we finally get round to making the attic bedrooms more homely. It's felt like camping out the last couple of nights. 'I got a bit confused with the picture Annie sent me earlier,' she continues. 'The one with the elephants.'

I know which photo she's talking about – the one with the Jeep in, too. 'I can't imagine being able to afford a trip like that,' I say. 'I took Tyler to the zoo when he was younger, and we saw elephants there. Not quite the same though.'

'How the other half live, eh?' Gina says, putting her phone in her pocket again. Then she hears the baby's cry coming from her cot, and Tommy, who's playing on the landing nearby, starts whining too, so she leaves me to finish getting the bedrooms ready alone.

I dust around and open the windows to let in some fresh air and, a few minutes later, when I know Gina is busy with the children two floors below, I head into the shower room next door and lift up my top, studying my bruises, squinting at them in the mirror. Then I pluck some make-up removing wipes from the packet and rub them all away.

SIXTEEN

GINA

Deciding to take a walk to the house where I grew up feels like a kind of self-punishment, but I'm hoping it will be cathartic – facing up to ghosts from the past that have been haunting me since we arrived a little over a week ago. Besides, I need to get out of the house.

I know it wasn't all bad, living here – far from it, in fact. My memories of growing up by the seaside are mainly happy. I'm an only child, and we weren't rich, but we weren't poor either, and what kid wouldn't love hanging out at the beach with their friends at the weekend – even if it was raining or blowing a gale most of the time?

It was only after Sara went missing that I couldn't wait to get away. Annie and Laura, too. Then, a few years later when Mum and Dad announced they were moving west along the coast to downsize to a flat in Eastbourne, there was simply no need to return. No need to deal with the ghosts any more. For a long time, I shut it all out.

But then came the night three years ago when Laura and I got straight on the phone to each other after we learnt the news.

'She's only gone and done it,' I said after Laura answered on the first ring.

'She always said she would,' came her reply.

Annie had sent us a photo of some keys dangling between her manicured fingers with a grand Georgian portico in the background on our three-way WhatsApp group. It was easy to zoom in and see the plaque beside the front door – Genoa House, Wessex Square.

Underneath, she'd simply written the message: *For you, Mum xxx*

She knew we'd understand.

As teenagers, we never imagined that Annie would follow through with her childhood promise to her mum, but now she had. Except her mum had died nearly fifteen years ago, never getting to see her only daughter hit the big time and become an award-winning singer and actress, which had enabled her to buy the house that her mother had always dreamt of owning.

We couldn't figure out why Annie had done it, given her mum wasn't here to live in the house any more. Or why, out of all the beautiful homes Annie could have afforded anywhere in the country, she'd chosen this one.

We didn't understand why she'd want to come back.

'I'd love a place like that, I would,' I remember Marjory Stone, Annie's mum, saying on several occasions as we walked through the square, passing by what she called the 'posh people's houses' on the way down to the beach. She was a jolly woman and always had hordes of kids round at her place to play, never allowing anyone to leave hungry, feeding us up with something she'd baked that morning before taking us for games on the beach.

'When I'm a famous actress, Mummy, I'll buy it for you. You can have a housekeeper and a dog and everything,' Annie had once said.

'Oh no, no. If I had a grand house like that, I'd take delight in cleaning every inch of it myself. It would be an honour,' Marjory had replied.

All these thoughts from the past are rushing through my mind as I coax Tommy to eat his dinner. Gracie nods off in the nest of my arm, drunk on milk as her head lolls and her eyelids droop. Carefully, I lay her in her pram, gently manoeuvring her into her little coat.

'We're going out,' I tell Tommy in a hushed voice. 'Fresh air and a walk before bath time is just what the doctor ordered.'

'Is your son sick?' comes a voice from the top of the stairs as I fasten Tommy's shoes.

'Oh... no,' I say, glancing up. 'It's just an expression.'

Tyler comes down, standing over me. The skin on my neck prickles.

'It means it's good for you,' I add when he doesn't seem to cotton on.

'May I come with you?'

I decide that it's probably best I know where Tyler is rather than risk him following us and freaking me out in the twilight. Mary has gone out so it's also preferable to leaving him here alone, giving him the chance to snoop through our stuff while Matt is still away. 'Sure,' I tell him, thinking that I can show him what I'm going to show Tommy, too.

The street where I lived as a child isn't a great distance from Wessex Square as the crow flies, but these days it takes longer because the new flats built the other side of the abandoned land behind Genoa House have put paid to sneaking across the area like we sometimes used to as kids – though our parents didn't know. From further up the hill, where my family's modest, pebble-dashed house was located, cutting through the common – as it was always called back then – was a tempting short cut to the beach... but a short cut that my parents warned me never to take.

Dad recounted grim tales of flashers and 'bad men' loitering in the scrubby bushes to put me off cutting through the area. The thought of someone opening their raincoat then cupping a hand over my mouth and dragging me behind a tree terrified the life out of me, though I'd still sneak through occasionally, virtually holding my breath until I got to the other side.

As we walk, I peek into the pram to check on Gracie. Tommy is not happy about being strapped into his side of the buggy.

'Det out! Det *out!*' he wails, kicking his feet on the footrest.

'OK, Tommo, hang on,' I say, stopping to unbuckle him. He'll probably only walk a short way before he's begging to get back in again, but he's going to wake Gracie at this rate. 'Hold my hand, there's a good boy.' The road is much busier these days than it used to be.

I grip my son's fingers, but he starts whining again, tugging away from me.

'Hold Tyler hand...' he squeaks, whipping free from me before slipping it into the older boy's outstretched fingers.

I'm about to protest, especially after what happened at the playground, but I know that Tommy is already on the verge of a tantrum, and my insisting will tip him over the edge.

'Don't worry,' Tyler says, giving me a sideways look that I'm not sure how to interpret. 'I'll hold on tight.'

I give him a nod as we walk on, making sure to keep between my son and the road. I don't remember the cars coming down here so fast when we were kids.

'Tyler, did your mum tell you that her boss and I grew up here together?' I say above the traffic noise. 'And our other friend, Laura, too. We were thick as thieves, us lot.' I let out an awkward laugh, not knowing what else to chat about. I feel bad not mentioning Sara, but I don't want to have to explain what happened.

Tyler just nods, staring down at Tommy beside him with a half-smile on his face.

'That was my house,' I say a few moments later, pointing to an unremarkable semi as we draw closer. 'It's not changed that much.'

'Cat!' Tommy suddenly cries, pointing at a tabby sitting on a wall across the street.

I'm about to tell him about the grey cat we used to have, but my heart is suddenly in my mouth when Tyler says, 'Go and stroke the pussycat.'

Before I can stop him, my son is hurtling towards the road, his arms outstretched.

'*Stop!* Tommy... *no!*'

I abandon the pram on the pavement, hurling myself after Tommy as he steps out onto the carriageway, cars speeding past as one swerves and another hoots its horn loudly. I lunge forward, grabbing the hood of Tommy's coat, yanking him from danger just in time.

We both fall backwards onto the pavement as a large van speeds past, a rush of wind ringing in my ears as I'm left shaking on the ground.

'Oh my God, oh my *God...*' I wail into my son's hair, pressing my face against him. I feel like the worst mother in the world, trusting Tyler to keep Tommy safe. I look up, ready to give him a serious telling-off, but another burst of adrenaline surges through me.

'Shit, the *buggy!* Get the buggy!' I scream up at Tyler, who's now looming over me. Sitting in the gutter with Tommy, it's like I'm frozen as I watch it rolling slowly towards the road.

I manage to scramble to my feet, keeping a firm hold of Tommy as I race off behind Tyler, who, thank *God*, grabs the pushchair a foot from the kerb.

'Jesus Christ!' I yell, shaking as I jam on the pram brake. 'What were you *thinking*, telling Tommy to stroke the cat?' I don't even want to hear his reply as I strap my son back into his seat.

'I did not say that,' he says in a monotone voice. 'I said you *can't* stroke the cat. You misheard me. It is not my fault if your son—'

'Just stop,' I say, turning to face him. I take a series of slow breaths, forcing myself to calm down. 'Tyler, for some reason you seem intent on hurting my son and I'm sick of your excuses. Just keep away from us, OK?'

'But you're wrong. I—'

I raise my palm at him. 'Let's just carry on walking before I do something I'll regret.' I glare over at him, tempted to shove *him* into the road, though I manage to control my rage, gripping the pram handle until my knuckles turn white.

Tyler shrugs before plucking his phone from his pocket, staring at the screen as though nothing has happened.

'Look, Tommy,' I say, still trembling as I lean down to the buggy. 'That's the house where Mummy used to live when she was a little girl.'

To my surprise, Tommy looks up, grinning and pointing. 'Dat house?' he says, shoving a toy dinosaur in his mouth.

'Yes, darling. And that window up there was Mummy's bedroom.' I smile at him, shuddering at the close call we just had.

Another shiver shoots through me as I remember how, as a teenager, I used to experiment with make-up and hairstyles in that very bedroom... *hoping he'd notice me*. I remember in exact detail what I wore that fateful night – a short denim skirt, sleeveless check shirt knotted at the waist, padded bra and high-heeled silver cowboy boots. My hair was slicked back into a tight ponytail that swished from side to side when I walked.

As I stand here now, I can almost see myself sneaking out of the front door, my parents oblivious as they sat watching telly with cups of tea. 'I'll see you in the morning...' I tentatively called out, clicking the front door shut behind me.

Earlier, I'd bluffed to them that Annie's dad was picking me up and taking us to the school disco, that I was staying over at her place afterwards. They had no reason to disbelieve me, especially as I'd claimed the same thing at the end of the previous year, pretending to go to a youth club disco, when really I'd gone to Matt's New Year's Eve party instead. The little white lies didn't seem so bad.

I walked as fast as I could, feeling excited. It was almost 9 p.m. and, being the end of the autumn term, it had been dark for a few hours. I was head-over-heels crazy for Matt – we all were – and we were looking forward to dancing and letting our hair down. It was almost the end of term and I'd heard there was going to be plenty of booze.

We were only fifteen.

But that night, there was no school disco. There wasn't much booze or dancing, either. And by the end of the evening, our GALS mantra of *big love, true friends, no secrets* had somehow twisted into a sickening knot of hate, backstabbing and lies.

SEVENTEEN

GINA

'Oh...!' I say, stopping in our bedroom doorway.

Mary whips round, startled, but she's quick to regain her composure. 'So sorry to intrude, Gina,' she says calmly, though I notice the slight clench of her jaw. She sweeps back her ash-blonde hair, tucking the silky strands behind her ear, and continues to rummage through the pile of worn clothes heaped on the dressing table stool.

'I'm odd-sock hunting,' she says, her back now turned as she makes a show of shaking out each pair of Matt's trousers that he's left lying there for the last few days. He's not the tidiest husband in the world.

'Where do they all go, these odd socks?' I joke, laughing and going in. But my humour is only a cover because Mary being in our bedroom outside of her working hours and not wearing her uniform is giving me a weird feeling in my stomach. 'Look, I'll take care of it,' I say, gathering up the dirty washing that she seems so intent on exploring. 'No need for you to bother with our clothes.'

'But laundry is in my contract with Annie,' she replies, turning to face me. Her eyes flick down to the bundle in my arms. 'Including that of house guests. It's important I fulfil my duties.'

'Really, there's no need,' I say, taking a few steps back as Mary approaches me, seeming intent on getting her hands on our dirty clothes. The stuff Matt wore to our house at the weekend is still in there, the tarry stink of smoke creeping up my nostrils. 'Honestly, Annie won't mind,' I continue. 'I'll sort this lot in the morning, but I really need to get Tommy and Gracie into bed now.' I drop the items into the laundry hamper and then head to the bedroom door, holding it wide open so that Mary takes the hint to leave.

She does, but only after a moment's pause, mumbling another apology before padding across the carpet in her bare feet and heading up the second flight of stairs to her attic bedroom, giving me a sideways look as she goes.

'Nothing was missing, so I don't think she was out to steal from us,' I say to Matt on the phone later. Even so, I decide not to tell him what I found on the floor of our bedroom shortly after Mary had gone up to her room.

It made my blood run cold when I spotted it, and I'm still trying to work out what it means.

'Well, we don't have much left to steal,' Matt jokes. However much we try to distract ourselves with other things, the fire is always at the back of our minds. And while the fire investigators did their work thoroughly, leaving no stone unturned to rule out arson, I know Matt would almost prefer that it *had* been deliberate.

As things stand, the blaze was entirely his fault.

I was barely able to absorb what the officer had said when he explained the results of their investigation.

'These photos illustrate what happened the best,' he said, pointing to a zoomed-in section of our charred ceiling. 'Trust me, your hallway light was where the fire started. I'm surprised it hadn't gone up before, to be honest.'

Matt sat perfectly still for a few moments, barely breathing. I explained to the officer that apart from briefly testing the ceiling light after Matt had put it up, we'd not yet used it, preferring to flick on the hall table light after dark instead.

The hundred and fifty quid we'd saved by not waiting a couple of weeks for an electrician had ended up costing us our home.

Finally, Matt's head dropped into his hands. 'Shit...' he muttered. 'I fitted the light. It's my fault the house caught fire.'

The fire officer made a sympathetic face. 'Just be thankful you weren't all upstairs asleep.'

I shuddered at the thought of us all being trapped. Not a day has gone by that I haven't thanked Laura for inviting us to hers that night, offering for us to stay over.

'Well, maybe Mary really was just looking for odd socks,' Matt suggests on the phone now. 'Sometimes things are as simple as they appear to be.'

'Maybe,' I say, pausing, wondering if I *should* tell him what I discovered in our bedroom after I'd put the kids to bed. 'What's weird is that I found—'

But I stop short. I don't want to worry him. Not while he's away on a work trip. He'll only fret about us and come back early, and I don't want him jeopardising this job. It's an important contract, potentially leading to a lot more work if this project goes well. We really need the money if we're to extend our house while it's being fixed up. And as a surveyor, Matt can't afford to take his eye off the ball – which is what made the fire investigator's conclusion an even more bitter pill to swallow.

'I just don't get it,' Matt said time and time again back in our hotel room that night. Gracie was unsettled and Tommy had the devil inside him. Everything in our lives felt wrong, derailed, in limbo. 'It's not bloody rocket science, wiring a light fitting into an existing point. I've done it loads of times before. How the hell did I mess up so bad?'

Thank God we were fully covered by insurance. We could have had a longer-term rental property paid for, but we were struggling to find one and then Annie's offer of her house by the sea came up. Initially, we were both wary about accepting – Matt especially so – though the more I thought about it, the more it made sense.

'It's an hour and a half's drive from our house,' Matt grumbled. 'It's going to make it much harder to monitor progress on the building works. And I really don't want to be... *beholden* to Annie, if it's all the same to you.'

'Annie's more than happy to help,' I reminded him, showing him her gushing texts. 'She's one of my dearest friends, Matt.'

'Yeah, *your* dearest friend,' he retorted. 'It'll feel weird being in her house without her, not to mention being in Hastings. I don't like it.'

It wasn't going to be easy for either of us, but eventually I wore Matt down, convincing him that a few months by the sea would be great for the kids, not to mention living in such a luxurious house. So, determined to put the ghosts from the past to the back of my mind, I messaged Annie and accepted.

'Sorry... you found what?' Matt says now on the phone through a yawn, going back to what I'd started to tell him.

'Oh, nothing,' I reply with a reciprocal yawn, changing the subject and telling him how I took the kids on a walk to see my old house instead – though I decide not to mention about Tommy running into the road, how it was Tyler's fault. He'd flip at me for being irresponsible – and rightly so.

After we've said goodnight and hung up, I put my phone on charge. Then I look at what I found on the floor under the dressing table stool earlier. It had caught my eye as I'd been picking up a wet towel, my heartbeat quickening when it dawned on me what it was. But then Matt had phoned.

I turn it over and over, weaving the tarnished chain between my fingers. The brassy metal links are caked with mud, and the pendant is mottled with rust. When I compare it to my own necklace, placing the two pendant halves side by side, the zigzag edges lock together to make a complete heart.

Best Friends is etched across the faded gold plating. One word on each half of the friendship necklace. I've not seen the *Friends* side to match my *Best* in many years. Probably not since we were all at school together. The four of us had two identical necklaces between us – one half of a heart pendant each. A GALS mascot to cement our friendship.

A few years ago, when I asked her about it, Annie admitted to not knowing where hers was any more – like Sara, she'd had a *Friends* half. And Laura said that her *Best* half was probably in an old jewellery box somewhere, though she couldn't be sure.

Am I the only one who's treasured my pendant all this time – carrying it around as a lucky charm, wearing it on my wrist, keeping it safe even after the fire stole most of our belongings?

I stare at the chain. This must be Annie's, somehow materialised on the bedroom floor – but I have no idea why it's so rusty and caked in mud.

I go over to the window, staring out at the neat back garden and into the overgrown land behind, hardly able to believe that it's been almost twenty-five years since Sara died. Then Mary is on my mind again – how I caught her nosing around in here, wondering if this necklace is what she was looking for.

EIGHTEEN
THE PAST

Gina hadn't meant to ask Matt out on a date, but it was that or admit she'd been spying on him.

Mortifying.

She'd got a hunch that he'd started dating someone, and she damn well wanted to find out who it was. Suss out the competition. She wouldn't admit to the others that she'd been snooping, but she would take delight in breaking the news: *Oh my God, you'll never guess what... Matt Dalton is going out with so-and-so... I saw them and... and...*

Well, maybe not *actual* delight. Devastation, more like. In fact, all of them would be gutted, instantly plotting how to split him and whoever she was up. Gina suspected it was Katie Johns from Matt's year. She'd overheard a couple of his friends talking about her flirting and hanging around him like a bad smell, and there was rumour of Matt having someone over to his house on Saturday afternoon while his parents were out. With a bit of gentle probing and false eyelash fluttering, Gina had got Matt's mate, Evan, to spill where Matt lived under the pretence of dropping off a maths books for a project they were working on together.

So there Gina was, hiding behind a bush in Matt's front garden waiting for evidence that Katie Johns was inside the house with him. Maybe she'd catch sight of them through the living room window, or perhaps she'd witness Katie leaving, the pair kissing on the doorstep. But as it happened, she didn't see any of these things.

She needed the loo desperately and, after crouching behind the bush for at least an hour and a half, she was fed up, cold and bored, and had all but convinced herself that maybe she didn't fancy Matt that much after all. It was clear he didn't fancy any of *them*.

The coast seemed clear, so Gina left the cover of her hiding place in a half-crouch, half-run, scuttling towards the car that was parked on the drive.

The front door opened just as she was midway between the bush and the car.

'Gina?' a voice called out.

She froze. Then she turned. Matt was standing in the doorway. Her face went from stunned to a twisted, pained grin. 'Hi.' She gave a little wave.

'What are you doing here?' He seemed perplexed but also amused. He was wearing jeans and a faded black T-shirt, and his black curly hair was mussed up as though he'd just got out of bed. His feet were bare, and, for some reason, Gina noticed that he had really long toes.

'I... I just came to... well...'

Shit.

What was she supposed to say? She'd not banked on being caught out so hadn't prepared any clever excuses. Looking for her cat wouldn't wash because she lived too far across town for it to have wandered this way. And she couldn't claim she was delivering flyers or the newspaper because she didn't have any on her. So she said the first thing that came to mind.

'I've come to ask you out,' she announced with a forced grin, her heart thumping wildly. 'On a date. Would you like to go out with me, Matt?' She held her head up high and walked towards the door, knowing he'd say no, but at least it would stop him calling her a stalker weirdo and give her a reason for being there. She would laugh about it with the others later, while simultaneously dying inside. She felt her cheeks burn scarlet as she prayed the ground would swallow her up.

Then someone appeared in the doorway beside Matt. A girl. A girl that wasn't Katie Johns.

'Sara?' Gina squeaked. 'What are *you* doing here?'

Sara said something then looked up at Matt, a nervous expression on her face.

Gina didn't hear her, so she crept closer – each step tentative like a cat approaching its prey. Though right now, she felt more like the quarry – walking into an ambush.

'What did you say, Sara?' she asked. It sounded accusatory, though she hadn't intended it that way. She was shocked to see one of her best friends – one of the GALS – standing there beside Matt and looking up at him adoringly. At least she thought that's what it was. Sara seemed... somehow on edge, almost reticent, as though she'd rather be anywhere else. Gina was even more shocked when she looked down to see their fingers linked together. So much for *no secrets*.

'I'm with Matt,' Sara repeated softly. She looked up at him again and smiled – an uneasy smile as if she wasn't sure what she wanted. 'How are you, Gina?'

Small mercies that Sara hadn't asked her what she was doing here, forcing her to repeat that she'd come to ask Matt out, even though she hadn't. She'd have literally curled up and died on the driveway. Instead, she said, 'Are you two...' she flicked a finger between them, 'like... *together* together?'

If they were seeing each other, then why the *hell* hadn't Sara said anything? She was one of the GALS, after all, and knew how they all felt about Matt, the four of them discussing him together, wondering if any of them was in with a chance, figuring out ways to get him to notice they were even alive. They shared everything. *No fucking secrets.*

Yet here Sara was – with a whopper. Quietly betraying them all.

Gina swallowed down the sick feeling creeping up her gullet. This was treachery of the worst kind, and she didn't like it one bit. The others would be livid.

Sara smiled coyly as Matt wrapped his hand around hers. He pressed himself closer to her side and said, looking a bit awkward, 'It's early days. But yeah, I guess we are...' He tentatively kissed the top of her head as if to prove it.

For some reason, Gina thought Sara seemed slightly crestfallen at his vague reply, despite the kiss.

'I've come round to study,' Sara said, almost having to shout so that her voice would carry the six feet or so between her and Gina. Her face lit up as she gazed at Matt.

'And have you done much... *studying* yet?' Gina swayed from one foot to the other, unable to believe that she'd just asked that. But if there was anything good to be gleaned from this excruciating situation, it had at least taken the heat off her having to explain why she was lurking in the bushes, convinced that she was about to find evidence of Katie Johns being Matt's new girlfriend. She'd never expected this in a million years. How wrong could she have been?

When neither of them replied, to break the silence Gina said, 'Well, you're a dark horse, aren't you, Sara Shaw?'

The couple shared a knowing look, which made Gina feel stupid, as though she was losing a friend as well as all hope of ever standing a chance with Matt. 'Have a good time then,' she said, giving them a little salute, turning to go.

As she walked off down the drive, Gina gulped back the

tears that were brewing. *Just get around the corner before you cry*. Her nails dug into her palms.

'Geen,' Sara yelled out. 'Geen, wait.'

Gina stopped in her tracks and slowly looked back. 'Don't tell the others about this, eh?' she continued, suddenly finding her voice. 'Not yet.'

Gina gave a little nod before heading off again. When she reached the end of the street, she bit into the sleeve of her denim jacket and screamed for all she was worth.

Annie was sprawled on Gina's bed, her legs up in the air and her arms spread wide. Britney was blaring out of the CD player full-blast, and they'd no doubt get told to turn it down when Gina's mum came home. Thank God her dad was out in his shed mending something or other. It was all so Saturday afternoon in the suburbs. So much more wretched with this news.

'I feel sick,' Gina said.

'Tell me exactly what happened again.' Annie sat up, jaw grinding as she pummelled the flavour out of her gum. She took a swig from the Coke can on the cabinet beside the bed. She still couldn't believe it.

Gina repeated the story. For about the tenth time.

'And they were deffo, you know, together? Sara? *Our* Sara?'

'Jesus, Annie. It's not like I didn't recognise her.'

They'd been talking in circles about the same thing for the last hour. They'd phoned Laura at her house to tell her to come over, but there'd been no reply. Then they'd remembered she and her family had gone away for the weekend to visit cousins or something.

'I love Sara, I *really* do,' Annie said. 'But... but *her* with Matt? You know what I'm saying, right?' She blew out a breath slowly, incredulously.

Both girls stared at the carpet, each feeling like a bitch for thinking what they were thinking. But they were feeling betrayed. Stabbed in the back. They reckoned their thoughts were justified.

'Apart from anything, she should have bloody told us. We're her GALS. Like, what happened to *no secrets*, right?'

Those two words triggered their secret handshake – performed with little enthusiasm as they brushed knuckles and linked fingers one by one. Their hands flopped back onto the bed.

Big love, true friends, no secrets – the mantra the four of them lived by. And yet how easily had Sara's betrayal happened?

'I hate her for this, but I still love her, too,' Gina said. 'That's what makes it so damned hard.'

'There are other boys in the world,' Annie said flatly.

'Not Matt Dalton, though,' Gina replied. 'At least you get to kiss him in the play. And anyway, that's hardly the point. Sara lied to us by omission.'

Annie got up and went over to the CD player to change the track. 'What do you think will be going through my mind now when I have to do the stage kiss?' She turned, hands on hips. 'I'll tell you what – that our supposed bestie Sara bloody Shaw got her poisonous little tongue in there first. *Fucking hell.*' She stamped her foot.

Gina went over and gave Annie a hug, resting her head on her shoulder. They swayed together in time to the mood-matching song that Annie had put on – the emotional lyrics all about broken hearts and first loves.

'Can I tell you a secret?' Gina whispered, not daring to look her in the eye. She felt Annie nod her head. 'I've been seriously crushing on Matt for ages.'

A laugh. 'Join the queue.'

'No, but like, *seriously* crushing. I honestly thought he felt the same. You know, the signals I was getting.'

'Signals?' Annie turned round, holding Gina at arm's length so she could see her face. She lifted up her chin and saw the tears in her eyes. 'Oh, Geen,' she said, pulling her close.

'I feel so stupid.' Gina let out a sob, noticing how Annie's shoulders suddenly felt tenser than before.

'Look, let Sara have her fun, eh?' Annie said. 'We all know that her home life's a bit rubbish right now, not to mention her being ill at the end of last term and most of the summer holidays. This might give her the boost she needs. And I'm sorry to sound like a bitch...' she lowered her voice, 'but we both know it's not going to last.' The pair shared a look.

'Spoken like a true friend,' Gina said with a laugh as she wiped a finger under her eyes, being careful not to smudge her mascara. 'And you're right, of course.' She grinned, deciding not to tell Annie that she'd literally been prepared to do *anything* to get rid of Katie Johns or whoever Matt's mystery girlfriend might have been when she'd lurked outside his house earlier.

NINETEEN

GINA

'Good morning, dear!'

At first, I can't place where the voice is coming from. I scan the back windows of Annie's house from where I'm pegging out washing in the garden – having finally convinced Mary that I will take care of my family's laundry – but there's no sign of Mary or anyone else calling out to me.

'Oh, hi!' I call back, a hand at my brow as I suddenly spot the head bobbing up over the garden wall. The woman, mid- to late sixties, must be balancing on something on the other side of the wall separating Genoa House from next door. It's too tall to see over otherwise. I give her a neighbourly smile then turn to get on with hanging out Gracie's sleepsuits.

'She's rarely here, that one,' the woman continues. 'Such a shame that she never gets time to sit in her garden.' The woman, wearing a khaki camouflaged army-style hat – looking totally out of place sitting over her pale, softly powdered face with her peach lipstick – bobs her head towards the house. 'Annie,' she adds when I give her a quizzical look.

'Oh... I see.' Another smile from me. 'The price of fame, I

guess. She travels a lot.' I peg out one of Gracie's little cotton dresses.

'She's famous?' The woman suddenly grabs hold of the coping stones as if whatever she's standing on has just wobbled. But then she seems to get even higher, perhaps climbing another rung on a step ladder, revealing that she's wearing denim dungarees with a white shirt beneath, the collar turned up around her neck.

'She is these days, yes. She's been in all sorts of things over the years, including lead roles in a few blockbuster cinema releases. Have you seen the latest series of her Netflix drama? It's a black comedy called *Left Field* and she totally owns it.'

'I'm more of a book person,' the neighbour reveals. 'And I play bridge three nights a week.' Then she holds up a pair of secateurs and snips at the air a couple of times. 'I like to get out in the garden when it's fine. Good for the joints.'

'Thought I'd take advantage of the dry weather, too,' I reply, signalling to the washing line.

'A baby in the house?' she asks, noticing the tiny clothes.

'Yes, a little girl, Gracie, and Tommy who's three.'

'Are you staying long?'

'We'll be here a few weeks,' I add, not wanting to go into the details why.

'That's nice, dear. Billy and I always wanted children, but God never blessed us.' She lets out a deep sigh. 'Billy wasn't able to...' She trails off wistfully, deciding not to reveal her husband's medical history, for which I'm grateful. 'These houses were built for families.'

She glances up at the back of her property, the brickwork glowing russet-red and gold in the early-autumn light, her eyes lingering on the top floor dormer window. I follow her gaze and, for a moment, I think I catch sight of a face behind the glass – perhaps Billy watching us – but it must have been the sun or a reflection because there's no one there now.

'Well, it's just nice to see Genoa House being used. Filled with happy sounds for a change. That housekeeper of hers never says much the couple of times I've seen her.' The woman tuts and rolls her eyes.

'You mean Mary?'

'That's her name, is it? We've crossed paths once or twice out the front, and I've said hello, but all I've got back is a rude stare before she scuttles off.' The woman pauses to catch her breath. 'And you can tell her from me...' she pauses to wag a finger over the wall, 'don't think I don't notice what she's been getting up to out the back at all hours of the day and night.' Then she points towards the patch of derelict land behind the gardens. 'Billy and I keep our eye on things around here, you know. We might be getting on, but we're not blind.'

'Oh?' I say, curiosity getting the better of me. 'What do you mean by *getting up to*?'

If Mary is involved in dodgy goings-on, then I have a right to know. She's living with my two small children, after all. Then I remember how I found the gate in the back fence open the other day, when Mary had taken my children to the beach without permission.

'Searching,' the woman says in a hushed voice, her fingers gripping the coping stones as she leans over the wall. 'She has her head down and gets on with her hunting, pushing through all the brambles, using a torch after dark.' Then she shrugs. 'She's not done it these last couple of days though.'

'I see,' I say, unsure if I'm feeling relieved or slightly disappointed that she hasn't spotted Mary carrying out a ritual sacrifice or meeting a drug dealer. Annie wouldn't stand for any nonsense and would fire Mary immediately. I feel ashamed for wishing she'd lose her job, but I'd prefer if it was just our family living here.

'What was she looking for?' I've already decided I'm going to take a look out there myself when both kids are having their afternoon naps. The baby monitor works where I am now, so will hopefully reach a bit further.

'I've no idea,' the woman says. 'But I'll be keeping my eye on her, that's for sure. There's something not right about her. When you get to my age, you just get a feeling. I'm Bridget, by the way.' She reaches a hand over the wall, and I go up to her, stretching up to shake it. Her skin is cool and papery, her long fingers strong and capable.

'I'm Gina,' I say in return. 'And my husband is Matt. He's a commercial building surveyor and away for work right now, but he's back tomorrow. You'll have to meet him.'

'I'd like that,' Bridget says, pulling the brim of her hat lower. 'Why don't you both come round for morning coffee on Thursday? Does ten o'clock suit? My husband loves children, so bring them, too. And you can tell me all about that famous neighbour of mine.'

And with that, the woman from next door drops down behind the wall again, and a moment later, I hear the *snip snip snip* of her secateurs, though it's soon drowned out when Gracie's shrill cry sounds from the monitor, cutting through the air.

TWENTY

MARY

As soon as she opens the door, I barge in. Head down, I can't muster any pleasantries as I slide sideways past her in the narrow hallway of my mother's two-up two-down terraced house. The grubby UPVC door opens straight on to the street and, as a kid, I remember lying on the floor, cheek to doormat, watching the shadows of people's feet pass under the gap of the old wooden door we had back then. Then I'd scuttle back upstairs when *he* came home.

'What's up with you?' My mother fills the kettle and lights a cigarette. She pushes the top of the kitchen window open, puffing her smoke out. 'You look like a wet weekend.'

'I lost the necklace.'

At this, she growls out a laugh and blows smoke into the room, a noxious cloud billowing around me.

'Careless,' she says, twisting the cap on a half-bottle of no-brand vodka. 'You only just found it.' Mother's face wrinkles as she takes a swig. It won't be her first drink of the day. She works that bottle like a drip, twenty-four seven.

I close my eyes long enough to see myself frantically scrabbling in Gina's bedroom in case I'd dropped it when I was in there – then I see myself caught red-handed.

'I'll get it back,' I say, not bothering to explain that it must have got caught up in a pile of clothes somehow while I was doing my stupid job. She'd tell me I was *useless, a waste of space, a loser...* proving that all the names she and my father used to call me are still true.

Mother takes another drag on her Benson and spews out a hacking cough. It turns into a laugh. 'You always were stupid. Get Ty to look for it instead,' she says predictably, although I'm invincible to the pain now, the words sliding off me whenever she hurls them. 'He'll find it.'

'I wish you'd quit all that,' I say, eyeing the bottle and her cigarette. 'You'll get lung cancer or liver failure.'

Another rattly laugh from my mother. 'My organs have held up for seventy years, Mary, my sweet. Ain't them that's going to send me to my grave.' Her lips contort into a nasty sneer, triggering a feeling inside that I've long since learnt to block out. A skill that got me through the years.

Was it *her* way to get through, too? To go along with everything that happened, turning her own blind eye, shutting it all out? I should hate her, cut her out of my life, plot murder for what she allowed to happen. But I don't. Like me, she was a victim. She just didn't see it at the time. Whatever happened, she's still my mother.

'Don't worry about the necklace,' I tell her, playing it down. 'That's the least of my concerns right now. We're in the house, at least.'

'And what about... you know?' My mother taps the side of her nose. Cagey is her middle name.

'It'll be OK,' I tell her in a shaky voice, though I don't let on that what I've done keeps me awake at night, sweating in a tangle of sheets through bad dreams in which the police come, handcuffing me and throwing me in the back of a van. In the last nightmare, I was shoved in a prison cell right next door to my father. Tyler was screaming out that I've let him down, that he hates me, that he never wants to see me again. Truth is, he's all I've got left.

'You don't sound sure,' my mother snaps. 'It's either OK or it isn't.'

And just like that, back I go, down a wormhole to when, aged nine, I was standing in this very room, my mother looming over me, a fag hanging out of her mouth and a spiral of smoke twisting upwards. She had a permanent squint because of it.

'It either happened or it didn't.' Her thumbs were hooked through the belt loops of her flared, hipster jeans – the shape of her pert, braless breasts visible beneath the fabric of her vest top, her spiralling blonde hair making her so different to my friends' mums, who all wore sensible skirts and worked as secretaries or nurses. Mother was a looker, yet she was ugly, too. If it wasn't for the poison inside, she'd have turned heads. As things stood, it was only my father who had eyes for her – for his *Pammie*. Well, her and all the others he had eyes for, though she was his favourite. She was the only one who'd given him children.

Her grilling of me continued until I cried, backtracked and truly believed that I'd imagined it all like she was insisting. She forced me into confessing that I'd had a bad dream. That I must have been mistaken about the blood between my legs, that there was no man in my bed, that it should all be forgotten. It was easier for my mother to deal with it that way.

'I said it's OK,' I repeat now, backing away as I get a faceful of smoke. 'It's all going to plan.' I peel open my denim jacket, beneath which is my cross-body bag. From it I take three rolled-up twenty-pound notes, handing them to my mother. It nearly kills me, giving it to her, as I don't have a lot to spare, but for her it's what this is all about. Money. Money for fags, for booze, for the slots and for bingo. I mete it out, like a parent giving their child pocket money. She wouldn't survive otherwise.

I pull open the rusting fridge door. 'Jesus,' I say, recoiling as I peer inside. I remove a block of cheese with green circles of mould growing on it, and similarly I chuck out an opened pack of bacon that I know has sat there for at least two months. 'Are you eating?'

My mother shrugs. 'Val calls round. We go chippy.' She stubs out her cigarette in a saucer by the sink.

'Have you seen Dennis recently?' Not that I particularly want to talk about my father.

'The fare's expensive.' She eyes my bag. Like the mug that I am, I take out another forty pounds and give it to her.

'Go and see him,' I say, knowing the prison visits keep her going. 'And buy extra food this week with what's left over. You've lost more weight.' Somehow, she seems hunched and shorter, too, and there are more bald patches within her stringy, nicotine-stained grey hair.

'Thanks, sweet,' she says, rolling up the notes and tucking them in her hoodie pocket – a worn, shell-suit-type top that I swear she had when I was a kid. 'I'll send your dad your love.'

I stare at her, eventually replying, 'Please don't do that.'

TWENTY-ONE

GINA

I didn't anticipate bringing Tommy with me on my recce this afternoon, but if nothing else, it's confirmed he has a sixth sense. Usually, he can't keep his eyes open after lunch and always has a nap, but today it's as though he's been mainlining sugar or has managed to operate the coffee machine because he's bouncing around the kitchen with his toy aeroplane and is as wide awake as I've ever seen him.

'Cwash landing!' he announces, hurling the plastic toy at the polished surface of Annie's expensive dining table.

'I said *pretend* there's an airport, Tommo. You'll scratch Aunty Annie's nice things playing rough like that.' I inspect the tabletop, wincing as I see a couple of dull lines in the sheen. But sorting that will have to wait. While Gracie is napping in her pram in the study, I want to have a proper scout around the common to see if I can work out what Mary has been up to, taking the opportunity while she and Tyler are out.

'Grab your wellies, Tommy,' I say, but I end up fetching them from the hallway myself, along with the baby monitor. Once he's padded up in coat and boots, I lift him up and plant him on my hip, but he squirms, trying to hurl himself to the floor until I convince him we're going to search for fairies, as well as plying him with a chocolate biscuit.

Outside, the gate at the end of Annie's neat garden leading through to the common takes a bit of yanking to get open but eventually it gives.

'Fare*wees*,' Tommy mutters, licking the chocolate off his biscuit as I carry him.

'That's right, kiddo. Keep your eyes peeled.'

As I'd discovered the other day in my panicked state, there's not a lot to see back here apart from weeds, brambles, a few dying trees and years of neglect. Leading directly from the gate is a sort of path where the undergrowth has been broken and trampled. I follow the flattened weeds, heading deeper into the common, wondering if it was Mary who carved out the route.

'Someone's been having a bonfire, look,' I say, spotting the blackened area in a small clearing. 'Perhaps it was the fairies.' Anything to keep Tommy engaged.

The trail takes me further away from Annie's house, though I'm relieved to hear the occasional snuffle from Gracie still coming through on the baby monitor. We head towards several gnarled trees huddled together with a clump of thorny bushes beneath. Everywhere I look, it's either thigh-high grasses turned brown and gone to seed or impenetrable brambles blocking my way.

'Farewee!' Tommy shrieks in my ear, making me jump. He sticks his hand out, pointing, dropping his biscuit into the weeds. Then he bursts into tears, wriggling to get down.

'Wait, we'll find it together,' I say, but it's too late. Tommy, who gets stronger every day, pushes against me so I'm forced to free him and let him slide down me to the ground. He lands on the remains of his biscuit, which triggers a shrill wail that I imagine everyone in the neighbourhood hears.

But I'm only barely conscious of my son's meltdown.

Because while it's not fairies that Tommy has spotted, it's certainly bordering on the surreal.

Over in a corner of the common, shrouded by the pale fluttering leaves of a small silver birch tree, is what looks like, at first glance, some kind of shrine. Faded cloth bunting of all colours hangs in the lower branches of the birch, some of it tangled and torn as it flaps in the breeze. Beneath the tree, someone has separated off a circular area about five feet in diameter with old bricks, laying them end to end in a wobbly curve. And around the edge of them is a decorative border of carefully set-out pebbles.

'How bizarre,' I whisper, keeping a firm hold on Tommy's hand as we walk closer. He's still crying about his dropped biscuit. 'You can have the whole packet when we get back,' I tell him. 'Just let Mummy look at this for a moment.' When his grizzling continues, I pretend to gasp loudly, 'Oh, Tommy, *look!* Fairy tracks!'

That does the trick, and he follows quietly beside me, enthralled, peering at the ground and walking in a semi-crouch as we approach what does, weirdly, resemble some kind of abandoned grotto.

'If you're really, *really* quiet, we might see some little fairies,' I tell him to maintain the calm. Miraculously, it works.

Within the bricked-off circle, there's an old tree stump and the ground around it has been cleared to expose the bare earth beneath. Strangely, there are patches of pea shingle placed in random piles with a few unrecognisable wildflower petals scattered here and there – and the petals appear to be fresh. A few weeds poke through the soil, but then I notice a small heap of pulled-up dandelions and thistles off to the side, as though someone has recently tugged them out.

'Farewee house,' Tommy says, pointing again. He's right. The old, gnarly tree stump in the centre of the circle, about knee height, has enough crevices and holes to house an entire population of fairies.

Before I can stop him, Tommy yanks his hand free of mine and steps inside the circle, crouching down at the log, peering inside it. He shoves his little hand into one of the holes, worming his arm elbow-deep.

'Did you see a fairy?' I ask, stepping closer to him, careful not to disturb anything. The whole area is giving me the creeps, and I wouldn't be surprised to see sheep skulls hanging from the branches above me, or pagan symbols carved into the tree trunk.

'Der!' Tommy says, pulling something out of the trunk and holding it up. It's the stump of a candle about three inches high with a blackened wick. 'More!' he squeals, excited to be raiding the fairy house.

'No, wait,' I say, grabbing his hand as he goes to put it in the hole again. 'Mummy will do it,' I say, expecting another tantrum. But Tommy stays calm. I don't want him finding drugs paraphernalia, given the types that used to hang out here. I'm not risking my son being jabbed by a needle.

I put my hand into one of the bigger holes at the base of the rotten log, my fingers searching around inside. At first all I feel is rotting leaves and mud, but as I push deeper, I come across something that feels hard... and flat. Just managing to reach it, I tug and wiggle it out of the hole, brushing the muck and soil from it.

I frown, staring at the tarnished silver picture frame, only about three inches by four, with cracked glass and a faded photograph inside. I wipe my fingers over it, revealing a faded picture of a teenage girl.

'Oh my *God*...' I whisper, letting out a gasp when I see her face. Then the little frame falls from my fingers and tumbles to the ground.

TWENTY-TWO

GINA

Pick up, for God's sake pick up... I'm about to send her a message when she answers.

'Geen, five missed calls? I've just stepped out of a meeting. What's up?'

Now I've got her, I don't know where to begin. Dredging up stuff that's been buried for so long isn't a prospect I'm relishing.

'I found Sara,' I blurt out, which leads to silence at the other end of the line.

Eventually, I hear, '*What?*'

'She was buried... no, *hidden*. In the common. Creepy as fuck, like with candles and bunting and flowers, but it looked old. That's a good sign, right?' I hear myself panting and gasping as my heart beats at twice its normal speed. 'She was filthy. Covered in mud.'

'Gina, calm down,' Laura replies. 'I've no idea what you're talking about. What do you mean, you *found* Sara?' I know her immediate thought will be the police... that we must contact them. Report this. Tell them everything. Reopen the case.

'Not actually *her*, of course. I... I found a photo. An old photo of *Sara*.'

'Jesus, Gina. I thought you meant...'

Voices in the background, then the sound of a door opening and closing, heels clicking on concrete. Birds singing. Traffic. She's gone outside.

'I took a photo of it.' A couple of taps and it's on Laura's phone with two blue ticks appearing immediately as she views it. I hear her exhale, making a slight whistle through her front teeth. 'I know, right?'

'Bless her,' Laura whispers. 'Her little face.'

'You agree it's her then? I mean, it's faded. It's dirty. I was hoping you'd say I was imagining things. That it was someone else.'

'No. No, it's her.'

'What do we do?' I pace about the kitchen, keeping one eye on Gracie as she sits in her bouncy chair watching Tommy play, while also flashing looks at the front door in case Mary and Tyler come back. This conversation isn't for anyone else.

Then I tell Laura about the rusty necklace I found on my bedroom floor.

'So, that means it's either Annie's pendant or...' I don't want to say it.

'Or Sara's.'

'Yeah.'

'Look, given that you're in Annie's house, it's most likely hers, right? That would be the simplest answer.'

'Why does everyone keep *saying* that to me?' Then Matt is on my mind again. How I miss him. How I wish he was here right now. While I don't want to tell him about this, at least it would give me a strong pair of arms to fall into until I've figured out what to do. But I don't need to because Laura lays out exactly what my next steps are.

'Right, you're going to message Annie. Ask her where her necklace is. Tell her that being in Hastings has made you feel all sentimental and you want a picture of the necklaces reunited... or something like that. If you find it wherever she tells you to look, then we have a problem – like, where the hell did this *other* necklace come from?'

'But if I don't find Annie's necklace,' I say, 'then we're still no further forward. It might be... or it might *not* be hers. Besides, they're common as anything.'

The unspoken subtext hanging between us says it's not as straightforward as we were hoping – that Annie's necklace, if it *is* in this house, is not going to be rusty or caked in mud as if it's been outside for years. Rather it'll be stashed, tangled up, in an old jewellery box or similar. And not being able to find it doesn't mean it doesn't exist somewhere in the house or get me any closer to an explanation.

'I wish we'd never agreed to move in here,' I say, still pacing about. 'I wish our bloody house had never caught fire.' I bang my fist against my thigh.

'I know, I know. You've been through hell, Geen. And it's not surprising that ghosts are surfacing. I'd get the shivers, too. It's understandable.'

'Come down here, Laura,' I say suddenly. 'Come and stay. Like, this weekend. Will you? *Please*?'

Silence.

'Work's a bit mad right now,' Laura eventually replies. 'Talking of which, I need to get back into the meeting. My tits'll be served on a platter if I don't.'

A bit more begging from me about coming to stay, which she acknowledges with an awkward *maybe*, and then she's gone, the line dead. I immediately text Annie while Tommy hurls a toy train at the bifold doors, Gracie whines and squirms, and a dirty nappy smell drifts my way.

Hi Annie, any idea where your GALS friendship necklace might be? I'm feeling all sentimental and would love to reunite the two halves. Insta gold lol. BLTFNS xx

Thing is, I rarely post on Instagram, and Annie would know this. I mainly use the app to stalk and keep up with her, to be honest, plus I follow a few accounts about parenting and healthy food, which invariably make me feel inadequate about my messy house and ready meals – though I'd take mess over burnt ruins any day. So my message to Annie is probably going to trigger questions, though I'll deal with them when I have to.

Then, twenty minutes later, with me perched at the kitchen island still staring at my phone as I wait for Annie's reply, the front door opens and my heart sinks. Mary and Tyler are back, their voices and laughter filling the hallway.

It's another two hours before I get a reply from Annie.

Christ, necklace could be anywhere. Not seen it in years. Probs lost in move. Sorry. All OK back at base camp? xoxo

On a whim, I press the call button on our WhatsApp thread, hearing the ringing sound in my ear as clearly as if she was down the road, not on safari in Kenya.

When there's no reply, I hang up. Then I see Annie typing.

Sorry, can't talk right now, heading off on trek. Try my dressing room for necklace. Top shelf, boxes full of sentimental stuff xx

It's something, at least. A place to start. I go upstairs, hovering on the landing outside Annie's bedroom suite, knowing Mary goes in there regularly to check on things, dust around and water the plants. Apart from the sound of Tyler frantically clicking buttons on his games console in the attic bedroom, I don't hear any other noises coming from the top floor. I've no idea what Mary does with herself while she's up there. She doesn't even have a television to watch.

Holding my breath, I turn the old brass doorknob on Annie's bedroom door, cautiously peeking inside. The plush, ivory-coloured carpet is freshly striped from vacuuming, making me concerned I'll leave footprints. But then, why am I even bothered about what Mary thinks? Sprucing it up is what she's paid to do, after all, and I have a text from Annie to prove that she doesn't mind me looking for the necklace. But despite that, it still feels like I'm snooping.

I head straight to the dressing room, noticing the faint smell of Annie's perfume – light and floral – as well as freshly laundered sheets. Everything in the room is neat and set perfectly in its place, and the linen bedding and velvet bedspread give an upmarket hotel feel.

In the dressing room, I slide open one of the mirror-fronted doors, coming face to face with rails of neatly hung, colour-coordinated clothes. A world apart from my little bedroom at home. How I long to be sleeping back there with the wonky pine wardrobe that Matt and I shared, his few work shirts and trousers fighting for space against my bargain store finds.

Standing on tiptoe, I'm just able to reach the top shelf. I smile at the sight of all Annie's hats up there, most of them stored in circular, candy-striped boxes. She's always dressed stylishly, even back when we were schoolkids relying on a few quid of pocket money a week. Her wardrobe bordered on the theatrical, stuffed with charity shop finds that she'd customised herself.

'That could be it,' I say to myself, spotting a tatty shoebox that looks out of place among Annie's other things. I stretch up even further, my fingers just managing to slide it to the front of the shelf, but suddenly I hear a shrill scream right behind me, making me knock the box onto the floor, its contents spilling out at my feet.

My heart races as I spin round, my eyes locking with Mary's for a split second before she slams the dressing room door.

'What the *hell*? What are you doing?' I cry out, running over and grabbing the handle, yanking it hard as I hear the key turning in the lock on the other side. I tug and pull and shout and thump, but it's no good – the door is not budging. Mary has locked me in.

TWENTY-THREE
THE PAST

Gina, Annie and Laura had organised a secret meeting – its very occurrence and exclusion of Sara instantly breaking the GALS' golden rule: *no secrets*. The three of them were sitting on a seafront bench, freezing and shivering despite being wrapped up in their coats. Their noses dripped in the biting wind that swept along the prom, and their shoulders were up around their ears.

'It would literally *kill* her if she knew we were doing this. You know how sensitive she is.' Annie pulled her hat down lower over her ears and stared out at the gunmetal churn of the sea, fixing her gaze on the horizon.

'Sara kept a secret first,' Laura pointed out. Always the one to consider both sides of an argument, she corralled her long brown hair with one hand, deftly slipping an elastic around it with the other. 'So she can't exactly diss us for meeting up without her.'

Gina watched a seagull perch on the railings between them and the shingle beach, its wings brown and speckled, thinking Laura sounded more like she was twenty-five, not fifteen. Now *there* was someone who knew what she wanted in life, as well as knowing the path to get there – decent A levels, law school, a plum job in a big city firm. Everything by the book for Laura Draper.

As for Annie, Gina knew she had her sights firmly fixed on the stage, her future visions illuminated by a far-reaching spotlight. It would no doubt be a tortuous and character-building journey to get there, fraught with disappointment and self-loathing, an alcohol addiction and a drugs habit while living in a squat with other thespians or art school types.

Even Sara was sorting herself out now. She'd always been quietly clever, despite whatever troubles she had at home – not that they knew much about those because none of the GALS had ever been invited back to her house. Oddly, though, they suspected that was *why* she was a grade A student – because she threw herself into her studies to avoid the turmoil. While she didn't know what she wanted to do when she left school, her intelligence gave her options. And because her family had no money, she'd likely get scholarships and funding to help her along the way.

Oh, and not forgetting that Sara now had the hottest and most popular boy in school as her boyfriend. There was that. *There was fucking that.*

Gina stared at the stupid seagull as it pecked around her ankles, almost admiring its bravery. If she had any food, she knew the blasted thing would be all over her, lunging at her with its greedy beak. She'd once had an entire bag of chips taken from her by a dive-bombing gull. Sara had been with her, and she'd handed over her chips to Gina without hesitation. 'We can share,' she'd said. Sweet Sara.

Sweet, lying Sara.

'I say we do nothing,' Laura continued. 'It's our *Saz*, after all. Good on her if she's pulled Matt Dalton. Though...' Laura trailed off, a pained expression on her face, 'I hate to be the one to say this, but I don't think it'll last.'

'Too late, we've already said it.' Annie stared out to sea, chin in hands. The sun was low in the sky, branding the horizon with a white-hot line that shimmered over the grey waters. 'If she wants to hold onto Matt, she should, you know, do more with herself. Her hair and make-up for a start.'

'Maybe we could help her,' Gina said, shooing the gull away as it came closer. 'Give her a makeover.' Her shoulders were hunched, and she had an empty feeling in the pit of her belly, as though nothing had a point any more now that Matt was off the market.

'I love Sara, of course I do,' Laura said. 'But there's just something so... see-through about her. You know?' Bitchiness wasn't her thing, but she reeked of it now.

'God, you're right, that's exactly what it is,' Annie chimed back. 'Like, she's almost a ghost. She never says much these days when we're together. And she never asks us round to hers. It makes me wonder if she even *wants* to be one of the GALS any more. Like she thinks she's better than us.'

A snort from Laura as she agreed.

'Thing is, we'd still be GAL without her,' Gina said. 'And cos there's three of us, that technically still makes us GALs.' There was no way she'd admit it to the others, but she didn't like the thought of Sara leaving the group. It wouldn't be the same without her.

The other two laughed, but without much verve. The light was fading and that meant their mums would be freaking out if they weren't home soon. Gina stood up and walked over to the railings separating them from the beach and sea beyond. The gull followed her, squawking and flapping its ugly wings when she wafted her hands at it. But it just came back again.

Annie took a pack of Embassy from her denim jacket pocket, and she and Laura joined Gina at the railings. 'So, what are we gonna do then?' she asked. 'Does Sara stay in GALS?'

'I say yes,' Gina piped up. 'She needs our friendship.' She

surprised herself by saying this, despite how much it stung about Matt. But several times recently she'd seen bruises around Sara's upper arms, noticed how she rarely ate lunch at school because she had no money. She didn't know Sara's sister very well, since she was a few years younger than them, but just last week she'd spotted her in a clothes shop nicking underwear. Seeing the fear and desperation in the girl's bloodshot eyes, she'd kept quiet and turned away, minding her own business.

'I still can't believe that Sara has done us all over,' Annie said, kicking a crumpled Coke can onto the beach. 'That she lied to us.'

'I vote for keeping her in because then we get the lowdown on Matt,' Laura said in her serious, analytical tone. 'When things go tits up, which they will, then we'll be here to support her, and one of you can take her place. I'm more into girls right now, so count me out.' Laura being bi wasn't news to Gina or Annie, though she hadn't come out to anyone else, not even her parents. She was still figuring herself out.

'OK, so Sara stays,' Annie decided, twisting her foot on her dog-end. The others nodded solemnly. 'Big love, true friends, no secrets,' she added, and the others chimed in, their fists and fingers entwining for the handshake.

As they walked back up into town, the stiff sea breeze biting at their backs, Laura and Annie chatted about the school play and the upcoming stage kiss. But Gina was silent, caught up in her thoughts. She hated that they'd met up behind Sara's back.

She turned, looking down to the seafront where they'd been sitting. The seagull with the brown speckled wing was still perched on the railings, its beady eyes seeming to track them as they walked home. But then it spread its wings and took to the air, navigating the downdraught as it circled overhead a few times. Finally, it squawked loudly and turned into a steep dive before sweeping out to sea.

Gina shook her head and continued walking, but something

kept nagging at the back of her mind, pecking away as the insistent voice told her that the seagull's presence was an omen, a warning, a portent of something bad. But by the time she'd got home, she'd convinced herself that she was being stupid. That it was nothing more than an annoying bird.

TWENTY-FOUR

GINA

Matt smells of home when I hug him. Not of my burnt-out house in Crawley, or even Annie's fresh-smelling house, but rather my *soul's* home – the place where I belong. And it's exactly what I need after the day I've had. As soon as he walks in through the front door, I press my face into the hollow where his shoulder meets his neck, fighting back tears.

'Thank *God* you're back,' I mumble against the fabric of his shirt.

'Need the loo, Geen,' he whispers. 'Long journey.'

Reluctantly, I release him. 'I've missed you so much,' I tell him, tracking him to the downstairs toilet, hovering outside the door that he leaves ajar. 'I didn't like it here without you.' Which is an understatement, considering everything that's happened.

The loo flushes, a quick swill of his hands, and then Matt is in the kitchen with me, cooing over Gracie and hoisting Tommy up to his chest. 'My big man,' he says in a deep voice that sends tingles through me and makes Tommy giggle. 'How's everything been?' he asks, grabbing a beer from the fridge.

'Fine,' I say through gritted teeth, giving Matt a look that tells him things haven't been fine at all. I'm desperate to tell him that I've been on edge ever since Mary locked me up – but I wait for him to put Tommy down.

'Anyway, it was all because she saw a spider in Annie's dressing room, can you believe?' I say when I've explained. I keep my voice low so Mary doesn't overhear from wherever she is in the house. 'A bloody *spider* that turned her into a madwoman and made her lock me up. I swear she had a smirk on her face when she let me out.' *And I still didn't find the necklace*, I think, lifting Gracie out of her cradle chair and holding her up to Matt for a kiss. My little family in a safe huddle, making my heart warm.

Matt takes Gracie from me, stifling a laugh, his expression falling serious when I scowl at him. 'I'm sorry that happened to you, love. Sounds scary. I'll go up and hunt for the spider if you like. I know my worth around here.' He grins.

'Don't be silly,' I say. 'I'm not incapable. I would have been happy to get it in a glass and put it outside. But... there was no spider. Not that I could see, anyway.' I shrug, pulling the corkscrew from the kitchen drawer. 'Honestly? I don't think that's the reason she locked me in the dressing room.'

Matt frowns. 'Do you think she made the spider up... so she could freak you out?'

I'm about to tell him that's exactly what I think, but I stop myself, widening my eyes at Matt to warn him. Mary is standing behind him in the doorway.

'Oh, hi, Mary...' I say, trying to sound casual.

Her glance flicks suspiciously between the pair of us, but then she goes up behind Matt and, to my horror, she slides a hand onto his shoulder, pressing herself against him as she coos at Gracie. I see Matt tense up, but he doesn't move away.

'I... I was just explaining about the spider,' I say to Mary, frowning at her. 'And that you locked me in the dressing room.' My tone is harsh, but I don't care. She's pushing my limits here.

She gives me a terse little smile in return, her fingers still kneading into Matt's shoulder – the same spot where I had my face buried just a few moments ago.

'I'm so sorry, Gina,' she says, sounding earnest. 'I overreacted, but I'm literally *terrified* of spiders. It started in childhood,' she says. 'It was a gut reaction to lock the door. So silly of me, really.' She rests her head down on my husband's shoulder, her eyes still locked onto mine, making me wonder if I'm imagining what I'm seeing because it's so brazen. Matt can't see her face, but Mary's smile has turned into another smirk aimed directly at me.

'They're not my favourite bugs, either,' I say, forcing myself to play it cool and not rise to her bait. 'Wine?' I hold up the bottle but, thankfully, she shakes her head. Perhaps she'll go back upstairs and leave us alone.

'Did you find what you were looking for in Annie's dressing room?' she asks instead.

'No, I didn't,' I reply, relieved to see her finally prising herself off my husband. Though she's still cooing over my baby.

'Maybe I can help?' she suggests.

'It's nothing. It was just a silly thing from when we were kids.'

'Such as?'

Mary's stare gives me the chills. I flash a look at Matt, but he's pacing about with Gracie over by the fireplace, probably glad to be away from Mary's clutches. Tommy hurls wooden bricks around on the shaggy rug, trying to get his dad's attention.

'Really, it was nothing,' I say, not wanting to explain about the necklace – especially as I'm certain she has something to do with it appearing in my bedroom.

'You can tell me, Gina. I'm interested to know.' To my horror, Mary slides onto a cream leather bar stool, leaning forward on her forearms. 'I think I will have that wine, after all.'

She gives me a look that, on the surface, is pleasant, but for some reason, it sends another chill down my spine.

Reluctantly, I pour her a glass, willing Matt to catch my eye so he can get down here and help me out. I know Mary's in a difficult situation, and that Annie wants to help her out by letting her stay here, but after everything that's happened recently, I hate sharing our space with a virtual stranger and her son.

'I'm all ears,' Mary adds, taking a long sip.

'It's... it's nothing really. Just that when we were kids, we had this... well, gang, I suppose,' I start explaining, in the hope it will get rid of her. 'No, it was more of a club. Gang sounds sinister.' I hold up my glass in a lacklustre 'cheers' when Mary raises hers. 'There were four of us.'

'Were you the mean girls at your school?' Mary asks, staring at me over the rim of her glass. 'Picking on the less popular kids?'

'What?' I pause, not knowing if she's joking or not. 'No, *no*, of course not. We were just four friends living our best teenage lives here in Hastings. It was all about boys, clothes and make-up.' I add in a laugh that sounds as forced as it is.

'Sorry,' Mary says. 'I didn't mean to sound... rude. More of that childhood trauma right there.' She drinks half of her wine in one go. 'As you can probably guess, *I* was the one picked on at school.' She polishes off the rest of her measure and shoves her glass towards me for more. 'There were some nasty girls in my year.'

Reluctantly, I top up her glass.

'Well, the "GALS" weren't like that,' I say through finger quotes, not wanting her to get maudlin.

'GALS?'

I half smile, feeling a bit embarrassed about telling her. 'Gina, Annie, Laura and Sara.'

She nods her head in a slow arc, a smile spreading on her face. 'That's cool,' she says. 'Wish I'd had friends like that.'

'The four of us were inseparable,' I say, feeling a stab of guilt rocket through my heart. *Until we weren't...*

'Is that the Laura who's coming to stay this weekend?' Mary says, getting stuck into her second glass. 'I couldn't help overhearing the other day when you were on the phone. Don't worry though, housekeeper's code.' She taps the side of her nose. 'I never spill the beans.'

'It is. But I don't think she's coming.'

'Oh, that's a shame. I'm not in touch with anyone from school. Thank God.'

I bite my bottom lip and give her a nod, desperately wanting this exchange to end.

'I'll start dinner in a moment,' I call out to Matt, hoping Mary will take the hint, but he doesn't turn round. He's got his phone pinned to his ear – not talking, rather just listening. Probably voicemail.

'So where's the other girl, Sara?' Mary asks.

To avoid responding, I turn my back and take out a few bits from the fridge, putting the oven on to warm up, taking a knife from the block. But it's hard to focus with her staring at me, waiting for an answer to her question – *where's Sara?* My hands are shaking, and my vision goes blurry, almost as though I'm underwater.

It's similar to the dream I have every couple of months – or rather the nightmare. The one where I'm at the party. Faces leering at me, everyone's eyes distorted and misshapen as though I've taken drugs and have no control over my body as I fight my way through the crowd. Then, as always happens in this nightmare, I'm suddenly outside, walking – no, *flying*, looking down from above. I go along the seafront, seeing everything familiar, though somehow it appears like another world, another time, another chance to get things right – everything dark with the moonlight glinting off the waves.

Then Sara appears, naked and alone as she runs through the night, screaming and terrified, her bare feet covered in blood, her hair flying behind her and tears streaming down her face. But all I do is watch her from way up high, doing nothing to help her as she runs to her fate – whatever that might be. Finally, I wake up, gasping for breath as if someone has their hands around my throat.

And it's as I'm gasping now – the kitchen slowly coming back into focus – that I see the knife in Mary's hand, her eyes huge and distorted, and her teeth bared as she approaches. It happens in slow motion – the blade coming towards me – and I let out a throat-burning scream, yelling for Matt to help.

TWENTY-FIVE

GINA

'... Gina? Gina, are you OK? Calm down, it's OK, love...'

It's the sound of my baby crying rather than Matt's voice that jolts me back to the moment, snapping me from the waking nightmare.

'Oh my God, I'm so sorry. Yes, yes... I'm OK,' I say breathlessly, trying to brush off what just happened. One hand grips the worktop, and the other comes up to my head as I refocus on the room. Everything inside me is vibrating and on edge.

'I was just trying to give you this back,' Mary says, indicating the knife as she holds it out to me, handle first. 'You dropped it.' When I don't take it, when I just stare at her, she says, 'I'll give it a wash then.' She swills it under the tap and places it back on the chopping board, looking at me as if I'm mad. 'You're a bit pale, Gina. Are you *sure* you're feeling OK?'

'I'll be fine.'

Though Matt clearly doesn't believe me as he's fussing over me now, telling me to go and sit, giving me my insulin kit so I can test my blood and inject before I eat. Then he insists he'll take care of dinner, that I should relax and have a cuddle with Gracie.

'Look, why don't I cook?' Mary suddenly pipes up, sidling into the preparation area. 'It's the least I can do to make up for what happened in the dressing room. How does a stir-fry sound?'

'Actually, that sounds amazing,' Matt replies with a quick glance and a nod at me as I settle on the sofa. 'You do look pale, love,' he says. 'Maybe you're anaemic? Breastfeeding might be taking more out of you than you realise.'

I have an urge to snap at him – that I've barely recovered from giving birth, let alone from the upheaval and shock of losing our home and moving here, so it's no wonder that keeping another human alive with my body is draining me. But I restrain myself, quickly checking my blood sugar then injecting myself in the stomach. I'm so used to doing it, it hardly takes any time at all.

'Honestly, I'm fine,' I say, once my kit is packed away. I unbutton my shirt and release the flap on my nursing bra, then Matt hands Gracie to me. She snuffles and grunts with excitement, knowing a feed is coming. Thankfully, I gave Tommy his tea before Matt arrived home. As my baby suckles, I rest my head back and close my eyes, drifting off, and it barely seems a minute later that I jolt awake again.

Bleary-eyed, I turn round to see if Matt is there, but I can't believe my eyes, almost convinced I'm having another nightmare.

Mary and Matt are standing together at the glass doors, looking out into the garden – her arm wrapped around his waist.

For some reason, Matt turns, pulling away from Mary when he sees I'm watching. My mouth drops open, but nothing comes out, and I swear I saw his hand around her waist too – though in my sleepy state, I could be mistaken.

'Dinner's ready, love,' he says, sounding as if nothing's happened. 'And the kids are bathed and tucked up in bed. We were... we were just admiring the garden,' he adds, seeing my frown.

'Sorry, you were *what*...?' I mumble, still not fully awake. It takes me a moment to realise that the weight of my baby isn't pressing down on my chest any more. I don't like that I didn't wake up when she was taken from me, even if it was by her father. I button up my top and stand, scowling at my husband.

'You were out for the count,' he says, bringing the wok over to the dining table. I'm pleased to see there's a tablecloth on it now, along with place mats – *three* place mats to be precise. Then to my horror, Mary sits down at the head.

I eye her for a moment, deciding I'm too exhausted to grill her about what I just saw – or tell her that we'd rather eat alone. Mary serves out portions of rice for each of us, handing me a large spoon to serve the beef and vegetables.

'No Tyler?' Matt asks.

'He's gone out,' Mary replies, serving some stir-fry for herself. 'To the cinema with a mate.'

'That's what he's told *you*,' Matt quips. 'You know what lads are like.'

Mary's head whips up, a scowl on her face. 'It's the girls you have to watch out for,' she says, turning to me as she slowly forks rice into her mouth. 'They can be right evil bitches.'

By the time we've finished eating, I decide I don't have the energy for a showdown with Matt about getting too close to Mary. I remind myself that he's my husband and I trust him.

As we're loading the dishwasher – I convinced Mary to leave it to us and thankfully she went upstairs – my phone pings from the other end of the room.

'Oh, amazing news!' I say, my eyes skimming the WhatsApp message. 'It's from Laura. She says she's going to come and visit after all.' I can't help the grin.

Matt glances up from wiping the worktop. 'I thought we were going to Crawley to get on with sorting the house this weekend?' He dries his hands. 'You said your parents were having the kids again. The builders are getting stuck in next week and—'

'Can't we just have one weekend not thinking about the bloody house?' I say, instantly regretting it when I see the look on his face. 'Sorry, I know you've got big plans, and believe me, I want to move back home as soon as possible, but...' I trail off, deciding to keep my thoughts to myself because they invariably lead back to, *If only you'd just paid for an electrician...*

We rarely argue, Matt and I. Rather a layer of sour air hangs between us until one of us clears it, which, as the evening wears on, is exactly what happens as the silence between us thickens. In the end, I abandon the idea of a cosy evening of Netflix together and get up off the sofa – the sofa we're sitting at opposite ends of. 'Think I'm going to get an early night,' I say.

Upstairs, instead of doing any of my night-time rituals, I check on Gracie in her cot beside the bed before lowering myself down onto the expensive cotton quilt. I'm not ready for sleep yet, so I open Instagram and scroll through my feed. The usual accounts flow past – mostly stuff about babies and toddler activities and healthy recipes for the family. But one set of images makes me smile – Annie has posted a few pictures of her safari, one of which is the photo she sent me.

The golden savanna has a fiery-red sky flaring up from the horizon with a line of silhouetted elephants behind it. The caption reads: *It's all about the sunsets, lions, elephants and the huge night sky, folks. Sometimes you just need a break. Series six of* Left Field *begins filming as soon as I'm back xxx*

I smile. Classic Annie. She only posted this twenty minutes ago and she's already had over fourteen hundred likes and ninety-seven comments – but that's not surprising given that she has nearly half a million followers.

I start typing out a comment, ending with the initials that only Annie, Laura and I will understand. And Sara, if she were here. *BLTFNS*. But I stop before posting. Instead, I go onto Annie's Instagram profile and scroll back through her pictures.

The safari shots were her first post in a while, though she usually updates for her fans several times a week. Previous photos show her in hair and make-up at the studios, some on set, some with the other actors chilling out or posing at an awards dinner. Dotted throughout her grid are promotional graphics and video trailers for whatever her latest movie or series is, and the occasional interview reel or story. I know she hates all the 'showing off' as she calls it and would much rather get on with the business that she's paid to do, the work she loves so much. But these days, people want to know everything about the stars they admire – whether that be about their love lives – Annie has so far managed to keep that simple by staying single – or their home and family.

'Good old Annie,' I whisper, feeling a deep sense of pride at what my friend has achieved. 'She only went and bloody did it.'

As I scroll further back through her pictures, I notice that there are a few photos of the kitchen extension shortly after it was finished in the spring. I must have missed them when she first put them up. No one would be able to work out the house's location from the few internal shots and photos of the garden. Annie values her privacy greatly.

One of the photos catches my eye. It's obviously not long after Annie moved into the new extension because her furniture is in the shot, but the place is a mess. The kitchen surfaces are covered in dirty plates, glasses and takeaway boxes; the sofas are strewn with random clothes; and the dining table is littered with papers and files and piles of scripts. There are also several overflowing bin bags near the bifold doors.

Seriously guys, I need a housekeeper... Apply within... the caption reads, followed by laughing and praying emojis. A quick glance at a few of the nine hundred or so comments she received, and it's clear that her fans absolutely loved her honesty.

I'll be your maid, one fan wrote.

Me me me, I'll clean up for you! reads another.

Love it, ur so real, we love u annie... is the theme of a few posts.

Wildies to the rescue... someone else says, with Wildies being what her fans call themselves since she released her first solo music album.

The comments are overwhelmingly supportive, offering Annie help or cleaning hacks, with only one or two trolls chipping her for being lazy or too candid about her life and how no one wants to see her dirty laundry.

A genius move by Annie to relate to her fans and followers... but something about the post is bothering me. Something doesn't quite add up.

Not able to pinpoint what it is, I go back to her latest safari post and add a couple of kisses after *BLTFNS*. I smile to myself as I post my comment, and then I send Annie a WhatsApp message.

You'll never flipping guess what – Laura coming to stay at weekend! Wish you were here too. Big love etc xxx

I get up and pad quietly to the bathroom to clean my teeth. It's as I'm brushing that I realise what was wrong with Annie's messy kitchen post from April.

Mary told me that she has worked here for over a year. So why was the place in such a mess in Annie's pictures only five months ago? And why was the caption asking for a housekeeper if she already had one?

TWENTY-SIX

GINA

By the next morning, the strained atmosphere between me and Matt is forgotten when we're woken by Gracie's snuffles, knowing she'll soon build up to a full-blown cry if she isn't picked up. Though as I open my eyes, I remember what I discovered on Instagram last night, feeling sickened that someone is lying. While I don't believe that 'someone' is Annie, I have no idea why Mary wouldn't be honest about the length of her employment here.

I groan, rolling over and pulling the pillow over my head, wanting to block it all out. Given we have bigger issues to tackle, I decide to keep quiet about it for now, but I'll be keeping a closer eye on Annie's housekeeper, that's for certain.

'I got her,' Matt says, giving me a kiss on my neck before going over to Gracie's cot in his boxers and T-shirt. I'm surprised he volunteered, given he was tossing and turning all night, mumbling in his sleep.

'Come here, little miss,' he says, scooping her up in his big hands, holding her against his shoulder.

'I forgot to mention,' I say, suddenly realising it's Thursday.

'Bridget, the neighbour, invited us round for coffee this morning. Do you fancy going?'

Matt bobs up and down gently, his hand supporting the back of Gracie's downy head. 'Really? I didn't sleep that well,' he admits.

I watch him with our baby – he's so gentle and good with her. But I see the tiredness in his eyes, too. 'More nightmares?'

Matt nods.

Since I've known him, he's gone through spates of bad dreams for no apparent reason. Night-time relaxation apps and wind-down routines, counselling, even antidepressants haven't made much of a difference. In the past when I've asked him about the cause, he's been vague. But more recently, since the fire, he's hinted that it's linked to his claustrophobia and fear of being smothered or not being able to breathe.

'But I'll live,' he adds. 'And sure, let's go meet the neighbours. Work owes me some time, so I can take an hour off.'

We all head downstairs to have breakfast – thankfully, there's no sign of Mary or Tyler yet – and after we've eaten, I bring Tommy back up to dress him. He's becoming fiercely independent these days, wanting to do everything himself, so it takes forever.

'Where is Tyler, Mummy?' he asks, struggling with his trousers. He bats my hand out of the way when I try to help.

'I think he's still asleep, darling,' I tell him. 'Why?'

'Tyler hurt Tommy,' he says, pausing to show me his arm. There are no marks that I can see.

'What do you mean, he hurt you?' My stomach knots at the thought of anyone harming my son. 'Show me where, darling.'

Tommy stares up at me, his big blue eyes filling with tears as he waves his finger around. 'Tyler hurt me here,' he says, though it's not exactly clear where he's pointing.

I ask him again, but he touches his head then his knee and then his leg in quick succession, followed by a giggle. But still, a chill sweeps through me given that my son has brought it up. I'll be keeping a closer eye than ever on him.

Tommy is still struggling with his little trousers, so I offer to help but, again, he shoves my hand away. As he eventually pulls them on, I hear Mary pushing the vacuum cleaner around downstairs, which makes me grab Tommy's T-shirt, insisting I help him so that she's not left alone with my husband too long. On top of what Tommy just said, I can't get the look she gave me yesterday out of my mind, when she was draped all over Matt – not to mention seeing them standing in an embrace at the window together when I woke from feeding Gracie.

God, what a mess! My mind is all over the place, trying to work out what Tommy meant, as well as what Mary is playing at, and then I'm fast-forwarding to this weekend – Laura's visit clashing with Matt wanting us to go to back to the house.

It's as I'm popping a sweatshirt on Tommy and Matt comes into the bedroom that I get the idea.

'And you really don't mind?' Matt replies after I've suggested it to him.

'Of *course* I don't mind,' I say, knowing how much he misses his lads' nights out. Besides, it's two days that Mary can't be throwing herself at him. 'Especially as Evan offered to come down and help with the clear-out, and Dave's only round the corner from our place and always willing. You and Evan can have a shower at Dave's before heading out. You guys deserve a blowout.'

As much as I dislike Evan, one of Matt's good friends from school, only tolerating him for Matt's sake, and even though I don't really want to be apart from my husband for the entire weekend, I also want to spend some much-needed time with Laura.

Matt pulls a thoughtful face as we go downstairs. 'It has been a while since we got together,' he admits, warming to the idea. 'We could get a curry in town like old times, then crash on Dave's sofa. His missus won't mind.'

'See if the guys are up for it,' I say as we're about to head next door. Mary is in the kitchen, so I make a point of sliding an arm around my husband's back, giving her a long stare when she glances up. She has the vacuum cleaner beside her, and her phone clutched in her hands as she thumbs out a text. She tucks the phone under her cardigan when she sees us, giving me a small smile as we leave.

'I'm very pleased to meet you,' Bridget says when I introduce her to Matt. Her hallway is a mirror image of Annie's impressive entrance with a similar black-and-white chequerboard floor, high ceilings and sweeping staircase. 'This is Billy, my husband.'

Pleasantries over with, Bridget leads us through to what she calls her 'morning room', her husband limping slowly beside her with his stick.

'Tommy, no,' I hiss down at my son, who's already getting into mischief by pulling a shopping bag off the bottom stair. A few items spill out and, by the looks of them, I think Bridget has left them there to be taken up. I grab the shampoo bottle and packet of soap, stuffing them back in the carrier, and gather up the shaving foam that's rolled away. 'Give me those,' I whisper to Tommy, who's hugging a packet of sanitary pads to his chest.

'Mine!' he shrieks when I try to take them off him. He swivels away from me, clutching the purple packet.

'Tommy, give them to me now!' I try to keep my voice low, and when I promise him sweeties later – something I hate doing – my son relinquishes the pads. I shove them back in the carrier bag, and Matt and I share an eyeroll.

The morning room is stuffed full of expensive-looking antiques and ornaments, making me feel on edge with Tommy being in a particularly boisterous mood today. A large wooden clock ticks loudly on the marble mantelpiece, and Bridget seats us at a table beside the French doors overlooking the back garden. Long net curtains hang at the window, and there's a small, raised terrace immediately outside with wrought iron-work spanning the width of the house – the same spot where Annie has built her large extension next door.

'Those are beautiful houseplants,' I say, noticing all the different types. I lift Tommy up and sit him on my knee, making sure to keep my arms firmly around his waist. There's a lot to destroy in here.

'Too many bloody plants, if you ask me,' Billy comments as he lowers himself into a cane chair with a grunt, resting his walking stick against the arm. Beneath his tweed jacket, he's wearing a mustard waistcoat buttoned up around a bulging middle. A grey handlebar moustache completes his country gent vibe, replete with supercilious attitude. I can't help thinking he'd get along famously with my father.

Bridget soon returns with a pot of coffee on a tray, along with cups and a plate of pastries. Tommy reaches out, straining forward with clawing fingers before she's had a chance to put the tray down.

'Ooh, no, you don't want those, young man,' she says, taking a saucer of pills off the tray and handing them to Billy, who pops them in his mouth. 'They're heart pills and not good for little boys.' She puts a custard tart on a paper napkin and hands it to Tommy. 'That's much tastier. And don't mind any mess, Gina dear. It keeps Hattie, my cleaning lady, gainfully employed.' She tucks back a strand of grey hair that's spiralled loose from the knot on her head, and her kind face breaks into a sunrise of soft wrinkles as she pours the coffee.

'Be careful, Tommo,' I whisper in his ear, picking up a few crumbs that spill onto my lap. 'Does Hattie know Mary, Annie's housekeeper?' I ask. It might also throw some light on the discrepancy of how long Mary has been working for Annie. Not that it really matters, I suppose, but on top of everything else, I don't like the thought of her lying to me. I can't think of a single reason why she would, but it makes me wonder what else she's lying about.

I notice the way Bridget stiffens and looks at her husband, as if she wants him to handle my question.

'I just thought they might be friends,' I add, wondering if Annie's housekeeper has rubbed them up the wrong way more than Bridget previously implied. 'I'm sure Mary could do with the company after her relationship break-up.' I don't mention that it was abusive.

'No,' she says finally. The single syllable delivered with conviction. 'They aren't friends. And I don't know about any relationship break-up. I heard that she was single.'

'Mary is living in at Annie's house for the time being,' I explain. 'She's had a bit of a tough time and Annie was happy to offer her a place to stay.' It takes a lot of effort to hold back what I really want to say about her.

'Pah,' Billy spouts. He bites into an iced bun, leaving crumbs in his moustache. 'The woman who bought next door needs to mind her own business.' His voice is scathing and gruff. 'Newcomers moving in, bringing all and sundry with them...' He ends with a throaty growl, dabbing at his mouth with a fancy cotton handkerchief.

My hackles are raised now, ready to stick up for my oldest friend, but I manage to keep my voice light. 'Actually, Annie grew up in Hastings, so she's not a newcomer. And so did I, just so you know. Annie's mum and dad loved Genoa House back in the day, which is why Annie bought it.' I'm bristling as Matt puts his hand on top of mine.

'These DFLs are all the same,' Billy pipes up, clearly not having heard a word of what I said. 'No regard for those who've lived here all our lives.'

'What's a DFL?' Matt whispers, giving my hand a squeeze.

'Down from Londons,' I reply as quietly as I can manage, holding back an exasperated sigh – mainly for Bridget's sake. 'It sounds like Annie has upset you in some way, but she's a genuine local,' I say instead, hoping that will get the message across. 'Born and bred.'

'Oh, it's not *Annie*, love,' Bridget says, sipping her coffee. 'Truth be known, we hardly see her, and she seems pleasant enough. And her builders were very considerate for the nine months they were here.'

'Travesty, adding on that glass monstrosity,' Billy chimes predictably.

'Many people are adding similar extensions to these old properties,' Matt says. 'I'm a building surveyor, you see. Mostly commercial these days, but occasionally domestic.'

'It's nothing to do with the extension,' Bridget says. 'No, dear, it's Annie's *housekeeper* making us concerned. Her behaviour is... well, it's been *strange* to say the least. And she's not at all friendly.'

'What do you mean, strange?' I ask, my ears pricking up as I'm reminded of what Bridget said the other day – that they'd seen her out on the common searching for something.

'Look, I'm not one to gossip,' Bridget says as she places her coffee cup on the table. She clamps her bony arms around herself, as if she's suddenly cold. 'And I know the girl's only been working there for a couple of weeks or so, but... after Annie left for her trip – rather suddenly I might add – her new housekeeper brought some quite unsavoury visitors to the house. Not the type of person we usually see in this neighbourhood, put it that way.'

'We don't want their type around here, full stop,' Billy grumbles, followed by a hacking cough. 'It's a good area now,' he says. 'Not like it used to be.'

'Wait... are you sure that Mary has only been Annie's

housekeeper for a couple of *weeks*?' I ask, Annie's Instagram post fresh in my mind.

'Certain,' Bridget replies. 'She introduced herself to me on her first day when our paths crossed in the front gardens. It's about the only time she's ever spoken to me. And I know exactly what day it was – the second of September – because it was my birthday. It was just over two weeks ago.'

'I see,' I say, giving Matt a glance, though he's engrossed in showing Tommy something on his phone to keep him entertained. He knows nothing about the necklace or what it means, and I didn't tell him about the photo I found on the common either. 'What do you mean by *unsavoury visitors*?' I ask, not sure I even want to know. Though Annie probably should.

'A rude boy, that's who,' Billy chips in. 'He was lanky as a piece of string and needed a damn good haircut. Not to mention a couple of years in the army. That'd sort him out.'

Bridget gives her husband a scowl. 'We all look out for each other around here, so when we saw him going inside next door, I naturally asked who he was. He said his name was Tyler. He was with a much older woman too – a nasty-looking character. She was smoking a cigarette and when I asked who she was, she told me to... well, she told me to mind my own business. Though I can't repeat her exact words.' Bridget clears her throat, glancing at Tommy. 'She went right on inside the house with that thing hanging out of her mouth.'

'I don't know who the older woman might have been, but Tyler is Mary's son,' I tell Bridget. An image of Tyler taking Tommy off into the wooded area at the park suddenly fills my mind, as well as what Tommy told me earlier when he was getting dressed.

'No, no, you're wrong,' Bridget says confidently. 'I asked him about that, and the boy told me that Mary is not his mother.'

TWENTY-SEVEN

MARY

'What are you up to?' I say, tapping on Tyler's door. Silly question, really, because I know he'll be gaming or programming.

As I step inside the top-floor bedroom with its creaky boards and sloping ceilings, it occurs to me how easily we've settled in here, even though it's only been a few days.

Finally, a home that's almost ours.

Soon enough, we won't be holed up in these attic rooms that were once used by the servants. I shudder, knowing that's the role I must play for now – the dutiful housekeeper, the loyal cleaner, the ever-helpful staff. Upstairs-downstairs. Makes me sick.

I pick up a PlayStation controller and sit down on the bed. Gina and her family have gone next door for a coffee, so it's a good time to skive the cleaning. 'Let's play,' I say, leaning over and giving Tyler a nudge where he's sitting at his computer.

He doesn't say a word, and nor does he look at me. Rather, he clicks his controller deftly, staring intently at the monitor, and I know he's in his happy place... a fantasy world where nothing else matters. Quite different to the game I'm playing. One wrong move and it's all over. No second chances.

I feel the vibration of a message coming in, so I take my phone from my uniform pocket. I don't get fun texts from friends inviting me to the pub or to go for a walk on the beach. Those things have never been part of my life.

'You playing then, or what?' Tyler says when I've read it. '*Call of Duty?*'

'Sure,' I say, tucking the phone in my pocket again. I smile, not wanting to reply to her straight away – that wouldn't look good. I need to be extra careful in my response, somehow nipping this little issue in the bud while moving things forward. But it wasn't as if I didn't expect problems along the way. I'm not that naive. It's a big leap up to the next level.

'Here you go, Mary,' Tyler says, holding out the controller. 'It's my favourite game.' He only calls me 'Mum' in front of other people – promising me that he's stuck to the plan and not referred to me as Mary or told anyone that I'm not his real mother. I want to trust him, but given his stupidity with Tommy in the park, I'm concerned about him keeping up the charade for much longer.

Ten minutes into the game, there's a noise from downstairs – the piercing shriek of Gina's toddler as they arrive back. He's not a bad kid as three-year-olds go, but I'm not a fan of children. I was only a kid myself when Tyler was born, though I never knew him back then.

Since he's lived with me, I've done whatever's been needed to keep us fed and with some kind of roof over our heads. Cash-in-hand jobs here and there, and a bit of nicking when I'm short. I lived in a car for nearly a year when Tyler was about to turn nine. That's when I took my chances and grabbed him from the supermarket, sneaking him back to the rusty old Ford in the field where he lived with me for nearly a week. We ate Haribo and drank milk huddled under blankets while I told him stories about the past.

But the heat was on – helicopters day and night, search dogs, flyers on lampposts, his name on the news hourly, police everywhere in town. After he got bored of the sweets, Tyler cried for his mummy, so I let him go, leaving him at a busy bus stop, knowing he'd soon be found, making him promise he wouldn't tell a soul about me. Hood up, head down and weaving between the CCTV cameras to break the trail ensured I never got caught, cutting a flighty path back to my car. Having no fixed abode, job, friends or family that I had contact with at the time came in useful. I kept myself to myself. I didn't need anyone else.

Over the years, I watched him from time to time, giving him a little smile or a wave if he looked my way in a shop or at the beach or when he turned round on the bus to see me sitting two seats behind him.

After the car, I upgraded to living in an abandoned caravan in a field until a storm brought down a tree, crushing one end of it with me asleep inside. It wasn't the worst thing to have ever happened to me at night.

Hostels and homeless shelters have been my friends over the years, too, though since Tyler's been with me, I've tried to avoid them. He likes his privacy. We're well known on the streets, though we've not had to sleep underneath the railway bridge for a while now. The staff at the local sports centre have always turned a blind eye to us using their showers, letting us through the turnstile for free when we've needed a wash. Tyler has sorted their computer network many times in return.

'We'll have to finish the game later,' I say to Tyler, putting down the controller and going to the door. 'I'd better go down and pretend to do some work.'

Tyler turns to me, a trusting look in his eyes. 'When is it

happening, Mary?' he asks, the tremor in his voice betraying his nerves.

'Soon,' I say, putting my finger over my lips. 'Soon enough.'

The hand on my shoulder makes me jump. I stifle a squeal.

'Sorry, Mary,' Gina says, a worried look on her face. 'I didn't mean to scare you.'

I switch off the vacuum cleaner and it wheezes to a stop. Gina is rocking from one foot to the other, her baby cradled in her arms. I can't help looking at Gracie's tiny head – all soft downy curls, wispy and fine, with that little soft spot making her so vulnerable and helpless.

No... stop! Get off her...! Thrashing arms, spit flying... Biting, kicking, screaming... The little girl so vulnerable and helpless...

'Mary... Mary, are you OK?' Her voice snaps me back to the moment.

'Sorry, yes. I'm just a bit tired.' I make a show of wiping my brow, laughing it off.

'Come and sit down. Maybe have some water,' she says, leading me over to a stool at the kitchen island and pouring me a glass from the filter jug. 'There's something I want to ask you.'

Suddenly my heart is leaping in my chest, my blood pumping furiously. That familiar feeling of wanting to run away rushes through me, but I stand my ground, looking her in the eye, my head tilted to one side. 'Of course,' I say sweetly.

Does she know?

'I just had a coffee with Bridget next door,' she continues.

That old bag. I smooth down my starched dress, sipping the water in the hope it will buy me a few seconds to think, to be ready with a smart response that easily explains whatever is on her mind.

'Lovely couple, her and Billy,' I say with a fake smile. I've only encountered him once, but for some reason, the man gives me the creeps.

'It's a bit awkward...' Gina hesitates, an anxious look on her face, 'and it's probably me getting muddled, but Bridget mentioned that you've only been working as Annie's house-keeper for a couple of weeks. I swear you said you'd been here over a year.' More jiggling and changing the baby's position as she whines in her mother's arms, Gina getting more flustered. 'I mean... you know, it doesn't really matter, but...' A nervous shrug as she tries oh so hard to be blasé about what she's discovered, but really, she's terrified that there's an untrustworthy stranger in the house living with her and her children.

That would never do.

And while she's right to be concerned, I'm relieved that's all she's worried about. I can easily deal with this.

'Oh, poor Bridget,' I say, pulling a pitying face. 'Bless her,' I add for good measure, sipping more water. 'It's really sad, but she's getting more and more muddled these days. And Billy's going the same way. They're such a sweet old couple, but their son lives in France and isn't around to look after them. I feel I should check in on them more. Maybe even do some cleaning for them.'

'Cleaning? But they've got Hattie,' Gina says, not yet seeming convinced by my explanation.

'Oh, yes, of course. Hattie,' I say, covering my tracks when I have no idea who Hattie is. 'And look, I understand your concerns – I'd be the same – but I've been working for Annie for just over a year now. You wouldn't want any old random off the street living with you and your children now, would you?' A little laugh from me.

'Well, quite,' Gina says, looking a little more relieved as she adds her own tinkly laugh.

'Tell you what, why don't you text Annie to confirm it? I

won't be at all offended. If I thought my live-in housekeeper wasn't telling the truth, I'd be all over it too. I bet she'll send you a copy of my DBS certificate if you ask. I'd rather know that you're totally comfortable with this arrangement. I know that me and Ty living here wasn't exactly what you signed up for.'

'Oh... well, I'm sure that won't be necessary,' Gina replies, distracted by her now whingeing baby. 'And I'm sorry to sound... well, you know... anxious.' She shrugs. 'I'll let you get on with your work.'

I nod and return to the vacuum, flicking it on with my foot and pushing it randomly around the floor while Gina heads upstairs.

A few minutes later, I feel the phone in my pocket vibrate as a message comes in. I pull it out, a small smile growing as I read the notification on the screen.

Hey Annie, just remind me how long Mary has been working for you? Is it just over a year? And you've had her fully vetted, right? BLTFNS xx

I tuck the phone away again, deciding to leave it a while before replying, finishing off the kitchen floors and emptying all the rubbish into the bins outside first. Then I water the downstairs plants before ducking into the toilet to tap out my reply.

Hi, yes, Mary's been with me just over a year now. Fully checked out. Total godsend! Love her to bits.

My finger hovers over the keys, wondering why she keeps putting those letters at the end of her texts. Am I supposed to do the same? I scroll back up the message thread, so I can mimic Annie's style, but all she's ever written in the past is *Big love*, so I add that and a couple of kisses, attaching a random safari photo I found online for good measure – making damned sure there are no car number plates in the shot this time. I can't afford to make any more mistakes.

TWENTY-EIGHT
THE PAST

When it came down to it, Gina couldn't watch them kiss on-stage. She'd thought of nothing else during the first few scenes of *West Side Story*, building herself up for Annie stealing the moment that she could only dream about. *Damn Matt and his soulful eyes and his dark hair and strong hands. Damn him for not even looking at me and damn him for ever coming to Collingwood High last year!*

She sat in the cramped seating in the school's gym that had been turned into a theatre, with Laura and Sara pressed either side of her. She screwed up her eyes when Matt's lips came down on Annie's with the violin section of the school orchestra playing everyone's heartstrings.

To get through it, Gina recreated the scene in her mind, but instead of Annie, she imagined it was her and Matt sharing a kiss by the sea, in her bedroom, round the back of Davy's Chippy – she didn't care where as long as she didn't have to witness her best friend kissing the boy she was madly in love with. The boy who was dating her *other* best friend currently sitting to her left.

Life was *so* unfair.

Finally, when she looked again, instead of seeing Annie standing on-stage, she imagined herself there with Matt, her fingers sliding from his as they pulled apart, looking bereft as their kiss was cut short.

Oh dear, what a fucking shame, Gina thought bitterly when Tony, Matt's character, was eventually shot. She was horrified to feel tears streaming down her cheeks at the outstanding performance given by Annie and, when the curtain fell, she was first on her feet as the cast took their bows, frantically clapping and whooping as the rest of the audience followed suit for a standing ovation. Despite the pangs of jealousy, the opening night of the school musical was a roaring success.

'Oh my God, oh my *God*...' Gina, Laura and Sara chimed in unison once they'd filed out of the gym and found Annie in the locker rooms where she was changing out of her costume. Their feet stamped in excitement as they grabbed each other in a group hug.

'You were bloody awesome,' Gina said, flinging her arms around her. Momentarily, she thought about planting a kiss on Annie's lips to see if she could catch a trace of Matt, but she held back.

'You really liked it?' Annie's coyness wasn't fooling anyone. The glow within oozed from her.

After Annie had taken off her make-up and changed, they walked in a line down to Davy's on the seafront with Annie promising the shakes were on her. 'I get to do it all again tomorrow night for the parents,' Annie crooned happily. 'I could get used to this acting life. Being on-stage is all I want to do.'

While they were waiting for their drinks, Sara stood up from their table, seeming even quieter than usual, and headed for the toilets. Annie's eyes tracked her across the café. 'Guess what, guys?' she crowed as soon as she was out of sight. Laura and Gina huddled closer over the table, eyebrows raised, breath held as they waited for Annie to spill. They leant back briefly as the waitress brought their shakes.

'Matt bloody Dalton is only having one of his legendary bloody parties this weekend,' Annie revealed in a low, breathy voice. Another glance to the loos. 'It's on the down-low, but we're all invited.'

'*All?*' Laura said. 'Like, the four of us?'

'Not technically,' Annie replied. She made a face, her eyes flicking over to the toilet door again.

'What did Matt say?' Gina asked, confused. Surely Sara must already know about it. Matt was her boyfriend.

'He told me to spread the word about the party. His parents are away for the weekend so it's all round to his on Saturday night after the final show performance. It's going to be amazing. A repeat of New Year's Eve.'

'Does Sara know?' Laura asked.

'She must do, surely,' Gina said, not liking where this conversation was heading, though Matt's illicit parties were indeed legendary. Despite them being in the year below Matt and his friends, the four of them had somehow wangled invites to his end-of-year party last New Year's Eve, though thinking back, she didn't remember Sara enjoying herself that much. For some reason, she'd left before midnight.

Annie was never one to redden from embarrassment or shock, but at that moment her cheeks burnt scarlet. 'No. Sara doesn't know.' She hesitated, leaning in closer. 'Matt said he... well, he said he wasn't certain things were going to last between them.'

'Jeez,' Gina said, sitting back in her chair. 'Poor Sara.'

She surprised herself that her first thought wasn't that Matt might soon be single, *available*, rather it was that Sara would be heartbroken. Destroyed, even. She knew how much he meant to her, despite their relationship being so unlikely.

He was an escape hatch for Sara, a way out of a life that

Gina was beginning to think was more awful than Sara'd ever let on. She'd seen the bruises on her thighs when they'd been changing for PE the other day, the way Sara never showered after hockey because she didn't want to show off her body. And she'd taken a load of time off school at the end of last term for a mystery illness, which had lasted all through the summer holidays. While no one really knew what was wrong with her, it didn't take much to work out her home life was shit, and that her dad had been in trouble with the law. When they'd phoned her house and left messages with her mother, Sara had never returned their calls.

And since Sara had returned to school this autumn term, not wanting to talk about what had been wrong with her, Matt had become a hand in the darkness for her. Someone to grip onto. Someone to make her days a little brighter. Something to live for. And now he was about to let her go.

'That really sucks,' Gina added. 'She's besotted with him. And she has no idea yet – about the break-up *or* the party?'

Annie shook her head. Another glance over at the loos. 'After he ends things with her, he doesn't want her at the party being morose and spoiling the evening. He said it's what she did on New Year's Eve – she got drunk and ruined it for him.'

'What the hell does he mean by *that*? She was hardly drunk,' Gina said, thinking back. They'd all been fawning and giggling over Matt, Sara included, as well as dancing and having a great night. At one point, she remembered Sara going off alone to get some fresh air, but they were together most of the night apart from that. She didn't remember anyone causing a scene at all. 'So why did he ask her out in the first place then?' Gina said, feeling more and more annoyed with him. 'Just to wind her up? Maybe we should boycott his stupid party in solidarity,' she added, feeling incensed on Sara's behalf.

Annie scoffed. 'It's almost the end of term, and the end of

show week, Geen. The cast need a blowout. We've worked insanely hard on this production. There's no way *I'm* not going.'

'But no thought for Sara's feelings?' None of this sat comfortably with Gina. Was their *big love, true friends, no secrets* mantra so meaningless and disposable to the others – to *Annie*? If so, it made her wonder what secrets they'd kept from *her*. She didn't like these new feelings one bit. Tiny fractures in their friendship.

'I can kind of see Annie's point,' Laura chipped in, shocking Gina even more. 'It's hardly our fault if Matt breaks up with her, and we shouldn't have to miss the party because of that. It'll be an amazing night. And don't forget, Sara hid her relationship from us in the first place.'

And why did she feel she had to do that...? Gina questioned, feeling the anger building. *Has anyone ever asked Sara the reason why she kept such a big secret from us?*

'Look, if Sara doesn't get invited to the party, then I'm not going.' Gina pinched her thigh to make sure she was actually saying these words, because she knew she'd have to stick to them. 'Imagine if this was happening to one of us. I'd be livid if you kept this from me and went behind my back.'

'To be fair, Gina also has a point,' Laura said to Annie, tipping the balance. 'You'd be bloody murderous if we betrayed you.'

Annie thought about this for a moment, her blush deepening as she stood steadfast in her thoughts. 'I would indeed be murderous,' she replied. 'But there's no way I'm missing out to protect Sara's feelings. Not when she chose to lie to us in the first place. I am damn well going to Matt's party, whatever happens to Sara.'

TWENTY-NINE

GINA

After Tommy and Gracie decided to out-squawk each other at Bridget and Billy's house, Matt and I called time on the coffee morning before things got messy. I'm glad we met the neighbours, but I returned with more concerns and questions than I'd gone with.

Mary was busy vacuuming when we got back, and I decided to keep my powder dry and not grill her *too* much about what Bridget had told me – but I couldn't resist picking the scab a little more. 'Just remind me how long you've been working here again,' I asked, tapping her on the shoulder and making her jump.

In reply, Mary was adamant that it was just over a year and said the neighbours were getting muddled. I didn't mention anything about Tyler not being her son – that felt like a step too far, and I wanted to check with Annie first. So I sent her a message.

Now, relief sweeps through me as I see her reply pop up on my screen a short while later, making me feel overly paranoid as I read her words.

*Hi, yes, Mary's been with me just over a year now. Fully
checked out. Total godsend! Love her to bits. Big love xx*

And she's sent me another picture – giraffes this time.

I smile, showing the animals to Tommy, but then *Peppa Pig*
catches his eye on the huge TV, making him toddle off to
watch it.

I tap back a reply to Annie while I know she's still active on
her phone.

*Do you know much about Tyler? Is he really Mary's son? It's
just that he*

I stop, deleting what I've written. I'm basically accusing the
housekeeper that Annie has employed and trusted for a year of
lying, based on something an older lady who apparently has
memory problems has told me. Though to be fair, it was Mary
who mentioned Bridget's unreliability, so she could be lying
about that, too.

I sit down next to Tommy, deciding that *Peppa Pig* seems
preferable to bothering Annie again while she's on holiday, but
then if it were me and my housekeeper was potentially hiding
things, I'd want to know.

I type out a new message.

*Do you know much about Tyler? Your neighbour said that he's
not Mary's son. Weird right? Soz to bother you again on hols.
Tommy loved the giraffes! BLTFNS xx*

I hit send and, thankfully, Annie is quick to reply. I'm
tempted to phone her, but with Mary still busying around the
house, I don't want to risk being overheard.

Relax, Gina. Bridget is a nosy old bag with a bad memory. I've met Tyler, he's def her son. A good lad who's been through a lot. He's your man for IT troubles. Just heading off to airport. Next stop Bangkok! Big luv xx

I'm not sure if it's a pang of envy about Annie heading to Thailand, or the lingering suspicion about what Bridget told me, but something is still nagging at me – something pecking at the back of my mind. Bridget sounded so certain about Mary not being Tyler's mother – convinced by what Tyler himself had told her – plus, I didn't like the sound of that unsavoury-looking woman with a cigarette that Bridget described coming inside Annie's house.

But I rein myself in when I reply. I don't want to spoil Annie's holiday, so I wish her a bon voyage and ask her to let me know when she gets to Thailand safely. It's only as I'm putting my phone away that I realise the way she spelt 'love' in her last message is most un-Annie-like. I shrug, figuring she must be in a rush to get to the airport.

It's an hour later when I'm coming back from the shop that I catch sight of Mary walking down the hill away from the house in Wessex Square, having just finished her shift. With Matt working from home, he offered to watch the kids while I nipped out, making my dash to Spar a whole lot quicker. Everything takes three times as long with the kids in tow.

For some reason, I hang back behind a tree when I see her. Mary's on her phone and hasn't spotted me as she strides away from the house, wearing skinny jeans and Nikes, a baggy grey hoodie on top. Changed out of her neat uniform, she blends in, appears unremarkable, just like any other young woman going about her business. Head down, large sunglasses on, she's released the bun she wears for work and her loose blonde hair whips around her face in the stiff sea breeze.

I don't know what makes me follow her, but I keep a safe distance, ready to duck into an alley or put my head down and pretend to check my phone if she should turn round.

Before she reaches the bottom of the hill, Mary turns right, cutting along a road that runs parallel to the beach a quarter of a mile away. Further along the road, the terraced houses give way to post-war semis and, after another five minutes' brisk walk, Mary glances left and right before darting over a busier road, then turning right again and heading inland. It's a familiar area to me and not far from my childhood home.

I'm half expecting her to hop on a bus – perhaps she's off to meet friends or go to an out-of-town shopping area, or maybe she's just getting some exercise.

But Mary does none of these things. She continues along for another few minutes before veering off down a road with smaller, much more run-down houses – tiny, squashed-in, red-brick terraces with front doors opening directly on to the uneven pavement, and battered old cars with flat tyres that look as though they've been parked there for years. The vibe of the area is a far cry from Wessex Square less than a mile away.

Adrenaline makes my heart pound as I follow Mary. She's walking fast, despite the incline. It's as she reaches the end of the street, where the road ends in metal, prison-like railings with scrubby ground at the back of an industrial estate beyond, that she stops, turning to face one of the tiny terraced houses located at the end.

I keep my head down, ready to turn the other way and walk off should she look in my direction. But she doesn't. Mary raps on the door, and, shortly after, she ducks inside the house, the door slamming behind her.

After a few moments, I venture further along the street, daring to get a closer look at the house. The bricks are mottled with damp patches, the downpipes are broken and corroded, and weeds are growing from the guttering. The front door and windows are grimy with condensation dripping down the inside of the glass.

As I edge up to its frontage, I can't help wondering if this is the home of Mary's abusive partner, maybe the place from which she and Tyler have recently escaped. If that's the case, I hope she's not being drawn back into the relationship, that she's just come back to grab some possessions before leaving for good.

Nervously, I venture closer to the front window. There are nicotine-stained net curtains shrouding the glass, one side sagging and torn, leaving just enough of a gap for me to get a quick glimpse into the front room. I walk past as casually as I can with my hand shielding my face, pretending to be on my phone as I steal a quick look inside.

What I see is only fleeting, but I catch sight of two shadowy figures in the small living room – one of them is Mary gesticulating wildly, bending forward as if she's shouting to make a point. And the other is an older woman with a pinched and angry-looking face, a cigarette hanging out of her mouth.

THIRTY

GINA

I've been wanting to tell Matt what I saw yesterday afternoon – about Mary going into that house the other side of town – but the words won't come. I'm concerned it'll lead to me mentioning the necklace I found in our bedroom, and the photo of Sara in the weird shrine on the common, neither of which I'm ready to talk about. Not when I know they'll lead directly back to Sara.

In the past, each of us dealt with her death in our own way, and Matt and I have only ever talked about what happened a few times – and certainly not recently. These days, it almost feels as though she never existed at all.

That's not to say I don't think about her privately, because I do, and even more so since we've been back in this town. Her ghost is everywhere. I imagine the type of woman she'd have become, if she'd have married, had kids, gone travelling, wondering about what job she'd have as she created the perfect little life for herself – a far cry from her childhood. I remember her once telling me that she wanted to be a scientist, a vet or a nurse. Sara was bursting with good.

Maybe it's because the police never found her body that we

hoped and prayed she might one day knock on the door, turn up as if she'd just popped out to run an errand and time had simply got away from her.

I still can't believe she's gone.

'Gina, sit down, there's no one out there,' Matt insists as I get up off the sofa yet again. It's Friday night and Laura is arriving in the morning at about the same time Matt will set off for Crawley. The kids are in bed, and Mary has taken Tyler to the cinema, so it's just me and Matt downstairs. But I can't help feeling that the walls have ears, that somehow Mary is watching us, listening in. For some reason I get the sense that we're not alone.

'I *swear* I saw something,' I tell him, going over to the patio doors and staring out into the night. A couple of upstairs lights in the houses across the other side of the common are just visible, but other than that, it's pitch dark out there – apart from the shadow of whatever, or *who*ever, it was I saw creeping through the garden a few moments ago.

'Relax, love. It'll just be our reflection you saw.'

'But neither of us was moving,' I tell him, cupping my hands around the glass. 'The thing out there *was*.'

'A reflection of the TV, then?'

'It wasn't turned on when I saw it,' I remind him, swinging round to face him. 'Look, I'm telling you, someone was out there. Will you go out and check?'

Matt sighs. 'Really? Why don't we just watch a movie?' he says, his eyes tracking me as I pad to the kitchen. 'OK, OK,' he finally says when I glare at him.

He unlocks the glass doors and goes outside, shining his phone torch around the garden, the shaft of light sweeping over bushes. I catch a glimpse of the gate leading out to the common, gasping when I see it's ajar. Earlier, I'd made sure it was shut.

'Literally nothing out there,' Matt says, wiping his feet as he locks up again. 'I closed the back gate, so stop worrying. Will you come and sit down now?'

I check the sliding door is properly locked. 'OK, sorry,' I say, giving his hand a squeeze. 'I'm just a bit on edge.' I go over to the other side of the room and flick the switch to bring down the electric blinds. If anyone is still out there, I don't want them staring in.

The blinds are only partway down when they stop in their tracks – at exactly the same moment the ceiling lights flicker a few times overhead.

'What the hell…?' I move the switch up and down again, on and off, but nothing happens. Matt comes over, trying the switch himself. 'I don't think it's my technique,' I tell him sourly, rolling my eyes. 'It's the bloody electrics again.'

Just as I say it, the lights flicker a couple more times, making my heart race. 'Do you think it's safe?' I grip Matt's arm, thinking about our own light fitting at home, wondering if it did the same before catching fire while we were out at Laura's house.

'It is a bit odd, I admit,' Matt says, turning the main ceiling spotlights on and off a few times. 'They seem OK now,' he says with a shrug. 'Maybe a couple of the bulbs are about to blow.' He tries the blinds switch again and, thankfully, they jump to life and continue to close.

'It was *all* the ceiling lights flashing, though,' I tell him. 'Surely the bulbs wouldn't all blow together? And why did it happen just as I was lowering the blinds?' I can't help the slight panic rising inside. Knowing that there are potential electrical issues in Annie's house makes me want to grab the kids and go back to the hotel again – not to mention the thought of someone lurking outside. 'How am I going to sleep knowing there's dodgy wiring?'

'Relax,' Matt says, giving me a hug. 'Maybe it was a surge in the main power supply. The extension is brand new and will have been signed off by building regs. There'll be certificates for everything. I can't imagine Annie cutting corners.'

'I know... you're right,' I say, trying to be rational, but then I also want to remind him that *our* light fitting was brand new, came from a decent shop, and Matt knew exactly what he was doing when he wired it in. Problems still happen. Houses still burn down.

'Look, let's put a comedy on or something to cheer you up. You fancy a glass of wine?'

I shake my head. 'Not really,' I say, wanting to keep my wits about me. 'I'll have a cup of tea instead.' Matt puts the kettle on and drops two bags into mugs. 'Will you check the fuse board or whatever it is that controls the electrics? Make sure it all looks safe?' I ask him when we've sat down again. 'I won't relax otherwise.'

Matt laughs, shaking his head, though quickly stops when I scowl at him. He knows my fears are real. 'I have no idea where the consumer unit is, love. Anyway, I don't see what good that's going to do.'

'Maybe it's in the hallway? Or the utility room? Can't you just look?'

Matt sighs and puts down his tea, getting up. 'I'm not going to get any peace until I check it, am I?' He heads off to look with me trailing after him as he opens the walk-in cleaning cupboard in the utility room, then checks another small cupboard by the front door as well as the downstairs toilet. He then tries the door at the back of the stairs in the hallway, revealing an inner lobby behind it with a much more modern and secure door behind that.

'That's the entrance to what was once the basement,' I explain. 'Annie's recording studio is down there now. She keeps it locked because of all her expensive equipment,' I tell him.

Matt has a quick glance about but shakes his head. 'Nothing in here either. Maybe ask Annie where the consumer unit is,' he says, sounding exasperated. 'Because if it's down in the base-ment and no one can easily get to it, then whoever designed the layout wants a stern talking-to.' Matt follows me back to the kitchen as I quickly tap out a message to Annie, waiting to see if she comes online, but she doesn't. In fact, her message remains undelivered.

It's only when Mary returns with Tyler from the cinema that we get any answers.

The pair stand beside the kitchen island, with Tyler clutching a large box of half-finished popcorn as Matt asks Mary what she knows about the electrics in the house. While I see a definite resemblance between her and Tyler – similar dimples in their cheeks, almost identical eyes, ash-blonde hair – age-wise, I can't help thinking that they look more like brother and sister than mother and son. And I can't get Bridget's words out of my head either: *The boy told me Mary is not his mother.*

'All the electrical stuff is downstairs in the basement,' Mary confirms. 'I saw it when she let me down there to clean. There's a keypad at the top of the stairs. I'll text Annie and ask her for the code,' she says. 'I'm sure she'll give me access if it's an emergency.'

'Well, it'll take a while for us to guess the number other-wise,' Matt says, folding his arms and rolling his eyes.

'Do you want to know what the maximum number of attempts is that it would take for you to hit upon the correct six-digit code?' Tyler suddenly pipes up. 'That's making the assumption you literally stumbled across the correct number last.'

Mary turns round to him, shaking her head. 'Not now, Ty,' she says.

'Probably more attempts than I have time for.' Matt turns off the TV. 'I'm ready for bed, love,' he says to me. 'I'll see you upstairs.'

Before I have a chance to protest, I find myself alone with

Mary and Tyler – and a growing sense of unease. How on earth does Matt expect me to sleep knowing there's an electrical fault somewhere in the house?

I explain to Mary that I've already texted Annie but haven't had a reply yet, though when I check my messages, I see it's now delivered. I glance at my watch, trying to figure out what time it would be in Thailand.

'I can call an electrician in the morning,' Mary says. 'Though I bet Annie will have replied by then. She's usually very good at getting house issues sorted.'

I smile, trying to convince myself that everything will be OK, that I won't need to lie awake all night sniffing the air to check for smouldering or planning our exit route in case the fire alarms sound. But as we're about to go upstairs, I stop, turning back to Mary.

'Have *you* ever noticed any issues with the kitchen lights, or had the blinds stop working before?' I ask glancing up at the inset ceiling lights, almost hoping she says yes. It would prove to me that it's nothing more than a minor glitch that happens all the time and it's nothing to worry about.

Tyler slides past me, heading up to bed, while Mary and I stand facing each other in the kitchen. It's as she's shaking her head, a frown growing between her eyes, that the lights overhead flicker three times in a row.

THIRTY-ONE

GINA

The next morning, after not much sleep, I stand on the doorstep with Tommy balanced on my hip, waving to Matt as he heads off in the car to Crawley. I've barely had a chance to go back in before the doorbell rings again. When I open it, Laura is standing there and an Uber is pulling off the drive.

'Oh. My. God,' we each chant in unison. Then comes the hug as we engulf each other in a mesh of arms and squeals. 'Bloody hell, Laur. It's wickedly good to see you.' The last time we were together was the night of the fire.

'Likewise, Gina. *Likewise.*' Then she glances up at the facade of the house. 'Bloody hell, Annie,' she exclaims, taking in the property – the first time she's visited. 'Our girl did good.'

We grin at each other as we stand on the top step of the house beneath the grand portico, staring at each other like loons, our hands linked as we laugh and discuss the weekend's plans – all of which will have to take place on foot or by public transport, I explain to Laura, given that Matt has taken the car.

'A small price to pay for a man-free zone,' she laughs.

'Well, there's a wild boy toddler and... a... a teenage boy to contend with inside,' I say, not knowing how to sum up Tyler. I was going to say 'grumpy' but he's not particularly. And he doesn't fit surly or moody or disorganised or lazy as might befit other lads his age. In my head, I settle on 'creepy'.

'Come in, come in,' I say, ushering her inside and taking her holdall from her. 'Mmm, you smell lovely,' I add as I get a whiff of her perfume wafting in after her.

She laughs. 'I don't know why,' she says. 'I'm not wearing any scent, and the train journey made me hot and sweaty.'

It's as I'm closing the front door that I smell it again – such an evocative, sweet aroma, reminding me of something from the past, though I can't quite pinpoint what.

After I give Laura a quick tour of the house, showing her to the second guest bedroom so she can dump her bag, I make us a coffee and we sit on the corner sofa by the fireplace. Tommy shows off his aeroplane collection to Laura, who is endlessly patient with him.

'Wow, Tommo,' she says, holding up yet another plastic aircraft. 'This one looks super-fast.'

'Is faaast!' Tommy replies, grabbing it back as he scrabbles to his feet and charges about with it, making a vrooming noise. I sit feeding Gracie while we chat.

'Annie certainly has a beautiful home,' Laura says, gazing around the impressive extension. I recognise the tone in her voice – I was the same when I first saw the place. It's a long way from jealousy – rather it's more an *imagine if I lived here* kind of wistfulness, knowing we'll never be in such a position. 'But...' Laura hesitates, a frown on her face, 'I mean...' She stops, sighing. Frowning more.

I laugh, making Gracie squirm in my arms. 'I mean... *exactly*,' I say, shaking my head. 'I totally get what you're trying to say.'

'Why here, in *this* town? It's a gorgeous house, obviously, and I know her mum always loved it, but surely Annie is mainly in London with her work these days. And *surely* she'd want to get away from...'

'I agree with all of that, too. She comes down here at weekends as much as she can, but also spends a lot of money on hotels in London. Though she told me that she recorded her new album here when the studio was finished a few months ago. Apparently, she does loads of voiceover work downstairs, too. I think being by the sea inspires her.'

'I guess,' Laura replies. 'I dunno, maybe it's just me.' She shifts her position, uncrossing her legs and leaning closer. 'It's just that after what happened... after we lost Sara, I can't imagine ever wanting to live back here again. Facing all the stirred-up feelings every day – of how we could have helped her but didn't. Not knowing the truth about what really happened that night.'

'I know, I *know*...' I say, agreeing entirely. 'But look, you know Annie. She's as stubborn as they come.' I glance at the door, knowing that Mary is upstairs with Tyler, though I've not seen either of them this morning. 'There's some stuff I need to tell you,' I whisper. 'Annie has a housekeeper who—'

Right on cue, Mary appears in the kitchen, her arms full of laundry. 'Good morning!' she calls down the room to us, peering over the top of tangled-up sheets. I'm about to introduce her to Laura, but she whips through to the utility room.

I widen my eyes at Laura, my heart racing as I realise how close I came to Mary overhearing my suspicions. *I'll tell you later*, I mouth, and while Gracie finishes her feed, Laura fills me in on Patrick's latest cycling trip to Lanzarote.

'Like this,' Laura says an hour later, crouching down as she shows Tommy how to hold the flat beach pebble. 'Then bring your arm back and throw it at the waves as hard as you can, keeping the angle at ninety degrees to—'

'Laur, he's three,' I say, laughing as I wipe a string of snot from my son's nose. 'He's not big on geometry.'

'Best they learn crucial life skills early,' Laura replies with a grin as she stands up and skims her own stone into the sea. It skips five times off the top of the breakers before dropping beneath the surface. Tommy whoops and claps while I hand Laura her coffee from the cup holder on the buggy. We sit on the pebbles sipping our hot drinks while Tommy chucks stones into the foam.

'You see, *this* is why Annie bought Genoa House,' Laura says, spreading her hand wide and gazing around. Colourful fishing boats are racked up on the Stade further along the shore, their nets stacked and draped over them like swathes of scarves with gulls circling overhead and the iconic fishermen's huts looming beyond. 'We *must* stop off at the fresh fish kiosk on the way back and get something to cook later. God, I miss being by the sea so much.'

'Me too.' Though I know she is thinking, like me, that if we ever did live by the coast again it couldn't be around here. 'Look, about what I wanted to say earlier... Weird things have been happening since we arrived,' I tell her, keeping my voice only just audible above the sound of the waves. I don't want Tommy picking up on a single word and risk him repeating it in front of Mary.

'Such as?'

I explain everything, including what Bridget, the neighbour, told me, as well as how Mary locked me in the dressing room, her coming on to Matt, the dirt in my bed, Tommy saying that Tyler hurt him somehow, as well as me being convinced there was an intruder in the garden.

'My God, that's a lot to deal with, Geen,' Laura says, looking shocked, but I don't get a chance to reply as my phone pings.

'Talk of the devil, it's Annie,' I say, opening WhatsApp.

'God, that's a relief.' I quickly explain about the electrical issues. 'She says not to worry, the weird flickering happens all the time and it's not urgent. It'll be fixed when she's back from Thailand.'

Laura stares blankly at me, slowly shaking her head. 'I can't believe how calm you're being about everything. Not to mention that picture you found in the tree stump. It's *Sara* for God's sake. Have you told the police? What do you think it means? It could be some crackpot, obsessed with her case – or someone obsessed with little girls,' she adds, pulling a disgusted face. 'But it could also be a lead, Gina. The police might reopen the case.'

I hear the wobble in her voice and can almost read her mind as she's beginning to wish she'd never come to visit now, not if Sara's ghost is going to be with us for the entire weekend.

'I know... I *know*, you're right,' I say. 'But listen... I swear that Annie's housekeeper knows something about it. According to Bridget, Mary has been out on the common a lot recently, searching for something. Look, this is what I told you about.'

I reach into my bag and take out the rusty heart necklace, holding it up. 'Mary looked guilty as hell when I caught her in my bedroom. My theory is that she lost it in there earlier and had come back to find it. And I also think it's what she was looking for out on the common. I bet it was with the photo.'

The smile drops off Laura's face as she reaches out to take the necklace, letting it trail between her fingers.

'I never found Annie's necklace in the dressing room, you see. Given everything else that's happened, I really think this could be Sara's necklace,' I say solemnly. 'And no,' I add, leaning closer, whispering in her ear, 'of *course* I didn't report it to the bloody police.'

THIRTY-TWO

MARY

My intention was never to kill Annie. It was more a case of wanting her out of the way. But sometimes plans change, things go wrong, fate intervenes, and people never behave the way you expect. It's a good job I'm a quick thinker and adaptable. I'll stop at nothing to get what I want. It's finally time for payback.

After I put a load of laundry on earlier, Gina briefly introduced me to her friend, Laura. What she doesn't realise is that I'm already very familiar with her and probably know more about her current life than Gina does – that Laura and her husband, Patrick, attend marriage counselling once a week, that Laura has been having a secret affair with a partner in her law firm for the last six months, and I swear something is going on between Patrick and a much younger woman in his cycling club, though I can't be totally sure. Tyler's hacking skills have turned out extremely useful, and he never asks difficult questions or accuses me of being immoral because he understands that I'm doing it all for him.

But I still smiled sweetly and shook Laura's hand, engaging in a few minutes of chit-chat as I was introduced formally.

'What a shame Annie isn't here, too,' I said after Gina needlessly explained about their childhood friendship group that Laura was also a part of. I almost feel like I belonged to it myself. 'It would have been a lovely reunion.'

I watched their faces, the way their brows frowned just a little, the quick glance they shared with each other, the simultaneous thoughts whipping between them that said, *No, it wouldn't be a reunion because one of us would still be missing.*

But, of course, they don't know I know that.

Gina then went on to tell me how she and Laura don't live too far apart these days and that they last saw each other a few weeks ago.

The night of the fire, I thought, but kept quiet about that, too.

Another thing they don't know is that Laura only came to stay for the weekend because of me. She didn't really want to trek down to the South Coast, having already made plans to spend time with her lover while Patrick is away on a cycling trip. But a friend in need...

I'm really worried about Gina, my WhatsApp message to Laura had stated. Rather, it had been *Annie's* WhatsApp message as far as Laura was concerned. My words sent from Annie's phone, which has been in my possession for a while now. I changed the passcode and face recognition as soon as I got it.

Poor Annie won't be needing it any more.

Oh no, why? had come Laura's reply.

She won't admit it, but she's not holding things together, had been my – sorry, Annie's – response. *She's obsessed with the past and is super anxious. Might be postnatal depression, too. Wish I could be there for her. She needs support. Would you go visit her?*

Consider it done, Laura had replied without hesitation. *I'll go this weekend.*

I'd sent another message, suggesting she take her friendship necklace with her as it would bring comfort to Gina when they reminisced, and Laura had agreed. In fact, it had been far easier than I'd thought to get the two of them together – and much easier for me, considering their fate, to have them under the same roof.

I bide my time until they go out for the day. From up in my attic bedroom, I hear their excited chatter as, two floors below, they get the children ready. I imagine the scene in the hallway – the two women dressed in their jeans and Chelsea boots – Gina perhaps in that green bomber jacket she wears, and Laura in the navy wool coat she arrived in as though she was heading off to a business meeting. Tommy with a fistful of toys and his excited babble as his mother zips up his red anorak, pulling a woolly hat onto his head. The baby snug in her pram.

Then silence once the front door closes. I admit, the two children are a problem. Their innocence in all of this is relatable – kids caught in the crosshairs. At best, they'll end up in care, which puts a smile on my face as I slip down to the middle floor to rummage through the stuff Laura brought for the weekend. There's something full-circle and karmic about those kids being fostered out. But at worst... well, I can't think about that now. There'll be enough mess to clean up as it is.

I head straight for Laura's make-up bag, which has been left on the shelf above the basin in the adjoining bathroom, and unzip it, immediately finding what I'm after. The necklace is tangled around an eyeliner pencil and a tube of lip gloss. Carefully, I unravel the chain, holding it up like a prize. I imagine Laura hunting high and low for it before she left her house, wondering how it could possibly help Gina and cursing me – *Annie* – for suggesting she bring it. I run my finger down the jagged line of the heart – the metal cheap and tarnished. The word *Best* is engraved across the centre.

'Best friends...' I whisper, stuffing the chain in my back pocket. '*Traitors*, more like.'

Then I head back into Gina's room to see if I can find her

necklace – my mistake was not taking it the first time I saw it, though I didn't want to reveal my hand too soon when she realised it was gone. Plus, I now need to find Sara's chain again. I can't believe I was so careless with it. Of course, I already have Annie's *Friends* heart hidden away safely, found in a drawer in her study before Gina even arrived.

As I head back onto the landing, I smile to myself knowing that very soon I will have the complete set of four.

A couple of hours later, my mother is not pleased to see me. But then, she never is. I'm the first to admit that my visits are driven by a sense of duty and co-dependence. Apart from Tyler, she's all I've got.

She stands in her usual position beside the kitchen sink, flicking her ash down the plughole and blowing her smoke out of the open window. Her skin is sallow, and her fingernails are stained yellow as she brings the cigarette to her thin, wrinkled pout.

'So?' she says expectantly in that gravelly voice that I once hoped and prayed as a child would save me, protect me.

Get off her... Leave her alone... It's OK, Mary, you're safe... I'll look after you...

But those words never came. My mother was too much of a coward to speak up. Too concerned for her own well-being and what would become of *her* if she stood up to him or the others. Instead, she turned a blind eye. Let bad things happen.

'So...' I say, unzipping my cross-body bag, shoving my hand in and taking out the three necklaces – Laura's, Annie's and Gina's. 'I'll have to find the other one later,' I tell her, holding up the chains, which have become tangled together.

'Dunno why you're so hung up on them damn things,' my mother says, unimpressed. She flicks her ash, staring at me. 'Those bits of metal ain't worth nothing.' She draws a line across her neck with her finger, ash dropping down her top. 'Not gonna put food on that boy's plate, or booze in me belly, are they?'

'I know, I just thought that...' But I trail off, realising I'm on a hiding to nothing trying to explain what they mean to me, why I'm so intent on possessing them. This woman is not interested in me or what happened in the past. She is not interested in revenge or finally getting the best for Tyler. All she's interested in is knowing where her next packet of fags is coming from and if she has enough money to buy a six-pack or a cheap bottle of voddie. 'Did you see Dennis?' I ask, changing the subject. I can't bring myself to call him *Dad*.

My mother nods, a grin breaking on her face, exposing more gaps than teeth. Apart from visiting Dennis in prison, she has little to smile about – more co-dependency right there. Money in our bank accounts or not, my mother is destined to be miserable and bitter.

It's no wonder she numbs herself with alcohol. I remember the clouts she also used to get from Dennis when I was a child, the dull thuds and thwacks coming from their bedroom. She never yelped or cried or screamed or fought back. She just took his beatings, covering the bruises the next day with make-up. Perhaps she believed that if he took his anger out on her, it wouldn't end up elsewhere. Except it did. He had a lot of it to give.

'Your dad wants to know when we're going to get the dosh. He's up for parole next year and reckons he'll get it. He wants to know he's got something to come back to. Something to look forward to.'

I stare at my mother – at Pammie. Pam. My Pamela. Dennis would call her all those things, depending on his mood. The once golden-haired beauty with a tiny waist and a heart of stone. My own heart clenches at the thought of my father being released from prison. The pair of them rubbing their hands over imagined wodges of cash.

When I don't reply, my mother continues, 'It was me who found her, after all.' She lights another cigarette, her eyes closing briefly as she inhales. 'That Annie Wilde. If it weren't for me recognising her smug face on the telly, spouting off like she was at that awards ceremony, bragging to everyone like she was the Queen of fucking Sheba, we'd not be getting nothing,' she continues. 'She's got a lot to answer for, that one. I want my dues.'

So, to tide her over, I take one of the heart pendants and drape it around her neck, doing up the clasp at the back, resisting the urge to pull it so tight that she can't breathe.

THIRTY-THREE

GINA

After I tell Laura how I followed Mary the other day, and where I ended up, she insists we're going for a walk. She wants to retrace my steps to the run-down house that Mary went into.

'Yeah, this is definitely the road,' I say when we get there, wishing my heart would stop racing. 'I remember that shop.' I point to Sunny's – a tiny newsagent's on the corner with trays of vegetables racked up on the pavement alongside crates of fizzy pop and bags of coal.

Laura gives me a solemn nod, double-checking Tommy's safety harness is fastened.

'Laur?' I say, holding back as she sets off down the street, the collar of her coat pulled up. 'Wait. What are you hoping to achieve?' I ask, though I'm not certain I really want to know the answer.

'It's a hunch,' she replies over her shoulder in a terse whisper, even though we're still at the opposite end of the street to the house Mary went into. 'Just indulge me.' She beckons me with a tip of her head, face set in determination, so I follow on, zipping up my jacket and bowing my head – not that either of those things affords me protection or anonymity, but it makes me feel better.

'Which house?' Laura asks, stopping halfway down the street. Tommy is humming to himself – a meaningless tune as he holds his aeroplane up high, kicking his boots against the footrest of the buggy, while Gracie stirs and squirms in her pram beside him.

'Near the end on the left,' I tell her in a low voice. 'Dirty white front door,' I add, certain I recall that detail.

'You don't remember the house number?'

I shake my head as we set off again, nearing the metal railings that surround the industrial estate beyond. Four teenage boys are scuffing a football about in the dead end, idly kicking it between them, hoods up, tracksuit bottoms hanging low, hands shoved in pockets. One of them is smoking a joint on the sidelines and he looks up, watching us through narrowed eyes as we approach.

Laura glances back as I follow behind with the buggy. Her long, dark coat billows out behind her, with her smart white shirt giving her an official look – certainly not a look that belongs down this type of street. It's only her jeans – albeit designer ones – that prevent her from looking like a government official on serious business.

'It's that house there,' I hiss in a whisper as we draw closer.

Laura follows my finger as I point at the door with number forty-five daubed on the bricks beside it in flaking white paint.

'Look like Dennis got 'imself in the shit again, bros,' one of the boys crows loudly to the others.

'Nah, still in the nick, innit, man,' another corrects, booting the ball at the metal railings. Several dogs start barking from nearby houses, followed by a male voice yelling, 'Shut up!'

'What are you even looking for?' I whisper to Laura as we walk slowly past the front window. She's to my left now, taking a long glance inside. It appears dark and deserted within.

'I don't know exactly,' she admits in a cautious voice. After we pass the next two houses, we reach the metal railings, drawing to a halt only a few feet away from the teenagers, who are still kicking the ball about.

'Oi, watch it,' Laura calls out as their ball skims the wheel of the buggy. 'There's a baby in there, you know.' She scowls at them, kicking the ball back in their direction.

'Sorry,' one of the boys calls out. 'Nice shot, missus. Wanna play?'

'Dat your babby, bro? You get someone up the duff, man?' another boy says, causing the other three to break into raucous laughter.

'I wouldn't want to show you up,' Laura replies, shocking me by going up to them. 'Who lives in that place then, eh?' She points at number forty-five. 'Any of you lot?'

Silence as the boys draw close to each other, their eyes falling suspiciously on Laura. Her questions have put them into defensive mode as they form a pack, edging towards her.

'Nah, not us,' one of them replies, his eyes big and glassy as he sucks on a joint. 'Who wants to know?'

'I do,' Laura says, hands on hips, her long coat pinned back, her chin stuck in the air. Slowly, dragging the buggy behind me, I walk up to her side.

'It's them old folks, innit,' the youngest-looking of the boys says, tipping his head towards the terraced house. 'But he's gone down. A lifer, I heard, innit.' He glances to the others.

'Paedo scum,' the one with the joint says, spitting on the ground.

Laura flashes a glance at me. 'Who lives there now?' she asks, but the group of boys suddenly look over to number forty-five as they hear someone coming out of the front door.

'Talk of the devil,' one boy laughs. 'That's her. She lives there. Old hag, innit,' he adds, sneering in her direction.

'I'd get yer kids out the way, missus,' spliff boy taunts in a loud voice, making the older woman stop in her tracks. She turns slowly, a cigarette hanging out of her mouth with an inch-long column of ash attached to the tip.

'Fuck off, you lot!' she yells, cigarette bobbing. The ash drops down her grubby white vest top, beneath which her breasts hang braless almost reaching her navel. She waves her hands above her head, the wrinkled and loose skin on her arms rippling as she shoves her hands on her hips. Squinting and screwing up her nose, she glares over at Laura and me. Then, to my horror, she walks over.

'I said feck off, you feckers!' Another waft of her hand at the four boys, her voice gravelly and determined, but they stand their ground, watching what I suspect is about to become a showdown – a showdown that I fear is going to include us. 'And whaddya you pair want, lurking about? I see you out here, snooping.' She jabs a finger at Laura and me.

The woman wipes her nose on the back of her hand before pulling out a torn tissue from her baggy jeans pocket. She stares at it for a moment before dropping it to the ground, then folds her arms. Her feet are bare and the nails on her toes are yellowed and long, almost curling down to the ground like claws. Even though she's a slight woman – possibly only five foot three or four – she commands a strong presence. I would not want to get on the wrong side of her, though I suspect we already are.

'I said, whaddya want?' She comes closer, and I get a whiff of her cigarette. Instinctively, I turn the buggy to face the other way, so Tommy won't have nightmares about her. She's giving off evil witch vibes at the very least.

'How long have you lived here?' Laura asks, making me want to prod her. What the hell is she doing – trying to rile her on purpose? We just need to leave. As it is, between the woman and the group of lads, we're hemmed in at the dead end. Unless Laura fancies hauling the buggy and two kids over the six-foot metal fence that's topped with spikes, then our getaway route is, currently, severely compromised.

'I think what my friend means...' I begin, 'is that it seems like a nice street and... and we're thinking of viewing a property that's for sale.'

The woman pulls back her chin. 'What property?' she growls. 'Ain't no property for sale around here.' She takes a step closer, making my heart race even faster. Something about her isn't sitting right with me, though I can't work out what. 'Tell me what you pair are *really* after or clear off. I know your type.'

'Cops, innit,' one of the boys pipes up.

The woman shoots a look at him, then back at us. 'Are ya?' she barks. 'You look like cops. I know what the fuzz looks like, and you look like the fucking fuzz.'

'Smell like the feds too,' comes another boy's voice.

'We're not police,' Laura says boldly. 'I don't believe they take their kids to work, so relax. We're just looking for someone.'

'Your lucky day, Kane,' one of the boys chants, shoving his mate in the side. The others laugh and jeer.

'Are we?' I whisper to Laura, tugging on her sleeve. 'Let's just go. This is stupid,' I say, wishing we'd never come. We could be sitting in a café eating cake and catching up with our news right now, not feeling trapped and threatened by a bunch of angry strangers who don't want us on their turf.

'And who might that be then?' the woman says, coming even closer. I catch a whiff of stale body odour as she stands, hands on hips.

'We're looking for Sara,' Laura announces, staring the woman down. 'She was our best friend from school.'

At this, the woman suddenly lurches towards us, her fists raised and angry, with something unintelligible spewing out of her mouth.

Then, instead of turning to go, instead of fleeing and getting my children to safety, I realise what it is that's been making me feel even more on edge. I stare at the chain around her neck, unable to take my eyes off the jagged heart pendant until, finally, we make a run for it.

THIRTY-FOUR

GINA

'I didn't have *that* on my bingo card this morning,' I say to Laura, my heart still racing as we sit in the steamy seafront café. It's not Davy's, where the four of us used to hang out – that has long since closed down – but a place with a similar vibe.

'I *knew* it as soon as I saw her,' Laura admits, sitting back in her chair and folding her arms. 'Same eyes. Same sad expression, albeit fleeting beneath that tough exterior. I'd bet my life on her being Sara's mother.'

'The only sad thing about that woman was her toenails,' I comment, still freaked out, though I immediately want to retract it, feeling mean. If she really is who Laura believes her to be, then she's suffered immeasurable loss in her life. 'As soon as you mentioned Sara's name, her expression changed. It was weird – her eyes went black and empty.' I lean over to Tommy, holding his milkshake steady as he sucks through the straw. 'You know what, though? It was that heart pendant that sealed it for me.'

Laura is thoughtful for a moment. 'It *must* be Sara's.'

I shake my head. 'But that would mean the rusty one I found in my room *isn't* Sara's like I thought.' My hands are still shaking as I bring my mug of coffee to my lips.

'You say you never found Annie's necklace when you went looking for it?' Laura asks.

I shake my head again, reminding her how Mary locked me in the dressing room because of some make-believe spider. 'What if she'd already taken Annie's pendant and given it to that woman?'

'Why on earth would Annie's housekeeper steal a cheap necklace?' Laura replies, shrugging. 'Surely there are far more valuable things she could take.'

'It doesn't make any sense,' I say, my mind spinning from it all. 'I mean, how do they even know each other? They seem so different.' We sit in thought for a moment, the sounds of the busy café around us – with me thinking about Mary's neat, precise ways, her immaculate turnout for work, her carefully applied make-up, and how totally opposite she is, on the surface at least, to the woman at number forty-five. I peer into the pram when I hear Gracie stirring from her nap.

'It's really got to me, you know,' Laura continues. 'The look in her eyes. She reminded me so much of Sara, the brave face she'd often put on. And I swear Sara once told me she lived on a street that sounded a lot like Waites or Water or Watling Avenue. Not that she ever let any of us visit. She was always so careful to keep us separate from her home life, never inviting us back to hers, even when we told her it was her turn to have us round for a change. I'm beginning to realise why.'

'Laura…' I hesitate, not wanting to bring it up, but it's been playing on my mind for years. 'Why *didn't* we do anything about Sara's so-called "brave face" back then? We weren't good friends, were we?'

'We were teenagers ourselves, Geen, and far too wrapped up in our own problems to realise what was going on,' Laura admits. And she's right – we didn't know any better, even if our own problems were merely about spots or boys or missed homework. Abuse wasn't a term we were familiar with. 'It wasn't our responsibility to carry out welfare checks on her.'

I'm taken aback by the slightly cold, dismissive edge to Laura's voice, but it's probably her guilt coming out. The same kind of self-protection and self-justification that I wrestle with. We all let Sara down.

'She never made a fuss,' I say, keeping my voice low so Tommy doesn't pick up on anything. 'And she was always so grateful for the little things,' I say, thinking back. 'I paid for her cinema ticket and bought her a drink and a chocolate bar once, and it was like she'd won the lottery. She didn't stop thanking me for a month.'

Laura bites her lip in thought. 'I suspect it wasn't so much about the ticket or the chocolate, and more that you thought to include her. You showed her kindness.'

'I don't think she got much of that at home,' I reply, wishing I'd done more for her, but by the time we realised she needed help, it was too late. 'When Matt... when he said he was going to end things with her,' I whisper, leaning closer, 'that's when it all went wrong. Like she fell apart, as though he was her only way out of a shit life, but he'd left and locked the door behind him.' I can't believe I just said that – betraying my own husband. I glance at Tommy, but thankfully, he seems lost in his own world, landing his aeroplane on the café table.

'Do you two ever talk about it?' Laura asks. 'About what happened?'

I shake my head. 'No. Never. To be honest, I wish we did. Much of that night is a blur. Fifteen-year-olds and vodka really don't mix.' We share a sheepish look. 'Sometimes I think I want to hear Matt's side of things, what *he* remembers rather than what the papers wrote, but mostly I just want it all to go away.'

'The police interviewed him too, didn't they?'

'Several times, like they did us,' I reply, nodding. 'Thing is, Matt's recollection of the evening fits perfectly with ours.'

Laura sips her coffee, looking pensive as we each think back. I remember it was threatening rain that night, and my main concern was to not get my hair drenched on the walk to Matt's party, or ruin my make-up.

He'd told us to arrive just after 9 p.m., to give him and the rest of the cast time to get back after the show finished. He'd said he planned to load up on some pre-party drinks in the interval, and I know that included Annie and a couple of the others.

If I'd told my parents where I was going that Saturday night, they'd never have let me leave the house. I was fifteen – three months off being sixteen – and I'd never kissed a boy, let alone had a boyfriend. I was madly in love with Matthew Dalton, not that I'd ever have admitted that to anyone – especially not Sara.

'You've *got* to come, Geenie,' Annie had said to me on the phone the morning of the party when I still wasn't sure if I'd boycott it or not. 'The whole night will be ruined for me if you're not there. It's the final show and I want all the GALS together.'

As we each realised the implications of what she'd just said, that we *wouldn't* all be together, there was silence down the line – me battling with my conscience about Sara not being invited, but also because I was nervous about sneaking out, not wanting my parents to overhear and ground me for the rest of my life.

But the longer I stayed on the phone to Annie, a hairline crack was beginning to form inside me. A chink. Something for her to work on and prise open.

'Matt said he wants you to come.'

And there it was. She'd found my weak spot. My Achilles heel.

I wavered, going over the details again. It was awful that Sara hadn't been invited by Matt – in fact, she didn't even *know* about the party – but mainly, it was awful because he'd been a coward and hadn't broken up with her yet. Annie told me he was doing it that morning, as though Sara was something he'd stepped in, something to be scraped off his shoe. Just a bit of a nuisance.

I took a deep breath, picking at the skin around my thumb as I pressed the phone to my ear. I was angry, sad and upset for Sara, tempted to tip off Matt's parents myself. But then the party would be cancelled, and I didn't want to spoil it for Annie and Laura, knowing how much they'd been looking forward to a blowout. It was almost the end of term and would soon be Christmas. Everyone was ready for the winter break.

'OK,' I whispered down the line. My head was filled with Matt and only Matt – *he wants you to come* – and my body tingled at the thought.

'Who are you talking to all this time?' my mother said, making me jump as she appeared behind me on her way through the hallway.

I shook my head, bowing my face. 'No one. Just Annie.' My cheeks burnt blood-red as Mum rolled her eyes and headed into the kitchen.

'Really?' I heard Annie squeal down the phone. 'You're *coming*?'

'Yes, yes, I will,' I whispered again, screwing up my eyes at the thought of betraying Sara.

THIRTY-FIVE
THE PAST

Matt breathed her in, feeling her breasts press against his chest as he pulled her close. Knowing that all eyes were on them as they stood centre stage gave him a thrill like no other.

He'd almost got used to kissing her now – when he'd first properly noticed her at the beginning of term, he'd never thought he'd ever get to claim *that* – and he certainly wasn't as nervous as he had been that first time their lips had met. This was their fourth performance after all, plus rehearsals. But *damn* this was the last time they'd get to do it. No reason going forward for him to be close to Annie after tonight's show. No reason for them to kiss ever again unless he made one.

Cue secret party.

When he'd reluctantly started dating Sara a few weeks ago, he'd consoled himself in the belief that at least it might bring him closer to Annie, allowing him to discover new things about her, hang out in her company more, ignite her interest in him. But he'd been wrong. In fact, all it had achieved was making him look like a twat in front of his classmates. A source of ridicule for dating the mouse girl.

A part of him felt sorry for Sara and the way everyone spoke about her behind her back. And of course, he knew things about her that no one else did. Things he didn't *want* to know. Things he couldn't ever erase from his mind.

Matt was used to being the cool guy, the one who had all the girls begging for his attention, always captain of the rugby team, and he seemed to fly through his classes with ease. He knew it was all because of the way he looked – tall, pretty-boy handsome, a fit body and a dazzling smile. Boys like him were privileged, right? Everything landed in his lap. Blessed with a charm that would melt an iceberg, his teachers and classmates adored him.

He supposed that would have all been true if it wasn't for the crippling anxiety that shredded him from the inside out every time he stepped outside his house and had to speak to anyone – especially girls.

No one knew that Matt went to throw up in the toilets because of his nerves, or that he sometimes hid away when a panic attack swept through him. No one suspected, either, that it took every brain cell he possessed to do well in exams, and he often only got three or four hours' sleep a night because he was studying late.

So yeah, he felt sorry for Sara. And, if he was honest about it, he felt bad for everything that had happened to her. But he didn't want to be dating her.

Matt focused. Concentrated on Annie's beautiful face gazing up at him for the last time as they stood in the spotlight. He knew every inch of her features – the softness of her eyes, the symmetrical angles of her cheekbones, her pronounced jawline, her brilliant red hair. The audience was silent, enraptured by the pair of them on-stage sharing the delicious kiss that was about to be halted by Maria's irate brother at any moment now...

And there it was. Matt's shoulder yanked back by Tim, the boy from the year below playing the part of Bernardo.

Matt responded to his cue, staggering away from Annie, their eyes still locked, their pulses beating to the same rhythm as their hands slid away from each other. Had she felt it too? Was it just an act any more?

Annie's lips were glistening, and her pupils were huge, and, for a horrible moment, he thought she'd forgotten her lines. Matt took a breath, gathered himself, filled his mind with his next few lines rather than the feelings stirring inside him, waiting for the prompter in the wings to nudge her along.

God, I want her so bad.

But no prompt was needed as Annie, after what seemed like an age, delivered her speech with power. Matt felt himself dissolving inside as she begged for his love, pleaded with her brother to leave them be, to let young love blossom. *What a performance...* he thought, though at the same time he was gutted that's all it was. An act. Fake. She didn't mean a word of it.

Or did she?

'Oi, oi, Mattie boy... the stage was sizz-*liin*' tonight!' someone crowed – a boy from the chorus giving him a nudge as they filtered off into the wings for the final time.

'*Right*?' a girl who'd done the make-up said, jumping up and down excitedly at his side. 'Red-hot performance, Mattie!'

Matt squirmed inside, looking around the excited cast as they hugged each other in groups, heading for the dressing rooms in a flurry of energy, relief and sadness that it was all over. All the hard work they'd put into the show during the last term had come to a head tonight – culminating in their best performance yet. The applause had only just finished, continuing well after the curtain had dropped to a standing ovation.

'Cheers, mate,' Matt said, high-fiving some others as they all congratulated each other on the way to get changed. He'd no idea where Annie had disappeared to – he'd been scanning around for her since they'd left the stage.

But Matt's enthusiasm to his peers was nothing more than a brave face – a shiny one, a well-worn one, a familiar mask he'd long become used to wearing. The only time he ever took it off was when he was alone in his bedroom and, at a push, when it was just him and his parents. They were decent people, his mother and father, though his dad did his best to keep a lid on those 'blasted emotion things' as he'd once called them when he'd found Matt upset and shedding a few tears – about what, he couldn't even recall. And his mum had always encouraged him to keep a stiff upper lip, hold his chin high, be a man like his dad.

He was getting tired of all that now. He didn't *want* to be the sporty, popular, academic one. The poster boy for middle-class teenagers everywhere. He wanted to experience the messy side of life, have people gossip about him for all the wrong reasons, date the bad girls, and earn his broken heart the hard way. He wanted his parents to be pissed off at him, to ground him, to despair of him and threaten to kick him out.

He wanted everything he deserved.

But more than anything, he wanted Annie – the girl he'd fallen so deeply in love with from the first moment he'd properly noticed her across the school canteen ten weeks ago, so deep that it physically hurt his bones to know that she probably wouldn't give him the time of day if they'd not been in the musical together. And especially not if she knew what he was really like – a total loser with no confidence wrapped up in lucky good looks.

'Time to party, Matt!' Evan, who'd become one of his best mates over the last year, said as they pulled off their costumes. 'I've got something to spice things up a bit.' He winked, laying a hand on his backpack.

Matt hesitated. Did he mean *drugs*?

Weed might be OK, he supposed, but what if Evan meant something harder? That was when things were more likely to get messy. People doing stupid things. Stuff getting stolen or smashed. Fights breaking out. Emotions running high – or low.

Matt felt nauseous as he was reminded of the last party he'd had at New Year's when his folks had gone to Scotland to stay with his mum's sister. There'd been drugs then, too. He shuddered at the memory, beginning to wish he'd never planned another stupid piss-up. He leant against the wall, feeling physically sick.

The logic behind tonight's gathering was to get closer to Annie. He hadn't had the guts to ask her out on a date. Nor had he had the guts to finish things with Sara first. That would never happen – *could* never happen. Rather, it was something she would have to do herself. He just needed her to hate him enough first.

'Cool, great...' Matt found himself replying to Evan, praying it wasn't drugs. 'I've got the booze stashed in my bedroom,' he added, hoping he might get the hint that it was a party to get pissed at, have a dance and snog a few girls at, rather to get stoned or high at. And for him to perhaps... *maybe*... if things went well... tell Annie how he felt.

On the walk back to his house ahead of all the others, Matt thought about what he could say to Annie to let her know how much he liked her – without actually telling her he liked her in case she laughed in his face. He scuffed the pavement as he walked, head down, hands shoved into his pockets.

'Oi, Matt,' a voice called out. He was nearly home and needed to get on with setting up the party before everyone arrived. His parents, who'd come to watch last night's show, had left during the afternoon so the coast would be clear. 'Wait up!'

Evan ran up to him, breathless. 'I just saw your girlfriend.' He shoved Matt in the back.

Matt continued walking, biting down hard, his jaw tense.

'She looked right angry.'

She's not my girlfriend, he wanted to yell. But, as things stood, she was.

'How come?' Matt asked as they went up the drive, his parents' car gone. Perhaps she was getting fed up of him already – he'd been avoiding her the last day or two. Good.

'She was asking everyone where you were. Looked right pissed off, she did.'

'And?'

Evan sprayed out laughter. 'Calm your bollocks. No one said anything. Most just ignored her as usual. Dunno what you see in her, mate. You could do way better.'

Matt shoved his key into the lock, wanting to spew out to Evan that he didn't see anything in her, apart from a lost soul who came from a bad family.

He shuddered, pushing open the front door. Inside smelt like home – the comforting scent of his mother's floral perfume as well as the neat, homely environment she provided. Freshly vacuumed carpet. Meals for him to reheat in the fridge. His father's golf clubs sat in the hallway, his shiny black work shoes positioned under the telephone table ready for Monday morning. Familiar things. Nice things. Their things.

What the fuck was I thinking, inviting a load of teenagers back here to get drunk?

'Where's the booze then, mate?' Evan said, hurling himself onto the sofa. 'I'm gonna get well hammered.'

Matt ran upstairs to his bedroom. He opened the wardrobe and brought down the two carrier bags of alcohol he'd had hidden in there for a week.

'That it?' Evan said, peering inside each bag. 'A bottle of vodka, two bottles of Strongbow and a couple of six-packs?' He looked up at Matt.

'Yeah, why?' Matt cursed himself inwardly. Evan was right. That amount of booze was going nowhere fast. Fact was, he'd not had the cash to buy any more, and hadn't really considered how much his mates would drink, figuring they'd bring some too. If he thought even harder about it, they weren't even his proper mates, really. It was obvious they were just coming for the free drink.

'Not gonna cut it, pal.' Evan smirked. 'You still got time to get to the offy before everyone comes. Here, use this.' He fished about in his back pocket and handed Matt his fake ID. 'Get double, triple this lot. As much as you can carry. I'll hold the fort and let everyone in when they arrive.'

Matt nodded without even thinking about where the money would come from to pay for it. He already knew. If he didn't put on a good party, everyone would out him as the loser he was – including Annie. He dashed to the kitchen and took the Tupperware box from the back of the cupboard where his mum kept the housekeeping money: a little over a hundred pounds.

He closed his eyes briefly as he shoved it in his pocket, thanking God for small mercies as he grabbed his jacket and headed down the hill towards the cheapest booze shop in town.

THIRTY-SIX

GINA

Laura helps me lift the buggy up the stone steps of Genoa House when we arrive back from the café, and we head inside, dumping all our coats and shoes in the hallway.

I pause, listening out, wondering if Mary and Tyler are home, but it's a futile exercise as Tommy roars off to the kitchen making a din, and Gracie begins to cry, quickly building to an urgent hunger wail.

'I'll fix up some lunch,' Laura offers while I get comfortable on the sofa to feed my baby and inject my rapid-acting insulin before we eat. The mood between us hangs sombre as we process the events of this morning.

When Gracie has finished feeding, drunk as a lord with her eyelids drooping, I lay her down in the buggy, wheeling her into the study where it's dark and quiet. Laura has warmed up some soup and made sandwiches.

'This is what we're dealing with back home,' I whisper when a text from Matt comes in, showing her the picture he's sent of our house.

'Jesus,' Laura replies when she sees our blackened living room.

I make a *sshh* sound, flashing a look at Tommy. I've already told her I don't go into detail about the fire in front of him. The last thing I want is him having nightmares. As far as he's concerned, the house is poorly and being 'made better' for us to live in again.

After lunch, Tommy rests in front of the TV and is soon nodding off. Laura covers him with a blanket and helps me load the few plates into the dishwasher. 'No sign of Annie's house-keeper?' she asks.

I shake my head quickly. 'Don't think she's here.'

'Should we do it now then?'

A single nod from me has us creeping up the stairs and hovering on the first-floor landing. As we pass each bedroom door, I listen out just in case she's in there cleaning – perhaps doing overtime on a Saturday. Or snooping about as I'm certain she was before.

'Mary?' I call out when we reach the bottom of the attic stairs. 'Are you home?'

Nothing.

'Tyler?' I try. 'It's Gina. Are you up there?'

Nothing again. No gaming sounds, either.

'Check in your room for your necklace,' Laura says. 'I'll check for mine, too. If they're still where we left them, then it's most likely just a coincidence that woman was wearing one.'

We each head off to our rooms, and I search through my bedside table drawer. When there's no sign of my necklace, I check Matt's side just in case I was mistaken about where I put it, but, as I suspected, it's not there either. I still have the rusty one in my bag.

Once I've hunted through all my stuff on the dressing table, I meet Laura on the landing, hands on hips. 'Gone, as I thought.'

'Mine too,' Laura says, looking concerned.

'It *must* have been Mary,' I say, feeling even more creeped out. 'Matt wouldn't be interested in them and besides, he left before you arrived.'

Laura nods solemnly. 'Right, let's do this then. I'll keep an ear out while you search up in her room.'

The thought of being caught makes me sweat. I stop for a moment, listening out for Gracie, peering over the balustrade and down to the chequerboard tiles in the hall below. All is quiet.

I give Laura a nervous look before gingerly treading up the narrow attic stairs, trying to convince myself this is necessary, that Annie would want to know if her housekeeper is a thief.

'Give me plenty of warning if you hear her coming back. Distract her if you must, just don't let her catch me up here.'

Another nod from Laura as she stops halfway up the attic stairs behind me – close enough to warn me of Mary's return, but still with a view down the stairwell to the ground floor should the front door open.

I go into Mary's room first. The single bed is neatly made – plain white cotton sheets and plumped-up pillows. A pair of flat black shoes is positioned neatly at the end of the bed – the shoes I know she wears for work – and her now empty holdall is stashed on top of the wardrobe. I pull open the doors to reveal a couple of tops and hoodies, a pair of jeans, and the smarter clothes she wore when we went to the restaurant all neatly hung alongside two clean and pressed uniforms ready for work next week. There's nothing else in there.

The chest of drawers underneath the dormer window doesn't provide much in the way of evidence either, containing a small selection of plain underwear, some socks and a couple of T-shirts. It's true to say that Mary did not bring many belongings after fleeing her abusive ex.

'Still all clear?' I hiss out of the door, catching sight of Laura, tense, on the stairs.

She gives me a thumbs up, ushering me back into the bedroom.

I rummage through Mary's wash bag sitting on top of the chest of drawers, but all it contains is a few bits of make-up. Beside it lies a hairbrush with a few strands of blonde hair stuck in the bristles, and a comb with some missing teeth. But no sign of any necklaces. A quick look through the nightstand, and it's on to the bathroom she shares with Tyler. Again, there's nothing of interest to be found.

'Did you check under her mattress?' Laura hisses up the stairs.

'I want to look in Tyler's room first,' I say, opening the door a crack to double-check he's not in there. But I suddenly freeze, hand on the knob. 'What was that?' I whip round to Laura.

She's perfectly still, listening downstairs. Then she shakes her head. 'It's fine. Just the house creaking.'

I continue into Tyler's room, surprised at how neat and tidy it is. I suppose it's easy for a teenager to keep things in order when he barely owns anything. The main items in his room are his computer and games console, plus the controllers and various accessories.

I creep over to the dressing table that he's using as a desk, scanning over everything and looking behind his two monitors. There's nothing much to see – just a tangle of cables and a power adaptor. His bed is also neatly made – the blue and white striped cotton duvet smoothed neatly with a towel hung over the metal end post.

I'm about to head out again when I hear a buzz. Something vibrating. Unmistakably a phone.

I swing around, my eyes flicking over every surface, wondering if I missed Tyler's phone lying about – though he's usually glued to it. But there's no sign of one. I can't imagine a teenager as addicted to tech as he is leaving it behind.

The vibrating sound again.

Coming from the dressing table.

I hold my breath, listening.

The two drawers are empty, so I pull them out completely, feeling around beneath the top of the dressing table. Nothing. I lift up the games console, shoving all the wires out of the way, then I check underneath Tyler's keyboard and...

...and there it is. An iPhone – its screen lighting up as another message alert comes in.

I don't realise at first why the pace of my heart speeds up and my spine tingles from top to bottom. But gradually, it dawns on me that it's not Tyler's phone at all – and that there's no reason for him to have a photo of Annie's parents when they were younger as his wallpaper. No reason at all for him to be receiving messages from someone called Bryan Adler, who I know to be Annie's agent.

Slowly, I reach out and pick up the phone – the latest model in a white silicone case.

I hardly dare breathe as I take the phone out to the landing.

'Have you got your phone on you?' I whisper to Laura, my voice breathy and weak. She nods up at me, looking puzzled. 'Send a text to Annie. Anything – just send anything. *Now*, hurry!'

With a confused expression, Laura does as she's told and, a second later, the phone in my hand buzzes with an alert from Laura Draper:

Hey Annie...

'*Oh my God...*' I say, hardly able to believe what I'm seeing. I swipe to open the phone, but of course it's locked. I angle the screen so Laura can see. 'This was hidden in Tyler's room,' I whisper, but we both suddenly freeze, listening out as a loud noise comes from downstairs.

It's the front door opening and closing.

'Hello! We're home...' a voice calls out. And, when I dare to peek over the edge of the banisters, I see Mary heading up the first flight of stairs.

THIRTY-SEVEN

MARY

Something doesn't feel right. Something is off.

No one replies to my hello as I come through the door, though I know they're home because their shoes are in the hallway. It's almost a... *smell* that I'm picking up on. The scent of mistrust.

Tyler goes upstairs ahead of me, his long legs easily carrying him up, but I'm more cautious. He's got a bag full of sausage rolls that I picked up from Greggs before I met him at the arcade after I'd left my mother's. It's the best place for him to wait while I visit her – I don't want any of her influence rubbing off on him.

But when I turn the corner to go up the final staircase, I'm met with a log-jam. Tyler has stopped on his way up to the attic, and Gina and her friend are standing on the landing above him. The uncertain expressions they both have tell me they've been caught red-handed – but doing what?

'Hi,' I say as breezily as I can manage, not wanting to show I'm rattled. 'Did you have a nice morning?' They've obviously been snooping in our rooms – though they won't have found anything, I'm sure of that. And my mother insisted she didn't give anything away when she confronted them outside her house earlier, but a part of me is beginning to doubt that now. I wish she'd just left well alone and stayed inside.

'We went to the beach, but it was a bit breezy,' Gina tells me, her voice faltering as her eyes flick across to her friend. 'We had a quick coffee at that place opposite the mini-golf. Do you know it?'

'No, I don't,' I reply, as Tyler slides past them, disappearing into his bedroom. I step back, gesturing to the women to come down first, offering my best smile as they pass. I just need them out of my way while I decide what to do. 'I'll have to check it out,' I add, wincing at how fake I sound. 'I have some family emails to send, so I'll maybe see you ladies later. Have a good afternoon,' I add as they head down the next flight of stairs, casting doubting looks back up at me as they go.

Once alone, I stalk around my room, checking to see if anything has been disturbed. Nothing appears to have moved or been taken, so I head into Tyler's room.

'Close call,' I say, though he won't understand my concern. *World of Warcraft* is on his screen as he sets up for a game, chewing on a potato and cheese pasty.

'Do we *have* to live here any more?' he asks, glancing up at me, a worried look on his face. Then he points to the wall behind his bed.

'More noises?' I say, trying to sound sympathetic, even though it'll just be his mind playing tricks on him.

He nods.

'I told you, Ty, these old places make all kinds of creaky sounds. Pipes rattling, floorboards creaking, windows banging. Honestly, there's no need to worry.'

'But it's none of those things. It sounds more like... like flapping. Something trapped.'

To show willing, I go over to the wall and put my ear against the plaster. 'Yup, I hear pigeons roosting,' I lie. 'That's all it is. They can make a hell of a din.'

'Well, I don't like it,' he says, turning back to his computer. 'What if it's a ghost?'

'If it helps, we can swap rooms,' I suggest, knowing how much little sounds or annoyances can ruffle him. 'Anyway, I came to get the phone,' I whisper, but Tyler is focused on his monitor again. 'Ty, can you give it to me?' I nudge him, making him swing round.

'What?'

Can I have the phone? I mouth at him, not wanting to be overheard.

His head arcs in acknowledgement as he turns back to his desk, lifting up his keyboard.

'What are you doing?' I ask, confused.

But Tyler just sits there, staring at the empty space on his desk.

'Forget it, I'll get it myself,' I say, going over to where his jacket is hanging on the back of the door. I didn't want to invade his privacy by going through it, but he's clearly in one of his less than helpful moods. I check each of the outside pockets before shoving my hand into the inside pocket of his padded coat. 'Ty, where is it?'

He turns to face me, a blank expression on his face.

'When we were out earlier, you told me that you had the phone,' I remind him. I'd given it to him several hours before we left the house, instructing him to keep it safe while I had a shower. I didn't want it left unattended even for a second. 'Were you lying to me?'

'No, I was not lying,' Tyler finally replies. 'You asked me if I had the phone.'

'Shhh,' I hiss at him, scowling as I close the door. 'Yes, and you told me you'd got it.'

'Got it in my *possession*,' he says, tapping the space on his desk. 'As in, I'd hidden it here, under my keyboard. So technically I'd got it as it was in *my* room concealed under *my* belongings and—'

'Tyler...' My voice quivers. 'Where is the goddamn phone?'

'I cannot answer that,' he says, putting the keyboard back on his desk. He's about to put his headphones on, but I grab them from around his neck.

'Oh no you don't,' I hiss into his ear. Then I drop to my knees beside his chair, knowing he'll clam up and likely not speak for three days if I get angry with him. 'Ty, you're not in trouble. Just tell me where the phone is. Is it in this room somewhere? *Please*...' I grab his hands and stare up at him.

'Given that I left the phone on this desk, and it is now not here, its absence would suggest it is not in this room any more.'

'Then where is it, Tyler?' I ask. 'What have you done with it?'

Tyler frowns. 'Nothing. It's a mystery.'

I stand up, pacing up and down the small bedroom. I drag my fingers through my hair. 'It's not a mystery, Ty,' I say under my breath, knowing he won't have made the connection with what Gina and her friend were doing up here.

Oblivious to my angst, Tyler puts his headphones on and gets on with his game. I go back to my bedroom, trying to convince myself that it's not a disaster, that things will simply have to be brought forward – *urgently*. In a way, it's positive and I'll reach the end goal sooner than I'd anticipated.

I grab my own phone from my back pocket, half expecting to hear sirens screaming down the street as I make a call to my mother.

'They know,' I say when she answers.

Silence down the line, apart from her sighing out heavily as she blows out a cloud of smoke. 'What d'you mean, *they know*?'

'Tell me the truth about what happened when you saw them out on the street,' I demand.

When I was at my mother's house earlier, handing over yet more of my wages, I'd glimpsed Gina and Laura walking past the front window. It was my fault for reacting, for telling my mother who they were, but I was shocked to see them. I hung back inside the house so they didn't see me, but my mother marched out there bold as brass.

'I'll sort 'em out. Leave it to me,' she said, not even bothering to put any shoes on. I stood behind the open front door, out of sight and listening as she barked at a group of lads to bugger off. But as she got further away, I couldn't make out much else.

'I didn't say nothing to 'em, I already told you that. I said one of them looked like a cop. I asked what they was doing and that were that.'

'I don't believe you,' I hiss into my phone. 'Why were they sniffing around your house in the first place?'

'How would I know?' my mother says. 'You're the one caused all this, not me.'

I bite my tongue, refusing to rise to her bait.

'They said they was looking at a house to buy,' my mother says. 'That's the truth.'

I decide not to mention that Annie's phone has gone missing, that I suspect Gina and Laura took it and are therefore probably close to discovering her fate. I don't doubt that the minute they piece it all together, they'll be calling the police – if they haven't alerted them already.

'I'm bringing everything forward,' I tell her. 'Do you understand?'

''Bout time,' is my mother's curt reply before she lets out a long, hacking cough. 'Can't understand what you're waiting for. Just get it over with. We need the money.'

There's no way I'm about to explain to her that for me it's not about money – money will never make things right. It's about making people pay for what they did. An eye for an eye. But getting my mother to comprehend my desire for revenge is beyond her low-grade intelligence.

'I'll let you know when I've done it,' I say, about to hang up.

'Wait, before you go, there is one other thing them women said,' my mother tells me, taking another drag on her cigarette. 'They said they was looking for Sara.'

THIRTY-EIGHT

GINA

The next morning, the first thing Laura does when she sees me is grab me by the shoulders. 'For God's sake, calm down,' she insists when I garble out that Matt has been arrested, that he just called to tell me. 'You'll scare the kids.'

'He... he said he didn't want to worry me last night,' I tell her, clutching at my hair.

She looks at me earnestly, but I pull away, checking around the kitchen for my insulin kit. Then I remember I left it upstairs, rushing down here in a panic straight after Matt's call.

I pace about the kitchen, not knowing which way to turn, my throat still burning from the screech that burst out of me after Matt had hung up. I feel ashamed for frightening Tommy.

'Just sit down and breathe a moment,' Laura says, pressing me down onto the sofa. 'Let's not overreact.'

'My husband has been *arrested*...' I hiss, not wanting Tommy to hear as he plays nearby. 'How can I stay calm? He said it was something to do with a fight breaking out last night. But Matt's a gentle giant – there's no way he'd kick off with anyone... never *ever*. He's being held in custody at Crawley police station. They only let him speak to me for a moment. I need to go to him now. Laura, will you stay and look after the kids?' I grab a cushion, pressing it against my face to stop another scream coming out. No wonder he didn't respond to my WhatsApp message last night – I'd just assumed he was out having a good time.

'Of *course* I'll help.' Laura sits down beside me. 'Look, I think it sounds more dramatic than it really is. It'll just be a drunk and disorderly thing and they bunged him in a cell to sober up. You'll both be laughing it off in a few days. Matt's not a big drinker, is he? Evan probably encouraged him to have a few too many.'

I drop the cushion into my lap, looking at her. 'Do you think so?'

Laura has never liked Evan, and I've only tolerated him for Matt's sake over the years. At school, he was always the trouble-maker, the one egging others on, lurking in the background as his mates took the punishment for his wrongdoings. Memories of Matt's New Year's Eve party when we were teenagers creep into my mind – Evan behaving appallingly, mocking Matt, taunting him. I've never forgotten how vile he was.

'It's entirely plausible,' Laura replies. 'Now look, stop worrying. God knows, Patrick has white-lied his way out of many a scrape over the years. Usually when he's been overseas and his dirty laundry reeks of perfume. The most insulting thing is that he thinks I believe his pathetic fibs.' Her expression suddenly turns bitter.

'Oh Laura, I'm so sorry...' The distraction works briefly, but then I'm thinking about Matt holed up in a police cell again. 'I need to drive to Crawley and... Oh *shit*.' That's when I remember that I don't have the car. 'An Uber will cost a fortune. I'll call Dad. He'll come and fetch me. Then I'll drive Matt back in our car – wherever *that* is right now,' I add, trying to work out the logistics. I'm so upset that my weekend with Laura is ruined.

'Good plan,' Laura says, reaching out and squeezing my hands. 'You'll be back in no time, and we can still have a nice evening later. It's a good thing I booked tomorrow off work. Matt can babysit as penance while we go out!' She gives me a reassuring hug. 'I'll stay here with the kids while you're gone. They'll have a fine old time with Aunty Laura, won't you, Tommo?' she says, getting down on the rug to play with my son while I phone Dad.

'Damn – voicemail,' I say, hanging up. I try Mum's number but it's the same. 'Now what?'

'Looks like it's a taxi then,' she says. 'If money's tight, I'll help with the fare,' she offers, but before I get a chance to reply, a voice rings out from the kitchen end of the room.

'Anyone fancy a cuppa?' Mary trills, holding up a couple of mugs.

Laura and I stare blankly at her, but then I get up and go over to her, my mind having gone down the same route as Laura's, judging by the look she gives me.

'You don't have access to a car, do you?' I say hopefully. '*Annie's* car, perhaps?'

I hold my breath, waiting for Mary's reply, trying to put out of my mind that yesterday I found Annie's phone in her son's bedroom, and that it's currently tucked inside my handbag. If it rings or vibrates, I'll just have to pretend it's mine.

Last night, Laura and I pondered what it meant, sending several more messages to Annie, which we saw appear on her phone. Given that she'd been replying to me perfectly normally up until now, we concluded that perhaps Annie had given Tyler her old phone as a gift, and that he hadn't yet got round to linking it to his own account – that it wasn't sinister or suspicious at all, and that Annie must have a new phone on her with call and message forwarding that wasn't working right now because she was in Thailand and... and...

I'd stressed myself out coming up with various reasons why Annie's phone had been in Tyler's room, until Laura told me to stop, that she wanted to hear no more about it, that there'd be a perfectly reasonable explanation. 'Geen, don't waste the whole weekend twisting yourself into knots. Let's just enjoy tonight, eh?' she said before ordering the takeaway.

She was right, of course, and we did have a good night, though it's still bothering me this morning. But until I've made sure Matt is safe and I've got him home, I'll simply have to continue convincing myself that it means nothing.

The alternative is too unthinkable.

Mary stares at me, standing perfectly still as she grips the mugs, her eyes narrowing ever so slightly.

'How come you need a car?' she says, not committing herself to an answer. 'You're not planning on leaving, are you?' Slowly, she puts down the mugs and comes out from behind the kitchen island.

A strange choice of words, I think, but, like the phone, I force myself to ignore it.

'I need to get to Crawley urgently,' I say, going up to her. I don't want to tell her what's happened to Matt, but I've little choice, so I play it down. 'Matt got himself in a spot of bother last night so I need to go to him. My parents aren't picking up their phones.'

'I hope he's OK,' Mary says slowly, her eyes fixed on mine as she sizes me up. 'But don't worry, I'll drive you. Annie's Mercedes is in the garage.'

'Oh God, thank you *so* much,' I say, hating how grateful I am to her given what I found upstairs. 'You're a lifesaver.'

'It's no problem. That's what I'm here for, after all,' she says with a smile. 'The keys are upstairs, so I'll go and get them.'

I give Laura a quick glance, praying that she picks up on my thoughts: *Don't mention finding Annie's phone.* I can't risk upsetting Mary and being alone in the car with her for an hour and a half, having to explain why we were snooping in her and Tyler's rooms.

'I'll grab my things, too,' I say. 'And Laura,' I call back over my shoulder, 'there's enough of my milk in the freezer for two, maybe three feeds,' I tell her, thanking God I expressed some the last couple of nights.

'On it,' Laura says. 'I'll look after those kids as if they're my own,' she says. 'You'll text me when you get there safely, right?'

'Of course,' I say, rushing off to get my coat and boots. I grab my handbag from the hook in the hallway, knowing there's a spare insulin kit in there. I'll inject in the car and grab something to eat from a garage on the way. I duck into the study to check on Gracie, who's starting to squirm and wake up in her pram. I lift her up gently, breathing in her soft scent. 'Daddy's been a silly man,' I whisper to her. 'So Mummy's going to go and bring him home. I'll be back in a few hours.' I kiss her cheek and take her with me back to the kitchen, handing her over to Laura.

Laura jiggles Gracie about as she starts to snuffle and whimper, building up to a grizzle.

'Right, let's go down to the car,' Mary says, appearing in the kitchen and dangling the Mercedes keys at me. 'We have to go through the basement.'

'Any trouble with the kids, just call me,' I say, giving Tommy and Gracie another quick kiss.

'We'll be fine,' Laura says, cradling Gracie as she sits down where Tommy is playing.

'Bye-bye, Mummy,' my little boy calls out from the rug, holding his dinosaur up at me.

I wave and grin, though my smile falls away when Tyler skulks past me into the kitchen, his eyes wide and searching as he sizes up what's going on.

I stop a moment, watching him, before flashing a concerned look at Laura. She waves me on, mouthing, *It's fine*, so I reluctantly follow Mary to the doorway beneath the stairs. She pulls it open to reveal the inner lobby that Matt and I found when we were looking for the fuse board, beyond which is the security door leading to the basement.

'Thank goodness Annie replied with the code,' Mary says, glancing back over her shoulder as she fiddles with the entry system, the keypad obscured by her body as she punches in the number. 'It's all soundproofed from here on in – for her recording work,' she tells me with a smile, glancing back. There's a beep followed by a click as the heavy door unlocks, and Mary pulls it slowly open, revealing a dark space beyond.

'Wow, no expense spared,' I say as neon-blue low-level lighting automatically illuminates the staircase. The stairwell looks sleek and modern, and everything – even my footsteps and breathing – suddenly sounds very, very silent.

'That's our Annie,' Mary says, stepping aside and gesturing for me to head down first. 'Only the best will do.' She gives me another small smile.

As I venture down, turning left down a dogleg in the staircase, I hear a dull thud as the door above swings closed, the lock clicking into place. 'Is there a proper light down here?' I ask, looking up to see if Mary is following me. 'Oh, my voice sounds really weird,' I say with a nervous laugh, wondering where she is.

'That'll be the sound deadening,' Mary replies, suddenly appearing beside me with a halo of blue light behind her from the LEDs. 'The studio is through there.' She gestures to another doorway. 'Want to have a quick look? I'm sure Annie won't mind.'

'Oh... well, we'd probably better head off,' I say, seeing another door that I presume leads into the garage. 'Another time.' I just want to get to Matt.

'Nonsense, I won't hear of it,' Mary says in a voice that sounds... well, different. *Strange*, even. I tell myself it's the weird acoustics down here making her seem sinister and cold, almost as if we're in a padded cell. Then Matt is on my mind again, stuck in an actual cell at the police station. Before I can protest about wanting to get on the road again, Mary pulls some keys from her pocket, putting one in the lock and turning it. Then, in the semi-darkness, she pulls the studio door slightly open.

It all happens so fast – her grabbing me by the arm, yanking me so hard that my head whips back, disorientating me. My shocked scream doesn't sound like my own when it comes out – rather it feels like it's trapped inside my head, as though someone is hammering on my skull.

'What the *hell*—' but I don't get the chance to finish or even fight back as I feel my handbag snatched from my shoulder before I'm shoved roughly inside the room behind the door. I'm plunged into total blackness as I trip on something and fall over, my hands coming out to save me as I go down.

Something hard smashes against my head, disorientating me for a moment – although my senses are utterly confused by the strange silence down here, the pitch darkness and... the pungent *smell*.

I lie there for a moment, waiting to either black out completely or for the ringing in my ears to stop. Then I hear something behind me – the dull thud sounding an awful lot like a door closing.

I groan, touching my head as I lie prone in the pitch blackness, my head throbbing. Gradually, I sit up, feeling nauseous. 'Mary?' I call out, willing myself to believe I was just clumsy and tripped and fell into this room because of my own stupidity – that she didn't shove me in here at all. 'Are you in here? I stumbled and...' I trail off, sniffing the air. 'Mary, where are you?'

Perfume. I smell sweet, floral perfume. As if someone has sprayed an entire bottle of it nearby.

And then I hear a voice. A voice that's not my own. A voice that's not Mary's.

Deadened and quiet, coming from a few feet away, someone says, '*Hello?*'

THIRTY-NINE
GINA

'Hello?' I reply cautiously, my voice wavering. 'Who's that?'

Silence.

I feel around with my hands, coming across something hard and cold with sharp metal edges. It feels like a square wastebin. Beyond that, there's what seems to be the leg of a piece of furniture – something hard, solid and upright. I use it to haul myself to a standing position, the pain in my head biting into my skull. When I touch my temple, it feels sticky and wet. *Blood.*

'Mary?' I call out again. 'Is that you? Can you put the light on? I'm hurt.'

'She'll be long gone,' the other voice says, making me freeze.

I recognise it yet... yet at the same time, I *don't* recognise it – perhaps the sound-altering acoustics again.

'Who's there?' I ask, supporting myself on what feels like the edge of a table or desk.

'Who's *that*?' the voice – female – says back. She sounds fearful and weak, almost childlike with her thin, barely-there words.

'It's Gina,' I reply. 'Gina Dalton. I think there's been some mistake. I was on the way to the garage with Mary but seem to have—'

'There's no mistake,' she says, sounding resigned – almost as though she's given up. 'And there's also no way out.'

I stop, taking in what she said. Processing who I now realise she *is*. Not wanting to believe it.

'Oh my God, *Annie*?' I whisper incredulously, wondering if I've blacked out after my fall and I'm imagining it's her. Of *course* it's not Annie.

Annie is on holiday. Annie has been on a safari. Annie has not long flown to Thailand. Annie is enjoying the beaches of Koh Samui.

But then... *Annie's phone was in Tyler's bedroom.*

A chill sweeps through me.

'Gina...' the voice comes back. 'Yes, it's me. Annie.'

I swallow hard, forcing down the sick that's about to come up. I don't know if the nausea is from shock or from hitting my head or disorientation in the sheer blackness of wherever I am.

'What... what in God's name are you doing down here, Annie? I mean *why*... where... shit, I have so many questions I don't know where to begin.'

I feel around for something, *anything* to make me realise this is a bad dream, not real. I can't believe it's happening; can't believe what I'm hearing.

'It was Mary... just now, she was... one moment we were going to the car, and now this. She'll be back any moment to let us out, I swear—'

'Gina, stop,' Annie says with a grunting sound, as though she's struggling to get up. 'Whenever Mary comes back, it won't be to let you out. Anyway, more to the point, what are *you* doing here?'

I'm silent for a moment, taking in what she's telling me. Not wanting to believe her.

'We're staying here... after the fire... your text, you offered,' I say, garbling everything out. 'Where... where are you? I need to touch you.' I suddenly have an overwhelming urge to cling onto another human – to find an anchor in what is surely a nightmare. I'm shaking uncontrollably.

'I'm over here. Stay put, I'll come to you.'

I feel around the desk which, further up, seems to be a bank covered in hundreds of knobs and switches. 'I think I'm at your mixing desk,' I tell her, hoping she'll be drawn to my voice, as dulled as it sounds.

'Close your eyes,' Annie says, sounding as if she's only a few feet away now, near the door where I stumbled in. Suddenly, the room is filled with light, making me screw up my eyes and cover them with my hand. 'I did warn you,' she adds.

Gradually, I open them, taking in my surroundings. As I thought, I'm right next to a huge mixing desk with several monitors in a room that's about twelve feet square with various other bits of technical equipment, some of which have their front covers pulled off and wires ripped out. There are a few instruments stored around the perimeter of the room, including several smashed guitars. There are a couple of chairs at the desk and, in the corner, is a water cooler. Above the mixing desk with its many controls is a small pane of thick glass with a view into another room.

But I'm not interested in all that. Rather, I'm focused on the pale, gaunt and broken woman standing beside me wearing baggy grey sweatpants and a pale-green T-shirt. She has mushroom-coloured rings beneath her eyes and sores on her lips – as if she's been biting the skin. Her usually vibrant red hair is greasy and matted, and a sour smell surrounds her – a contrast to the sweet perfume hanging in the air.

'Oh my God, *Annie*...' I cry, falling against her as she opens her arms. We hug – she feels skeletal – whimpering into each other's hair, but then I pull back, holding her at arm's length. 'What the fuck's going on? Why are you down here? Why the hell has Mary done this? Your phone, I found it earlier... and Mary...' I shake my head, remembering. 'I followed her to this random house across town and there was an older woman who looked... and the necklaces and...'

I trail off, suddenly realising the true horror of the situation.

'Oh my God, oh my *God*... my kids are up there with *her*...' My heart thunders at a thousand miles an hour as the reality hits me. 'It's OK, it's OK,' I try to convince myself, clutching at my head as I force myself to get a grip, taking a deep breath. 'It's all going to be OK. Laura is looking after them. As soon as she realises that I never made it to Crawley, she'll raise the alarm. I promised I'd text her when I got there and—'

'*Laura's* here?'

I nod, then say, 'Oh *no*...' My mind races, but the more I try to work out what the hell is going on, the more confusing it becomes. 'Laura said she came because *you* texted her that I needed help,' I explain. 'She said that you were worried about me.'

'But I didn't text her,' Annie says breathlessly, as though it's a struggle for her to talk. 'I've been stuck down here for several weeks... no phone – maybe it's several months, I don't even know. I have no idea when it's day or night. That's why I turn the lights off sometimes – to help me sleep.'

'*Exactly*,' I continue. 'It *wasn't* you texting her. Which means it was someone else using your phone...' I trail off, bracing myself before telling her. 'I found your phone in Tyler's room earlier.'

'*Tyler*?' Annie asks.

'He's Mary's son,' I explain. 'Well, I'm not sure if he is or not. Though... though I don't think it was him doing the messaging.' I shake my head. 'If you met him, you'd know why. The language... it was from a woman.'

Annie seems confused at what I'm telling her, her eyes

empty, while I try to accept the sudden new reality of what's happened – and right under our noses.

'It must have been Mary texting Laura from your phone. *And* me... Jesus Christ, all those messages I sent you questioning Mary's integrity were going directly to *her*.' *No wonder she's locked me down here as well*, I think, but keep quiet about that. 'Mary has engineered this whole thing. But what *is* this whole thing, and *why* is she doing it?'

Annie takes a deep breath, as if she's about to explain everything, but we freeze as the door to the outer chamber of the basement suddenly clicks and then opens – the soundproofing having blocked any warning noises.

'Gina is through this way,' Mary's voice suddenly says as the door swings inwards a couple of feet. 'She was insisting you come down to help her before we left. She seemed so upset. I think she really needs you.'

Then I hear confused mumblings from Laura, which I interrupt by yelling out, 'No! Laura, *no!*' at the top of my voice, lunging towards the open door as soon as I realise what's happening.

Annie is further away than me, so it makes sense for me to take my chances, but before I even make it across the studio, Laura stumbles into the room as if she's been shoved, just like I was, grabbing onto the mixing desk before she trips over. When she straightens up, her face is a picture of horror as she sees me standing there with blood on my forehead. Her eyes flick between Annie and me.

I make a grab for the door while it's still open about a foot – wide enough for me to hear my baby crying upstairs, the sound travelling down the stairwell.

'*Tyler!* Deal with those *bloody* kids once and for all, will you?' Mary yells from just behind the door, her words spurring me on.

But I'm too late. I don't get a strong enough hold, and the

door clunks closed again with a dull thud, followed by the click of it being locked.

'Annie... Oh my God, *Annie!*' Laura cries, grabbing the desk for support. She's gasping for breath as though she's been thrown into freezing water.

I bang on the door with both fists, yelling until my throat hurts. 'Mary... Ma-*ry!* Sto-*op!* Come back! Let us out... *Please,* we can sort this out... Ma-*ry...*'

'Forget it,' Annie says flatly, dropping down onto one of the swivel chairs. 'She can't hear you.'

Laura starts with the questions... ranting and mumbling and whimpering and spouting exactly the same things as I did just ten minutes ago... bordering on the hysterical as she shoves me out of the way, yanking at the door's handle.

'Who in their right mind put the lock on the *outside...*' she spits, swinging round to face Annie. 'What the hell is going on? Why are we even in here?'

'Oh, well excuse me for wanting to protect hundreds of thousands of pounds worth of equipment with a lock,' Annie says, barely looking up.

'Just forget all that,' I say, quietly at first, but when the pair begin to bicker and argue about locks and whose fault this is, I raise my voice. 'I said *forget* it, you two!'

They both pipe down, staring at me.

'All *I* care about is that *you* were supposed to be looking after my kids, Laura, and now you're down here without them.' I'm shaking, spit collecting at the corners of my mouth, hair stuck to my cheeks. 'What do you suggest I do now, eh?' I grab her by the arms.

'But... but Mary told me you needed me down here urgently, that there'd been another call from Matt and that you were in pieces. I was coming to help you.'

I drop my head down, muttering silently under my breath. 'Where are my children, Laura? Where were they when you came down here?' I'm trying so hard not to scream at her.

I imagine Gracie somehow rolling off the edge of the sofa, Tommy trampling wildly around her and hurling his toys overhead. Then, in my crazed mind, I imagine Mary packing up all her stuff and driving off with my children... changing their names, bringing them up as her own, Matt coming back to an empty house, and me never seeing them again and... and...

Suddenly I can't focus. My eyes fill with anger and tears and a rage so deep it cuts through all my senses.

'I *have* to get to my children!' I scream, thumping the door over and over. My knees buckle and, between them, Laura and Annie lower me to the ground as I drop down in a heap, sobbing.

But then I fall silent when I hear Laura say, 'Oh God, Gina... I left them with Tyler...'

FORTY

THE PAST

'I don't like it one bit,' Gina said as she and Annie headed to Matt's party, arms linked. It was pitch dark, the streetlamps casting cones of yellow light as they walked, and Gina wished she'd worn flat shoes. 'Keeping things from Sara – it doesn't feel right. She's our friend.'

The pair had met at the junction by the main road down the hill, with Annie coming straight from the performance at school.

'I *really* don't like it,' she said again, drawing to a halt. She was on the verge of going home.

'Geen, I *need* you here. You're my wing-woman. I've got a good feeling about tonight... You know, with Matt.' Annie nudged Gina, turning to face her. She'd still got some of her stage make-up on but had added her trademark cat-flick eyeliner and blood-red lipstick for the party. She'd changed into her own clothes in the dressing room – a short, black ruffled skirt with tights underneath, an AC/DC T-shirt that she'd hacked into a crop top, along with her faded black denim jacket. And, of course, her favourite Doc Martens. She'd doused herself in a sickly-sweet floral perfume, which Annie loved but Gina thought smelt like the one her mum used.

Gina stared down at the pavement. They were nearly at Matt's house – still time for her to turn and go home, pretend to the others she had a headache. She would just forget her stupid crush on Matt, give up hoping that he was *ever* going to notice her – especially now that Annie's intentions towards him were clear. There's no way she'd be able to compete. It was best she bowed out while she still had a shred of dignity left.

Or... she supposed she could walk up to that front door, go inside, chat with her other friends, have a couple of drinks, a few dances, maybe a snog with a different boy... though she couldn't get out of her head that she'd probably have to watch Annie and Matt doing the same.

'I just think Sara should know about the party, that's all I'm saying,' Gina said as they walked on again. 'She's had a tough year and it'll be horrible for her to hear about it second-hand on Monday. Matt *still* hasn't had the decency to break up with her.'

'You don't *know* that he's not dumped her yet,' Annie replied, sounding as if she knew something Gina didn't. 'And we don't really know if Sara's had a tough year or not because she never confides in us.' They'd reached Matt's house now and stopped outside. The sound of loud music pumped from the house. 'I sometimes wonder if she even wants to be friends with us at all.'

'Jesus, Annie!' Gina snapped. 'If you stopped thinking about yourself for a moment, you might have noticed that things have been really rubbish for Sara lately. She was off school for *weeks* last term and not well over the summer.'

Gina shook her head, on the verge of turning and striding off as she remembered how her mum had tried to phone Sara's mum to see if they could visit her, or even send a get well soon card. But she couldn't get through.

'Look, I think we'd know by now if he'd dumped her,' Gina continued. 'Sara would be in pieces. She'd have phoned one of us for support.'

Annie nodded then shrugged. Matt had told her he was going to break up with her, and whether he had or not was hardly her problem. As far as she was concerned, he was as good as single now and fair game. 'Come on,' she said, grabbing Gina's hand and leading her up to the front door with a grin. 'Don't be a misery guts. Let's go party!'

Sara was in her tiny bedroom, sitting on the bottom bunk, shivering from the cold. Anger simmered inside her. Her hands were clamped over her ears – partly to block out the yelling coming from downstairs, and partly to silence the voices in her head.

But she could still hear both – her father's angry shouts, the occasional dull thud and piercing scream as he lashed out at her mother, and the jeering and cruel laughter of her inner voice telling her that she was a loser, ugly, friendless, fat, disgusting, worthless and deserved to die.

She was on the verge of something – though she wasn't sure what. It could be anger, or it could be fear. She'd learnt there was a thin line between the two.

Sara had gone out looking for Matt earlier, hoping to catch him after the last performance, but no one knew where he was. It seemed he'd disappeared from the dressing room in a hurry, which fitted in with the gossip she'd heard from a few of his friends. Word was that Matt was having a party. A party to which she'd not been invited.

Sara sat on her bed, staring at the peeling wallpaper, clawing at her wrist with her fingernails as she willed herself not to go hunting for a razor blade. She didn't know what to do to make things OK. She felt numb. Abandoned. Worthless and desperate.

Her little sister came into the room they shared, no words needed as she crept up to Sara and curled up on the bottom bunk, burying her face in her lap. Sara wrapped her arms around her shoulders, rocking her gently, wishing she could make everything better.

Stupidly, she'd believed that when she'd started dating Matt, it would mark the end of all her problems... making her feel whole and wanted, eventually leading to a better life for her and her sister away from this hell-hole. But it hadn't. In fact, it had made everything worse.

Their first date was a walk along the prom – hot chocolate and holding hands in a gale – but Matt had spent most of the time asking her questions about Annie. *Which boys does she like at school? When is her birthday? Does she ever talk about me? Who is her favourite band?*

The time after that, they'd met at Davy's to share a cone of chips – with Matt constantly asking if Annie would be there, if she knew her movements, where she'd be later. For the two hours they'd sat there, Matt had been staring out of the window, swinging round to the door every time it opened, looking disappointed when a new customer came in and it wasn't Annie.

She'd gone to Matt's house to study on several occasions, too – including the time when Gina had called round out of the blue, seemingly lurking in the front garden. That was awkward, given she'd not told the other GALS about her few dates with Matt, but Gina had been kind, non-judgemental, and she reckoned she'd kept it a secret. Not that it felt much like she and Matt were dating if she was honest. They'd not made out at the cinema or gone on any picnics or proper romantic walks where they could be totally alone, and she hadn't even had a peck on the cheek yet, let alone a proper kiss. She'd not met his mum and dad either, with Matt sneaking her upstairs the couple of times she'd been round to his.

Then came the blow yesterday at school when one of Matt's mates, Evan, had whispered something in her ear as they'd passed in the corridor – something that made her blood run cold.

'Matt's gonna dump you,' was all he'd said as he'd swept past, his laugh ringing in her ears as he rushed off to his next lesson.

'I hate it here,' Sara's little sister whispered up at her now, her head still in her lap.

'Me too,' Sara replied, stroking her mousy fringe back off her forehead. 'Me too.'

'Dad said they're coming for me later,' she told Sara. Her young eyes were sunken and tired, and the skin on her face was sallow and pale. 'I heard him talking to that man. The one with the moustache.'

It had been going on for as long as they could remember, right back to when they were little – sometimes once a week or, if they were lucky, every few months. It was always one of the same two or three men – *my good friends*, their father said, which, he'd told them, made it OK. On handing over either one of his daughters for a few hours, their father would get paid. The extra cash meant their parents could buy booze and drugs and tobacco. Sometimes they'd even buy food.

Sara knew which man her sister meant – the one whose clothes smelt as if they'd sat in the washing machine too long. The one whose hands were rough and scaly. The one with the beady eyes that burnt their skin when he looked at them naked. Her father said they must do as they were told, that they mustn't cause a fuss, that they must never tell a soul.

The woman from social services had been again recently – it happened every six months or so. During her last visit, their mother had been on her best behaviour, telling her that their father was out looking for work, that her daughters were well fed, clean and going to school happy.

The girls, holding hands, had stood in the doorway, nodding and smiling when the woman asked if this was true. Just as their mother had told them to do. Sara had desperately wanted to say something, to beg her to help them, to take them away, but the stakes were too high, the punishment too severe. And she couldn't risk them being split up in different foster homes. So instead, Sara had given her a lopsided smile that she prayed would be interpreted as anything but happiness.

The social worker, who hadn't even had time to sit down or have a cup of tea, had, after a moment of staring at them, frowned slightly, her lips parting as if she'd been about to speak. But she'd changed her mind and given them a satisfied smile in return, ticked off something on a form, and rushed off to her next case.

'I won't let them take you tonight,' Sara told her little sister now. 'I'll go instead. I'll tell them you've got your first period.' She was resigned to sacrificing herself again – it was what she did. While she wanted to sort things out with Matt, go to his house to find out if he *was* having a party, she couldn't stand the thought of her little sister being taken.

'I'm running away tonight,' her little sister suddenly said, sitting up and staring into Sara's eyes. Her voice sounded too old and weary for a girl who was barely twelve. 'Come with me?'

She'd threatened it before, and had done it once or twice, not getting any further than the bus station with her plastic bag of clothes. Once she was brought home by a cop, another time she was hauled back from the seafront by their father where she'd made a bed on a bench, and the other time she'd come back by herself after a few hours, hungry and cold. But for some reason, this time Sara sensed her little sister meant it. That she was finally leaving for good.

FORTY-ONE

MARY

Despite the fear creeping through me, the terror that I've messed up, got things badly wrong, made everything so much worse for Tyler, I need to stay calm. I'm standing in Annie's kitchen, my fingers knotted together, staring out of the glass doors while trying to work out what to do next.

Fuck...

I claw my fingers down my face. Everything seemed so much easier in my mind when our plans were taking shape months ago, but the reality of achieving them now feels very different. But too many people have got away with too much for too long. It's time to set things straight.

I clench my fists, wishing I was able to erase the past from my mind – that I had no memories to avenge, that I could simply live my life and look after Tyler, set him up for a decent future. I made a promise to his mother, after all. But it doesn't work like that. There's a fire inside me – a burning need to put things straight, to make those guilty finally pay for what they did.

Their suffering will end mine, and if no one confesses, then they will *all* have to die.

I take a sharp breath as the enormity of the situation hits me. I have three women locked up in the basement. Three women whose survival depends on my next move. And not only that but two children to get rid of.

The voice in my head barrages me with endless chatter – *Do it... don't do it... they deserve it... it's not their fault... kill them... let them go...* – until I clamp my hands over my ears and shake my head, screwing up my eyes.

What the hell have I done?

I hear a noise from behind – the soft murmurings of the baby.

'You're a natural,' I say, swinging round to face Tyler, watching as he cradles the baby's head in the nook of his elbow. In a panic, Laura had handed her over to him as I lured her downstairs with the fake emergency. 'But these kids are a problem,' I tell him. 'We can't keep them.'

Tyler looks at me – that empty look in his eyes. He gives me a single nod, telling me he understands what I mean. 'I'll sort the children. Don't worry.'

Then Tommy launches himself at Tyler's legs, waving a picture book up at him. 'Want storwy!' the little boy grizzles. 'Read storwy now!' He's on the verge of what sounds like a tantrum, his cheeks red and his bottom lip quivering. 'Want Mummy,' he adds in a whimper.

'Do what you must with them both,' I tell Tyler. 'There's something I need to do.'

Tyler snatches the book from the toddler – there's a little red fire engine on the cover; a book no doubt bought by Gina to help explain to her son what happened to their house – then Tyler grabs hold of Tommy's wrist. I can't help the smirk as I head to the sliding glass door, closing it softly behind me as I step outside.

The autumn sun slices over the red-brick wall, casting golden shadows as I walk down the garden. I hear Bridget next door snipping her plants. Then, as I approach the end of the garden where the gate leads on to the common, I hear her husband's gruff tones as he says something to her. It's as I'm tugging the gate open that I pause, seeing the spotted cotton handkerchief dropped on the ground – a man's handkerchief, wet and muddy, partly concealed by the grass. A heavy feeling creeps through me like a hand tightening around my neck, its fingers digging into my veins, the pressure slowing my heartbeat as the past reaches into the present.

I force it all from my mind as I go through the gate into the overgrown patch of land, half expecting to see a little girl running across the common in her grubby school skirt, her happy, gleeful giggle heard by no one except me – soon replaced by piercing screams as she cries out for help... followed by silence as her life is snuffed out. This is the soundtrack that has filled my nightmares since the night she didn't come home.

I pick up a fallen stick, using it to beat a path through the nettles and weeds that have sprung up, though I can't help wondering if someone else has been out here since my last visit. There are patches of snapped stems and trodden-down greenery where there weren't before.

Instinctively, I glance back over my shoulder, wondering if I'm being followed – if Gina and her nosy friend have stalked me. But then I remember – they're locked up with Annie. I imagine them frantically trying to work out what's going on, why I've imprisoned them, praying it's a mistake, a misunderstanding, convinced that I'll soon let them out, their voices growing louder as they talk over each other, turning into futile screams and throat-burning yells.

Tyler and I tested out the soundproofing when we first arrived, while Annie was still unconscious.

'My voice sounds most like hers,' I told him. 'Lock me in the basement and see if you can hear me yelling. Then go outside and listen from the street. If you hear anything, record it on your phone.'

I was wary of the ventilation, too, having tried to work out where the shaft exited the house, but I couldn't find it. I didn't want to leave anything to chance with even the slightest sound alerting the postman or people walking past the house or, of course, Gina or her husband when Annie offered – or rather when *I* offered – for them to stay here. They'd taken the bait as I'd hoped.

At the other side of the common, I sit down inside the brick circle, cross-legged beside the old tree stump. 'Hello, Sara,' I whisper, pushing my fingers through the soft earth. In my head, this is where I imagine she lives now. 'I'm trying to do everything right for Tyler, but it's really, *really* hard.'

I choke back the tears, cradling my legs, resting my chin on my knees as I sit on the scrubby grass beside the makeshift grave or shrine or whatever I thought it was when I made it as a child. This place isn't filled with good memories – the opposite, in fact – and I can't even stand to think about the horrors that used to happen here. But I needed somewhere private that wouldn't be disturbed.

When I became Annie's housekeeper, it took me a few days to find the tree stump again, beating a path through the undergrowth as I searched. Apart from being more overgrown, nothing much here has changed. I'm glad I made this little memorial all those years ago – it's all I have left of her now. The photograph of Sara was still here, but the envelope containing the lock of Tyler's baby hair had been nibbled by mice, its contents gone.

I push my hand inside the tree stump to find her picture, familiar with all the gnarly twists and turns within. But when I feel around, I can't find it, so I get to my knees, rooting around inside, cursing when I realise it's gone. I stand up, kicking the ground, betting it was Gina who took it.

'Fucking *bitch*!' I growl, marching back to the house, angry as hell with her – angry as hell with *all* the women locked in the basement. One of them knows what happened all those years ago, and it's time for the truth to come out. I don't care about any money – that would all be for Tyler – but I *do* care about revenge.

One of them is going to pay. One of them is going to die.

I yank open the sliding door to the kitchen, closing it with a bang. I scan around for Tyler, but he is not here. There is no baby, and there is no Tommy, either.

Good. He's doing what I told him to do. Taking care of those brats.

Then I hear a sound coming from the front door – someone letting themselves in.

I freeze, not knowing what to do. My mind racing, I creep into the kitchen area, taking one of the chef's knives from the block, slipping it under my hoodie.

Then, from the hallway, I hear a familiar voice call out, 'Gina? It's me. I'm home! The police let me go.'

Matt is back.

FORTY-TWO

GINA

'You did *what?*' I say when I've taken on board what Laura just told me. 'You left my kids with *Tyler?*' I feel as though I'm about to pass out. I shove one of the swivel chairs hard at the mixing desk to get my anger out, but it tips and drops onto its side with a dull thud. Mary's words echo through my mind... *Deal with those bloody kids once and for all...*

This can't be happening – someone tell me that I'm in a nightmare, that my children aren't with a monster, that I'll wake up any moment. *Dear God, please keep them safe.*

'I didn't exactly have much choice,' Laura says with a wobble in her voice. 'Tommy was fine... I left him playing on the rug. He wanted me to read him a story. And Gracie was on the verge of sleep. Tyler... he seemed happy to hold her. I only thought I'd be down here for a few minutes, for Christ's sake!' Laura covers her face and lets out a pitiful sob. 'Mary told me there'd been some emergency and you needed my help. If you must know, I was going to persuade you to come back upstairs and I was going to suggest that *I* went to fetch Matt.' She's on the edge of tears.

Without saying a word, I stand the chair upright again and

drop down onto it, cradling my head in my hands, elbows on the edge of the mixing desk. A searing pain cuts across my forehead as I dig the heels of my hands against my skull, trying to work out what's happened, how I can get to my kids – rather, *rescue* my kids, because that's what it feels like I need to do.

I whip up my head. 'I didn't think we were going to get locked in a bloody basement with our friend who's meant to be six thousand miles away, did I? I didn't think a lot of things, actually. Did *you*?' I stand up suddenly, squaring up to her, but drop down into the chair again, overwhelmed by the pounding in my head as the pressure shoots down my spine. I feel light-headed and shaky, and my heart is racing, reminding me that I've not had my insulin shot yet today. *Shit*, I think, suddenly realising that my medical kit is in my handbag. The bag that Mary snatched away from me when she shoved me in here.

'You both need to shut up,' comes Annie's voice from where she's slumped down on the floor beside the door. Her legs are drawn up, her feet apart as she stares up at us. 'We need to work together, figure out who the hell this woman is and what she wants.'

'Yes... yes, Annie's right, Gina. We mustn't argue or blame each other or—'

'Wait, you're telling me you don't even have a *clue* who Mary is?' I wheel myself closer to Annie on the chair, looming over her. I daren't stand up, I feel so shaky.

'I don't,' Annie replies.

'She's... she's not your housekeeper then?' Laura says.

Annie gives her a look, her eyelids heavy as she stares up at her, slowly shaking her head. 'Fuck's sake, Laura, keep up.' Then, on all fours, she crawls over to the water cooler in the corner, putting her mouth beneath the tap and turning it on. Water dribbles down her chin as she drinks, while the large plastic container above glugs and gurgles a few times.

'I need some of that,' I say, going over to the half-empty

container. 'I'm really thirsty.' I kneel down and drink from the tap. 'Tell me this isn't all the water we've got.' I wipe my mouth on my arm and sit back down, leaning against the wall again.

'There's a kitchenette through there with a sink and tap,' Annie replies, pointing to another door opposite where we came in. 'She hasn't brought me any food in a while, but maybe she will now you're both here. Who knows?' Annie gives a resigned shrug.

'What about...' Laura looks around the studio, 'the toilet?'

'There's one off the kitchen,' Annie tells us.

'Can you get to the garage through there?' I ask. 'Can we get out that way?' I feel an all-over sweat breaking out – desperately needing my insulin. I've been late with it a couple of times in the past, but there's always been someone on hand to help – Matt, or my mum when I was younger – and I'm never far from my kit. If my blood glucose levels rise too high, it can be extremely dangerous.

Annie gives me the same look she gave Laura. 'Oh, yeah, silly me. I forgot all about the escape route through the fucking garage.' She tips her head back against the wall, her jaw clenched.

'Annie, love, it's OK, we understand your anger. We'd be the same if we'd been stuck down here for so long, too.' Laura gives me a look. 'Geen, are you OK? You don't look well. You're very pale.' She reaches down to touch me, but Annie swings round and snaps, as if she's about to bite her. Laura jumps back.

'I'll be OK,' I say, not wanting to worry her. 'Just in shock.' My stomach twists in knots again as I think about my kids left alone with Tyler and Mary. 'We... we need a plan,' I say, feeling even more light-headed. 'Work out what's going on before Mary comes back. Annie, tell us exactly what happened when you first encountered Mary. Everything leading up to the time when she locked you down here.'

I wipe my sleeve across my face to mop up the sweat, and

Annie stares up at me. She looks so thin I swear I wouldn't have recognised her if she walked past me on the street. But there's also a tinge of something lucid in her eyes. The fire still burning within.

'It started with an advert,' she says. 'I put a notice for a housekeeper on the community board in the local post office. Bridget next door gave me the idea, saying it's how she found her cleaner, Hattie.'

She rests her head back against the wall again, taking a few breaths as if each one is an effort. Laura and I share a quick glance.

'I had a few phone calls and interviewed two applicants, but they were no good. Then Mary applied and I arranged a time for her to come to the house. It's weird, because as soon as I opened the door to her, I swear I recognised her.'

'Where from?' I ask, wanting to know every detail. If nothing else, it keeps me distracted until I can somehow get to my children. I'm not feeling at all well.

'I wasn't sure at first. Mary said that we'd bumped into each other in the post office when I was putting up the notice, but...' Annie trails off, suddenly coughing, holding her stomach. 'But it was more than that. I'd seen her around somewhere else. Maybe even hanging about the square, hidden in the trees. At first, I thought she must live around here but... well, she didn't look the type, if I'm honest. I didn't think much more about it and was just glad to have someone decent apply.'

'What next? You gave her the job?' I ask.

Annie is silent for a moment, her jaw tensing as she thinks back. Then her head starts to shake as she looks up at each of us in turn. 'No. We never got that far.'

'Then what, Annie, for God's sake, *what*?' I drop to my knees beside her, wobbling and feeling woozy as I grab her by the upper arms, giving her a little shake.

'I showed her around the house,' Annie tells us. 'She was

asking all these questions. It felt more like she was interviewing me than the other way around.'

'What sort of questions?' Laura says, joining us on the floor. She takes hold of Annie's hand and strokes it. I take her other one, trying to encourage her.

Annie swallows dryly. 'Stuff about the past – about any boyfriends I'd had, my parents, who my friends were. When I mentioned your names, she was asking about you, too.'

'Did that not ring alarm bells?' I say, trying to keep it together.

'Not particularly. She seemed so... so *normal*. And she had this knack of prising things out of me.'

'Jesus Christ, Annie, and you *still* gave her the job?' I flop back onto my heels, grabbing the chair for support.

But Annie is shaking her head again. 'No, like I said, I never *gave* her the job,' she states quite clearly. 'I'd shown her around the house, and then she asked if she could look down here in the studio. She knew about my work, obviously, and told me she was a budding musician, learning the guitar. We'd been chatting about different bands, musicals and stuff, so it seemed a reasonable enough request.'

'Then what?' I can't believe what I'm hearing – that Annie has been just a few feet below us for the past couple of weeks. A prisoner in her own home while we've been living life above her, oblivious to her presence. It's impossible to believe.

'I was going to offer her the job,' Annie continues. 'I'd already decided that. She seemed... orderly and together. And calm – so calm. Yes, that's it. As if she was super in control of herself and her life. I figured it wouldn't hurt to let her have a look down here, given she'd be cleaning these rooms too.' Annie pauses, scanning around the studio, her eyes heavy and tired. One deck is smashed with wires hanging out all over the place, while several control panels on the wall are in a similar state.

'Especially when she said she liked my music. I was flattered, I guess.'

'Christ, you should have just gone through an agency to get a housekeeper,' Laura pipes up. 'Someone as well-known as you can't just go hiring some random off the street.'

I give Laura a tap on the arm, shaking my head and scowling.

'I know, I *know*...' Annie says, hanging her head. 'But I don't want to be some out-of-touch celeb who doesn't live in the real world. Do you not get it?' Annie has a lump in her throat, her voice sounding tight and on the edge of tears. 'I *hate* being famous.' She lets out a choked sob.

'It's OK,' I say, cradling an arm around her. 'You thought you were doing the right thing. Tell us what happened next.' Laura puts an arm round her too.

But Annie doesn't get a chance to reply because we suddenly hear a noise. Our heads whip round. A clicking sound as the door unlocks – and a second later, it slowly wheezes open.

FORTY-THREE

GINA

Instead of screaming or lunging at the door to attack, for a split second we're all frozen, terrified as the door opens, none of us daring to breathe.

I see her hand first, her fingers creeping round the edge of the door. Then we get a glimpse of her body as she stands sideways, as though she's waiting for someone to pass through.

Now, I'm screaming in my head, willing the words to come out. *Now... Laura, you're closer – grab her! Punch her! Pull her to the ground while I get hold of the door! Anything!*

But Laura and I just crouch there in shock beside Annie on the floor, all of us mute and motionless as Matt strides in, a sheepish grin on his face as he sizes up what's going on. His skin is a sallow grey colour, he has dark circles under his eyes, and his hair is a mess.

'Ladies...' he says, cheerfully at first, though I can tell from his bloodshot eyes that he's expecting a telling-off from me. But as he takes in the scene, a frown pinches his face. 'What are you doing—'

Before he finishes, I force my shaking and sweating body into action, hurling myself past Matt towards the door before it closes, screaming for all I'm worth, praying he'll cotton on and help me.

'Stop her! Stop her! Matt...!'

I grab the edge of the door with my right hand, yanking it back open with all my might – which isn't much, considering how ill I'm feeling. And if the kitchen knife hadn't caught my wrist – Mary jabbing the blade at me with one hand as she pulled back hard on the door – and if Matt had been quicker, we might have stood a chance of overpowering her.

Instead, pain slices up my arm, causing me to let go of the door just as she slams it shut again, trapping my fingers before I yank them out at the last moment. Too stunned to cry out, I watch a thin line of blood seep from my skin. Then I flop down, feeling as if I'm about to pass out.

'Jesus *Christ*, Geen,' I hear Matt say, his arms looping around my waist. Strong arms to hold me up. 'You don't look well. What the fuck's going on?' He shoots a panicked look at Laura and me. 'I just got back, and she told me you were down here fiddling with the electrics, trying to fix the flickering lights, and that I needed to get down here fast before you electrocuted yourself. What's going on?'

Laura quickly unwinds a cotton scarf from her neck and bandages it around my wrist to stem the bleeding. She ties it tightly while I'm staring up at my husband, watching his eyes dart about the studio. His brain is trying to piece everything together, especially since Laura is down here, too. But it's only when he takes a proper look at who's sitting on the floor that he realises the horror of our situation.

'*Annie?*' he says, looking as though he's seen a ghost. 'But I thought you were in...' He trails off, going over to the door, tugging hard on the handle, wiggling it over and over. But it doesn't budge. 'Fuck,' is all he says before leaning against the soundproofed wall and tipping back his head.

. . .

'You didn't come down here to fix the lights then?' Matt says for about the third time.

'Matt...' I say, exasperated and breathless. My vision is starting to go blurry, and I can barely hold my head up. 'No...' I whisper. 'My... my insulin. It's upstairs... and the kids...'

'But Mary said—'

'Forget what Mary said,' I tell him. 'It's all been a lie. She's not Annie's housekeeper and she's certainly not our friend.' I clutch at my head with a trembling hand. 'Did... did you see the kids?' I ask him. 'Were they OK? What the fuck's going on up there? Have you got your phone on you? Did she say anything to you? Why were you arrested?' I have so many questions, but it takes all my effort to speak.

'Whoa, calm down, love,' Matt says, taking hold of my hands. I can tell his brain is processing things slowly after too much alcohol and no sleep last night. 'I didn't see the kids, no. Are they OK?'

'I don't *know*, that's the whole bloody point of me asking *you*!' I snap back, feeling frantic with worry. 'Laura left them with Tyler. Is he not in the house with them? Mary spun her some bullshit to get her down here, too, and now we're *all* locked in!' I can't help the sobs, but they're not for me. They're for my children.

'OK, OK, I'll get us out,' Matt says, suddenly sounding in control. Out of habit, he pats the back pocket of his jeans. '*Shit*. My phone... it's on the hall table. I left it there with my keys when I came in.' He closes his eyes for a moment, taking a deep breath. 'I saw an electronic keypad on the outside of the door,' he says to Annie, rattling the handle again. 'Which electrical circuit is it connected to? Is the consumer unit in here?'

Annie stares up at him blankly. 'Forget it,' she tells him. 'She must have overridden the keypad and is using the manual key. There's some kind of electrical unit at the bottom of the stairwell, but it's the other side of this door,' she says, sounding as if she's given up all hope of ever getting out. 'It controls the entire house. I've had problems with the damn thing from the start. If I had too much equipment running at the same time down here, the lights would flicker up in the new extension,' she tells us. 'Since Mary locked me down here, I've been turning everything on – all the decks, all the equipment, including my instruments, trying to overload the system and make the lights in the house flicker. Then I tried to short everything out by ripping out some of the wires and reconnecting them.'

I feel a chill creeping over my skin as Matt and I share a glance. 'Jesus, Annie, that was *you*?'

'Did it work? Did the lights go on and off?'

I nod, feeling terrible that we didn't investigate the problem further. 'Oh, *Annie*...' I say, unable to imagine how hard it has been for her locked down here all alone.

'I kept turning the water on and off, too. Another cock-up by the builders. Whenever the tap down here is running, the kitchen tap pressure drops. I was trying to remember Morse code for SOS but couldn't, so I just turned it on and off in a set pattern every so often in the hope that it would get noticed.'

'Oh, it got noticed,' Matt confirms, dropping down into one of the swivel chairs. 'We just thought it was an annoying plumbing quirk.'

'How long have you been down here?' Laura asks, unzipping her hoodie. It's getting hot and airless in the small space.

'I don't know,' Annie replies. 'It seems like weeks. When I brought Mary down here, we spent a while talking about the equipment, how the recording booth works.' She points through the small window to the other room. 'She seemed particularly interested in the soundproofing.'

'She had it all planned out, didn't she?' I say, racking my brains as to why she wants us all down here, but my thoughts are fuzzy and confused.

Annie nods, confirming my fears. 'When she locked me

down here – it all happened so fast. At first, I didn't realise what she'd done. One minute she was behind me peering over my shoulder as I explained the equipment to her, then she disappeared. I got distracted in the recording booth, then when I came back in here to find her, the exit door was locked. Normally I can open it from the inside, but there's also another lock that needs a key. I started looking for my fob – the master set for the whole house – but quickly realised it was gone. I swear I left it on the corner of the desk here.'

'Jesus Christ,' Matt says, blowing out through his teeth. 'Tell me I'll wake up back in the police cell any moment.'

'Yes, about that...' I say, not even wanting to hear his excuses right now.

'I'm innocent, just so you know,' Matt says, holding up his hands. 'I nursed two pints the entire evening. Evan, however, went over the top as usual and got himself into a fight with a group of lads, so I went to his defence. The police came and scooped the lot of us up.'

I want to take Matt's hand, to give it a squeeze and console him, but I don't have the energy. Whatever happened last night will have to wait.

'When did you interview Mary for the job?' Laura asks Annie. 'Can you remember the date?'

'Towards the end of August. Perhaps the twenty-eighth? I'm not sure exactly.'

'It's the twenty-second of September today,' Laura continues. 'Gina, when did you hear from Annie about coming to stay here – well, *Mary* as we now know it was.'

'Check your phone for the date,' Matt suggests.

'I don't *have* my phone,' I say, glancing at my husband. 'And neither does Laura. You don't think we'd have thought to use them before now? When Mary shoved me in here, she grabbed my bag. It's got my insulin in it and... I don't want to worry you guys, but I really, *really* need my medication.' I take a few deep breaths, trying to calm my racing heart. 'From memory, I think I got the text at the very end of August, perhaps the start of September. We'd been staying in the hotel a week, maybe ten days.'

'Even if you had your phones, there's no reception down here anyway,' Annie says. 'And you can bet she turned off the studio Wi-Fi. It's on a separate system to the rest of the house and easy to do.'

'Of *course* it bloody is,' Laura says, scuffing at the floor with her foot because, apart from one of us, there's nothing much else to kick.

'The fire...' I whisper, thinking back. 'Matt, do you think Mary *knew* about it? Maybe she saw the piece in the local paper and realised we'd need somewhere to stay.' I daren't even bring myself to think that it was all a set-up, that she knew exactly what had happened to us and took advantage of our situation.

I see Matt's mouth open as he's about to reply, but he doesn't get a chance because we're suddenly plunged into darkness as the lights go out.

FORTY-FOUR

THE PAST

'Someone needs to dim the lights,' Annie said, nudging Gina as they walked into the living room, weaving their way through everyone at the party 'It's too bright. No atmosphere.'

Gina looked about to see if she could spot Matt. There were more people at the party than she'd reckoned, with some hanging out in the kitchen. She'd only been inside Matt's house once before for his New Year's Eve party, and she thought it looked homely and beige. Something her mum would like.

'Anyone got more beer?' someone called out – a lad Gina recognised from the year above. He was decent enough looking, she thought, giving him the eye as Annie led her by the hand towards the kitchen. He gave her a smile back just as Annie flicked off the lights, leaving only a couple of table lamps for illumination. A few voices whooped above the music and a couple of girls started dancing.

'Jesus, where's all the booze?' Annie asked as she scanned the kitchen worktop, elbowing her way between two girls from their year as she inspected a bottle of vodka. There was only an inch or two of it left, so she divided it between two paper cups and sloshed in some Coke on top, handing one to Gina.

'Matt's gone to get supplies from the offy,' a voice behind them said. Gina felt a hand on her waist and turned to see Evan leering at them. His cheeks were flushed, his eyes glassy and staring as he slung his other arm around Annie. 'Expect things to get lively very soon,' he beamed. 'Meantime...' He tapped his top pocket. 'I've got something to spice things up if you fancy it.' He pulled out a tiny plastic baggie with some white powder inside.

'Fuck off, Evan,' Annie said, her eyes whipping about the kitchen.

Gina was shocked but secretly proud of her friend. She didn't like Evan and liked him even less now that he'd just offered them drugs. She'd barely ever touched alcohol before, let alone anything like that. She sidled away from Evan's sweaty hand, which was still sitting on the small of her back, and watched as Annie's eyes darted everywhere at once. She was also on the lookout for Matt.

'C'mon, Geen,' Annie said, leading her back into the living room. 'I'm gonna get so shitfaced tonight,' she whispered in Gina's ear when they were away from Evan. She grinned, bobbing her head to the music, closing her eyes and swaying to the beat. 'Let me know if you see Matt,' she said, her eyes still closed.

'I will,' Gina replied, shouting above the noise. 'I'll keep an eye out for Sara, too,' she added, wondering if Matt had gone to her house to do the right thing while he was out. Gina was concerned that if Sara turned up here, it would be either because she'd heard about the party and was coming to have it out with Matt, or that she'd taken the break-up badly and wanted to give him a piece of her mind. Either way, it wouldn't be good. Gina didn't plan on drinking much. She wanted to be sober in case Sara needed her.

'Y'all right, girls,' that boy who Gina had smiled at on the way in said to them both as he sidled over with his mate. Gina was about to introduce herself, but he turned to Annie. 'You were awesome in the play,' he said, shuffling closer. His not so good-looking mate stood beside Gina. She felt his breath on her cheek as he said something to her, but she ignored him while Annie flirted with the other guy.

'Want some of this?' Gina heard him say to Annie. The lad, who'd introduced himself as Gaz, pulled out a small bottle of something green from under his denim jacket, giving Annie a wink. He drizzled the liquid into her paper cup before holding the bottle up to Gina.

Gina shook her head, scowling. 'What is it?' she whispered to Annie.

'No idea, but if it helps me get shitfaced, I'm in.' Her laugh was shrill.

While Annie chatted with Gaz, the pair of them eventually peeling away to dance, Gina finished her drink, making the bare minimum of chit-chat with Gaz's friend before telling him she'd see him around and heading upstairs to find the toilet.

The bathroom was empty, so she locked the door behind her, shutting out the din of the party, and went to sit on the toilet lid. She opened her small shoulder bag and took out a couple of medical items from the kit she always carried, laying them on her knee before testing then injecting herself with insulin. Having been diagnosed aged eleven, she was used to doing it now.

Afterwards, she cradled her head in her hands. They'd only been here half an hour and she was already wishing she hadn't come. She could have stayed home, perhaps given Sara a call to see how she was – not that anyone ever picked up the phone at her house – or just sat with her mum and dad and watched a rerun of *Family Fortunes* on the telly. They loved that show.

But no. Here she was at Matt's house, perched on the lid of his toilet without even having set eyes on him yet, and worried sick about her friend. Something wasn't right with Sara these days, and she didn't just mean her relationship with Matt. She'd mentioned her concerns to Laura a couple of times this term, who, in practical mode as ever, had suggested Gina tell the school nurse. She'd thought this a sensible idea, but when she'd got to her office, she'd been issued with a stern 'mind your own business' and a hard stare, which had sent her scuttling back to her classroom for afternoon lessons.

Someone wiggled the bathroom doorknob, then banged impatiently. 'Anyone in there?' a voice called out.

'Just a minute,' Gina replied, standing up and flushing the loo, even though she hadn't used it.

She let the basin tap run for a few moments, looking at herself in the bathroom cabinet mirror, wincing at her reflection. She'd thought she looked nice when she'd got ready at home earlier, but here, in the harsh fluorescent light, her make-up appeared thick and cakey, her black lashes clumped together.

She broke off several bits of toilet paper and wiped away her lipstick, thinking it looked cheap and vampy. Who was she trying to kid? Matt wasn't going to notice her, not when Annie was here. Anyway, Matt wasn't even at his own party yet, which gave her another reason to go home.

As she unlocked the bathroom door, she made a pact with herself. If Annie was too busy with that other boy, and if Matt wasn't back from the off-licence yet, then she was going home. This party couldn't get any lamer.

Matt walked slowly down the hill towards the off-licence, dragging his heels. He'd made up his mind how he was going to deal with Sara tonight.

Avoid her. Do absolutely nothing.

Some would say it was cowardly, but he'd been waiting for tonight too long to risk ruining his chances with Annie.

He *had* to let her know how he felt.

His pace picked up as he walked, the wodge of cash in his pocket burning more of a guilty hole in him than his decision about Sara. His mum would have a fit when she found out the money was missing, and his dad... that didn't bear thinking about. But they wouldn't be able to prove it was him who'd taken it, and by the time they returned home, the party would be long cleaned up. All evidence erased.

Matt looked at his watch. He should hurry. Annie and her friends would be at his place soon. When he reached the cross-roads, he hesitated, deciding to take the short cut through the land behind the big houses on Wessex Square. It would shave a good ten minutes off his walk, giving him an extra twenty minutes of Annie time, he reasoned, darting over the road.

The road leading into the square was deserted with only a couple of streetlights illuminating the grand houses, one of which had been derelict for years. He knew this was the route Annie and her friends sometimes took to get down to the seafront, and that their parents had strictly warned them off the short cut he was about to take. Being a guy, he figured it was different. If anyone saw him, they'd not pay him any attention or give him any hassle.

Matt cut across the green area at the centre of Wessex Square, veering off down the narrow road that led around the backs of the houses on the west side. For some reason, there were no streetlights down this section of road, and it felt creepy and desolate, having a bad reputation for attracting sex workers and drug dealers. But tonight, there was no one about, with just the overflowing dustbins lining the way. Then up ahead, Matt swore he saw the flash of a pair of fox's eyes, though it was diffi-cult to tell in the dark.

He glanced back over his shoulder as he ducked down the alley leading to the common, pausing a moment when he thought he heard footsteps behind him. He must have been mistaken, knowing that if he turned back now, it would take even longer to get to the shop. He decided to press on, even if it meant coming back the long way.

Matt stifled a yelp when the man stepped out in front of him, zipping up his trousers and glaring out from beneath a dishevelled mop of hair as he ducked out of a narrow, litter-filled gateway. The whole area stank of urine as Matt quickly walked on.

Shit... shit... shit... he thought but kept his head down, shoving his hands in his pockets as he continued, his fingers curling around the cash. When he next looked up, the man was gone. He just had to get to the entrance to the common and then dart across it. After that, once he emerged on the other side, he'd almost be at the shop.

Matt suddenly stopped in his tracks when he heard what sounded like a scream. A shrill but brief screech cutting through the night air.

'It's just a fox,' he muttered, having heard their haunting cries before. He carried on walking.

There. Again. Another cry... *Was* it a fox?

Of course *it's a fox*, he convinced himself, continuing on. He just wanted to get back to the party and celebrate the end of show week – and hopefully the start of something good with Annie. *At least this will make a good story for the others later*, he laughed to himself, straining up ahead to see where the alley turn-off was.

This time, it wasn't a scream or a fox that made him come to an abrupt halt. It was a person. A girl – loitering up ahead.

'Shit,' he cursed under his breath, immediately recognising her – the only girl in the entire world he didn't want to see right now.

Sara.

What the fuck is she doing alone out here at night? he wondered, slamming himself flat against the brick wall of the alley, praying that she was going to veer off into the common and wouldn't have to walk past him. If he waited for her to go, he could carry on at a distance behind her, avoiding seeing her.

Then the blasted fox shrieked again – it *was* a fox, wasn't it? – though it sounded more distant this time, muffled and even more human-like. Matt held his breath, slowly turning his head sideways to try and see what was going on, waiting for the figure lurking up ahead to finally disappear.

But wait... was that someone *else* with Sara now? It was hard to get a decent view and it was almost pitch dark... Yes, someone else was there – a man, much taller than Sara, though he couldn't see her properly now. It wasn't the man he'd just seen urinating. Matt flattened himself against the wall again, not daring to breathe, waiting, waiting, waiting for what seemed like an age.

It was the loudest and most piercing scream yet that flushed him out of the alley, chilling him to his bones as it seared through his head.

He didn't care if she saw him now – he'd say a quick hello and walk on. He just wanted out of this godforsaken area and to get to the off-licence. It was the next blood-curdling scream as he ran into the common – faced with the expanse of overgrown weeds, a rough path trampled through the middle – that made him cover his ears with both hands. There was no sign of anyone here, at least.

Picking up his pace, he fixed his sights on the lights just visible on the street the other side of the common – the row of shops where the offy was located. But then something caught his eye – something over to his left, towards the back of the big old townhouses on Wessex Square, behind the abandoned house on the corner. Was that something moving in the under-growth? No – it was doing more than moving. It was thrashing.

He stopped and stared, squinting into the darkness, unable

to believe what he was seeing. A girl's arm flailing. The arch of a man's back as he crouched over something. Some*one*.

Matt felt the swell of saliva collecting in his mouth as the nausea inside him rose. No, he was wrong. He was mistaken. *Surely*, he was seeing things. His breathing quickened as he convinced himself it was nothing – nothing untoward going on at all. There was no one there...

Matt began to run, ignoring another chilling scream – a scream that had the potential to haunt him for the rest of his life.

He gave a quick glance to his left as he hurtled past whatever was over there, about twenty feet away in the shadows of the abandoned house and... and Jesus Christ, it *was* her...

He saw her... *Sara*... and she'd seen him, too.

Their eyes met... locked together for a second as he hesitated, almost stopped. Hers were pleading, bloodshot, terrified. His were wide and disbelieving. She was on the ground... writhing. Screaming. Pleading. Her hand reaching out.

'Fuck, fuck, fuck, keep running...'

Matt panted out the words over and over in time with his breathing as his legs kicked off again.

'Just run, run, run...'

It seemed like ten miles, but a few minutes later he stumbled out of the common and over the zebra crossing towards the brightly lit shop. He stood on the pavement a few feet away outside, hands on knees, head down, screwing up his eyes and praying like he'd never prayed before that what he'd just heard was only a fox, and what he'd seen was a figment of his imagination. The stuff of nightmares. He cupped his hand over his mouth trying to stop it, but the puke came up anyway, splattering down his jeans and onto the ground.

FORTY-FIVE

GINA

'Stay calm, stay calm...' Matt's deep voice says through the darkness, though I hear the panic behind his words. His fear of small spaces, especially in the dark, is being put to the test.

'Jesus Christ,' I hear Annie say, followed by the deadened thump of a fist on a wall. 'She's taking the fucking piss now.'

'It might not be Mary,' Laura pipes up. 'It could just be a power cut. The lights will probably come back on in a few minutes.'

'Wake up, Laura,' Annie snaps. 'Of *course* it's not a power cut. The bitch has done it on purpose. Which means she's just outside the door here because that's where the consumer unit is. She'll have flicked a switch to knock out the lighting circuit for this level.'

In the blackness, I focus on my breathing, forcing myself to stay calm even though every cell in my body is shaking and buzzing. My ears are ringing and my head pounding. And now I'm getting griping abdominal pains – a sure sign that things aren't right. Then, nearby, I hear a noise – something scuffing, a chair dragging, a grunt and groan. It sounds like Annie is getting to her feet.

'I know you're out there, bitch!' she yells from over by the door. 'And I know what you're doing.' Then there's more thumping as she pounds on it.

'She's not going to hear you, Annie,' I remind her just as something hits my leg. '*Oww!*'

'What's happening?' Matt says from over to my right, his voice filled with fear. My eyes grow saucer-wide, hoping to pick up the tiniest dots of light. But there's nothing. It's totally black. Totally terrifying. This must be what it feels like to be blind.

'I'm OK,' I reply to Matt, knowing Annie must have kicked something, which then hit me – the metal wastebin, I think. I shove it back under the desk.

'Mary is trying to scare us, to get us to argue among ourselves,' Laura says through the blackness that seems to be swallowing us all up.

'But *why?*' I ask whoever will answer, but I have a creeping sense that it's not a coincidence that Mary has locked all three of us up together.

'Because she's a fucking psycho, that's why,' Annie says, bumping into me as she tries to find the swivel chair. I feel around, steadying it while she sits down.

'She wants something,' Laura says, trying to reason it out. 'And it's either going to be something *one* of us has, or something we *all* have collectively. By "we", I mean Annie, Gina and me. Matt, I think you're collateral here. In the wrong place at the wrong time.'

'I know it's wrong to wish I was back in the police cell,' he pipes up, 'but I wish I was back in the police cell.'

'Jesus, I just want to get to my kids,' I sob, doubling up with physical pain at the thought of them up there with Tyler – or possibly worse, not being looked after at all. I take a breath, trying to stay calm as my heart pounds, making me feel sick. I'm no good to anyone in a panic, and I'm certain my blood ketone levels are rising, putting me in grave danger of diabetic ketoacidosis. But I can't focus on that now. 'You thought she might be after something that *one* of us has,' I say, thinking Laura's logic makes sense, 'but why lock us *all* up, if that's the case?'

Silence as we think.

'Because she doesn't know which one of us has whatever it is she wants?' Laura suggests.

'That makes sense. But if it's Gina who has it, then it's not money,' Matt gets in first.

'And if it's money she wants, then there'd be no need to lock up Gina *or* me,' Laura says. 'She'd go straight to Annie for that.'

'I'm asset-rich at the moment,' Annie says seriously. 'If it's cash she's after, there's not much of that. I spent most of what I had on this place and the renovations.'

'Mary wouldn't necessarily know that, though, would she?' Matt says. 'I need some water. My head is pounding.'

'Would you get me some, too?' I ask him. My mouth is rasping and dry – another common symptom, but I keep quiet, not wanting to worry the others. Matt knows how serious it is if I don't get my medication, though he doesn't seem to have fully caught on to how fast I'm going downhill.

'There aren't any paper cups left for the cooler,' Annie tells him. 'Go through the door on the opposite wall and there's a kitchen area with a sink and a tap. There are glasses on the draining board.'

I take Matt's hand and guide him past me, remembering how much of a gap there is between me and the mixing deck. 'Here,' I say, putting his hand on the doorknob. 'Through that way.'

'Go forward about three paces and the sink is directly opposite,' Annie tells him. When he's gone, the rest of us fall silent, though our thoughts are loud.

Sara...

'Is anyone thinking what I'm thinking?' Laura eventually says.

We hear the tap running behind the semi-open door.

'Yes,' Annie and I both whisper in unison.

'What else do us three have in common apart from... *that*?' I say, stating the obvious.

'School?' Laura suggests. 'And friendship.'

'Which still leads back to...' I trail off.

'But who the fuck *is* she? And why now, after all this time?' Annie says in a strained whisper.

'Maybe there's no logic to it,' I suggest. 'Maybe it's nothing to do with...' I fall short of saying her name when I hear the tap stop running and Matt comes back into the small room. 'Maybe it's totally random and Mary's simply a psycho who took a shine to Annie's big house.'

'Or a crazy fan?' Laura suggests. 'Has anyone stalked or harassed you lately, Annie?'

'Oh, great,' I hear Matt say before Annie gets a chance to answer. 'So while Mad Mary is living up there in psycholand, we're all stuck down here until...' He trails off, not wanting to say what we're all thinking. Instead, he feels around for my hand, wrapping my fingers around the cup. I drink greedily, knowing it won't be enough.

'Jesus, Matt, we *have* to get out. Our kids are up there,' I say, wiping my mouth, barely able to keep myself upright. I reach out to find Matt in the darkness, pressing myself up against his chest. He cradles my head.

'What's that smell?' he says a second or two after we hear a *tss-tss* sound.

I sniff the air, hoping the smell they're picking up on isn't coming from me. I've only come close to DKA once before and it was caught early, but I remember the doctor commenting on signs to watch out for. Sweet-smelling breath was one of them.

'Perfume,' Annie's voice says in the darkness. 'Last few squirts of it. Anyone want some?'

'What... *why?*' Matt asks, incredulous. 'How can you think of perfume at a time like this?'

'Because there's nothing else I can do right now!' she snaps angrily. 'I always keep a bottle down here... to spritz on myself to freshen up when I'm working. Gina knows the scent... it's the one I always wore from way back. I have loads of the stuff upstairs.'

'Oh my *God...*' I say, my fuzzy brain remembering. 'I smelt it on the front steps when Laura arrived,' I tell her. 'It's called... Flora or Floristique or something.'

'Florista,' Annie reminds me. 'So *that's* where the ventilation shaft comes out then. I sprayed most of the bottle into the air-conditioning duct to see if anyone picked up on the smell. The rest of it I've used to spray on myself because, after a couple of weeks down here, I stink.'

'Oh, Annie,' I say, wishing to God I'd noticed the signs. 'I'm so sorry I didn't do anything... But it did make me pause and think. I was reminded of our school days. It took me back to...'

'To the night of my party,' Matt chips in. 'After our show. You were wearing that perfume then, Annie.'

'*What?*' I say, unable to help the indignation in my voice. I clutch my stomach, grimacing through another wave of pain. 'You actually remember what *perfume* Annie was wearing that night?'

Silence for a moment, apart from the sound of Matt clearing his throat. 'Smells are evocative.' He clears his throat again, but it turns into a cough. 'Jeez, I don't feel too good, Gina,' he says, probably an attempt to hide his guilt.

'Sit down on the floor,' I say, ignoring my own pain. 'You're in shock.' I slide my hand down his arm and guide him over to the wall behind me. 'There's a spot there. It might be a bit cooler on the floor, too. It's getting so hot in here.'

'If it's any consolation, if I'm not home by tomorrow evening, Pat's going to flip his shit,' Laura says. 'For once, him being a controlling arse is a good thing. When he can't reach me, he'll know something's off. He'll be straight onto the police.' We all consider the implications of this. 'What else do you remember from the night of the party?' Laura says, sounding businesslike again.

'Why are you grilling *me*?' Matt asks.

'I was asking *anyone*,' Laura retorts. 'I'm trying to find a reason why we're all here. 'If it's to do with something in our pasts, then that night is as good a place as any to start. Unless you can think of another time when a friend of ours was murdered.'

'You don't know that she was murdered,' Matt says from down on the floor. 'They never found her body.'

'Missing presumed dead, then,' Annie states with an impatient sigh. 'The story was in the local papers almost seven years to the day after she disappeared. I was living in London when Mum sent me a newspaper clipping about how Sara's parents applied to the courts to have her death registered. It was disgusting to read. They were milking the story, trying to get on TV and all sorts. Nothing much came of it though, apart from highlighting what terrible parents Sara had. Her mother looked half-cut and her father has been in and out of prison.'

'I think we can safely say poor Sara never got to see the sun rise the morning after your party, Matt,' Laura says. 'Plus, it's most definitely *not* a coincidence that Mary recently visited a house on the street where Sara used to live.'

I quickly explain how I'd followed Mary the other day, then Laura and I went back to see who lived there, describing the gruff woman we encountered.

'She sounds exactly like Sara's mother in the newspaper clipping, right down to the fag hanging out of her mouth in her photo,' Annie replies.

'Sara had a younger sister, didn't she?' I ask. 'Does anyone remember much about her?' My thoughts are too fuzzy for me to recall details.

We're all silent again, thinking back, each lost in our own memories of Sara, our own version of the events of that night. How little we knew of her and the troubles she suffered at home. She must have felt so sidelined, so on the edge of our friendship group, so grateful for any crumbs of companionship we offered.

'She did have a sister, yes,' Matt says sheepishly, his voice quiet in the dark – probably because we all know he wasn't serious about dating her, that he was just leading her on, breaking her heart. Looking back, it all seems so fleeting – just a few weeks out of our lives – yet it cost one of us her *entire* life.

'A *younger* sister,' he adds slowly, and I get the sense there's something else on his mind.

'What was she called?' Laura asks. 'Do you remember?'

We're all silent, the only sound an annoying *tap-tap-tapping* coming from where Matt is sitting on the floor. I think it's his leg jiggling about, like he does when he's nervous.

'I do,' my husband says quietly before taking a deep breath. 'Sara told me that her name was Mary.'

FORTY-SIX
GINA

'I mean... it's a common enough name,' Matt says, breaking the silence. 'When Gina first mentioned what Annie's housekeeper was called, it didn't even register as a name from the past... I thought nothing of it. There are two Marys in my office alone, for God's sake.' His voice seems to go up a couple of pitches.

'One of Tommy's little friends at playgroup is called Mary-Ann,' I chip in, blindly defending Matt. There's no way he could have made the connection, not after all this time, and especially when none of us knew Sara's little sister.

'I only met her once when I was dating—' Matt stops, draws in a sharp breath. 'This isn't easy for me to talk about, OK? And I'm not proud of the way I behaved back then. I should have known better.' He clears his throat. 'I never meant to upset Sara.'

'Matt, mate, plenty of time for absolution when we're out of here,' Annie says sourly. 'Tell us what you know about her little sister, because I'm already pretty fucking convinced that she's the one who's locked us down here.'

'Like I said, she was younger than Sara,' Matt continues. 'But it was hard to tell. Both those girls were so... I dunno, they seemed so neglected. Pasty and thin. Uncared for. And there was a naivety about them, but also...' Matt groans and I imagine him pulling his knees up, resting his forehead on them. 'And just so you all know, Sara and I... we never... It wasn't like that.'

'We don't need to know your sexual history in detail, for God's sake, Matt.'

'Annie, *stop* it,' I tell her. 'And we don't need you chipping away at everyone. We have to work together here, or—'

'*Oww!*' someone yells – Laura. 'What the fuck? Who threw that?'

'I didn't mean for it to hit anyone,' Annie growls. 'It was just my shoe. I'm pissed off.'

'Just stop it, OK?' Matt says loudly. 'We need to figure out what's going on so next time that psycho bitch comes down here we can negotiate with her, perhaps tap into her vulnerable side.'

'Matt's right,' I say. 'Annie, just hear him out.'

'This one time, Sara and I went for a walk along the prom,' Matt says. 'It was a Saturday morning and really windy. Annie, we happened to bump into you, do you remember?'

'No... no, not really. But I do remember crossing paths with you in Davy's Chippy a couple of times when you were out with Sara. You sat there gawping at me most of the time.'

'Get on with it, Matt,' Laura says.

'After we'd had a quick chat with Annie on the prom, Sara spotted her sister down on the beach. She was standing at the shore, staring out to sea. The funny thing was, she was wearing regular shoes, but the water was lapping around her feet and ankles. She must have been soaked, and there was an icy wind.'

'Was she alone?' I ask, silently doubling up in the dark as another wave of pain hits me. I've never gone this long without my insulin before.

'No. That's the thing. There was a man with her. Mary was a skinny little thing like her sister, and this man seemed three times her size. A big looming shadow beside her. His arm was around her shoulders, I remember that.'

'Then what?' I ask.

'I just remember Sara saying, "Oh no," in a really worried voice before rushing off down to the beach, her arms flying. I decided to keep out of it and watched from up on the prom. It looked as though Sara gave this bloke a stern telling-off. She was waving her arms about, yelling at him – though I couldn't hear what she was saying. At one point, she shoved him away from her sister.'

'And you didn't go to help them?' Annie asks, making a *pftt* sound.

'Leave it, Annie,' I warn, though I was thinking the same myself.

Matt continues, 'Eventually, the man limped off, hands shoved in his pockets, head down. I didn't really get much of a look at him, but he was probably in his fifties, though it was hard to tell his age. He didn't look like he had any business being with a young girl.'

'I don't see how a trip down memory lane is helping us now,' Annie says.

'It's the only contact any of us has ever had with Sara's little sister, if our theory is right and that's who Mary is,' I say. 'So I suggest we listen to Matt for a moment. Go on, love,' I add.

'Sara led Mary back up to the promenade. She kept looking back over her shoulder to make sure that bloke wasn't following them. But he'd gone off in the other direction.'

'When was this?' Laura asks.

'Not long before the show started and I had the party,' Matt says. 'Probably a couple of weeks before.'

'Did Sara tell you who the man was? Did Mary say anything to you? What was she like? Did she look like house-keeper Mary?' I ask Matt, tripping over my words.

'Sara acted casual about it, telling me that the man had been bothering Mary,' Matt replies. 'But then Mary said something in a low voice to her sister. It was clear they were worried their dad would be angry because Sara had chased the man off, that they'd both get a good...' Matt hesitates. 'I'm pretty sure she said a good beating, but she also mentioned something about money.'

We're all silent a moment as we absorb what that might mean.

'As for what Mary looked like, I honestly can't remember,' Matt continues. 'She was one of those people who was easily forgettable, if I'm honest. A bit like Sara – sort of mouselike and insignificant.'

Suddenly there's a thwacking sound then Matt yells loudly.

'*Oiii*... I know, I *know*... I deserved that. But I'm just trying to be honest here. Help us build a picture.'

'The only picture I'm building is that you were an A-grade arsehole, Matthew Dalton,' Annie says.

'Stop it, the pair of you,' I say, racking my aching brains to remember anything useful. I've never had a headache like this before. It's making me want to throw up. 'I feel wretched that we never knew much about Sara's life outside of school. What I do know is that she had a heart of gold and would do anything for anyone.'

I recall the time she waited with me in the playground when I'd forgotten to bring my insulin to school. She met my mum at the school gates when she came with my kit, refusing to leave my side until I could inject.

I hug my arms around myself, suddenly feeling chilled, even though I'm sweating and it's muggy and airless in the studio.

'And I hate it that we've barely spoken about her since... since she died,' I say, trying to hide how breathless I am. 'It's like we all just pretended she never existed.'

'To ease a few guilty consciences, I suspect,' Laura mumbles.

More silence as we take in the enormity of our selfishness – how, collectively, our actions led to Sara losing her life with no one checking where she was, how she was feeling, if she was OK. And now it feels like we're about to lose *our* lives.

'What do you suggest we should have done then, Gina?' Annie shoots at me through the darkness. 'Go on, if you're such an expert, *you* tell us.'

'We should have told Sara about the party, for a start,' I say weakly. 'Instead of her finding out about it second-hand. And also...' *Dammit.* I can't say it. It's on the tip of my tongue, but the words won't come out.

When I met Matt again a few years after we'd left school – the others having gone through university while I'd worked low-pay jobs, either living at home or flat-sharing in dumps with people I didn't know – it felt like a different Matt I was meeting. And I was a totally different person by then, too – the hard knocks of life having shaved off my innocence. Sara's death was why I'd left school at sixteen, much to my parents' dismay. Failed apprenticeships led to dead-end jobs led to months on benefits. It was official. I was a loser. But it was still better than being dead.

'Matt, you should have broken up with her,' I blurt out, feeling even more light-headed. 'You took the coward's way out. Perhaps if you'd done the right thing, Sara wouldn't have been out that night – or maybe she'd have been having fun with us. And... and she'd still be alive today.'

There. I said it. I feel sick. *More* sick.

'And we wouldn't be stuck down here,' Annie adds.

'Wait, *Geen...* Christ, it wasn't like that. *Nooo...* c'mon,' Matt says, his voice sounding choked and indignant. 'We weren't even really dating. Not properly.' He lets out a nervous laugh. 'If anything, it was *you* who should have said something to her. You were her best friend.'

'Jesus, Matt,' I spit back, even though it takes all my effort. 'She was besotted with you, you bloody idiot.'

I'm reeling for having spoken out against my husband. I feel terrible, a traitor – but it needed to be said. I've been stewing on it all these years. Then the tears come hot and fast – I can't help it. They're for Sara and for my poor babies upstairs – and for me as I feel my body fading. An arm slides around me, but it doesn't feel like Matt's – it's thinner and lighter than his. When I lean against the body it's attached to, I smell Annie's perfume as she lets me sob against her shoulder.

FORTY-SEVEN

MARY

Once I'd got Matt locked up with the three women, I couldn't see or hear what was going on behind the soundproofed door, what they might be plotting or thinking. I'd sat on the basement steps leading back up to the hallway feeling drained and scared. The only source of light was from the neon-blue strip lights in the stairwell, making me feel as if I was in a different world. I was shaking and shivering, suddenly freezing cold as though I had a fever.

What was I *doing*? I could go to prison for this – and then what? Tyler would have nothing and be totally alone.

But then I reminded myself of who I was doing this for.

For my sister.

My *dead* sister. And her son.

Even in the half-light, I saw her sweet face as if she was sitting on the step beside me. Felt her arm slip around my shoulders, heard her soothing words in my ear to make everything all right like she always did.

There, there, Mary... It'll be OK, you'll see. Tomorrow's a new day...

Then one day, for Sara, tomorrow never came.

Tears stung my eyes as I thought back. She'd promised to take my place the night she disappeared, begging our father to let that revolting man take her instead of me.

But I didn't want her to sacrifice herself. I didn't want her to come back at midnight broken and silent like the other times she'd gone instead of me. I didn't want her to miss days off school because of the bruises – she *loved* school, loved her friends. Sara was clever, said she was going to study hard, get a good job and get us both out of there, away from our parents. Away from those men. And I believe she would have done, too.

It had been towards the end of the previous year when everything changed, though neither of us knew it at the time. In the spring, Sara had grumbled to me that she was getting fatter – so she stopped eating so that she could still fit into her school uniform. I didn't really understand why, even when, weeks later, she explained to me that a baby was coming. Our father was furious.

After Sara had had her son, after she'd come home from the hospital at the end of the school summer holidays, we'd lain on her bunk, the morning sun streaming over our faces, and she'd told me how she'd been allowed to hold him for one hour.

'The nurse said he was born a month early,' she'd told me. 'He was so tiny, but he still gave me enough love to last the rest of my life,' she'd said, smiling as I toyed with her fingers.

If only she'd known that the rest of her life was only three months long.

'Tyler!' I yell out as I come up from the basement. I listen out, wondering if he's back yet from dealing with Gina's kids. After searching around the house, finding all the rooms empty, I grab my phone and call him. But it goes straight to his voicemail.

I fetch Gina's handbag containing her phone and, as I suspected, Annie's phone, too. My instincts were right about her taking it. There are some message alerts – including several from Annie's agent, Bryan.

> *Annie, we need to talk about your schedule. Time getting tight.*
> *Have to let the network know where you stand. Call asap. Bry x*

And there are three missed calls from him, too. Until now, it was easy to deflect her colleagues and friends or anyone who might have contacted her.

Saying I – *Annie* – needed time to decompress, that I was on a much-needed holiday, worked a treat on friends. With a few Instagram posts of stock photos to back up her story, no one has questioned anything. Bryan, admittedly, was a little harder to convince about the wisdom of Annie's short-notice holiday, especially as I couldn't take his calls and had to tell him by email that I was taking a break. There's only so much time that I can stall him before he turns up here looking for her. She's one of his biggest clients and her well-being is his priority.

I also need to consider who will be looking for Gina, Matt and Laura. I suspect Laura's husband will miss her when she doesn't arrive home tomorrow evening, being the first to raise the alarm. While he will have made good use of a long weekend with his mistress, from what I know of him, he also likes to keep close tabs on his wife.

Gina's parents are unlikely to find anything amiss for a few days – if she doesn't respond to her mother's messages immediately, her parents will assume she's busy with the kids. Matt's work could be an issue, but not immediately given he seems to work from home a lot.

At best, I reckon I have about twenty-four hours to get a confession from one of the women locked in the basement. A confession from whoever killed my sister. Because I know it was one of them, and it's finally time to get the truth. Time to get revenge.

'Matt, just *drop* it,' I hear someone say. 'As long as we're stuck down here, we need to pull together.'

While the darkness is driving them insane, I'm fading fast. If I don't get some insulin soon, I won't make it out of here alive.

It's Laura speaking – practical, calm, ever-capable and competent Laura. The night of the party, she kept a low profile, and who can blame her considering the way things turned out. She had no interest in fawning over Matt like Annie and me. She had nothing to prove to any boy given that, at the time, she told us that she liked girls more.

She arrived at the party after us but didn't drink any alcohol or take any of the coke Evan was shoving at people. Looking back, I think she only went because she knew I was worried for Sara, and, like me, she wanted to make sure that if she turned up at the party, she'd be OK. Having all the GALS around her, as I'd said at Davy's earlier that week, was what she'd need to get through the break-up with Matt.

'God, Geen,' Matt says in response to my accusation that he treated Sara badly. 'You've got it all wrong. You need to listen to me...' I feel his hand reach out for me in the dark, trying to grab hold of mine, but I pull away. 'Look, Sara knew all about my party,' he goes on with a nervous laugh. 'I *invited* her, for God's sake.' He takes a breath. 'She told me she didn't want to come, OK? And there was no dumping to be done because we'd already ended things amicably earlier that day. She was fine about—'

'I'm feeling *really* rough, Matt.' I want so much to believe him, but I can't focus on that right now. 'I need my insulin before it's too late...'

'Well, you brought the subject up,' Matt snaps back, ignoring my comment about being unwell. I detect a wobble in his voice again. The sound of a man on the edge. A man scared. 'Like I said, *you* were her friend. And *you* should have been there for her. Whatever happened to her was *not* because of anything I did. There are plenty of creeps in the world.' Suddenly, Matt's voice changes, as though he's on the verge of one of his panic attacks. 'God, I... I need to get out of here. I can't breathe. And it's so fucking *dark*. Christ...' he chokes out. 'I'm going to die down here...'

I prise myself away from Annie, reaching out for my husband even though I feel as though I'm about to collapse, but he jumps as soon as I touch him.

'What's that? Get off me!' he shrieks, recoiling. 'I can't stand this!'

'Oww... *Matt*...' I yelp, jumping back as his arm thwacks me on the temple, adding to the pounding headache I already have. 'Jesus, keep it together, Matt. Please, I know this is freaking you out, but you have to calm down.' I lean in to whisper, but I don't think he's listening. 'Did you hear me before? I'm not trying to worry you, but I think my blood sugar is crazy high right now. I've not injected this morning.'

Matt doesn't reply. Instead, I hear his panicked breathing – the short, sharp breaths of hyperventilation.

'Look, these lights aren't coming back on any time soon,'

Annie says. 'I think there might be a torch somewhere in the kitchen area, or possibly in the recording booth, I can't remember where exactly.'

Laura and I groan together. '*Now* you tell us,' Laura chimes.

'It might be out of batteries, but it's worth a shot if it keeps him from freaking out,' Annie adds. 'Matt, why don't you come with me and help me find it? Let's have a change of scene.' She lets out a snort at the irony.

'I... I can't move. I can't breathe...' he says, his throat sounding tight. I can tell that he's slumped down onto the floor now by the direction his voice is coming from. 'Help!' he suddenly yells – but the sound seems to bounce off the walls and back into the room with a dull thud. 'Someone help us!'

'Mate, calm down.' I hear Laura shuffling over to him, but then she screams loudly when he lashes out again, knocking her into something and then stumbling back against me.

In turn, the weak yelp I make seems to send Matt over some kind of emotional precipice because he's suddenly on his feet and lashing out.

'Get off! Get *off* me!' he yells, sounding on the edge of hysteria. 'No... *nooo*...'

'Matt, stop!' I cry, ducking lower, banging my head on the mixing desk. I've never heard him like this before. Sweat drips off my face as my insides twist from pain. 'It's... it's going to be OK, Matt, just calm down! I need you to stay calm, *please*! Do it for our kids!' My voice is breathy as I reach out blindly for him, my arms grappling in the dark.

'I've got you,' Annie suddenly says. 'Matt... Matt... it's OK, I've got you.' I hear the effort in her voice as she tries to restrain him, and, gradually, he calms down.

Then it's just the sound of Matt sobbing – the sound of a broken man as he finally stills.

'Come on, mate. Let's get that torch,' Annie says. 'And some more water.'

'It's... it's being down here. The darkness... the screams... I can't stand it...' he mumbles through sobs – sobs that I've rarely heard in all the time we've been together. Matt never cries.

My cheek still stinging from where he hit me, I feel the heat of their bodies as they edge towards the door that leads out to the kitchen area, opposite to where we came in. From what Annie said, there's another door off that area leading into the recording booth – the much smaller room behind the glass partition window where Annie does her vocal and instrumental recordings, while the engineer sits in here where we are.

'I need to pee again,' I say, following them out and feeling my way to the small cubicle. After that, I find the tap in the kitchenette, drinking from it greedily. This is not a good sign.

Then I return to the studio, hearing Laura's shallow breaths nearby.

'That's not like Matt,' I say when I'm certain it's just me and her in here now. I'm still whispering even though they can't hear me. Annie shut the recording booth door behind them, silencing Matt's snivels. 'To lose it like that...'

'He's probably tired and hungover,' Laura states. She sounds on the edge of giving up – resigned and scared. 'I don't know what we're going to do, Geen. This is a fucking disaster. She can't leave us here until we literally die of starvation, can she? I mean... she must have a reason for putting us down here.'

'It's... it's about Sara,' I say, wiping my face with my sleeve, not that Laura can see the sweat pouring off me. 'It's got to be.'

'This is about us three, and Matt coming back earlier than expected has thrown her, I reckon. She's not following her script any more. She's acting irrationally.'

'But what *was* her script? And how long does it even take to die of starvation?' I ask, not wanting to know the answer because without my medical kit, I will be the first to go, slipping into a diabetic coma before my brain and heart give up. 'Jesus, I just want to get to my kids.' I thump the wall limply with my fist. 'Mum, Dad, if you can hear my thoughts, then please, *please* get yourselves over to the house...' I whimper. 'Honestly, Laura, I can't take much more. I *really* need my insulin. I'm fading fast, I can feel it. And Gracie needs feeding. I left a bit of milk in the freezer, but God knows if that bitch Mary will—'

I stop suddenly, holding my breath.

Laura is silent too as we hear the noise – our ears in hyper-vigilant mode since the lights went out. It's the soft, deadened sound of the door opening – the locked door through which we came in.

Oh my God, oh my God, oh my God... My heart thumps even harder as I edge closer to the mixing desk. I know the metal wastebin is on the floor just underneath it, and I also remember seeing an empty mug on the corner of the desk. Either would make a weapon – if I can muster the strength.

'Who's there?' Laura calls out, but there's no reply.

Then we see a faint blue light as the door opens, followed by a shadow slipping inside the room.

'Who is it?' Laura barks. Then, more quietly, she says, 'Mary, is that you?'

Whoever it is doesn't reply, but the blue light suddenly disappears as the door is closed again, then the dull click of it being locked.

Fuck, I wish Matt was here, but he and Annie are the other side of a soundproofed door. Whoever is in here with us now is perfectly silent – just the slow wheeze of their breath every few seconds.

My hands pat around the desk lightly to find the mug, but as I take a step forward, I accidentally kick the metal wastebin, knocking it over. Laura squeals as I stumble, steadying myself on the desk, almost grabbing the mug with my left hand just as I send it skidding onto the floor.

'Who are you?' I yell out. 'What the fuck do you wa—'

But I don't get to finish because an arm curls around my throat and a hand goes over my mouth.

FORTY-NINE

GINA

I thrash wildly, trying to escape the grip of whoever's got hold of me – but I'm so weak, I'm not able to put up much of a fight. I lose my balance in the darkness, tripping on something then buckling to the floor, jarring my shoulder as I go down.

'Laura, where are you?' I cry, clutching my arm, but before she gets a chance to answer, a pair of hands is yanking me upright and slamming me back against the mixing desk. My head bangs down on the knobs.

'I'm over here,' she says – though there's no way I can get to her. Not while I'm being pinned down. I hear breathing above me, but in the darkness it's impossible to tell who it is.

'Mary... is that you?' Laura says tentatively from the other side of the studio. 'I... I understand how upset you must be. We both do. We're on your side. We... we want to help you, but we can't while we're trapped down here.'

I let out a whimper as something cold presses against my throat – something that feels a lot like a knife.

'Talk to me, Mary,' Laura says. I hear a scuffling sound as if she's standing up.

Oh, Matt... where the hell are you...?

'Mary?' I dare to whisper. 'It... it doesn't have to be like this, you know. We can help you... just don't hurt me... my kids... *please*...' My words turn to sobs.

'Is this about Sara?' Laura says through the darkness. 'Is that why you're here?'

Silence. Just the cold blade pressing down on my neck.

'We know who you are, Mary,' Laura adds, but all it does is add to the thick tension that's growing in this pitch-black space.

My breaths are frantic, and my eyes are saucers as I stare up into the darkness, desperate to make out the face looming over me.

'We loved Sara too...' I whisper, not knowing what else to say. But I immediately wish I'd kept quiet.

'You don't fucking know *anything* about Sara...' a voice yells directly above me – *Mary's* voice. Globules of spit land on my cheek.

I scream, struggling to get free, but the weight of her above me is more than I can overcome in my weakened state. The blade digs deeper into my neck.

'Laura... she's... she's going to *kill* me...' I utter, though the words barely come out.

'Mary, it's OK,' Laura says, her voice suddenly closer. 'We understand...'

'You don't fucking understand!' Mary yells. 'You really, *really* don't.'

'OK, OK, we don't,' I whimper beneath her. 'You're right... we don't know anything,' I say, praying she believes me. 'Just tell me... are my children OK? Who is looking after them? Where are they now?' When I speak, my throat presses harder against the knife. It feels as though she's already drawn blood.

Mary lets out a nasty laugh. 'I have no idea where your bloody children are.'

'Oh *God...*' I stifle a scream. I can't afford to anger her any more. Not if I'm to ever see Tommy or Gracie again.

'But... but I left Tyler in charge of them when you... when you shoved me down here,' Laura says. 'Where the hell are they?'

'Laura, please... be careful,' I whisper, praying she'll get the message not to antagonise Mary. I just want to stall for time until Matt comes back. Laura and I could try to overpower her now, though with that knife at my throat, I can't risk taking chances. But between the four of us, we stand a chance. The keys to the door must be on her somewhere.

'Not a nice feeling, is it? Not to know where a loved one is, or if they're in danger or if they're even still alive,' she spits down at me. I hear the hurt beneath her words. 'Especially if the loved one is a child. Or child*ren*, in this case,' she adds.

'Mary, I'm begging you,' I say, trembling. 'Gracie is barely two months old. She needs me. She needs to be fed and looked after. And Tommy... he's just a toddler. He'll be scared without me.' I swallow, though my mouth is so dry. 'Please, *please* let us out so I can get to my children, I'm begging you.' Hot tears roll from my eyes and onto the mixing desk.

'Not a chance,' she says.

'Then... then will you get my insulin for me?' I ask. 'I need to inject—'

'Keep me here and let Gina out,' Laura demands. 'She needs medical help, for fuck's sake.'

I hold my breath waiting for a reply, but it's not what I want to hear, her words making me almost pass out.

'The children aren't in the house. They're gone. And I don't care about your stupid injections either.'

I didn't know I had so much rage inside me, but hearing her talk about my children like that sends it bubbling up to the surface like a volcano erupting. I don't stop to think of the consequences of being stabbed – all I care about is overpowering her and getting to Gracie and Tommy.

'You *bitch!*' I cry, using every last drop of energy I have left to bring a leg up, kicking Mary hard.

Not expecting it, she's knocked off balance and stumbles, releasing the knife from my throat and letting out a yelp as I grab hold of her hair, using it to haul myself up off the mixing desk. With a loud grunt, I hurl myself against her, frantically feeling about in the darkness, making a grab for her arm – and the hand that's holding the knife.

'*Oww!*' I scream, feeling something slice across my shoulder. But the pain doesn't stop me, nor does the feeling of wetness as blood dribbles out of the wound. In fact, it drives me on, making me find a strength I never knew I had – my final reserves before my body gives up.

'Gina... stop, you'll get hurt!' I hear Laura cry. 'Mary... get *off* her!' She's somewhere nearby – I feel her hands whip against me as she tries to intervene.

Suddenly there's a sharp pain in my right forearm as... 'Oh my God, she *bit* me!' I yank Mary's head again with the fistful of her hair, and we both stumble backwards as I slam her down onto the bank of controls and slider knobs.

Mary yells obscenities as she lies on the mixing desk, me pinning her down now, though I'm fast running out of strength. She's panting and I imagine her eyes are huge and venomous, staring up at me.

I'm sweating, my cheeks burning red with rage, and my hair is stuck to my face. I squeeze Mary's wrist hard, trying to make her drop the knife. I can't see it, but I sense it's pointing up at me. One wrong move and it'll be in my neck.

'Let us *out* of here!' I scream in her face, my mouth inches away from hers. 'Laura, get the keys... check her pockets,' I call out, but before she responds, Mary has a surge of energy and thrashes to one side, making me overbalance.

I shove my left hand out to stop myself falling over completely, releasing my grip on her. But we're both shocked motionless as the whole mixing desk suddenly lights up in an array of glowing buttons, knobs and controls. I've accidentally hit the master switch and turned the whole deck on, causing a gentle hum of equipment around us.

In the dim glow, I see Mary's panicked face, her hair matted over the controls. In her hand is the kitchen knife – the ten-inch blade glinting in the faint light. And in her eyes, there's terror, regret, remorse and fear.

But more than that – in her eyes, there's Sara.

'Oh my God, I see it now,' I whisper, wanting nothing more than to hug her, press my face into her neck and tell our dear friend how sorry we are, how we never meant for anything bad to happen to her. 'Sara...'

Mary lies silently below me, our faces close in the dim light as she pants short, sharp bursts of fear, staring up at me, unmoving. The terror in her eyes tells me she has no more idea what she's doing than I do. That she's acting out of raw instinct – her desire to avenge her sister's death. While my raw instinct is to save my children.

It's at that moment Mary suddenly twists sideways, rolling away from me.

'Nooo!' I yell, barely having the energy to stand upright, let alone fight back. I'm so weak now, it takes little effort for Mary to overpower me and shove me back down beneath her, reversing our positions before I have time to think. Then the blade is at my throat again.

At first, I don't realise what has caused the loud voices we suddenly hear all around us – two voices, one male, one female, seeming to be in heated debate coming through speakers positioned around the studio. Mary seems as puzzled as I am, her hate-filled eyes flicking about. But I quickly realise that in the struggle, my elbow has jammed down on a couple of switches near the edge of the mixing desk.

'For God's sake, get a grip, Matt,' the female says. The female I recognise to be Annie.

'I can't... I can't stand it...' Sobbing follows the male voice on the edge of despair. *Matt*. 'Being trapped down here... I'm... I'm claustrophobic.'

'Grow up, Matt,' Annie snaps, her voice crystal clear and sharp as it rings out through the speakers. 'We're not kids any more. And if you want to see *your* kids again, then I suggest you buck up and figure out what it's going to take to get out of here.'

Inadvertently, I appear to have turned on an intercom in the recording booth beyond the window.

I have no idea how it's all connected up, but I noticed a microphone on a stand in there earlier when the lights were on, and it makes sense that the engineer in here would need to communicate with the vocalist or musicians somehow.

'Jesus, what's going on...?' Laura says, like me, unable to believe her ears.

'It's Annie and—'

'Shut up and listen,' Mary yells, looming above me, the pair of us frozen in deadlock. Shadows from the mixing desk lights angle over her gaunt face, making her appear crazed and ghoulish.

'Can they hear *us*?' Laura whispers.

'No, I don't think so...' I say, keeping my eyes fixed on Mary above me. She's dead still as she listens intently to what's being said, the knife still pressed against my neck.

'Mary's never going to let us go, is she?' Matt snivels through the intercom. 'We're going to die down here...' More sobbing before Annie snaps at him to hold it together. 'I've only ever wanted you, Annie,' Matt continues. 'Did you know that?' he says in a voice that makes my blood run cold. 'I was in love with you from the first moment I saw you.'

His words cut me to the core as my heart pounds against my ribcage. Mary looms over me, pinning me down as I try to take in what Matt just said... *He's in love with Annie...*

But it's what my husband says next that causes my world to turn on its axis.

'I... I know what happened to Sara.'

FIFTY
GINA

'You *know*?' Annie says, her shock palpable. Her voice is choked but clear as her words come through the speakers in the studio. 'You've got to tell me what happened...'

'Just so you're aware,' Matt says, sounding pathetic, 'I never wanted to go out with her in the first place. Annie, don't you realise, I only ever wanted *you*. I was going to tell you how I felt the night of my party, but I never got the chance. I love you, Annie. I've *always* loved you.'

Silence followed by the sound of Annie exhaling.

'*Matt...*' Annie says, drawing out his name. 'You're not acting rationally. You don't sound... *well*. If you know what happened to Sara, you've got to tell me.'

'Shut up!' he snaps. 'You don't know what you're saying...'

'Matt, listen. It's OK, you can talk to me,' Annie says. 'No one can hear us. The room is soundproofed, and we're sealed in. Please, just tell me what happened that night.'

I feel sick, unable to believe what I'm hearing. I'm frozen with Mary pinning me down, the knife at my throat, her hand trembling as she also listens to the voices surrounding us.

'Look, Matt, if you won't tell me what happened,' Annie

continues to my husband, 'then when we get out of here, you've got to go to the police.'

'You think we'll *ever* get out of here?' Matt asks, a wobble in his voice again, like a toddler on the verge of tears.

'God knows,' Annie says. 'But I'm not going down without a fight.'

'When we're out of here and everything's died down, we can finally be together, right? Do you want that, too? I'll leave Gina. I earn more than her – I'll get custody of the kids. I've got it all worked out.'

Oh my God... I let out a stifled sob. My husband sounds pathetic. Grovelling for Annie's attention even though he has no idea where our children are or if they're even OK at this moment. He's destroyed our marriage with just a few words.

'I don't know, Matt,' Annie says. 'One step at a time, and—'

'No!' Matt yells, making us jump as his voice booms around us. 'That's *not* how this works, Annie. Not after everything. You and me... we belong together.'

'Things change, Matt. People change. You have a family, a new baby and—'

'That was Gina's dream, not mine. I never wanted any of it. Us being trapped down here, it's all her fault. If it wasn't for her, *none* of this would have happened. She's a liability, Annie. All I ever wanted was you...'

My head is swimming as Matt drones on about how awful his life with me is... how he's only ever loved Annie... how he thinks about her all the time, watches everything she's been in, listens to her music constantly...

I can't believe what I'm hearing. Matt is obsessed.

'Oh my God, oh my God...' I say on repeat, tears streaming from my eyes.

'Shut up and let me listen,' Mary snaps. Her eyes are filled with anger, and her breathing is fast and shallow. One move from her and I'm dead.

'Matt,' Annie continues, 'just tell me what happened the night of the party.'

'Annie, I love—'

'I remember you came back to your house after buying more alcohol – so much booze you could hardly carry it,' Annie presses on. 'And you were jittery as anything, I remember that. I thought you'd taken something, you were shaking so much. You downed about three beers in a row before hitting the vodka. Evan was egging you on, but I saw something else in your eyes as you drank—'

'Stop it! Stop it, no, you're wrong! *Stop it!*'

As Matt whimpers, I imagine him with his hands over his ears, head down, eyes screwed up as he paces about the small space of the recording booth.

'I can't stand it in here. I need to get out... It's driving me insane... There are ghosts, *so many ghosts*...' Matt sobs again, and I can barely believe it's my husband I'm hearing in stereo as my life falls apart around me.

'What do you mean, ghosts?' Annie asks. 'Where are the ghosts?'

Matt snivels. 'They're everywhere,' he says, sounding like a little boy. 'They're in my head. They're in my dreams. They're in my nightmares. And they're in the... *walls.*'

'What walls, Matt? What are you talking about?'

'These walls, Annie. *These* ones.' More snivelling from him as I dare to glance at Laura, the angles of our faces highlighted from the mixing deck's glow.

'Tell me more, Matt,' Annie urges.

'She's in *these* walls, Annie. Sara is here... I see her everywhere. Her ghost following me. Haunting me. Day and night. She's down here... I know it, she's down here with us.' More wailing and sobbing as Matt fully breaks down.

'Try to stay calm or you'll make yourself unwell,' Annie says in a neutral yet strangely coaxing voice. I've never heard her like this before – it's as though she's acting, but not acting. It's her, but also not her.

'Which direction is the back of your house?' Matt suddenly asks, sounding more coherent. 'I need to know.'

Annie hesitates. 'Er, this is the back of the house. In this room, the recording booth. Why?'

'And did there used to be... like, a window in a deep light well that led up to ground level? Like you see in basements? Or a coal chute maybe... something leading underground from the garden?'

'Matt... I don't see—'

'Just tell me!' Matt snaps, making us all jump again.

'Yes, there were both of those things. An underground window in a light well, and an old coal chute. Both got dug out and filled in with the renovations,' Annie says. 'But I don't understand, Matt. Why would you ask me that?'

The wailing is quiet at first – a low, pitiful sound of a man in pain. But its intensity soon grows, each breath drawn as if he's sucking in the ills of the world.

'Matt, what the fuck's going on? You need to tell me.'

'OK, OK...' he says through more snot and tears. 'I trust you, Annie. I *love* you.' He takes a breath. 'On the way to the shop that night, I saw Sara,' Matt admits, making us all gasp so loudly I swear they'll hear us through the glass.

'You *saw* her? Where? What happened?' Annie says in that same persuasive way. She must have found the torch because, when I twist round, straining to see through the viewing window above me, I see a cone of light illuminating Matt's face from under his chin.

'It wasn't good,' Matt admits. 'Not good at all. But when I was on my way back, it got much, much worse.'

FIFTY-ONE
THE PAST

What Matt remembered most about the shop where he bought the booze, apart from having thrown up just outside it, was how bright it was. After wiping his mouth, he glanced around to see who'd witnessed him vomiting. No one, by the looks of it. Through the shop window, he saw the old guy at the checkout chatting to some customers and the only other person on the street was walking in the opposite direction.

He went inside, squinting from the fluorescent strip lights, wondering if his eyes were smarting because of what he'd just seen.

No... no... no... He'd seen nothing. He'd take the long way home and that would be that. He was mistaken. Panicked by the foxes. Jumpy from seeing that man zipping up his flies. Scared of the dark.

'Y'all right,' a voice said as Matt stared at the shelves of alcohol racked up not far from the checkout.

'All right,' Matt replied, grabbing a basket and loading it with as much beer and wine as he could carry. At the till, he asked the shopkeeper – a balding man with a round paunch and grubby overalls – for three bottles of vodka from the shelving behind him. 'And a pack of Bensons,' he added, clearing his throat.

The man hesitated, staring down at Matt. He was shaking, felt a sweat break out on his back, but it wasn't because he was buying booze aged sixteen. It was because of what he'd just witnessed.

No... I didn't witness anything...

Matt pulled out the fake ID from his back pocket, waving it at the shopkeeper.

'Y'all right lad, no need. I can see you're over eighteen.' He winked, taking the wodge of notes Matt held out. 'You 'ave a good night.'

As Matt left the shop, struggling through the door with the four bags, he felt pleased as punch at how easy it had been to get extra supplies for the party.

Let the good times begin...

It was only when he trod in his own vomit, almost slipping over by the lamppost, that he remembered what he'd seen on the common. He walked a few paces away from the shop, already feeling his fingers straining under the weight of all the booze he'd bought, wondering what to do.

Go back and check if he really *had* seen something? Or ignore and head home along the main road instead?

The long way back would add another ten, maybe fifteen minutes to his walk – a gruelling thought with the heavy bags. And it meant less time with Annie.

The short cut... going back that way made him feel sick again. But then, what the hell was he scared of? A stupid fox and a bit of darkness?

It was the thought of Annie wondering where he was, maybe even getting off with someone else, that made him cross over the road and head back towards the common, retracing his steps. While he couldn't run with the bags, he'd walk at a fast pace and get through to the other side quickly.

Whatever it was that he'd thought he'd seen would be gone by now.

Matt ducked through the old metal gate. He looked around. It was dark – but there was enough ambient street lighting as well as the moon, almost full, to guide him.

At least there are no screeching foxes now, he thought, heading back along the track through the overgrown area. To his right, he saw the looming shadows of the tall townhouses, several with lights on, though the one at the far end was in darkness. The rear fence separating its garden from the common was broken down. When he'd seen it in daylight, the place had always looked derelict.

Matt put his head down and kept walking. The bags seemed to get heavier with every step. It was hard to follow the trampled-down path among the undergrowth, but if he squinted up ahead, he could just make out the shape of the tree against the night sky, near the gate that led out to the alley – and then the road. He forged on.

Shit. What was that?

Matt was halfway across the common, level with the back of the derelict house, when he heard it. He stopped.

There. Crying. Definitely someone crying.

Help me... please...

Did he *really* hear that?

Shit. No. He didn't. It was his imagination tormenting him again.

Help... Oh God... please help...

Then more sobbing.

Slowly, as if his brain had lost control of his body, he put down the bags of alcohol and ventured off the path towards the back of the big house. One cautious step at a time.

What if that man was still there? Despite his lopsided gait, he'd looked grim, and Matt didn't want to get into a fight.

'Who's there?' he heard himself calling out as he got closer.

'Help me...' came the voice. Weak and barely audible.

He recognised the voice.

'Sara?' Matt called out in a hushed voice. 'Is that you?'

He knew it was. But didn't want to believe it. He walked closer to the sobbing sound, tripping on some broken bricks.

'Over here... *please* help... I need... hospital...'

Matt caught sight of an arm – then more pale flesh, highlighted silver when the moon came out from behind a cloud. Virtually naked and covered in mud and blood, Sara lay head down in a ditch behind the broken-down fence, her neck twisted at an impossible angle. Her face and hair were matted with vomit and her body was cut and bruised.

She barely looked human. More like a grotesque fantasy painting, gothic and repulsive. She was utterly helpless, yet she still had a power over him. Matt felt it, burning inside him. He loathed her yet couldn't stop staring at her naked body.

Her face lit up when she saw Matt standing above her.

Her fingers twitched as her hand reached up to him. *Help me...*

Matt peered down at her.

'It hurts,' she whispered. 'So much...'

Matt thought he was going to puke again. He cupped his hand over his mouth.

'You... party...' she said, her words a whisper, as if that was more important than her broken and bloody body lying in a ditch. 'Don't... leave me, Matt,' she uttered through breathy syllables. 'We... *us*... I love you...'

Staring down at her, feeling his lip curl into a sneer, Matt hated that those were her last actual spoken words.

I love you.

Sara made noises as he grabbed her – screamed when he almost yanked her shoulders from their sockets. He lugged her out of the ditch, and, when he was able to manhandle her properly, he clamped a hand over her mouth.

Look at her, his brain told his body, as it called him to action. *Just look at the disgusting state of her. No use to anyone now.* He didn't know what that man from earlier had done to her, or who he was, but it was bad. No one would want her like this. He was doing her a favour.

Sara's words – *Help me... I love you...* – raged through his mind as he dragged her towards the smashed-down fence of the derelict property. His conscience burnt. Chipped away at him. Slowed his progress.

Maybe he *should* help her. Go back to the shop and get the man to call an ambulance. Run home and use the phone. Flag down a motorist and beg them for help.

But his brain silenced his thoughts as he gathered up Sara's clothes strewn about nearby – he would take them back and burn them in the incinerator tomorrow. His father had always taught him not to show weakness, to hide his emotions. His mother wanted him to be a real man, a decisive go-getter.

Think, man, think.

If he got help now, if Sara survived, questions would be asked. Questions that Matt would not want to answer – including why he didn't get help the *first* time he'd seen her. Sara had witnessed him passing by earlier.

But if she didn't survive, there would be no questions. No one would ever know. And *all* his problems would be gone forever. More importantly, he'd be free to be with Annie.

These back-and-forth thoughts spun through Matt's mind as he grunted, hauling Sara over the rough ground, across some rubble and splintered wood with nails sticking out. Her screams barely registered they were so pathetic now.

He found the hole by accident, almost falling down it as he neared the back of the house. There was a huge pile of wood with a plank sticking out that had caused him to trip after he dragged Sara's dead weight across the overgrown garden. Next door's lights were on, affording a bit of visibility, and he convinced himself there was no one watching, that the face at the upstairs window was just his imagination. He heard the hum of something on next door's television – a comedy with canned laughter as he shoved and kicked and rolled Sara down into the deep hole.

She made a noise as she dropped down the ten feet or so, landing upside down and bent in half. There was a lot of other rubbish and weeds down there, which Matt hoped would hide her for a bit. But to be on the safe side, he piled a load of wood and dirt on top of her, filling in the hole. If she wasn't dead yet, she soon would be.

Afterwards, as he walked back through the garden, panting, he brushed his hands down his front to make sure there was no muck on him. Then, stepping back over the broken-down fence, passing by where he'd found Sara, something caught his eye.

It was near where he'd gathered up her clothes, where the weeds were flattened and trampled down. Somehow, he'd missed it before, only catching sight of it now as the moonlight glinted off it.

Matt bent down and picked up the cheap gold necklace, the one Sara always wore. It was a broken heart pendant with *Friends* etched across the front. He'd noticed Annie wearing one similar. He smiled to himself as he slipped the grubby necklace into his jeans pocket, grabbed the clothes and the bags of alcohol, and headed back to the party.

He liked the thought that, between them, they'd have a whole heart.

FIFTY-TWO

GINA

Matt is sobbing as he finishes telling his story. Laura and I hardly dare breathe, and Mary hasn't moved a muscle since he began talking. She's still pinning me down and staring through the viewing window, watching the scene beyond.

Matt does not sound like my husband any more. *Definitely* isn't my husband any more.

This man makes me feel sick. He's a stranger to me.

'When you got back to the party,' I hear Annie say, her voice somehow maintaining an even tone, despite Matt's confession, 'you got really drunk, really quickly.'

'I wanted to forget,' he replies.

'Do you remember we danced?' Annie asks. 'You grabbed me and held me like the world was about to end.'

'I'll never forget,' Matt says.

I grip onto the edges of the mixing desk to stop myself screaming out. As much as I hate Matt for what he's done, hearing this must be so much harder for Mary.

'It was a slow dance,' Annie says. 'You had your arms around my neck, and you kissed me.'

'Yes,' Matt says weakly. 'I remember that too.'

'While you were kissing me, do you know what I was doing?'

'No,' he replies. I imagine that his face is a picture of self-pitying fear and grief, believing that having confessed his crime to Annie, he will somehow be absolved. Then he can go back to living a life filled with lies.

'I had my arms slung around your back. Then I slipped a hand down into your jeans pocket.'

Matt remains silent.

'And in there, I found a heart pendant,' Annie continues. '*Sara's* pendant. I slid it out and kept it. All this time, I've had it. And when I bought this house and found someone had made what seemed like a shrine to Sara out on the common, I left the necklace there. It seemed the right thing to do.'

'It was *you* who took it?' Matt lowers his face, the shadows from the torchlight giving him the appearance of an old man. A broken old man.

'All these years, I've *desperately* wanted to believe that you were innocent, that you had no idea what happened to Sara.' Annie's words gain intensity as she shoves her face close to Matt's, the torch still shining between them. 'You swore on your life to me that you didn't know what happened, Matt. We all made statements to the police, for Christ's sake.'

She shoves him on the shoulder, making him flinch.

'But deep down, I always had my doubts about you,' she continues. 'The way you acted, carrying on with your life as though a weight had been lifted after that night, as if nothing had even happened.'

Matt hangs his head lower.

'I should have spoken up about my concerns to the police when they interviewed us the next day. I should have told them about the necklace. Told them that your clothes had mud on them. Told them that I saw blood under your fingernails when you held my hand.

'But at the time, they were more intent on questioning Sara's parents, her father especially. He was later arrested and sent to prison, branded a paedophile. I heard his other daughter was taken into care. So much about that night makes sense to me now, yet none of it did back then. I dunno, maybe I felt sorry for you, or maybe I even had a bit of a crush on you myself.' She pauses then, huffing out a laugh. 'Not as much as Gina, though. By God, that girl adored you.' Annie shakes her head.

'Annie, you've got to understand about Gina. She means nothing to me, not like you—'

'Shut the fuck up,' she says, shoving him again. 'Thing is, Matt, it's not too late for me to do the right thing. Not too late for me to tell the police what I found in your pocket that night. The world will listen to me now. Unlike Sara, I have a voice.'

Annie shines the light directly in his eyes.

'Tell me where she is, Matt,' she whispers, stalking around him, pacing slowly, keeping the torch aimed at him. Matt looks confused, panicked and filled with terror. *'Tell me!'*

Matt's hands come up to his face, tearing at his skin as his mouth falls open in a grimace.

'Do it, Matt. Go over to where she is and beg for her forgiveness. Grovel for your fucking life.' Annie kicks him, still shining the light in his eyes. Matt turns away, trying to avoid the glare, but she tracks him round. 'You were a coward, weren't you, Matt? You didn't have the guts to finish things with Sara, so you killed her instead, didn't you?' Annie yells. 'Admit it!'

'No... no... no, I didn't mean to. It wasn't like that,' Matt sobs as the tears start. 'I didn't know she was going to be on the common, I swear...'

'You left her there to die when you could have *saved* her.'

More sobs from Matt. 'Yes, yes, I did...' He walks to the back of the recording booth and drops to his knees, his back facing the viewing window as he stares up at the blank wall behind him. 'There...' he says, pointing at the wall. 'She's... she's some-where in there... that's where I left her.'

It's the wall that would have once housed the light well from the back garden. The light well that was since excavated and backfilled with concrete when Annie's renovations began.

I'm suddenly aware of a noise above me. When I look up, Mary is crying, her hand over her mouth as she gulps down her tears. Now is my chance to overpower her, if only I can muster the energy. Every minute without my insulin, my body is growing weaker, made worse by knowing that I married a monster. Nothing can surpass the horror of that – not even Mary with a kitchen knife at my throat.

'It was because of me...' Mary weeps, shaking her head, tears now streaming down her face. 'That night, he was coming for me... that revolting man.' Her voice sounds vacant, distant, as though she's deep in thought. 'Sara said she would go in my place, and I ran away. He must have taken her instead. He must have taken her to the common.'

Mary sucks in a breath, closing her eyes for a second, so I grab the opportunity and, using the final dregs of energy left in my body, I yank my right arm free from her grip, rolling side-ways off the mixing desk.

'Laura, quick!' I yell, suddenly realising that Mary has dropped the knife, but Mary snaps to her senses again and lunges for it. Her knuckles turn white as she grips it, turning to me and brandishing the blade with a terrifying look in her eyes.

This is it... this is the moment I die...

But then Mary swings round, pushing past me as she heads to the door that leads out to the kitchenette and on to the recording booth. The door that leads to Matt.

'Mary!' I call. 'Wait, no, let's talk about this. Upstairs. *Please*, unlock the door and let us out of here... I just want to get to my children.'

Mary stops, her back to me as she stands at the door. She

bows her head briefly before reaching into her pocket and pulling something out. Then she holds her hand out behind her.

Slowly, I step forward and take what she's offering me: the keys to get out of here. She disappears through the door, appearing shortly after on the other side of the viewing window.

'Oh my God, are you OK?' Laura says, breathless as she grabs hold of me. Before I can reply, Mary's voice blares through the speakers as she screams at Matt. Laura and I stand huddled together, our hearts racing as we stare through the glass into the booth.

'I don't feel at all well, Laura. I need my insulin, fast.' I grab her arm for support. 'Jesus Christ, what's happening in there?' I whisper, trying to work out what's going on as the torchlight jumps about and angry noises boom out of the speakers. With only the erratic torchlight, it's hard to see properly. 'I hate him... I fucking *hate* him for what he's done...' I say breathlessly, leaning on Laura's shoulder as more grunts and screams come through the speakers. 'But... but my kids need their father... Oh God...'

Feeling as though I'm about to pass out any moment, I clutch the keys in my hands – torn whether to turn left and go to Matt's aid or turn right and unlock the door to freedom.

In the end, I do nothing. Standing beside Laura, our mouths gaping as Annie shines the torch down on the small room from up high, I see my husband on his knees in front of Mary.

'Dear God, no,' he begs, his agonised face staring up at her. 'It wasn't my fault,' he wails. 'Gina and the others... they should have done something. They were her friends. Blame them, not me. And Sara... she brought it on herself, going to the common alone. You should have seen what she was wearing, going out dressed like that... a short skirt, skimpy top—'

'Get up!' Mary yells, making Matt flinch and stumble to his feet as she jabs him in the shoulder with the kitchen knife. He clutches the surface wound, trembling in front of her.

'You have no idea what my sister and I went through,' Mary roars. 'You have no idea of the despicable things that happened to us. Things that would break cowards like you within seconds. You're nothing but a weak man, Matthew Dalton, and I do not know what my sister ever saw in you.' She spits in his face.

'She saw an escape in him,' I whisper to Laura the other side of the glass, taking hold of her hand, the keys pressed between our palms. 'Sara wanted a way out of her life. But instead, she lost it.'

Almost as if she hears my words, Mary flies at Matt with the knife. I know there's no saving him when I see the blood splatter all over the glass, virtually obliterating our view. Then a second later, I witness his agonised face jammed up against the window, distorting his features.

Mary holds the knife above her head and plunges it into him over and over, stabbing his back and then slicing into his neck. A volcano of blood erupts from an artery, spraying everywhere.

Matt is gone.

'Gina!' I hear Laura calling above the ringing sound in my ears. 'Are you OK? Don't black out... Stay with me. Come on, Gina! Let's get out of here!'

I'm on the verge of unconsciousness. Without me even realising it, Laura has taken the keys and unlocked the door to the bottom of the stairs.

When I don't move, she comes back and grabs my arm, wrapping it around her shoulders as she supports me, pulling me towards the door. As we pass through it, I take a last look back over my shoulder, my vision blurry and my head lolling as I see Matt's grotesque face sliding down the glass in a trail of blood, his dead eyes wide and staring.

FIFTY-THREE

GINA

'Tommy... Gracie...' I mumble, semi-conscious as Laura half drags me up the stairs from the basement. As we emerge into the hallway, my legs buckle beneath me.

'You're doing great, Geen,' I hear Laura say as she guides me through to the big sofa, though her words float around me. 'I'm going to find your meds... I saw your handbag in the hallway... just hang in there...'

I flop back on the couch, my head thrumming and my body aching as I fight down the nausea. Before I know it, Laura is sitting beside me again, riffling through my insulin kit with shaking hands.

'Quick, what do I have to do?' she says in a panicked voice, staring at the items in the zip-up pouch. 'I don't know how to use this...' She holds up my insulin pen, a concerned look on her face.

I reach out, struggling to hold my head up, and slowly take the kit from her. I've injected myself thousands of times... I know the drill inside out... could do it blindfold... So why is my head swimming, my hands not doing as they're told?

I see the pen fall to the floor as I drop it, then Laura grabbing it for me.

'Cartridge,' I manage to say, pointing to the pouch. Laura hands me a new insulin vial and, somehow, I manage to get it inserted into the pen. Fumbling, I lift up my top, exposing my stomach and grabbing a pinch of flesh with my left hand. I don't bother wiping myself with alcohol, and I don't care which site I last used... I just need to get the stuff inside me.

I press the plunger on the pen until all the insulin is dispensed, then I hold the needle in place for a count of ten... though I keep losing my place. My head flops back.

I don't remember much else... wild dreams and fast breathing... images of my children and Matt's bloody face sliding down the glass. Three days could have passed, or perhaps just three minutes. But I wake to the sound of Laura's voice and, thank God, a head that feels less like it's been hit with a hammer.

'Geen, are you OK? Can you hear me?' she says. 'I'm going to call the police. We need to find the kids. I haven't checked everywhere, but I don't think they're here.'

'No, wait...' I grab her arm as everything filters back into my mind. I sit up, testing my body. It feels stronger, more like me, more alert and able to move. 'Do you think... do we *need* to call them? I mean... *Mary*?' My heart clenches at the thought of what she's been through. I take a few breaths, grounding myself, wiping my hands down my face.

'*What*?' Laura says, incredulous. 'Annie's still down there with her, and she's wielding a knife, for fuck's sake. We need to get help!'

I shake my head, standing up to check my legs feel OK, that I'm not going to pass out. 'It's not Annie that Mary was after. Until she heard Matt's confession, I don't think she knew *who* she was after. Speaking to the police will just delay things. My priority is finding my kids.'

For now, Laura agrees not to call them and, together, we search the house, yelling out their names, screaming out for Tyler, looking in every single room including the attic bedrooms.

'Please, Gina, let's just call the police,' Laura begs again when we're back in the hallway.

'Wait,' I say, looking at the shoe rack. 'Tommy's shoes are missing. And his coat.' I dart into the study to check what I must have missed earlier. 'And Gracie's double buggy isn't here either.'

'I think we've established that they're not in the house, Geen.'

'But you don't put shoes and a coat on a child you mean to harm, do you?' I say, thinking hard as I try to work it out. My thoughts are still a little fuzzy, but I don't have time to stop and think. 'If we run, we can be there in fifteen minutes.' Though I'm not sure my body is up to that yet.

'Run *where*?' Laura asks, but that's when I see the car keys dropped on the hall table, realising that the Toyota is back. I grab my phone from my bag.

'If you're coming, then hurry,' I say, praying I've got this right because there's no time to waste, but before Laura has made up her mind, I'm out of the door and in the driver's seat, starting the engine and pulling out onto the street. I know Laura will be calling the police, and for that, I don't blame her. But I think she's wrong. Matt is gone – there's no bringing him back – but if we send Mary down for his murder, then we also send Annie down, too, for withholding evidence all this time.

But there's no time to think about that right now. I just need to find my children.

Ten minutes later, I skid to a stop in the playground car park. A couple of mothers glare at me when I leap out, grabbing onto their toddlers and pulling them closer to avoid the crazy woman charging from her car, leaving the door gaping open.

I'm coming, Tommy... I'm coming, Gracie... I say to myself, running as fast as my recovering body will allow, my arms and legs pumping as I career past the swings and climbing frame.

For a split second, I pause by the playground equipment, just in case, my eyes scanning around. But it's approaching twilight now and everyone is leaving for home, the play area almost deserted.

I take the same path I took in a panic a few days ago when I lost Tommy, praying that my instincts are right, that Tyler has come back to what he called his 'special place'. Though I can't stand to think about the *special things* he said he did here... I pray I'm not too late.

The wooded area looms dark and menacing ahead, shrouding the far end of the park. Without stopping, I run straight into the trees, the light dropping away and the temperature falling as I enter the thick canopy.

'Tommy!' I scream out. 'Can you hear me?'

I stop and listen, hands on knees as I catch my breath, my heart racing. Nothing. Just the sound of a dog barking in the distance. A car droning by on the nearby road. A couple of birds roosting in a tree above me.

I press on, beginning to worry that I've got this horribly wrong, that my little boy and baby aren't here in the woods at all, and that Tyler has taken them somewhere else. From what Mary said, it sounded as though she'd told him to get rid of them somewhere – meaning he could have got on a bus or a train and be hundreds of miles away by now. If I don't find them in a few minutes, then I'm definitely calling the police, and Annie will just have to face whatever consequences come her way.

'Tommy!' I scream into the dark woods, scanning left and right as I head deeper into the trees. 'Are you here?' I stop to listen but keep going when there's no reply. 'Tyler!' I yell. 'You're not in trouble! I just want to see Tommy and Gracie!'

Twigs crack underfoot as I press on, scanning around all the while. It's getting darker the deeper I go, so I put my phone torch on, shining the beam all around me, which seems lost in the huge dark area. I only have two per cent battery left.

'Tommy! Gracie!' I call for my baby too, even though she won't answer. But if Tommy hears me yelling for his sister, it might trigger a response.

Wait... over there. What's that, caught in the light of my phone?

I pan around with my torch, trying to spot what I just saw – something bright on the ground. When I see it again, I rush over and pick it up from among the leaves and twigs, disappointed that it's just a red sweet wrapper rather than one of Tommy's small plastic toys as I'd hoped.

But it's as I'm standing up again that I notice the pink baby sock lying at the base of a tree. With a thumping heart, I go over and grab it, brushing the muck off it. I instantly recognise the little kangaroo embroidered on the cuff. A friend who emigrated to Australia sent them as a gift.

It's Gracie's little sock.

'Tommy! Tyler!' I scream, now knowing my instincts were right.

I stop, straining my ears, widening my eyes as I stare into the darkness as the trees seem to get closer together. Then I hear... crackling. Something popping. And... and I smell something, too. Something like *fire*... Something – or some*one* – burning.

I run deeper into the woods, finally seeing the orange glow of flames lighting up a small clearing within the trees. Sparks rain upwards to the twilit sky, and, in the firelight, I see the silhouette of a figure bent over the fire, poking it with a stick.

'Stop! *You!*' I scream, kicking off into a run again. I leap over some brambles, almost tripping, and as I get closer, I see the person beside the fire is Tyler. I charge up to him and shove him sideways, nearly knocking him into the flames.

'Where are my children?' I yell in his face, my entire body consumed with rage. 'What have you done with—'

'Mummy!' I feel something barge against my legs at the same time as I hear the most beautiful sound in the world – my son's little voice. I look down.

'Oh, *Tommy*,' I say, bending down to grab him, hoisting him up on my hip. I press my face into his hair, drinking him in and kissing him over and over. He smells of smoke and something sickly sweet.

'Where's my baby?' I bark at Tyler, but I don't wait for a reply because I spot the buggy a little way from the fire. I rush up to it, throwing back the hood to reveal my sleeping daughter. She stirs and makes a whimpering sound as I grab her up, checking her over and over as I hug both my children close. It's all I can do to remain upright.

Then the final image I had of Matt fills my mind, making me screw up my eyes. For the sake of my children, I stifle my cries.

'Tyler got mash-lows, Mummy,' Tommy says, pulling me back towards the fire by the hand. 'Want some?' He points down at the campfire contained within a circle of large stones and the packet of marshmallows and skewers beside it. 'Me toasty dem,' he adds proudly.

I look over at Tyler, who's standing perfectly still with his hands down by his sides, staring at us.

'I am sorry if I made you mad, Gina,' he says. 'I used to come here when I was a little boy. It's my special place, and I thought Tommy might like it here, too. There was so much... fuss at the house it was hurting my head. Everything was going wrong. Laura put me in charge of the children, and I couldn't leave them alone so brought them here with me. I warmed the baby's milk from the freezer, and she drank it before we left. We were having toasted marshmallows for dinner because I used to do that with Mary when she stole me away and we even slept here once. I know it's not healthy food, but it was just a special treat. Please don't be cross. Please don't be cross.'

Tyler is breathless when he's finished, his words spilling out in a stream, but I can't take them in. I need to get my children into the car and back to the house – to get my insulin and some of our stuff. Then I will go to my parents... or somewhere. I don't know yet. All I know is that I need to get far, far away from this place. After that, I have no idea.

'I'm not cross,' I say to Tyler, not having the energy to feel anything right now. I grab the pram handle and drag it behind me across the bumpy ground. Then I stop, turning. 'Are you coming back with me?' I call to him, now knowing he's not a threat.

He shakes his head, sitting down on the log beside the fire. 'I'll have a few more of these then I'll put out the fire,' he tells me. 'I'll walk.'

I nod and head off, Tommy's hand gripping mine on the pram handle, while I cradle Gracie in my left arm. 'Let's go home,' I say to my children, trying to sound as normal as possible, but not having a single idea where home is any more.

FIFTY-FOUR

MARY

My hands are covered in blood. My face and neck are covered in blood. The recording booth is covered in blood.

Matt is dead.

I killed him.

Oh God... oh God... oh God...

I'm standing in the main hallway of the house facing Annie, each of us in our underwear, staring at each other like crazed animals. We've barely spoken since we stood over Matt's lifeless body in the studio, each giving the other a knowing look that said far more than words ever could.

'Take your clothes off,' I told Annie before we came up. She knew by then that I was not going to hurt her. Truth is, I need her alive. 'I... I heard Matt's confession.' My entire body was trembling as I dropped the knife. 'Gina... she somehow turned on the intercom.' I shook my head, covering my face, thinking how close I'd come to killing her. I'd been convinced one of the three women was responsible for Sara's death – and I'd been ready to kill *all* of them if they didn't confess.

'I know,' Annie replied, expressionless. 'I saw the green light come on.' She pointed to a small control panel on the wall. 'I knew you were listening. That's why I pushed Matt to tell me what happened.' She was also shaking from head to toe, pressed up against the back of the small booth, having avoided most of the blood spatter. But invisible droplets travel. Like me, she'd be a walking crime scene.

After a bit more encouragement, she copied me as we removed our outer layers, dropping our clothes to the floor. Then we left the room, carefully stepping around Matt's lifeless body as Annie fought down a retch. The doors up to the main house had been left open, so we didn't have to touch anything, and here we are now, standing in our bras and pants in the hallway, trembling, fearful, our eyes locked.

'I admit, I was pretty certain it was you or Gina who'd killed my sister,' I tell her. 'Because you were jealous of Sara being with Matt. Sara told me everything, you know – how you and Gina were obsessed with Matt, constantly plotting ways to get his attention. She even overheard you once say that someone like her would never have a chance with him.' I shake my head in disgust. 'My sister believed you were her friends. But the truth is, you were mean, backstabbing little bitches, excluding her from your stupid gang. The worst part is that she *knew* what you were up to, yet she still wanted to be your friend. Matt asking her out gave her hope, a reason to live, something to look forward to. But she didn't want to hurt any of you, either, knowing how much you wanted him. In the end, her loyalty destroyed her.' She backs away from me, still wary – and rightly so. I've had her locked up for over two weeks. 'That's why I got you all together here – even Laura, who at the very least is guilty of keeping secrets. I had to know the truth. Get vengeance for Sara. I couldn't see another way.'

'What the *hell* are you talking about? You're a crazy woman. I'd *never* have hurt Sara! All I know is that one minute I was interviewing you for the housekeeping job, and the next I was...' Annie trails off, shaking her head, too traumatised to speak.

'Look, Tyler has been living with me for a few years, since he was eighteen,' I explain, knowing it's going to take a lot for her to forgive me. 'He's actually twenty-five but looks a lot younger. I couldn't tell you the truth about his age, or you'd never have believed he was my son. He's had a tough start in life, in and out of foster care, and he's vulnerable, too. From the moment I tracked him down and first met him as a little boy, he's been asking me questions about his birth mother. I promised him that one day I'd find out the truth. And believe me, with Tyler, a promise is a promise.'

I clamp my arms around my body, briefly explaining about our childhood, that Sara was Tyler's mother, that Tyler was the product of abuse.

'But I wasn't doing it *just* for Tyler,' I say, staring down at the floor as I fight back the tears. 'I had to know too. Sara was my sister. I loved her so much.'

'Oh my *God*,' Annie says, tears collecting in her eyes. 'I had no idea... and no idea that Sara had a baby... *None* of us did. Christ, the poor girl...'

I take a breath, forcing myself not to get emotional. 'I knew that getting inside your lives was the only way I stood a chance of finding out the truth. God knows, I've blamed myself enough since she died.'

Annie gives me an incredulous look. 'We have to call the police,' she says, her eyes flicking to the hall table to see if she can spot her phone – *any* phone. 'You've *killed* a man.'

'I agree,' a voice says. Laura comes out of the kitchen, approaching warily as though I might attack at any moment. She stands beside Annie, wrapping an arm around her shoulder.

I hold my hands up, showing her I have no weapon. 'The moment you call the police to arrest me, then Annie is also under suspicion and incriminated. Don't you see?'

The pair look at each other, their expressions telling me they hadn't thought of this.

'But I didn't do anything wrong. I didn't *murder* anyone!' Annie retorts. 'I got Matt to confess the truth, didn't I? I loved Sara, she was my friend.' She lets out a sob, and Laura pulls her closer.

'We all heard you confess about finding Sara's necklace, that you suspected Matt had something to do with her death, but you kept quiet all this time,' I remind her. 'Look, I'm willing to do a deal…' I pause, searching for the right words – the words that will convince her to do exactly as I say so I don't get sent down for murder. 'I'm willing to overlook this now that I finally have the truth about my sister,' I continue. 'Though I doubt the police would be quite so benevolent with you.'

Annie looks at Laura, each of them sharing the same concerned expression.

'When they interviewed you all those years ago about Sara going missing, why didn't you tell them you'd found her necklace in Matt's pocket at the party?'

Annie shakes her head.

'I mean… I get it… Matt was a charismatic guy. I can imagine you all being besotted with him. I know Sara was. But it was perverting the course of justice, Annie… concealing evidence from the police. You'd be in a *lot* of trouble. Not to mention them ordering the excavation of your studio, everything dug up as they exhume Sara's remains. The scandals about you in the papers would be off the scale. Everything would come out. They might even see you as an accomplice. Your career would be over.' I draw a line across my neck. 'You'd be completely cancelled.'

Annie whips up her head. 'But I was a *kid* when it happened,' she says, a tremble in her voice. 'And… and I was drunk… I didn't know what finding the necklace meant. Not really. Matt and Sara were dating, so I figured that's why he had her necklace. I don't know… It was all so awful.' Her face folds in panic.

'It's OK. It's OK. We can deal with it,' I say, taking hold of her hands. 'But no police. Right?'

'Actually, I have to agree with Mary,' Laura says, surprising me with her compliance.

Annie looks up slowly, nodding at me before sharing a concerned look with Laura. 'OK. No police.'

'Right, that's settled. I'll set to work cleaning up,' I say, before instructing Annie and Laura to take thorough showers. 'Wait, though,' I say. 'Out of interest, Annie… were you going to give me the housekeeping job?'

A pause. 'Yes, yes, I was,' she replies, giving me a single nod.

'In that case, I accept,' I say, just as the front door opens and Gina returns. A knot of tension eases inside me when I see both her children are with her. 'I assume it's a live-in position?' I add. 'For me and for Tyler?'

'Yes,' Annie nods, still ashen. Now that she knows who I am, it almost looks as if she's warming to the idea. 'It is.'

'Glad that's all sorted then,' I say, heading to the cupboard to gather up what I'll need. Like I said, I am very good at cleaning up after myself.

The next eight hours pass in a blur as I take on a long night shift of housekeeping duties. Tyler arrived back an hour after Gina, during which time I was aware of her getting her children to bed. Then the three women sat together drinking cups of tea, watching me furtively as, occasionally, I came up from the basement for more supplies or to dispose of waste.

'Gina,' I said, late into the evening, 'I'm glad your children are safe. Tyler would never have hurt them in a million years, just so you know. I instructed him to get the children out of the way for a while, to take care of them. I didn't want them getting upset.'

She gave me a single nod.

'He adores children. In fact, I think he relates to them far more than adults.' I smiled, hoping to elicit one from Gina, but she just sat there with her mug. 'And I'm so very, very sorry about Matt and—'

Her head whipped up. 'I'm not,' she stated. 'I can't believe it... everything he said. It's still rumbling around in my head like an earthquake, but... but I'm not sorry he's dead. After what I heard... What he *did*...' She shuddered and brought a hand to her mouth, looking upset again. 'I'll never unhear it. I'll *never* forgive him. I was married to a monster.'

Another look from Gina, and no further words were needed.

It's still dark out and time for the next stage. I head outside to the common with a shovel I found in the garage. Thankfully, the earth is soft and workable after the recent rain, though it still takes me a couple of hours to dig a pit deep enough for a body. I keep an eye open for nosy neighbours or people in their gardens, but it seems that no one else is up at this hour, and I'm pretty certain I'm hidden within the cover of the trees as I excavate a three-foot-deep grave right behind the fence. It's the perfect place to dispose of a body.

Matt is already wrapped and packaged in many layers of dustbin liners and a tarpaulin in the basement, and I've scrubbed and bleached the entire recording studio to my highest standards. I'm a dab hand at getting rid of blood stains.

'Are you ready?' I ask the others as they huddle together on the sofa. One by one, they follow me down to the studio.

The children and Tyler are thankfully still asleep as we haul the body up the stairs, through the house and out of the glass doors, dragging Matt's dead weight down the garden, through the gate and into the common just as the sun comes up. He falls into the grave with a dull thud, and, between us, he is soon covered with earth. Then we disguise the area with garden rubbish and other overgrowth, making it look almost as it had a few hours ago.

We stand back, staring down at the shallow grave. Annie takes Gina's hand in hers, giving it a squeeze. 'You OK?' I hear her whisper, but Gina just gives a single nod as she looks down at her husband's final resting place – the same spot where Matt first left my sister for dead.

'C'mon, let's go,' I say, knowing that the longer we're out here, the more chance there is of someone spotting us. The others follow me as we traipse back through the garden.

'Wait,' a voice says when we're halfway along the path. 'Anyone else see that?'

I swing round. It's Gina, pointing up at a back window next door.

'No, what?' Laura asks, drawing closer. Annie follows suit, all of us staring up.

'I swear I saw a face, watching us.'

'The neighbours?' I ask, urging them to hurry, to get back inside. 'They won't know what we're up to.' I glance up at the top window again, but all I see are panes of glass with blackness behind. 'If anyone says anything, just say we were out for an early-morning walk.'

But once we're back in the house, Gina is anxious and pacing about, not letting up about it, swearing blind she saw something. 'Whoever it was up there, they spotted us,' she insists. 'They... they were staring right at me. I'm telling you, they saw us *all*.'

FIFTY-FIVE

GINA

'We can't just do *nothing*,' I say to the others when we're back inside. Laura has made coffee, but I can't stomach anything right now. 'Do you believe me? Someone was at the top-floor window next door watching us, I'm in no doubt. What if they saw us... you know.' I glance out of the window, down the garden and towards the common.

Mary protests again, trying to convince me I'm being paranoid, that she didn't see anyone, while Annie and Laura remain quiet, as though they're pondering possible repercussions.

'I think we should go next door. Gauge Bridget and Billy's mood – see how they act in front of us,' I say, not wanting to go alone. 'As you say, it's probably nothing, but I'm not about to leave it to chance. They could be calling the police right now, for God's sake!'

As I hoped, the mention of the police is enough of a threat to get the others to come with me to test the waters. So here I am, knocking on the neighbours' front door with the others standing behind me.

'Hi, Bridget, we're so sorry to bother you this early,' I say when she answers the door, a surprised look on her face. 'We just thought... we thought you might like some company.' I force a smile, briefly turning back to the others. 'And we brought you these.' I hold out some shop-bought cookies arranged on a plate to make them look home-made.

I've left Tyler in charge of Gracie and Tommy, with Tommy confessing before bed last night that Tyler didn't hurt him at all, that it was all made up – for attention, I presume. His honesty has allowed me to downgrade my concern, at least while we go next door to investigate. Besides, after what has been swimming around my head all night, I'm worried about *way* more than us being spotted out on the common at dawn.

'Oh... good morning, ladies,' Bridget replies with a smile. 'This *is* a lovely surprise, but please excuse me still in my dressing gown.' She glances at her watch before touching her head – her hair concealed beneath a scarf and bound up in rollers. 'Would you like to come in for a coffee? I've just put some on.'

I'm grateful that she hasn't yet asked what we're all doing here en masse, even if she does seem a little surprised at our early and unplanned visit. But her politeness prevents her from saying anything – even when she spots Mary, who she has made no secret of disliking. We follow her through to the kitchen.

'Billy hasn't been feeling well, I'm afraid,' she tells us. 'He's been in bed for a couple of days. Doctor's orders.' She touches her heart and pulls a face, her eyes flicking between us as she gets some cups from a cupboard. 'His angina is playing up again. Annie, dear, how lovely to see you. You're home from your holiday.'

Annie, who has showered, changed and eaten and is looking a bit more like herself, glances at Mary – a shared under-standing hanging between them.

'She had a great time, by all accounts, didn't you, Annie?' I interject, giving her a sly look of my own.

'Come and tell me all about your travels in the morning

room, my dear,' Bridget says as Mary takes the tray of coffees from her, along with the cookies. 'Oh, thank you...' she adds, eyeing her warily.

For the next fifteen minutes, Annie's acting skills are put to the test as Bridget asks a stream of questions about her trip.

'I'll have to show you my photos when... when I've organised them all,' Annie says with a fake laugh, glancing at me. 'I took so many that I need to sort through them first.'

'And what about you, Gina? Will you and the family be heading off now that Annie is back?' Bridget asks, eyeing me over the rim of her cup.

I hesitate, not sure how to answer, but I'm also trying to read her tone. And as far as I can make out, she sounds normal, not in the least suspicious – albeit a little worried about Billy's health.

'I figured Annie wouldn't be able to keep away from her work for long, so yes, we've made other plans.' I leave it at that, finding it unbearable that my version of 'we' now doesn't include Matt. 'By the way, I hope we didn't wake you up first thing this morning,' I continue, ignoring the sudden glare Laura gives me. 'We were out the back doing a spot of early-morning yoga.' I add a cheerful laugh, which physically hurts inside. 'It ended up with us in fits of loud giggles, so I'm sorry if we disturbed you or Billy.' It's risky, but I need to know if either of them heard anything or is suspicious about our movements at dawn.

Bridget stares at me for a few seconds, her face finally breaking into a smile. 'No, no, you didn't wake either of us, dear,' she says. 'We both slept like logs. Billy needed the rest.'

I nod, shooting Annie a look, picking up on the almost imperceptible raise of her eyebrows as she looks as relieved as I feel. They didn't see us. I must have been wrong about the face at the window.

And yet... something still doesn't feel right. I know what I saw.

. . .

It's half an hour later, in the hallway as we're all gathered to leave, that I take my chance, knowing I might not get another one.

'Is it OK if I go up and use your bathroom quickly?' I ask Bridget, my mouth suddenly dry from nerves. 'I'm... I'm heading straight into town from here,' I add to explain why I don't just wait until I'm next door. I already know there isn't a downstairs toilet from my last visit.

The older woman halts, frowning briefly, perhaps wondering why I didn't use the toilet before I came, but then she smiles and ushers me on up. 'You know the way, dear.'

'Won't be a sec,' I say to the others, ignoring their stares as they no doubt wonder what the hell I'm doing.

But when I'm on the landing, I don't take the first door to the bathroom. Instead, I head past all the other doors, peeking around the front bedroom door that's been left ajar. Billy is lying propped up in bed, wearing stripy pyjamas, his eyes closed and his mouth hanging open.

It's a gut feeling that sends me creeping up the second flight of stairs to the attic rooms, to the room where I *swear* I saw someone at the window earlier – dark eyes set within a pale and gaunt face, watching us intently. The same room where I *know* I saw someone when I was talking to Bridget over the wall. At the time I'd just assumed it was Billy. But hearing that he's ill in bed, it can't have been him this morning.

'Hello?' I say, knocking gently on the closed door. Like in Annie's house, there are two bedrooms up here, once used by the servants. 'Anyone in there?'

Silence as I listen, one ear open for Bridget in case she comes up to check where I am.

I try the handle, but it's locked. I peek inside the other bedroom up here but there's nothing much to see – a single bed, an old wardrobe and a stack of boxes that tell me the room is used mainly for storage.

Mirroring Annie's house, there's also a small bathroom in the eaves, so I take a peek, surprised to see a toothbrush on the basin, along with toothpaste and a damp face cloth. There's a pot of moisturiser on a shelf, a hairbrush beside it, and a bar of soap in the shower.

My first thought is that Bridget sleeps up here, perhaps so she's not disturbed by Billy's snoring. But then I spot the period products beside the toilet, which disproves that theory. Bridget is too old to need pads.

My heart is now thumping at what this might mean, so I pick up the hairbrush and inspect it, pulling out several hairs from the bristles. My mouth falls open as I hold them up to the light – they're long and blonde, and nothing like Bridget's thicker grey hair.

I dash back to the locked room, tapping on it as loud as I dare. 'Hello... who's in there?' I hiss. 'Please, open the door. I'm not going to hurt you. It's Gina... I'm here to help you...'

My skin breaks out in goosebumps as I wait, but there's no sound from within. I shake my head, wondering for a moment if I've made a terrible mistake.

In a panic, I scan around the small landing area, hunting for a key. The door lock is old, so the key is likely to be large – and there aren't many places to hide anything up here with only one small chest of drawers on the landing. But it's not in there, so I feel over the tops of the three door frames, but again, nothing.

It's as I'm thinking what to do next, if I should give up and go back down before Bridget comes to find me, that I spot a section of loose and frayed carpet in the corner, where it looks as though it's been pulled up. I drop to my knees and peel back the worn floor covering, revealing the old boards beneath... and a key.

I grab it and shove it in the lock, breathing out a sigh of

relief when it fits. Then I turn it, hearing the lock slide across in the mechanism. Slowly, I twist the knob and push the door open a few inches.

The curtains are closed and it's dark inside the room. As my eyes grow accustomed to the dim light, a figure slowly resolves across the other side of the room. Shadows and vague highlights morph together to form the outline of a person – of a girl. No, wait – of a small and frail *woman* sitting on the bed, her knees drawn up under her chin as she stares at me through unblinking eyes, terrified as I approach her.

It's just as I'm about to ask who she is, if she's OK, and how I can help her that I hear a booming voice behind me.

'What the *hell* do you think you're doing, you nosy fucking bitch?'

When I swing round, Billy is standing there with an iron poker raised above his head. And it's aimed directly at me.

FIFTY-SIX

GINA

'Sara?' I shriek incredulously as I duck, dodging a blow from the poker as Billy brings it down hard. It skims across my shoulder, narrowly missing the side of my head.

I glance over at the frail woman again, not daring to go near her because it will only lead Billy towards her. Yes, yes, it really could be her... It really could be Sara huddled, terrified, on the bed.

She gives me a tiny nod just as Billy roars, his voice croaky as he raises the poker at me again, swinging it towards my head. But I'm too quick for the old man as he limps across the room towards me, dragging his bad foot behind him – the same limp that Matt described when he confessed about what had happened that terrible night. It's been nagging away at me ever since as I tried to piece things together.

'It's OK, Sara,' I call out. 'Just stay where you are.'

I reach out, trying to grab the poker from Billy, but he wields it away from me, coughing and clutching at his chest.

'Help!' I scream at the top of my voice. 'Annie, Laura, Mary! Get up here... help me!' I scream until my throat burns.

At the mention of Mary's name, I hear a little whimper from the bed as Sara realises her sister is here. All I want to do is hug her, dissolve onto the floor, sob in a puddle after everything that's happened during the last twenty-four hours. But I must stay strong for a while longer – until we can get help for Sara.

'Oh no you don't, old man,' I yell, darting around behind Billy as he lumbers closer to me, the poker aimed at me again. The skin on his face appears grey and sallow as I grab him by the shoulder, yanking his right arm and locking it behind his back. When I give his wrist a tight squeeze and pull the poker, he releases it, coughing and hacking as I grab it from him. Then I shove him away from me, rushing over to where Sara is on the bed, curled up and looking terrified. He won't dare come near us while I'm brandishing this in my hand.

'It's OK, it's OK, you're safe now...' I tell her, but she's not looking at me. She's looking over at the door, her eyes fixed on something, or some*one*, I realise, as I track her stare.

Mary is standing the other side of the attic room with Laura and Annie flanking her. None of the three women says a word as they take in the scene in front of them – me cradling a gaunt, ill-looking woman sitting on the bed, her bare legs curled up, knees tucked under her chin. She's wearing a thin cotton night-dress that's too small, straining across her bony shoulders, and men's socks that are too big on her feet. Her long hair is greasy and uncut, hanging in ratty strands around her face.

'Watch out!' I yell when I see Billy making a move towards the others.

They don't know he's dangerous, that *he* was the one who first hurt Sara the night she disappeared. After Matt buried her in the hole, Billy must have gone back to the scene and dug her out of the pit where she'd been left for dead, perhaps witnessing what happened from his upstairs window. Against all the odds, Sara had somehow survived. And now, all these years later, it was *her* face at the window that led me to find her.

'Quickly!' I yell. 'Grab him!'

When the others look puzzled, not understanding my urgency, I launch myself off the bed towards Billy, but just as I get to his side, he turns a strange shade of greyish green. His eyes fix straight ahead as he becomes rooted to the spot, his right hand suddenly coming up to his chest as he clutches at his heart.

'Owww... *Ayyy...*' he says through a pained grimace. 'God... *no...*'

Billy's face contorts into a series of crevices and wrinkles beneath his grey, stubbly skin. His thinning moustache hangs limply above his twisted mouth as he cries out in pain.

'What's wrong?' I say, taking him by the arms. 'Get Bridget,' I say, turning to the others. But she's already here, pushing between them to get to her husband.

Billy drops to his knees as he doubles up in pain, grabbing his chest, not knowing what to do with himself.

'I think he's having a heart attack,' I say as Bridget crouches down beside her husband, stroking his clammy forehead as he writhes in pain. His lips are turning blue, and his eyes are rolling back in his head. Spit is frothing from his mouth as I fumble in my back pocket for my phone. 'I'll call an ambulance, it's OK, Bridget, he'll be OK... don't worry...'

'No...' a small voice suddenly says from behind me. I turn. Sara is standing there looking like a child in her nightgown even though she's the same age as us. She's so pale and thin, as if she's never had the sun on her face. 'Do *not* help him!' Her voice sounds a little stronger now, more forceful as she steps forward.

'What? No, get help for him... *please...*' Bridget begs, staring up at Sara, then at me, her hands cradling her husband's head.

'I said *no!*' Sara yells. Her voice is a little croaky, as though she's not spoken in a while, but there's a power behind it. She steps forward and kicks Billy in the back. 'He deserves to *fucking die* for what he's done to me,' she screams. Then she spits down at him, a disgusted expression on her face as he groans in agony at her feet.

'I'm begging you...' Bridget cries. 'Help him! Do you know CPR? *Please*...' She stares up at us, her eyes scanning between me, Annie, Laura and Mary. But they're not taking any notice – instead their eyes are all firmly fixed on Sara.

'Oh my God...' Mary finally says, stepping over Billy to get to her. 'Is it *really* you? Sara? I... I don't believe it. I must be dreaming... I'm going to wake up and you won't be here... Let me just hold you before that happens...'

Tentatively, Mary reaches out and slides her hands onto Sara's – each of them jolting as if an electric shock has passed between them. They take a step closer to each other, looking so alike, yet also they couldn't be more different given the vast gap in the passage of their lives.

Slowly, Sara melts into her sister's arms as she presses her smaller frame against Mary's body, almost becoming one person as they absorb everything that's been missing between them for almost twenty-five years.

'He's dying... someone please help!' Bridget cries from the floor. Billy has stopped moving now, and when I bend down to check for a pulse, I can't find one.

'I'm sorry, Bridget, it's too late. He's gone.' I stand up, watching as she stares at him, unable to speak, her hands clasped under her chin. 'You *knew* about Sara, didn't you?' I whisper accusingly, remembering her bag of shopping on the stairs – the bag that contained bathroom items for Sara. 'You helped keep his dirty secret for all this time. You're disgusting and no better than he is.'

'No, no, I swear it's not like that,' Bridget says, leaning on a chair to get up off the floor. 'She is... she's like our daughter. We saved her! Don't you see? Billy said she had no one else, that no one wanted her, that she would die if we didn't take her in. He told me that she was ours to look after, that God had finally blessed us with a child and given us a daughter in the most unlikely of ways.' Bridget shudders as she recounts her twisted version of events, believing her own lies.

'I'm calling the police,' I say, shaking my head in disgust. And this time, no one stops me.

FIFTY-SEVEN

MARY

The morning passes with a swarm of paramedics and police as they take Billy's body away and begin to unravel the unbelievable mystery surrounding my sister. I can't take my eyes off her for even a second in case she disappears again.

'It's her,' I tell the police shakily, feeling on the verge of hysterics. 'It's *really* her...' But the two uniformed officers remain sceptical until they call for back-up and a pair of detectives come out to take statements, telling me they'll need to do a DNA test before they can confirm anything. The older of them remembers Sara's case from way back.

After that, Sara is taken by ambulance to hospital with a police escort – and me glued to her side. They're keeping her in for a day or two, monitoring her and running various medical checks. I've not let our mother know yet – I'll spare Sara one more night of not having to deal with her. I doubt she'll want to have anything to do with either of our parents – and I'll stand by her on that. They do not deserve their daughters.

. . .

Later in the day, after much talking and planning between us, Gina takes the step of reporting Matt missing to the police. About 6 p.m., two different uniformed officers come round to the house to take her statement. Laura, Annie and I keep out of the way, watching the children while remaining within earshot as Gina sits with the police.

'I'm so worried that he's going to do something stupid,' she says, shedding a few tears. 'He was already on the edge after our house burnt down, blaming himself for the fire.' She blows her nose. 'His mental health has been so bad these last few weeks.'

It's hard not to feel guilty when I hear this – and right on cue, Tyler walks into the kitchen, his ears pricking up at the mention of the fire.

I glare at him, slowly shaking my head, willing him not to say anything about what we did – how we broke into Gina and Matt's house when they were out at Laura and Patrick's for dinner, how Tyler knew exactly how to mess with the electrics in the light fitting so that it slowly smouldered, finally igniting. How else was I going to flush them out and get them here?

Tyler stares at me, his mouth opening then closing, a knowing look finally spreading over his face. He taps the side of his nose and pulls open the fridge.

'And then when Matt got arrested trying to protect his friend,' Gina goes on, explaining to the officers, 'I think it tipped him over the edge. He was so ashamed. When he got home from the station, he didn't stay here long. He was crying, telling me that he felt worthless and that he didn't deserve me and the kids. He told me he was going out for a walk, that I might never see him again, that I was better off without him. I begged him to stay, not to leave us, but he turned on me and got quite violent, shoving me away.' Gina shows the police the cuts and bruises on her arm – injuries from when she and I fought in the basement. 'I know he was hurting inside.'

'Has he ever threatened suicide before?' one of the officers asks.

'Yes, several years ago,' Gina says. 'When he was made redundant. He's always suffered with his mental health.' More sobs. 'He went to the GP about it recently.'

I glance over at Annie and we share a knowing look, impressed with Gina's acting skills.

'He didn't even take his phone or his wallet with him,' Gina adds, showing the officers the items.

Half an hour later, they leave, promising to open a missing persons case.

As we breathe a collective sigh of relief, we already know that they will never find Matt.

None of us slept well last night – apart from Tyler and the children – but today is a new day, the promise of a new future, even if normal is still a long way off.

Yesterday was draining and emotional to say the least, and today I expect more of the same as I take Tyler to the hospital to meet his mother – his *real* mother – for the first time. Few words are exchanged during the hour we're there and, for a while, I leave the pair alone with Tyler sitting beside Sara, her small hand clutched in his. As I head off to get a coffee, I glance back at them, the silent conversation they're having in the long, searching look they share enough for me to know they'll be OK. That they have each other now. That we *all* have each other.

Gina and her children are leaving tomorrow, going to stay with her parents while her house is being rebuilt, telling them that she's hopeful Matt will soon be found. As for the children, Gracie is too young to know what's going on, and, for now, Tommy seems to have accepted his mother's explanation that Daddy has gone away for a little while.

Over the coming months, we all know that Gina's fake hope

will have to wane, and she will learn to adapt to her new life as a single mother. Laura is also going home tomorrow, ready to divorce Patrick, so this is our last meal all together, though we've already made plans to meet up often. Tyler and I will be staying on here in Hastings, with me employed as Annie's live-in house-keeper. And Annie has said that Sara is welcome to stay for as long as she wants, until the police have finished their investigation and we decide what we're going to do longer term.

Plainclothes officers have been in and out all day, and Bridget and Billy's house next door has been sealed off as a crime scene since the discovery, with a few reporters sniffing about in the street, their camera flashes and questions raining down on us every time one of us goes out. Bridget was arrested and taken away in a police van not long after Billy's body was removed and, being an accomplice all these years, I doubt she'll be coming home again.

I place a big bowl of spaghetti Bolognese on the table, along with a salad – adding a bowl of plain pasta for Tyler.

'Food's up, you two,' Gina calls to Tyler and Tommy, who are playing with Duplo on the rug.

'Look at them,' I say. 'Getting on so well.'

Gina smiles. 'Like brothers,' she adds, cradling her baby as everyone sits down at the table.

'Hey, I've got something for you all,' I say after we've eaten and Tyler and Tommy have left the table. From my uniform pocket, I take the four 'Best Friends' heart necklaces, finally having the complete set since finding Sara's necklace tucked inside Gina's bag. I hand one each to Gina, Annie and Laura. The other I hand to Sara, who is sitting to my right.

I took back the pendant my mother was wearing when I visited yesterday. She was not pleased to see me, especially as the news about Sara was beginning to break. I left without giving her any information, and before she had a chance to guilt-trip me.

'Go on, put them on,' I say, watching as they all fasten the chains around their necks. Then I help Sara with hers. I cleaned it up and gave it a polish, so it almost looks as good as new.

'Here,' I say, holding out both hands, linking fingers with Sara and Annie. The others complete the circle in a chain of hands. 'Big love, true friends, no secrets,' I whisper, looking fondly at my sister, finally understanding what it means.

EPILOGUE

SARA

'Big love, true friends, no secrets,' Annie sang, shoving her hand in the middle of the group.

'I'm so pumped about the New Year's Eve party,' Gina said.

'Excited doesn't even come close,' I replied, though I don't think they heard me. I wanted next year to start with new hope, leave the past behind, study hard so I could one day make a new life for me and Mary. She was the most precious little sister and neither of us deserved the hand we'd been dealt. 'Big love,' I repeated, feeling it deep within, so grateful for my friends.

I wasn't exactly sure whose party we were going to – Matt someone, apparently, and he was in the year above us, according to Annie. We hadn't been invited by him directly – rather we'd heard about the get-together through a friend of a friend, that it was open house, everyone welcome. All I knew was that it was a chance to get out of *my* house, even if it meant leaving Mary alone for a few hours. But I knew our parents would be passed out from booze before long, and Mary would be upstairs safe in bed.

We were all getting ready at Annie's, with everyone lying to their parents that there was a youth club disco in town, that they were staying over with friends. It all seemed so easy, sneaking out for the night.

We were barely fifteen.

'Where are his parents?' I yelled in Gina's ear over the loud music when we'd gone inside. I was grinning from ear to ear, feeling so grown up.

'Away in Scotland, I think,' Annie said. 'Some of this crowd go to theatre club,' she added. 'We can hang out with them.' She looked pumped to be there.

It was my first proper party – the kind with alcohol, cool music, neighbours complaining and a whole lot of mess to clean up the next day. But I was loving it and wasted no time grabbing a drink and dancing with Laura. It was as though everything bad in my head melted away.

'Oh my God, is that the guy whose party this is?' Gina said later in the evening as we all stood in a huddle, surreptitiously pointing at a boy across the room.

'Yeah, that's Matt,' Annie confirmed. 'Hot, right?' She winked and we all giggled, standing together in our group of four. 'He only started our school at the beginning of term. All the girls are in love with him.'

'I can see why,' I admitted, blushing deeply when he stared our way. My head was spinning from the wine.

No, wait… he was staring *my* way.

At *me*.

Not the others.

He was with another boy who was staggering about, shoving Matt in my direction, egging him on and laughing as he pointed at me, jeering something I couldn't make out.

'Shit, he's coming over,' Annie said, turning inwards in our huddle.

We pretended to be discussing something about the hockey team and I remember thinking that I wished I'd got better clothes. Compared to my friends, I looked like a little kid in my pink dress with the ruffles on the sleeves.

'Hi, girls,' Matt said, sliding into our group. 'Happy New Year and all that.' He raised his beer bottle at us. 'Only forty minutes to go.' I thought I was going to pass out, but I managed to raise my paper cup back.

Then he looked at me again. 'I'm Matt,' he said, holding out a hand at me.

I froze. Then I felt Laura nudging me.

'I'm Sara,' I replied, reaching out to shake it.

But instead of a handshake, Matt pulled me and led me away from the group. My heart raced with excitement. I glanced back at the others, but they were already chatting to some other boys, going off to dance and not paying any attention to where I had gone.

Outside in the back garden, Matt lit a cigarette. 'Want one?'

I shook my head.

'There's some decent booze in the shed,' he told me. 'Over there.'

Further down the lawn, I spotted a wooden tool shed.

'Champagne for midnight,' he said.

'I've never had champagne before,' I giggled, imagining what the others would say when they heard about this. Matt took me by the wrist and led me across the lawn and into the cool, earthy interior of the shed.

I don't remember too much after that, as though my brain erased my memory to protect me. Afterwards, my back was sore and bleeding from where he'd rammed me against the rough wood wall. And I remember thinking that I'd get into trouble because he ripped off my knickers.

My father's friends had done plenty of bad things to me, and made me do bad things to them, but they'd never done *that* to me before. Afterwards, I cried, and Matt put a hand over my mouth.

It had hurt. It had hurt a lot.

Though it didn't hurt as much as when, nine months later, the baby came out.

Nor did it hurt as much as when they took him away from me.

After the school holidays, when I told Matt what had happened, that the reason I'd been off sick at the end of last term was because I was having his baby, that it felt as though I'd had my heart ripped out when he was taken into care, he refused to believe me. Refused to talk to me or look at me. It was almost as painful as when they'd taken my son.

And he really, *really* didn't want to go out with me when I asked him to be my boyfriend, telling him that us being together would help me feel closer to my lost child, and perhaps we could even have another son one day when we were a bit older... in love... married. Matt did not like this. He shoved me away, not understanding that despite the assault, he was the only person who could help me. I'd been abused all my life and wasn't about to lose the father of my son, too. I wasn't thinking clearly.

But Matt soon changed his mind when I threatened to tell his parents what he'd done. It was the only bit of power I had left. The only credibility available to me in a world where I had no voice. It gave me a few weeks of feeling like someone who mattered. Of feeling like there was a life left for me.

When it was over, when he'd zipped himself up in the shed that night, he'd wished me a happy New Year and gone back inside. Slumped on the floor, I'd sobbed when I heard everyone counting down, when I'd heard the whoops and yells at midnight, the fireworks overhead.

I'd cradled my knees, reaching a finger up to my neck,

touching my GALS necklace. I knew that when it came down to it, there was no big love, there were no true friends, though there were always plenty of secrets.

A LETTER FROM SAMANTHA

Dear Reader,

My heartfelt thanks to you for reading *Her Housekeeper*. I really hope it had you flying through the pages! A quick note to say that if you'd like to be kept up to date with my new releases, please click on the link below – you can unsubscribe at any time you want.

www.bookouture.com/samantha-hayes

Home should be a safe space, right? Especially when there are young children involved. So when I started writing this book, I knew I wanted to threaten Gina's home life right at its heart. After the fire, she was already on the back foot by relocating to a place filled with bad memories, so when Mary moves in, she's totally unprepared for the horror to follow.

Having a housekeeper is an unaffordable luxury for most, but how would you really know if someone is trustworthy or what their intentions are if you were to employ them – especially given that they'll be spending a lot of time in your home? Trusting someone to look after your house and family is a deeply personal step, and police checks can only go so far and don't predict what a person might do in the future.

In the initial stages of plotting this book, I was reminded of a friend I had as a teenager. Her family had various employees working at their large home – from live-in housekeeping staff to drivers to gardeners. I remember being fascinated by the situation – and in awe when I once visited! But I was shocked when she told me that their housekeeper had done a 'moonlight flit' and stolen valuable items from the home, including a much-loved pet.

I've never forgotten this tale – thankfully my friend was reunited with her cat! – and I'm sure it's a rare occurrence, but the essence of it is embedded at the core of *Her Housekeeper*. *They* let her in… *they* trusted her. I used this chink of vulnerability to crack open Gina's past, along with that of her friendship group, and, because I love nothing more than a dual timeline plot, it was the perfect opportunity to weave in secrets from the past, bringing them very much into the present.

If you enjoyed reading *Her Housekeeper*, then it would mean so much to me if you could leave a quick review so other readers know you loved it! It really does help spread the word.

And of course, meantime, I'm busy plotting my next novel – another nail-biting thriller – and very much cracking on with my own housekeeping duties!

With warm wishes,

Sam x

facebook.com/samanthahayesauthor

x.com/samhayes

instagram.com/samanthahayes.author

ACKNOWLEDGEMENTS

I'd like to say a massive thank you to my lovely editor, Jessie Botterill, for her editorial magic and inspiring brainstorming sessions, whipping this book into its best page-turning shape! Huge thanks, too, to Sarah Hardy and all the publicity team at Bookouture for getting my books out there, to DeAndra Lupu for copy editing, to Jenny Page for proofreading, and to Lisa Horton for fantastic cover design – it's all very much appreciated. And, as ever, my sincere thanks to everyone at Bookouture for publishing my books.

Grateful thanks to Oli Munson, my lovely agent, for looking after me, as well as the whole team at A. M. Heath.

Heartfelt thanks indeed to all the dedicated bloggers, reviewers and readers who are so very passionate about books, taking time to review and shout out favourite reads. We authors really do appreciate it greatly!

And much love to Ben, Polly and Lucy, as well as the rest of my family, for continued support.

Sam xx

PUBLISHING TEAM

Turning a manuscript into a book requires the efforts of many people. The publishing team at Bookouture would like to acknowledge everyone who contributed to this publication.

Audio
Alba Proko
Sinead O'Connor
Melissa Tran

Commercial
Lauren Morrissette
Hannah Richmond
Imogen Allport

Cover design
Lisa Horton

Data and analysis
Mark Alder
Mohamed Bussuri

Editorial
Jessie Botterill
Ria Clare

Copyeditor
DeAndra Lupu

Proofreader
Jenny Page

Marketing
Alex Crow
Melanie Price
Occy Carr
Cíara Rosney
Martyna Młynarska

Operations and distribution
Marina Valles
Stephanie Straub
Joe Morris

Production
Hannah Snetsinger
Mandy Kullar
Jen Shannon
Ria Clare

Publicity
Kim Nash
Noelle Holten
Jess Readett
Sarah Hardy

Rights and contracts
Peta Nightingale
Richard King
Saidah Graham

Milton Keynes UK
Ingram Content Group UK Ltd.
UKHW031455061124
450821UK00004B/351

9 781835 258989